# CHAMBERLAIN STREET

THE MURDER OF LADY PENELOPE

By Willow Hewett

Author of the 'Past My Time' series, 'The Taranock', and 'The Wishy Washy, Curly Wurly Dragon' series.

Copyright © 2024 by Willow Hewett

All rights reserved. No part of this publication may be reproduced, distributed or transmitted in any form or by any means, without prior written permission.

Willow Hewett
www.willowhewettauthor.co.uk
Front cover © 2024 Canva, Vecteezy, Willow Hewett

Publisher's Note: This is a work of fiction. Names, characters, places, and incidents are a product of the author's imagination. Locales, places, and public names are sometimes used for atmospheric purposes. Any resemblance to actual people, living or dead, or to businesses, companies, events, institutions, or locales is completely coincidental.

Book Layout © 2024 BookDesignTemplates.com

Chamberlain Street/ Willow Hewett. -- 1st ed.

# Dedication

This book is dedicated to my brothers and sister, and my mum. It is also dedicated to my friends, partner, and my children.

If I don't dedicate this to them, I'll get shouted at....

(Oh, and to my brother Loui, it was me who ruined your spaceship set many years ago... Sorry bro.)

I would like to also dedicate this book to all my author friends (You all know who you are), and to my amazing editor, Sarah. We are all in this strange writing world together, and I wouldn't pick anyone else to do it with.

To Seb, Sean, and Helen – I hope you enjoy this book.

# CONTENTS

Prologue

Chapter One – The Crime Scene

Chapter Two – Thornton's Pie Shop

Chapter Three – The Prowler

Chapter Four – Bailey

Chapter Five – Thornton

Chapter Six – Shelton's Townhouse

Chapter Seven – The Orphanage

Chapter Eight – The Bristol Docks

Chapter Nine – The Police Station

Chapter Ten – The Cheese Mongers

Chapter Eleven – The Rummer Pub

Chapter Twelve – Thornton's Secret

Chapter Thirteen – Bella

Chapter Fourteen – The Night of Bella's Death

Chapter Fifteen – The Hospital Mortuary – Present Day

Chapter Sixteen – The Morning After Robert's Disappearance

Chapter Seventeen – Inspector Acker's Office

Chapter Eighteen – The Night of Robert's Mistake

Chapter Nineteen – Acker's Residence

Chapter Twenty – An Arrest

Chapter Twenty-One – Bristol Cemetery – Night

Chapter Twenty-Two – The Missing Orphan

Chapter Twenty-Three – Royal York Crescent

Chapter Twenty-Four – Corn Street – Day Time

Chapter Twenty-Five – Lost & Found

Chapter Twenty-Six – The Interrogation

Chapter Twenty-Seven – Robert's Cover-up

Chapter Twenty-Eight – Shelton

Chapter Twenty-Nine – Thornton's Mistake

Chapter Thirty – Mary's Hand

Chapter Thirty-One – The Streets of Bristol

Chapter Thirty-Two – Lady Elspeth's Home

Chapter Thirty-Three – Harvard's Secret

Chapter Thirty-Four – The Docks

Chapter Thirty-Five – Taken

Chapter Thirty-Six – Robert's Findings

Chapter Thirty-Seven – Bailey's The Hero

Chapter Thirty-Eight – The Girl Is Found

Chapter Thirty-Nine – The Mortuary

Chapter Forty – Shelton's Interrogation

Chapter Forty-One – Murdered Who?

Chapter Forty-Two – Betty Returns

Chapter Forty-Three – Where Have They Gone?

Chapter Forty-Four – The Wrong Man

Chapter Forty-Five – Lady Elspeth

Chapter Forty-Six – Evelyn

Chapter Forty-Seven – Caught

Chapter Forty-Eight – Bailey's Confession

Chapter Forty-Nine – Creed

Chapter Fifty – The Plan

Chapter Fifty-One – A Knock at The Door

Chapter Fifty-Two – The Butler

Chapter Fifty-Three – Cuffed

Chapter Fifty-Four – A secret Uncovered

Chapter Fifty-Five – Banes

Chapter Fifty-Six – The Cells

Chapter Fifty-Seven – Claydon

Chapter Fifty-Eight – A Horrible Surprise

Chapter Fifty-Nine - Trapped

Chapter Sixty - The Photograph

Chapter Sixty-One – Fire

Chapter Sixty-Two – Don't Trust Anyone

Chapter Sixty-Three – Harvard and Banes

Chapter Sixty-Four – Dinner Laced with White

Chapter Sixty-Five – Murder at The Station

Chapter Sixty-Six – Keep Awake

Chapter Sixty-Seven – Superintendent Landrake

Chapter Sixty-Eight – The Wrong Shoe

Chapter Sixty-Nine – London

Chapter Seventy – Escape

Chapter Seventy-One – The Breakthrough

Chapter Seventy-Two – Landrake's Plan

Chapter Seventy-Three – Schizophrenia

Chapter Seventy-Four – Fate

Chapter Seventy-Five – The Time Is Up

# PROLOGUE

The spectre of Jack the Ripper's heinous crimes had cast a long shadow over cities far beyond the borders of London. Bristol, though miles away from the epicentre of the Ripper's terror, felt the ripple effects of fear and unease that swept across the nation.

In the wake of the gruesome murders, paranoia gripped the populace, and the once vibrant streets of Bristol became eerily deserted after nightfall. Residents, haunted by the chilling tales of the Ripper's brutality, hesitated to venture outside, even in the relative safety of their own neighbourhoods, miles away from where the murders had taken place.

The memory of those dark nights in Whitechapel loomed large in the collective consciousness, serving as a stark reminder of the fragility of life and the presence of unseen dangers lurking in the shadows. Despite efforts by local authorities to reassure the public, the pervasive fear persisted, leaving the streets empty and devoid of life long after the last echoes of the Ripper's reign of terror had faded.

And so, the desolation that now enveloped the streets of Bristol mirrored the lingering trauma inflicted by Jack the Ripper's grisly legacy, a sombre reminder of the enduring impact of violence and aggression on the communities.

As twilight descended upon the streets of Bristol, a sense of eerie quietness enveloped the surroundings. The once bustling thoroughfare now seemed frozen in time, its grandeur subdued by the encroaching darkness. Shadows danced whimsically under the dim glow of the iron gas lamps, creating an otherworldly atmosphere.

The occasional carriage rolled by, its wooden wheels creaking against the cobblestones, echoing hauntingly in the stillness. The rhythmic clatter of the horses' hooves added a melancholic soundtrack to the deserted scene, giving the homes residing nearby a sense of comfort.

Peering through the mist, the silhouette of the old pub stood like a sentinel on the corner of the street, its warm glow promising solace and refuge from the desolation outside. Yet, it remained hidden behind the row of houses, adding to the mysterious allure of the deserted street.

Across the street, a figure's footsteps led away from a small alleyway nestled between two townhouses. His knee-length coat flapped in the evening breeze as he wrapped it tightly around his waist to keep the winter chill at bay. His dark beady eyes darted from window to window, checking that no one was watching him. Anxious thoughts began flooding his mind, causing his bloodstained hands within his pockets to shake

The figure's clandestine movements betrayed a sense of desperation as he navigated the desolate streets of Bristol. His tattered coat and threadbare attire spoke volumes of his impoverished state, while his furtive glances betrayed a sense of paranoia that seemed to haunt his every step.

He paused to catch his breath, the house beside him catching his eye as the warm light from inside spilled out onto the street before him. As he peered through the illuminated window, a pang of longing and envy twisted in his gut at the sight of the family within, enjoying their meal in the warmth and comfort of their home. The contrast between their opulent surroundings and his own destitution only served to exacerbate his feelings of resentment and inadequacy.

For a fleeting moment, he allowed himself to indulge in fantasies of abundance and security, imagining himself as part of that idyllic scene. But reality soon came crashing down upon him, reminding him of the harsh truth of his existence.

Shivering not only from the biting cold but also from the gnawing hunger that plagued him incessantly, the figure turned away from the window, his heart heavy with bitterness and despair. In his world of deprivation and scarcity, the luxuries enjoyed by others seemed like cruel taunts, mocking his own lack of fortune.

With a heavy sigh, he continued his solitary journey through the deserted streets, and away from the scene of the happy family.

As the figure scurried across the road, a sinister smirk twisted his lips, reflecting the twisted satisfaction he derived from his nefarious deeds. In the shroud of darkness, he moved with the stealth of a predator, his whistling a discordant melody in the silence of the night.

His mind buzzed with the thrill of his actions, the adrenaline coursing through his veins as he relished the knowledge that he had left an indelible mark on the fabric of the city. The thought of his infamous act splashed across the headlines filled him with a perverse sense of accomplishment, a macabre validation of his twisted desires. He knew by morning that he would make the front page in the paper.

Despite the facade of callousness and satisfaction that the figure wore like armour, deep within the recesses of his conscience, a gnawing sense of guilt clawed at his heart. It was a flicker of humanity amidst the darkness that consumed him, a whisper of remorse for the crime he had just committed.

Yet, in the cruel dance of his own self-deception, he buried these feelings deep beneath layers of denial and rationalisation, clinging to the illusion of power and control that his acts of violence afforded him. He convinced himself that he was above such trivial emotions as guilt, that he was merely doing the city a favour.

With each step, the weight of the knife in his pocket served as a grim reminder of the crime, a tool that he wielded with chilling precision to sow fear and chaos in the heart of his unsuspecting victim.

He shook the guilt from his thoughts and disappeared into the labyrinth of alleys and shadows, leaving behind the faint smell of blood from his hands, and a lingering uncertainty of what was to become of him if anyone found out.

CHAPTER ONE

# The Crime Scene

The discovery of the woman's lifeless body sent shockwaves rippling through the crowd that had gathered in the dimly lit alleyway. Gasps and murmurs spread like wildfire as pub goers and passersby alike were drawn to the scene, their morbid curiosity piqued by the grisly tableau before them.

The woman's once elegant red dress now lay in disarray upon the cold cobblestones, a stark contrast to the pallor of her skin illuminated by the flickering glow of the gas lamps. Her vacant gaze seemed to fixate on the tattered poster of missing children on the wall, a haunting reminder of the countless tragedies that had befallen the city's streets.

One hand lay serenely upon her chest, as if in a final, futile attempt to shield herself from the cruelty of fate, while the other remained tightly clenched around her evening purse, a poignant symbol of her futile struggle for survival. The dark liquid oozing from her hair painted a macabre portrait of the violence that had befallen her, staining her once lustrous locks with the crimson hue of misfortune.

As the crowd whispered in hushed tones, a sense of unease hung heavy in the air, mingling with the palpable grief and disbelief that enveloped the scene. For in the stillness of that desolate alleyway, the spectre of death loomed large, casting a long shadow over the heart of the city.

Police officers had already begun cordoning off the crime scene and collecting the necessary evidence from the body before the detectives had even shown up. Rumours had already begun to circulate about the gruesome murder being one of Ripper's victims, casting a wave of fear across the growing crowd. The police fought tirelessly against the crowd, demanding them to go home, yet they remained, wanting to know who had committed such a crime and if the Ripper had moved his heinous ways to their city.

A smart-looking man in a sleek black suit pushed his way through the crowd, closely followed by another man dressed the same. Both men looked across at the growing crowd with solemn expressions, revealing no clue as to why they had been called there.

As the men, known as the "half-brothers," made their way through the throng of onlookers, an air of authority seemed to precede them. Their identical appearances and sombre expressions hinted at a shared sense of duty and purpose as they surveyed the scene before them.

The elder of the two, with a slight shadow of stubble adorning his chin, exuded an aura of seasoned experience, his weary eyes betraying the weight of countless investigations and crime scenes witnessed over the years. He stood with a commanding presence, his demeanour speaking volumes of his dedication to his profession.

Beside him, the younger half-brother emanated a youthful energy and enthusiasm, his mischievous glint belying the sharp intellect that lay beneath. Despite their outward similarities, each man possessed his own unique strengths and talents, complementing one another in their pursuit of justice.

Their reputation preceded them, their names whispered in hushed tones among the locals, a testament to their formidable reputation within the police force. Known for their relentless pursuit of truth and justice, they had earned both respect and fear in equal measure, their deep brown eyes holding secrets untold and mysteries yet unravelled.

As they surveyed the scene with practised scrutiny, it was clear that the half-brothers were more than just colleagues; they were partners bound by blood and shared purpose, determined to unravel the enigma that lay before them.

A drunken man stepped in front of the half-brothers, causing the glass of bitter in his hand to spill on the coat of the person beside him. The eldest brother maintained his composure with a steely resolve and confronted the man holding the pint of bitter, his authoritative voice cutting through the clamour.

"Inspector Acker, now move aside and let me through," he declared, brandishing his police badge as a symbol of his authority. His words carried the weight of law and order, demanding compliance from those who dared to challenge his presence.

The crowd faltered momentarily, taken aback by the inspector's commanding presence and unwavering demeanour. Reluctantly, the man with the pint of bitter begrudgingly stepped aside, allowing Inspector Acker and his younger half-brother to proceed unhindered.

As they made their way through the rest of the crowd, the tension in the air remained palpable, but the inspector pressed on undeterred, his focus unwavering as he approached the scene of the crime.

As Inspector Acker and his brother, Claydon, passed by the officers on the scene, a hushed anticipation rippled through the crowd, their curiosity piqued by the presence of the renowned detectives.

The inspector's ritualistic gesture of extracting a cigarette from his silver case, engraved with his initials, served as a familiar prelude to the task at hand. With practised finesse, he tapped the cigarette against the case before lighting it with a single fluid motion. It was something he would always do before analysing a crime scene.

Claydon, meanwhile, wasted no time in immersing himself in the investigation, his black leather notebook poised in his hand as he meticulously documented the evidence surrounding the pale-skinned victim. With a furrowed brow, he moved with swift efficiency, his keen eye discerning even the smallest details that might hold significance in unravelling the mystery before them.

As Acker took a contemplative drag from his cigarette, his gaze swept over the gathered crowd, his expression inscrutable behind a veil of smoke. Amidst the crowd, most of them watched with fearful expressions, wondering if the Ripper had set up base within their city.

Acker's keen eyes scanned the wall, searching for any trace of a pattern amidst the blood stains that marred its surface. Despite his thorough examination, he found no discernible clues to shed light on the grim tableau before them. With a resigned sigh, he turned to his brother, exhaling smoke in his direction as he awaited Claydon's assessment.

"So, sergeant, what do you think?" Acker inquired, his tone laced with a hint of anticipation.

Claydon, undeterred by his brother's impatience, knelt beside the victim to inspect the wounds up close. His brow furrowed in concentration as he meticulously examined the evidence before him, his sharp eyes taking in every detail with practised scrutiny.

"Give me a chance to look at her, Acker, and I'll let you know," Claydon grumbled in response, his focus unwavering as he began to piece together the puzzle laid out before him.

With a nod of acknowledgment, Acker stepped back, allowing his brother the space to conduct his examination. Despite their occasional differences in approach, the Acker brothers shared a mutual respect for each other's expertise.

Acker's frustration simmered beneath the surface as he watched the crowd, their prying eyes and whispered conversations fuelling his growing anger. He knew all too well the dangers of allowing speculation and gossip to cloud the integrity of an investigation, and he refused to let the scene be contaminated any further.

In a swift and decisive motion, he seized a nearby police officer and directed him toward the gathering throng. "Get these vultures away before they destroy any more evidence," he commanded, his voice cutting through the murmurs of the crowd with an authoritative edge.

The officer, recognizing the urgency in Acker's tone, sprang into action, marshalling his colleagues to disperse the onlookers and create an even bigger perimeter around the crime scene. With firm but measured gestures, they ushered the curious bystanders away.

As the crowd reluctantly began to disperse, their eager curiosity tempered by the presence of law enforcement, Acker's gaze remained fixed on the scene before him, his eyes flickering from the body to the old poster of missing children on the wall.

"How is the missing child case going?" he asked, puffing out another cloud of smoke, this time aimed at the dispersing crowd.

Claydon gave him a stern look. "It's a dead end, I'm afraid. The case has been put on the back burner for the time being until new evidence turns up, which I'm very much doubting at this point. The kids are orphans, Acker. They've been put in that hellhole for a reason. No one is bothered about it apart from us."

"Children go missing, and no one cares. It makes me sick to think that it could have been my own daughter going missing. You don't understand because you don't have any children."

Claydon looked grim as he turned away from Acker. "Thanks for reminding me."

A feeling of guilt washed over Acker as he realised he'd gone too far. He quickly changed the subject by pointing to the body. "Does anything spring to mind?"

"She suffered blunt force trauma to the head, a clean cut to the neck, and a few bruises on her arm. It looks to me like she had tried to fight back against her attacker," Claydon paused and searched around her, looking for the weapon. "The attacker has taken the weapon, but there is a bloodied footprint beside her that looks to be a size ten or eleven."

Inspector Acker listened intently as Sergeant Claydon relayed his findings. The details of the victim's injuries painted a grim picture of the violence that had befallen her, and Acker knew that time was of the essence in unravelling the mystery surrounding her death.

As Claydon mentioned the bloodied footprint and the missing weapon, Acker's mind raced with possibilities, his instincts honed by years of experience in the field. But before he could formulate a response, Claydon's urgent plea brought his attention back to the present reality.

"We have to get her out of here, Acker. Another crowd is forming, and I don't want a riot on our hands," Claydon insisted.

"Why would there be a riot on our hands?" Acker asked, his voice betraying a hint of apprehension.

His eyes narrowed in confusion at the notion of a potential riot, but before he could question it further, Claydon's next revelation sent a chill down his spine.

His grim expression said it all as he pulled back the woman's hair to reveal her face. Acker's breath caught in his throat as recognition dawned upon him, the weight of realisation settling heavily upon his shoulders.

"You do know who she is, right?" Claydon's words hung in the air, laden with unspoken implications that sent a ripple of unease through the inspector's core.

As the truth of the victim's identity sank in, Acker's mind raced with the implications of what her death could mean for the delicate balance of power within the city. With tensions already running high, the revelation threatened to ignite a powder keg of unrest, and Acker knew that they had to tread carefully if they were to prevent the situation from spiralling out of control.

"She's Lady Penelope from the opera house," Claydon announced.

Another wave of shock rippled through Acker, his mind reeling with the implications of her murder. The realisation that a prominent figure from the opera house had met such a tragic end only intensified the mystery. She was well-known for her interest in politics and charity. Everyone knew of her.

With a sense of urgency, Claydon swiftly covered the body with a blanket, shielding her from prying eyes as he directed the officers to transport her back to the station. The swarm of police officers moved with practised efficiency, carrying the stretcher away before any further onlookers could bear witness to the grim scene.

As the streetlamp cast its harsh light upon Lady Penelope's covered body, Acker's features contorted with disbelief. With his mind racing and his nerves on edge, he knew that they had to act swiftly to secure the crime scene and gather as much evidence as possible before the impending rain washed away any vital clues.

"We need to gather as much evidence as possible before it rains," Acker declared, his voice wavering slightly as he sought to regain control of the situation. With a trembling hand, he reached for another cigarette, seeking solace in its familiar embrace as he grappled with the shock of the noblewoman's untimely demise.

His thoughts churned with a multitude of questions, each more pressing than the last. "Are you sure she was murdered here?" he asked, his voice betraying a hint of uncertainty as he struggled to make sense of the senseless violence that had claimed Lady Penelope's life.

Claydon nodded. "Yes, you can tell by the blood on the ground. There's no doubt about it."

As Acker paced the alleyway, his eyes scanning the debris for any sign of evidence, his agitation grew palpable as he watched the crowd's attempts to breach the police barricade again.

Glancing at his brother Claydon, Acker's expression hardened with determination. They both knew that time was of the essence, and they couldn't afford to let distractions or interference derail their investigation.

"Alright, so Lady Penelope was hit from behind with..." Acker's voice trailed off as his gaze settled on a broken wooden beam hidden amidst the rubble. He retrieved the beam and examined it closely, his eyes narrowing at the telltale splatters of blood that stained one end.

"This," he declared, handing the beam to Claydon as he continued his search for further evidence. His mind raced with possibilities as he pieced together the sequence of events that had led to Lady Penelope's death.

"She then fought back until the assailant killed her with a knife and left her here," Acker concluded, his voice tinged with a grim resolve as he recounted the grisly details of the crime.

"He didn't just leave her here, Acker. He repositioned her hand carefully over her heart, which means-"

Claydon's observation about the positioning of Lady Penelope's hand elicited a surge of excitement from Acker, who recognized the significance of the detail.

"Which implies that whoever did this to her knew her.

Excellent work, Claydon," Acker exclaimed, his voice brimming with enthusiasm at the breakthrough. He acknowledged Claydon's contribution with a nod of appreciation.

Claydon's modest response belied his keen eye for detail, a trait that had often proven invaluable in their investigations. "I've always had a keen sense for detail," he admitted with a sheepish grin, acknowledging his own expertise.

Acker knelt beside Claydon to inspect the bloodied footprint. "We need a photographer and a sketcher here. Bring Heath to me right away and send someone to get Anthony. Wake him if needed. We can't have this print damaged in any way," he instructed, his tone authoritative.

Claydon vanished into the throng of police officers before reappearing with a young man. Acker greeted him with a nod of acknowledgment, his gaze unwavering as he observed the meticulous analysis of the footprint.

"Draw the design of this footprint as precisely as possible," Acker instructed.

The young sketcher, dressed in an oversized policeman's uniform, approached the crime scene with a focused intensity, his eyes trained on the bloody stain on the floor. With steady hands, he began to sketch the intricate pattern of the footprint, capturing every contour and detail with painstaking precision.

As he worked, the Acker brothers watched intently. With each stroke of the pencil, the sketcher brought the footprint to life on the page, transforming the abstract impression into tangible evidence that would help guide their investigation.

Claydon's expression softened as he offered his gratitude to the young sketcher, Heath, whose diligent work had proven invaluable time and time again.

"Thank you, Heath. Your work here is much appreciated," Claydon said warmly, his hand coming to rest reassuringly on the young man's shoulder.

Heath looked up from his sketch with a mixture of pride and exhaustion, his eyes reflecting the weight of the task he had undertaken. Despite the challenge of sketching quickly and precisely, he knew that his contribution would play a crucial role in advancing the investigation and bringing them one step closer to uncovering the truth. With a nod of acknowledgment, Heath offered a small but genuine smile, grateful for the opportunity to assist in the pursuit of justice alongside the seasoned detectives.

"I'll take this back to the station along with the other pieces of evidence." he stated, waving the sketch pad.

"Good work, Heath. Make sure it's kept safe," Claydon responded, nodding in approval as he glanced at the sketch pad containing the crucial evidence.

Heath carefully tucked the sketch pad under his arm, ensuring that it was secure before turning to leave the crime scene with a few of the other officers in tow.

"We need to clean this place up and leave. Dawn is approaching, and we don't want any evidence to be left behind," Claydon said, turning his attention to Acker.

As Acker donned his black leather gloves, the signal to depart was clear. With a sense of unease, he prepared to leave the crime scene behind, his mind already racing with new leads and possibilities.

"Get the men to clean this up. I'll meet you back at the station," Acker instructed, his voice firm as he turned to Claydon. "But don't clean anything until the photographer gets here and does his job. I want those photos."

Claydon watched his brother intently, a hint of concern etched upon his features. "Where are you going?" he called after him.

But Acker offered no immediate answer, his gaze fixed on a distant point beyond the throng of police officers and onlookers. With a determined stride, he disappeared into the crowd before Claydon could press further.

"I have a hunch about something. I'll see you later. Just make sure it's clean before sunrise," Acker's voice echoed back to Claydon, carrying with it the mystery of where he was heading off to.

Left standing amidst the remnants of the crime scene, Claydon watched as his brother vanished from sight, his mind already turning to the task at hand. With a deep breath, he turned to the assembled officers, ready to ensure that Acker's orders were carried out to the letter.

## CHAPTER TWO

# Thornton's Pie Shop

As the early morning sun cast its golden glow upon Chamberlain Street, the teeming thoroughfare came alive with activity. The vibrant hues of orange and yellow danced across the windows of the surrounding buildings, lending a warm and inviting ambiance to the bustling scene below.

Shoppers filled the streets, their footsteps echoing against the cobblestones as they perused the open stalls lining the sidewalks. The air was alive with the chatter of haggling and hawkers advertising their wares, the scent of freshly brewed coffee mingling with the tantalising aroma of baked goods and street food.

Amidst the throng of shoppers, pickpockets lurked in the shadows, their keen eyes scanning the crowd for unsuspecting targets. With nimble fingers and quick reflexes, they sought to seize upon the opportunity presented by the marketplace, their intentions veiled beneath a facade of anonymity and deception. But amidst the chaos and excitement of Chamberlain Street, there was an undercurrent of fear from the murder of Lady Penelope. A teenage paper boy stood in front of one of the stalls, shouting out the paper's headlines: MURDER, MURDER! RICH WOMAN

OFFED!

As the news of Lady Penelope's murder spread like wildfire through the city, the police station became a hive of activity, swarming with reporters and journalists hungry for a sensational story. Eager faces pressed against the windows, their cameras poised to capture every moment of the unfolding drama.

Within this chaos, the paperboy was navigating his way through, his arms laden with stacks of newspapers hot off the press. With each step, he deftly dodged the eager hands reaching out to snatch a copy, his eyes scanning the crowd for potential buyers. Coins rained down upon him from all directions, tossed by onlookers eager to get their hands on the latest scoop. In a matter of minutes, the stack of papers he held had vanished, leaving him empty-handed but satisfied with his success.

With a sense of accomplishment, the paperboy made his way back through the crowd, his pockets jingling with the coins he had collected. He felt confident that his boss would be pleased when he returned empty-handed.

A tall, stocky man appeared in front of him, wearing a blood-splattered leather apron. His shirt appeared to be clean and crisp, but his hands were caked in dried dough. He had a distinct aura about him, exuding confidence. He lowered his gaze to the boy, wrinkling his nose at his lack of cleanliness. "Are there any more newspapers, Billy?"

The tall, stocky man towered over Billy, his presence imposing as he loomed before the young paperboy. His blood-splattered leather apron hinted at a hard day's work, while his crisp shirt and confident demeanour spoke of a man accustomed to command.

His small, beady eyes bore into Billy's, their intensity causing the boy to shrink back instinctively. The man's disdain for Billy's appearance was evident in the wrinkling of his nose, a silent judgement that made the boy squirm under his gaze.

"N-no, sir, all of them have been bought," Billy stammered, his voice barely above a whisper as he struggled to meet the man's eyes. Sensing the man's displeasure, he began to fidget nervously, his broken shoes scuffing against the gravel as he sought to edge away.

But the man's smirk only widened, revealing a small dimple on his right cheek that belied his otherwise stern countenance. "You go ahead and do it, boy, and bring one to my shop. I'll be waiting for your return," he commanded, his tone leaving no room for argument.

With a trembling nod, Billy hastily turned on his heel and hurried away, eager to escape the oppressive atmosphere that surrounded the enigmatic figure. As he disappeared into the crowd, the man watched him go with a satisfied expression, his dark eyes glinting with a hint of mischief.

He sauntered away, his long legs quickly covering the ground to his shop in a matter of seconds. The man stood outside his shop, a sense of pride washing over him as he admired the clean, gleaming window of Thornton's Pork. The sign above the shop proudly proclaimed its name, while the window display showcased an array of homemade pies and slabs of meat, tantalisingly arranged despite the presence of flies buzzing around.

His keen eye caught a small smudge on the door handle, and with a swift motion, he wiped it away with the side of his apron, ensuring that none of his customers would notice any imperfections. Pleased with his handiwork, he pushed open the door with a proud smile, the bell above ringing loudly to announce his arrival.

Inside, the shop was buzzing with activity. A large counter dominated the space, covered in dough balls and bowls of cooked meat scattered across its surface. The aroma of freshly baked pies filled the air, mingling with the scent of burning wood from the small fireplace nestled in one corner.

As Thornton hummed loudly to himself and moved swiftly behind the counter, his sleeves rolled up in preparation for the task at hand, a sense of ease infused his every movement. With practised skill, he began crafting more pies for the oven, his hands working deftly as he expertly shaped the dough and filled it with savoury meat and rich, flavourful ingredients.

He knew he was renowned throughout the city for his culinary prowess, his pies a testament to his skill and dedication to his craft. The tantalising aroma that wafted from his shop drew customers from far and wide, each eager to sample his delicious creations.

But with success came envy and resentment from his peers and competitors, who viewed him with a mixture of admiration and disdain. He revelled in their glares and whispered gossip, knowing that his success only served to highlight their own struggles.

His arrogance grew with each passing day, fuelled by the knowledge that he was the best pie maker in the city and that his business thrived while others faltered. He took pleasure in the jealousy of those around him, relishing in the knowledge that he had achieved what they could only dream of.

Thornton's chirpy tune faltered, replaced with a scowl as the door abruptly swung open, admitting a large man with a sash full of coins. His presence filled the room, his protruding belly and round, chubby cheeks giving him a jovial appearance despite the stern expression on his face.

With a thick, grey beard covering his cheeks and wispy strands of hair escaping from beneath his cap, the man appeared older than his years. Dressed in a leather apron stained with creamy textures and a snug white linen shirt that struggled to contain his ample girth, he cut an imposing figure as he surveyed the shop with bright blue eyes.

Thornton's scowl deepened as their gazes met, a palpable tension filling the air between them. Despite the jovial atmosphere of the shop, there was an unmistakable sense of rivalry and animosity that simmered beneath the surface.

With a curt nod, the large man approached the counter, his sash of coins jingling with each step. His expression remained stoic as he addressed the shopkeeper, his voice carrying a hint of challenge.

"Thornton, my man, how goes it? Good, I hope," the large man announced.

Thornton brushed away a strand of dark brown hair with the back of his hand while eyeing the man up and down. "Good business, as usual, Robert. I suppose you're here for some more flour?"

"In fact, I'm here for some of your delicious-tasting meat."

Thornton raised a sleek, perfectly sculpted brow at Robert.

"What for?"

"I'm holding a celebration at the end of the week, and I need some scrumptious nibbles to keep my guests entertained," he chuckled as he juggled his stomach.

Thornton remained silent, instead giving him a fiery stare. Robert cleared his throat, becoming increasingly uneasy in Thornton's company. "I need a pound of mince."

Thornton's movements were deliberate as he stepped to the side of the counter, his hands deftly weighing out a pound of mince on the scales. With practised precision, he wrapped the meat in an old newspaper, his movements swift and efficient.

Without a word, Thornton slapped the package of meat aggressively into Robert's hand, his gaze lingering on the man's face with an intensity that made Robert's nerves flare. A flush crept up Robert's cheeks as he took an involuntary step back from Thornton, the palpable tension between them thickening the air.

"I appreciate it," Robert stuttered, his voice betraying his nervousness as he struggled to maintain his composure under Thornton's penetrating gaze. With a quick nod of acknowledgment, he turned on his heel and hurriedly made his way to the door, eager to escape the oppressive atmosphere of Thornton's shop.

Thornton's sly smile widened at Robert's quivering demeanour, relishing the discomfort he had caused. His tone was casual, but there was a hint of mischief in his words as he addressed Robert.

"You're welcome, friend," Thornton replied smoothly, his eyes gleaming with amusement. "Is this an invitation-only event, or is everyone welcome to attend?"

Robert's suspicion lingered as he turned back from the door, but he forced a smile in response to Thornton's inquiry. "You're more than welcome to appear if you'd like," he replied, his tone polite but guarded as he opened the door.

Thornton sneered. "I believe I will." He circled back around the counter and continued smacking the dough into place, putting an end to his conversation with Robert.

Robert juggled the meat and his satchel of coins in one hand, inadvertently dropping his money in the process of heading out the door.

As he exited Thornton's shop, Robert couldn't shake the feeling of unease that lingered from their interaction. He knew that Thornton's presence at the event would only add to the tension and rivalry that simmered between them, but he also understood that he had little choice in the matter. Thornton was not a man to be reckoned with. The man could rip his business away from him with a swift wave of his hand and he knew it. Thornton had everyone under his thumb, especially the ladies, and he knew what Robert was really like toward his wife. Beneath the jolly façade the cheesemonger expressed was a pure hatred toward women, especially successful women. To him, women were beneath him. They were weak and simple-minded, and men could do as they will with them. Thornton was the only one who knew that about Robert, and made sure to show him with their encounters.

As Robert shuffled off into the throng of people, the breeze cut through his shirt, sending a shiver down his spine. Thornton's snidey demeanour lingered in his mind, but he quickly dismissed it, his thoughts returning to the task at hand.

Thornton's meat was undeniably the best in the area, and Robert was determined to impress his guests with the quality of his offerings. With a renewed sense of purpose, he made his way back to his shop, the anticipation of the upcoming event driving him forward.

As he entered the shop, his wife greeted him from behind the counter, a warm smile on her face as she emerged from the basement trap door, holding a wheel of cheese. Her presence brought a sense of comfort and familiarity, easing the tension that had lingered from his encounter with Thornton.

"Returned so quickly?" Betty beamed as she set the cheese on the counter.

Betty's hands moved with practised precision as she deftly worked her way around the wheel of cheese, her movements confident and sure. With each slice, she ensured that the portions were uniform in size, a testament to her skill and attention to detail.

As she waited for Robert's response, her eyes met his with a warm smile, her greying hair tied tightly into a bun atop her head. She wore a long pinstriped dress that draped comfortably over her round belly, the apron tied securely around her waist.

Despite her simple appearance, there was a certain charm about Betty that endeared her to all who knew her. Her thick Somerset accent lent a sense of warmth and familiarity to her words, her voice filled with a genuine kindness that resonated with everyone she encountered.

As Betty continued to slice the cheese with practised precision, Robert couldn't help but feel a pang of guilt gnawing at him. He knew he had been blessed when she had said yes to marrying him, but that didn't stop him from abusing her.

Behind closed doors, their relationship was far from perfect. Nobody knew who the real Robert was, not even his closest acquaintances. To the outside world, they appeared to be the most loving and devoted couple, but the truth was far darker, and Thornton was one of the few who saw through the façade.

Thornton had witnessed the true nature of their relationship when he first returned to Bristol to open his pie shop. He had observed how Robert spoke to Betty in the street, his words laced with venom and disdain. And when Robert had pushed her headfirst into their shop, Thornton had seen nothing but evil in the man's eyes.

But Robert was cunning enough to recognize Thornton's scrutiny, and he had since shown him nothing but kindness to keep him quiet. He knew that his business was booming, and he couldn't afford anything to derail it, not even rumours about his relationship with his wife.

Despite the whispers and speculation that surrounded their marriage, Robert remained steadfast in his pursuit of success as the best cheesemonger in the city. And as he watched Betty work alongside him, her loving charisma belying the darkness that lurked beneath the surface, he couldn't help but feel a twinge of remorse for the secrets he kept hidden. But in the cutthroat world of business, he knew that sentimentality had no place, and he resolved to do whatever it took to protect his reputation and his livelihood.

Betty stopped cutting the cheese, giving him a puzzled look as he sighed loudly. "Betty, the man creeps me out. I can't stand being near him for very long."

She gave him a sympathetic look before returning to cutting her cheese. "Did you get any of the meat?"

"There's something off about him, something unsettling. I absolutely despise him."

As Robert's frustration boiled over, Betty paused in her task of cutting the cheese, giving him another sympathetic look. His words spilled out in a torrent of emotion, his face turning bright red with each passing second as he vented his frustrations about Thornton. But Betty's attempts to interject with questions were met with deaf ears as Robert went off on a tangent, his anger palpable in the air.

Ignoring Betty's question, Robert's thoughts spiralled into dark fantasies, his mind consumed by images of violence and revenge. The urge to lash out threatened to overwhelm him, but he forced himself to focus on the task at hand, desperate to distract himself from the dangerous thoughts that plagued him.

When Betty finally asked about the meat again, Robert's rage erupted, and he threw the package onto the counter with a snarl. His teeth bared in a display of aggression as he snapped at her, his words laced with venom.

Betty remained calm, her own patience wearing thin as she tried to placate him. She knew all too well the consequences of provoking his temper, and she didn't want to risk further harm to herself. With a forced smile, she assured him that she would begin making the pies right away, her heart heavy with the weight of their strained relationship.

She could hear his footsteps retreating to the basement and burst into tears the moment she realised she was safe. Betty's heart sank as she heard the doorbell chime behind her, the sound sending a shockwave of anxiety through her body. Wiping away her tears, she forced a smile onto her face before turning to greet her customer, only for her smile to falter when she saw Thornton standing in the doorway, holding Robert's satchel.

Robert, hearing the doorbell, quickly returned from the basement to see who it was. Spotting his satchel in Thornton's hand, he moved to retrieve it, but Thornton's cunning manoeuvre caught him off guard. With a snide smile, Thornton snatched the satchel away and held it out to Betty instead.

"Perhaps you should have it," he said, his tone dripping with sarcasm. "I'm sure you'll take better care of it than your husband."

Betty's cheeks flushed with embarrassment as Thornton's words hit her like a slap in the face. She felt a surge of anger and frustration rise within her, but she forced herself to maintain her composure.

Betty glanced at Robert's crimson face, looking for permission to take the satchel. Robert took a step back, allowing her to step forward. With a trembling hand, she reached out to take the satchel from Thornton, her eyes downcast to avoid his piercing gaze.

"Thank you," she murmured softly, her voice barely above a whisper. She could feel Thornton's gaze boring into her.

Thornton sneered when he noticed Robert's firm grip on Betty's shoulder. "This time, Robert, I recommend you keep a closer eye on it. If you lose it again, you might not be so lucky to get it back."

Thornton's sneer did not go unnoticed as he issued his warning to Robert, his words dripping with malice. Robert's response was terse, his teeth gritted in frustration as he thanked Thornton through clenched teeth.

Thornton grinned and tipped his hat toward Betty. "No problem. See you soon."

As Thornton sauntered out of the shop, his laughter echoing in the air, Betty braced herself for the inevitable backlash from Robert. But to her surprise, there was nothing but silence. Peering around cautiously, she realised that Robert had already retreated to the basement, leaving her alone with her thoughts. Her heart heavy with a mix of emotions, Betty hesitated for a moment before steeling herself and returning to her duties. With a deep breath, she pushed aside the lingering fear and anxiety, focusing on cutting the cheese.

## CHAPTER THREE

# The Prowler

As evening fell over the city of Bristol, the streets grew quiet and deserted, enveloped in the eerie stillness of the night. In the shadows of the street, the police lay in wait, their patience unwavering as they prepared to apprehend their elusive murderer.

The alleyway remained shrouded in darkness, a stark contrast to the warm glow emanating from the pub nearby. The sounds of laughter and chatter drifted through the air, a stark reminder of the bustling activity just beyond their reach.

Inspector Acker and Sergeant Claydon stood vigilant in the darkness, their senses heightened as they waited for any sign of movement. The light from the pub cast long shadows across the cobbled street, creating an atmosphere of tension and anticipation.

Every sound, every whisper of movement, put Acker and Claydon on high alert, their instincts honed for the slightest sign of their target. They knew that patience was key, that their moment would come when the murderer least expected it.

"Do you reckon he'll be back to kill again?" Claydon hissed.

Acker knelt and hid behind a large barrel of liquor. "He'll be back; I'm sure of it."

Claydon got up from his crouching position. "But it could just be a one-off murder, Acker. Even if he were to strike again, I highly doubt he'll strike in the same place."

Acker sighed, getting up slowly. He knew that his brother was right, but he didn't want to admit it. It was just a hunch of his that the murderer would return. "I hope you're right, Claydon, but once they get a taste for it, they can't stop until they're either caught or dead. You know that."

A noise from across the street interrupted Acker as a man dressed in a long cloak appeared from the street corner.

As the man in the cloak emerged from the street corner, Acker's senses sharpened, his instincts on high alert. The figure moved swiftly, attempting to blend into the shadows, but Acker's keen eyes caught sight of him.

The man stopped suddenly in his tracks and stared directly at them, his face securely hidden in the shadows of the street.

"You! Stop there!" Acker's voice rang out in the silence of the night.

But the figure showed no signs of compliance, his hood concealing his features in shadow. A sense of unease settled over Acker and Claydon as they watched the mysterious nightwalker, their hands poised on their weapons, ready for any sign of aggression.

With each passing moment, the tension in the air grew thicker, the weight of uncertainty pressing down upon them. As Acker and Claydon waited for a response, the night seemed to hold its breath, the stillness broken only by the faint sound of their own heartbeat. In the dim glow of the streetlight, the figure remained shrouded in mystery, a silent enigma that held the key to their next move.

The man suddenly bolted, Acker shouting after him, his footsteps slapping on the ground as he dashed through a maze of alleyways to escape.

"Come on, Claydon!" Acker bellowed.

As Acker and Claydon pursued the hooded man through the maze of alleyways, their footsteps echoed off the walls, the urgency of their pursuit driving them forward. With each turn, the gap between them and their target narrowed, their determination fuelling them.

But as they rounded the final corner, their hopes of apprehending the man were dashed. Before them lay a dead end, the alleyway flanked by derelict factory buildings and hemmed in by a tall wooden fence.

A sense of frustration washed over Acker as he realised their quarry had nowhere left to run. With a grim determination, he approached the fence, his mind racing with possibilities. Beyond the barrier lay the docks and the Bristol River, a tempting escape route for the fleeing suspect.

But Acker knew they couldn't afford to let him slip away. With a quick glance at Claydon and the other officers, he signalled for them to spread out and secure the perimeter, ensuring that no avenue of escape remained unguarded.

After a few moments, Claydon reappeared alone and out of breath. "I've told the officers to spread out and cover every entrance and exit," he puffed.

Acker cast a glance behind Claydon's back, distracted by something. He started sniffing the air, his face contorted with suspicion. "Can you smell that?"

"Smell what?" Claydon asked as he followed him to the end of the alleyway.

"There's a faint whiff of cooking, but I see no chimney smoking away, which means?" Acker looked at Claydon questioningly.

Claydon's face remained expressionless until he realised what his brother meant. His face brightened, and he looked around for a nearby smoking chimney. "The smell belongs to the hooded man."

"Excellent, Claydon. Gather the remaining officers quickly. I have a plan."

Acker's senses were on high alert as he scoured the alleyway, his keen eyes scanning every corner for any clues left behind by the hooded figure as he waited for his brother to round up the rest of the officers. With each step, he followed the faint trail of baked goods that lingered in the air, his nostrils flaring as he tried to discern its source.

His search led him to a pile of discarded crates, their wooden surfaces worn and weathered from years of neglect. Acker began to sift through the debris, his hands moving quickly as he searched for any trace of the hooded man's presence.

Suddenly, his fingers brushed against something cold and metallic, hidden among the rubble. With a sharp intake of breath, Acker carefully retrieved the object, his heart pounding in anticipation. It was nothing but an old rusty pipe. He threw it back into the rubble and sighed heavily before lighting up a cigarette and inhaling it deeply to calm his nerves.

He listened to the sound of approaching footsteps from his officers before stubbing out his cigarette and turning to them as they entered the alleyway, hot and breathless. "We may have a simpler solution. Gentlemen, gather around." He gestured for them to come closer. "Within a five-mile radius, I need a list of every bakery, pie shop, cheesemonger, and butcher. Whoever that man is, he has left behind a very distinct cooking smell, which means he works in a food establishment. I want this city turned upside down."

"Is he our killer?" one of the police officers asked.

Acker pulled out his pocket watch and checked the time. "I'm not sure, but this is what we want to find out. He ran away from us for a reason, so he is hiding something."

"Inspector, Sergeant!" a voice from the back called out. A man pushed his way to the front of the group, puffing loudly as he went. "I need to see Inspector Acker right away."

Acker and Claydon took a step forward to see who it was. They were taken aback by the presence of the red-faced, puffy man dressed in a police officer's uniform. Acker motioned for him to take a step forward, away from the others, so he could speak privately.

"What exactly is it, Jenkins?" Acker demanded, his voice low and whispered.

"Sir, the orphanage just reported another missing child who

was taken last night," Jenkins hissed, attempting to keep his voice quiet.

Acker's expression hardened as he absorbed Jenkins' words. Another missing child, taken under the cover of night. The gravity of the situation weighed heavily on him as he exchanged a concerned glance with Claydon.

"Was there any evidence of forced entry?" Acker inquired, his mind already racing with possibilities.

Jenkins shook his head, his face grim. "No, sir. The matron found nothing, apart from an empty bed."

A surge of anger welled up within Acker as he processed the information. The thought of innocent children being snatched from their beds filled him with a righteous fury.

"Claydon, we need to step up this investigation and find out what's going on at that orphanage. I don't believe the kids are fleeing. I believe they are being kidnapped. We have to go to the orphanage first thing tomorrow morning."

Claydon agreed with his brother. "That's the best idea I've heard all evening, sir."

Acker frowned at him before ordering the police officers to disperse. "You've all received your orders. Go ahead and do it, and don't return until you have something for me to work on."

"Sir, should we send Chapman to Lady Penelope's home tomorrow to talk to her husband? He may have some information that could help us with our investigation. We need to delve into her past to see if she had any enemies that wanted her dead." Claydon explained.

"Yes, let's bring Chapman in on this. We need as many men as possible if we want to solve both cases. Where is he now?"

"At the station, sir," Jenkins responded.

Acker rubbed his forehead, stressed by the amount of work he had. "Then it's back to the station. As for the rest of you, start searching. We need to find Lady Penelope's killer before he strikes again."

As the weary police officers emerged from the alleyway, their determination remained unwavering despite their fatigue. They set out into the city, their footsteps echoing against the cobblestone streets as they fanned out in search of any food establishment that might provide a clue to the whereabouts of the mysterious hooded man.

## CHAPTER FOUR

# Bailey

Horse-drawn carriages bustled up and down the street, kicking up dust from the gravel as they went. Bailey leant quietly against the wall, his weathered hands cupped in front of him as he gazed out at the crowded street with a mixture of longing and resignation. Despite his ragged appearance, there was a sense of dignity about him, a silent strength that belied the hardships he had endured.

As the horse-drawn carriages passed by, Bailey's eyes followed them wistfully, his thoughts drifting back to a time long ago when he had ridden proudly at the head of his regiment. But those days were nothing more than distant memories now, faded and worn like the tattered uniform he wore.

Despite his struggles, Bailey remained a familiar fixture in the lively city, his presence a testament to the resilience of the human spirit. Though many chose to avoid him, fearing the ghosts that haunted his past, there were those who still showed him kindness, offering him scraps of food or spare change when they could.

But as the day wore on and the sun began to sink below the horizon, Bailey knew it was time to retreat to the shadows once more, seeking solace in the quiet corners of the city where he could rest his weary bones. But before he moved, he took one last look around the market, hoping for a scrap of food to be dropped. He scanned the crowd of eager buyers at the stalls before focusing on Robert and Betty taking a slow stroll up the road behind a carriage. He watched Robert link his arm through Betty's and lovingly smiled down at her in front of onlookers. A man stepped in front of them, and they both stopped in their tracks, surprised as to why he was there. The man towered over Robert aggressively, and Bailey crept closer to get a better look at what was unfolding in front of him. The man swiped a horse fly from his sleek, black coat, his cold, dark eyes fixed on Robert. The man appeared flashy and expensive, with a gleaming gold pocket watch on display for all to see. He wore grey gloves that matched his silk waistcoat, and his black shoes were perfectly waxed.

Bailey listened intently as the conversation between the mysterious man and Robert unfolded before him. Though he remained hidden in the shadows, his curiosity burned brightly, compelling him to eavesdrop on their exchange.

As the man confronted Robert with an air of aggression, Bailey's heart quickened with anticipation. He strained to catch every word, his ears pricked for any hint of danger or intrigue.

The man's imposing presence contrasted sharply with Robert's more subdued demeanour, and Bailey couldn't help but feel a surge of sympathy for the couple caught in the midst of the confrontation. He watched as Betty's fake smile faltered, replaced by a look of uncertainty, and he wished he could intervene somehow, to protect them from whatever trouble lay ahead.

But as the conversation continued, Bailey's attention was drawn to the man's lavish attire and expensive accessories. A pang of envy gnawed at him as he compared his own worn clothes to the man's opulence, a stark reminder of the vast divide between them.

Despite his longing for a life of wealth and luxury, Bailey knew that such desires were futile. He had long since accepted his fate as a simple scavenger, resigned to a life of hardship and obscurity. And yet, as he watched the drama unfolding before him, a part of him couldn't help but yearn for something more, for a taste of the life he had never known.

But as quickly as the thought crossed his mind, Bailey pushed it aside, refocusing his attention on the scene unfolding before him. Whatever fate awaited Robert and Betty, he knew that he had no choice but to remain a silent observer, hidden in the shadows, as the drama of their lives played out before him.

"I have no idea what you're talking about, Shelton. Please step aside," Robert hissed angrily at the man.

Shelton took another step toward Robert, taunting him with his walking stick as he poked it into his stomach. "You know very well what I'm referring to, Robert. You were seen on the night of my wife's death."

Betty looked at Robert's reddening face, confused and upset. She took a step away from him while trying to compose herself in front of Shelton. "What does he mean, Robert?"

Robert started becoming flustered and he ran his hand through his hair, giving himself time to think clearly. His eyes were wide with terror, staring at Shelton glaring down at him. "For goodness' sake, I was in the pub next door, as were a lot of men! You should be questioning them, not me, or perhaps you should question Mr. Thornton, the pie maker!"

Bailey's heart raced as he listened to the confrontation between Robert and Shelton. The tension in the air was palpable, and he could sense the fear radiating from Robert as he struggled to defend himself against Shelton's accusations.

As Robert's voice wavered with panic, Bailey couldn't help but feel a surge of sympathy for him. He could see the desperation in Robert's eyes, the overwhelming sense of injustice as he was unfairly targeted by Shelton.

But as Bailey watched Betty's confusion and distress, he couldn't shake the feeling that there was more to the situation than met the eye. There was something about Shelton's demeanour, his aggressive stance and accusatory tone, that didn't sit right with him.

Shelton's gaze narrowed on Robert, completely oblivious to Betty's shocked expression. "When I find out who killed my wife, there will be a dead man on the streets."

Robert quickly escorted Betty away from Shelton as he pointed to a stall. "Can you get some fabric so that you can make a tablecloth? Ours are getting on in years."

"Nonsense, it's only a year old, Robert."

Robert gave her a cold stare, his intimidating stance scaring her into submission. "Do exactly what I say, Betty."

She looked at him, upset and hurt, before eventually moving slowly toward the stall, sighing loudly to herself. She was aware that her husband was attempting to conceal something but asking him questions could enrage him to the point of no return. She put on a happy face and went to the fabric stall as her husband had instructed.

Bailey watched with a heavy heart as Betty complied with Robert's demands, her shoulders slumped with resignation. He could see the pain and fear in her eyes, the silent plea for help that went unheeded as she obediently followed her husband's orders.

As Betty moved toward the fabric stall, Bailey felt a surge of anger rise within him. It was clear to him now that Robert was not the man Betty believed him to be, that behind his charming facade lurked a darker, more sinister figure.

But even as his heart ached for Betty, Bailey knew that he couldn't intervene directly. He was just a humble scavenger, a man of little consequence in the eyes of the world. And yet, as he watched Betty walk away, he made a silent vow to himself.

He may not have the power to confront Robert directly, but he could still make a difference in his own way. He could be a voice for those who had none, a silent guardian watching over the streets of Bristol, ready to intervene when justice demanded it.

Bailey observed Robert leaning into Shelton, his eyes turning dark and menacing. "If you don't think your wife deserved to be murdered, then you didn't know her well enough."

Shelton grabbed Robert by the collar and yanked him violently toward him. "What's that supposed to mean?"

Robert sneered at him, pushing him away. "It means that your wife's past is not all it seems, sir. If you want to find your killer, I recommend looking into her past to see what evil she has done and why someone dared to kill her. Unfortunately for you, it wasn't me that did it. I don't have the guts for blood and gore," he adjusted his collar and extended his arm toward Betty. "Come on, Betty, our discussion here is over."

Betty, fearful for her safety, reluctantly took Robert's arm as he smugly walked away with her, leaving a stunned-looking Shelton behind, wondering what Robert meant about his wife.

Bailey watched the scene unfold with a mixture of shock and disgust. It was clear to him now that Robert was not only capable of cruelty but also manipulation and deceit. The way he had twisted Shelton's grief to deflect suspicion from himself was a testament to his cunning and ruthlessness.

As Robert and Betty walked away, Bailey couldn't help but feel a surge of anger rise within him. It was one thing to witness injustice from a distance, but to see it happening right in front of him, to see a man use his power to manipulate and control those around him, was almost too much to bear.

But even as anger burned in his chest, Bailey knew that he had to be careful. He may have sworn to stand up for what was right, but he also knew that confronting someone like Robert head-on could be dangerous. He needed to bide his time, to gather evidence and allies before he could take action.

With a heavy heart, Bailey slipped back into the shadows, his mind racing with plans and possibilities. The streets of Bristol may be dark and dangerous, but he would not let fear hold him back. He would find a way to expose Robert for the villain he truly was, and bring justice to those he had wronged.

## CHAPTER FIVE

# Thornton

The 'Thornton Pie Shop' was empty as Thornton disappeared into a small cloakroom in the back. He hung up a black cloak on one of the hooks and smiled to himself as he stroked the material, admiring its softness.

"One day I'll stop," he muttered before grabbing another long coat and draping it over the cloak, hiding it from view.

He heard the doorbell chime and returned to the front of the shop with an excited spring in his step. When he looked up, he saw a remarkable-looking woman eyeing his pies. Her tight striped bodice accentuated her curvy figure, and the sound of her heels on the wooden floor sent a shiver up Thornton's spine. His eyes gleamed with temptation as he gave her his most dazzling smile, watching her elegant fingers brush across the counter. "May I assist you, madam?"

The woman glanced up, meeting Thornton's gaze with a coy smile. Her eyes sparkled with a hint of mischief as she surveyed the array of pies on display. "I'm in the mood for something... savoury," she replied, her voice smooth and alluring. "Perhaps you could recommend something?"

Thornton's smile widened, pleased by the woman's interest. "Of course, madam. Allow me to suggest our specialty: the beef and ale pie. It's a customer favourite, and I must say, it pairs quite nicely with a glass of red wine."

The woman's lips curved into a delighted grin. "Sounds perfect," she purred, reaching into her purse to retrieve some coins. "I'll take one, please. My husband has a tab with you and will pay by the end of the week."

Thornton moved the pie away from her grasp. He eyed her closely and pulled a leather-bound book from beneath the counter. "Name?" He asked, opening it and began searching through a list of names.

"Hilton," she replied.

He found the name and added twelve tally marks against it before snapping the book shut. "Your husband's adding up quite a tally, miss."

The woman's smile faltered slightly, a hint of surprise flickering in her eyes. She quickly recovered, though, her expression smoothing into a practised facade of nonchalance. "Oh, is he now?" she remarked casually, though her tone betrayed a touch of curiosity.

Thornton nodded, his gaze unwavering. "Yes, indeed," he replied, his voice taking on a knowing tone. "Seems he's quite fond of my pies."

The woman chuckled softly, a light, musical sound and placed her hand on top of his. "Well, I suppose everyone has their indulgences," she remarked, reaching for the pie once more. "Thank you."

Thornton felt another shiver run down his spine, making him quiver in her presence. He quickly gathered his thoughts and gently pulled her hand away from his, leaving it dangling in mid-air. "Make certain that your husband has paid by the end of the week," he said sternly as he began wrapping the pie in the old newspaper. "Is that all?"

The woman leant in closer to Thornton, stretching her legs as far as they would go. Thornton could see the lust and eagerness in her eyes as she gazed at him. "I suppose you've forgotten our evening together last week?"

Thornton's tone was firm, betraying no hint of emotion as he addressed her. "I believe you're mistaken, madam," he replied evenly, though a flicker of discomfort crossed his features. "I assure you, our interaction was purely for just one evening."

The woman's expression faltered, a mixture of disappointment and frustration clouding her features. She quickly masked it with a forced smile, though her eyes remained troubled. "Of course, Mr. Thornton," she murmured, her voice tinged with disappointment. "I must have misunderstood." With that, she turned and hurried out of the shop, leaving Thornton to grapple with the uneasy feeling that lingered in the air.

## CHAPTER SIX

# Shelton's Town House

Chapman had been able to determine which house belonged to Shelton without his boss's directions. With its polished porch and gleaming windows, it stood out from the rest of the street. Everything appeared tidy, right down to the primed hedges that surrounded the property. It stood tall and proud, towering over the surrounding buildings, arrogance seeping through the marble bricks.

"All right, here we go," Chapman mumbled to himself as he wrapped his old, tattered coat around his waist, before making his way up the steps to the front door. He gently knocked on the shiny black door and took off his faded bowler hat in respect of Shelton's presence. Acker had advised him to be cautious with Shelton and not enrage him. He wasn't sure why he had warned him about Shelton, but his words lingered in the back of his mind, giving him a nervous stomach.

As Chapman waited for a response, he couldn't help but feel a sense of trepidation. The imposing facade of Shelton's house seemed to loom over him, and the polished exterior only added to his unease. He shifted nervously from foot to foot, glancing around the quiet street as he waited for the door to open.

After what felt like an eternity, the door finally creaked open, revealing a well-dressed butler peering out at him with suspicion. "Yes, what do you want?" the butler asked curtly, eyeing Chapman up and down with disdain.

Chapman cleared his throat, trying to maintain his composure in the face of the butler's hostility. He pulled out his police identification card and showed it to the man. "I'm here to speak with the servants of the house," he explained, his voice faltering slightly. "I'm from the police department, investigating a matter of some urgency."

The butler's expression hardened at the mention of the police. "Wait here," he muttered, before closing the door abruptly in Chapman's face.

Feeling the weight of uncertainty bearing down on him, Chapman shifted uneasily on the doorstep. He glanced around the quiet street, acutely aware of the eyes that seemed to bore into him from the neighbouring houses. The air was heavy with tension, and Chapman couldn't shake the feeling of being an unwelcome intruder in this affluent neighbourhood.

As he waited, the minutes stretched on, each one feeling longer than the last. Chapman's nerves were stretched taut, and he found himself replaying Acker's warnings in his mind. He couldn't afford to mess this up—his career and reputation were on the line.

Finally, the door creaked open once again, and the butler reappeared. "Mr. Shelton will see you in a moment," he said gruffly, stepping aside to allow Chapman entry.

Chapman nodded gratefully and followed the servant into the opulent foyer of Shelton's home, steeling himself for the encounter ahead.

He nervously entered the large hallway with his hands clasped behind his back, waiting for the butler to gather the servants. He was astounded, but not surprised, to see the lavish decor of the house. Everything glistened and glittered, polished to perfection.

There were delicate Chinese ornaments everywhere he looked. Above him, the crystal chandelier twinkled and twirled slowly, casting warm beams of light across the foyer.

The butler noticed Chapman's awe and turned his nose up with a smirk. "This way, please, sir."

Chapman followed the butler into the lounge and waited by a large stone fireplace, situated in the middle of the room. The room was full of beautifully made, hand-carved furniture and the same Victorian decor as the foyer. The butler closed the door and left Chapman alone. He sighed and leant against the fireplace, watching the flames and wishing he had such a lavish home as this one.

As Chapman waited in the opulent lounge, his mind buzzed with a mix of awe and anxiety. The contrast between the grandeur of Shelton's home and his own modest living quarters was stark, and he couldn't help but feel a pang of envy at the thought of such luxury.

He wandered around the room, admiring the intricate details of the furnishings and the exquisite artwork adorning the walls. Each piece seemed to tell a story of wealth and privilege, a world far removed from his own.

The door opened again, interrupting his thoughts, and a line of terrified and confused servants entered. He straightened his back and turned to face the servants, observing each one as they walked slowly past him. He displayed his police identification and waited for their reaction. They all looked terrified, apart from one woman. She stood at the end of the line with a smile on her face. "I'm here today to ask each of you a few questions about your late mistress, Lady Penelope," he said as he put away his I.D.

As Chapman addressed the servants, he noted their varying reactions with a keen eye. Most of them appeared apprehensive, their faces etched with worry and uncertainty. But amidst the fear, the woman had a hint of obstinance in her demeanour, her smile almost defiant in the face of adversity.

He approached each servant in turn, asking them about their interactions with Lady Penelope, their whereabouts on the night of her death, and any other pertinent details they might have. Some answered nervously, stumbling over their words, while others remained tight-lipped, their expressions guarded and wary.

But it was the woman with the smile who caught Chapman's attention the most. Despite the solemn occasion, she seemed oddly composed, her gaze steady and unwavering as she met his eyes.

"And what is your name, madam?" Chapman inquired, his curiosity piqued by her demeanour.

The woman's smile widened slightly, a glimmer of amusement dancing in her eyes. "My name is Evelyn, sir," she replied, her voice calm and collected. "I served Lady Penelope faithfully for many years."

Chapman nodded, taking note of her response. There was something about Evelyn that intrigued him, a sense that she held more knowledge than she let on. But for now, he simply thanked her for her cooperation and moved on to the next servant in line, determined to unravel the mysteries surrounding Lady Penelope's death.

Chapman looked around at the servants and noticed a small, timid woman in the middle who appeared to be very uncomfortable in his presence. She moved her gaze away from him and began to pinch the side of her arm, becoming increasingly nervous with the cold stare Chapman was giving her. He pointed to her, knowing that she was hiding something. "You there, come here."

The servant girl took a hesitant step forward, her bottom lip quivering slightly as she avoided his gaze. She began to smooth her apron before wiping a few strands of hair away from her face. She looked plain, yet there was something about the way she stood—confident and eager to please.

"What's your name?" he asked.

She stared down at the floor, avoiding his gaze. "Bella, sir."

"What do you know of your mistress's past?"

As Chapman questioned the timid servant girl, he observed her closely, noting the telltale signs of nervousness that seemed to radiate from her every movement. Despite her attempts to appear composed, her trembling hands and downcast gaze betrayed her inner turmoil.

The girl fidgeted nervously under Chapman's scrutiny, her fingers twisting the fabric of her apron as she struggled to find her voice. When she finally spoke, her voice was barely a whisper, barely audible over the crackling of the fireplace.

"I... I don't know much, sir," she stammered, her words hesitant and halting. "I-I only started working for Lady Penelope a year ago. She... she was always kind to me, but..."

Chapman raised an eyebrow, sensing that there was more to the girl's story than she was letting on. "But?" he prompted gently, his tone encouraging.

The servant girl swallowed hard, her eyes darting nervously around the room before finally meeting Chapman's gaze. "But there were rumours, sir," she admitted reluctantly, her voice barely above a whisper. "Whispers of... of secrets and scandals from her past. I never paid them much mind, but... but perhaps there was truth to them after all."

Chapman's interest was piqued by her words, and he leaned in closer, his eyes narrowing thoughtfully. "What kind of rumours?" he pressed, eager to uncover any information that might shed light on Lady Penelope's mysterious past.

Bella quickly glanced around the room, searching. She knew that if she said anything more, she would get into trouble. She needed to say something to divert his attention away from her. She motioned to the woman with ginger hair at the end of the line. "I only know a few of them. Evelyn over there has seen far more than we have. She worked as a lady in waiting for the mistress."

Evelyn gave Bella a stern look before turning away sheepishly.

"Step forward, please, madam," he said, noticing for the second time her piercing blue eyes and elf-like features.

But before the servant girl could respond, the door to the lounge swung open, and a tall, imposing figure stepped into the room, casting a long shadow over the gathered servants. It was Shelton, Lady Penelope's husband, his expression dark and stormy as he fixed Chapman with a cold, unyielding gaze.

"You, sir. Enough of this debacle."

He then clicked his fingers, and the servants scarpered, leaving him and Chapman alone in the room. The butler took one last look at Chapman, smirking, before he closed the door behind him.

Chapman shifted his focus away from the door and toward Shelton. "Sir, I am investigating your wife's murder. Kindly step aside and let me do my job."

Chapman's tone was firm and unwavering as he addressed Shelton, his gaze steady despite the tension crackling in the air between them. He stood his ground, refusing to be intimidated by the imposing figure before him.

Shelton's expression remained impassive, his cold eyes fixed on Chapman with a steely intensity. "Investigating, are you?" he replied, his voice laced with thinly veiled contempt. "And what, pray tell, have you discovered thus far?"

Chapman squared his shoulders, meeting Shelton's gaze head-on. "I've uncovered some intriguing leads, sir," he replied evenly, careful to keep his cards close to his chest. "But I'm afraid I cannot divulge any specifics at this time."

Shelton's lip curled in a sneer, his scepticism evident in the curl of his lip. "How convenient," he muttered, his tone dripping with sarcasm. "Tell me, Constable, do you have any suspects in mind?"

Chapman hesitated for a moment, weighing his words carefully before responding. "It's too early to say, sir," he replied cautiously. "But rest assured, I will leave no stone unturned in my pursuit of justice for your late wife."

Shelton's gaze hardened, his jaw clenched with barely suppressed rage. "See that you do, Constable," he warned, his voice low and menacing. "I expect results, and I expect them soon."

Shelton sat down on one of the immaculate, auburn chairs and then pointed to the chair across from him, motioning for Chapman to sit down. "Scaring my servants into talking will only deter them further from telling you the truth."

Chapman took a seat, leaning back to settle in. "I'm simply doing my job."

As he sat there, Shelton's eyes narrowed into slits as he observed Chapman's nervous leg twitches. "Then do it properly, sir.

I want you to find my wife's murderer, not harass my servants. There is nothing for you to find here."

Chapman resisted the urge to fidget under Shelton's intense gaze, maintaining a composed demeanour as he listened to the man's words. "I understand your concern, Mr. Shelton," he replied evenly. "But it's my duty to thoroughly investigate all possible leads, no matter how inconsequential they may seem."

Shelton's expression remained stoic, but Chapman detected a flicker of irritation in his eyes. "I assure you, Constable, I have nothing to hide," he stated firmly. "My wife's death was a tragedy, and I want nothing more than to see her killer brought to justice. But I will not tolerate baseless accusations or unfounded suspicions."

Chapman nodded, absorbing Shelton's words carefully. "Of course, sir," he said diplomatically. "I'll do everything in my power to ensure a thorough and impartial investigation. If there's anything you can provide that might aid in our efforts, I would be grateful for your cooperation."

Shelton's demeanour softened slightly, though the steely edge remained in his voice. "Very well, Constable," he replied, his tone less hostile than before. "I'll do what I can to assist you. But mark my words, I expect results, and I won't tolerate any further disruptions to my household."

He pulled a pipe out of his pocket and filled it with tobacco. With a snooty look on his face, he reclined in his chair, blowing smoke rings into the air. He looked solemnly at Chapman, revealing nothing about what he was thinking. Chapman couldn't read him, and the clock was ticking. He had only a few minutes to figure out what Shelton was up to, and it didn't help that he was making him feel very uneasy with his contemptuous stares.

"I need to question the servants to learn more about your wife's background. They may be privy to information that you are not." Chapman's tone remained firm as he addressed Shelton, determined not to let the man's intimidating presence sway him. "As I mentioned earlier, Mr. Shelton, it's imperative that I gather as much information as possible to piece together the events leading up to Lady Penelope's death," he stated, his voice steady despite the unease prickling at the back of his neck. "The servants may hold vital clues that could prove invaluable to our investigation."

Shelton scoffed, almost choking on his pipe. "My servants know nothing of value, sir. The only thing you'll find is their loyalty to me. I suggest you look elsewhere."

Chapman leant forward, watching Shelton's every move. The man stared into the fire, silently blowing out smoke bubbles into the room, as if he were trying to think of something quick to say. Chapman had always been good at detecting lies, and he could tell that everything Shelton was saying to him was a lie. He simply needed more time to corner him and get the truth. "How do you know that? They might know more than you think," he pressed, trying to keep him talking.

Shelton rose from his chair and sauntered over to a small table piled high with liquor bottles. He poured himself a glass and downed it all at once. He looked at a painting of himself on the wall with his back to Chapman. "Sir, I am aware of every secret, whisper, and rumour that circulates in these halls. There is nothing here for you." He poured himself another glass, but this time he looked at Chapman with rage. "Now get out there and find my wife's murderer."

Chapman's suspicions only deepened as he watched Shelton's evasive behaviour. The man's quick dismissal and sudden shift in demeanour only fuelled Chapman's determination to uncover the truth. He remained seated, his gaze unwavering as he studied Shelton's every move. "With all due respect, sir, I cannot simply take your word for it," Chapman replied evenly, refusing to back down. "My duty is to pursue every lead and explore every avenue until justice is served for Lady Penelope."

Shelton's grip tightened around the glass, his knuckles turning white with anger. "You dare to question me, Constable?" he spat, his voice dripping with venom. "I suggest you remember your place before you overstep your boundaries."

Chapman held Shelton's gaze, unflinching in the face of the man's hostility. "I am simply doing my job, sir," he asserted calmly. "And rest assured, I will leave no stone unturned until the truth is revealed."

With that, Chapman rose from his chair, his resolve

unwavering as he prepared to continue his investigation. Shelton's icy glare followed him as he exited the room, leaving behind a palpable tension that hung in the air like a thick fog.

He closed the door softly and headed towards the front door, but Bella, the servant girl, appeared from the servant's quarters, catching him off guard. He rushed over to her, cornering her before she could escape. "Please, miss, I only require a few moments of your time."

Bella's eyes bulged with fear, glancing around the foyer to make sure no one was watching. "We cannot talk here, sir. Evelyn is dangerous to be around. Don't trust her. She knows our mistress's terrible past."

Chapman's heart quickened at Bella's words, his instincts screaming at him to pay attention to the young servant's warning. He leaned in closer, his voice hushed. "What do you mean, Bella? What terrible past are you referring to?"

Bella glanced around nervously once more before leaning in to whisper. "Mistress Penelope... she had secrets, sir. Dark secrets that she kept hidden from everyone. Evelyn... she knows more than she lets on. She was always close to Mistress Penelope, like a confidante. But I fear she may have been involved in things... things that no one should know about."

He placed a reassuring hand on her arm and squeezed it gently. "I need to know everything that could be connected to your mistress's death."

She took another nervous look around before speaking, keeping her voice as low as possible. "Her past is full of hatred, abuse, and revenge, and she didn't care about anyone, not even her husband. There's more to her than meets the eye. She used people in ways you couldn't imagine."

A noise from upstairs caused Bella to jump, and she quickly snatched her arm away from Chapman's grasp, revealing a cluster of red, raw scars on her arm. Chapman took notice, raising a brow at her.

She quickly pulled her sleeve back down, clearly embarrassed and upset. "As I said, I cannot speak here because it is too dangerous for me. I can meet you somewhere, but only in secret; I cannot tell anyone that I am with you."

He nodded eagerly. "Tonight, at dusk? At the docks? I'll wear a brown bowler hat, so you'll know it's me."

She agreed reluctantly before retreating from him. "All right, I'll see you there; now hurry up and go before someone notices us."

Chapman hurried to the door and smiled at her before vanishing from view. She sighed, leaning against the wall to support her quivering body. After a few moments of deep breathing to calm herself, she wiped her brow, straightened her uniform, and walked away, her gaze darting around the foyer to make sure no one was looking. She had to tread carefully to avoid being killed, but she also wanted the police to know the truth about Shelton and his wife's dark secrets. He couldn't get away with it any longer, and she knew just what to do to stop him. A noise coming from the top of the stairs stopped her in her tracks. She peered up, but there wasn't anything there. She entered the kitchen, not realising that Evelyn had heard every single word she and Chapman had said. A huge grin spread across Evelyn's face as she retreated around the corner, back to her room.

## CHAPTER SEVEN

# The Orphanage

In a horse-drawn carriage, Acker and Claydon sat silently across from each other. They entered through a large, rusted iron gate bearing the words 'Bristol Workhouse' in faded gold letters above. The sound of wheels churning against the gravel path echoed across the swampy moors as the coachman bellowed out "Whoa there!" to the horses.

"We're here, Acker," Claydon announced, looking up at the crumbling mansion, standing desperate and derelict before them. The light filtering out of the dusty mansion windows sent bleak rays into the overgrown garden, full of weeds and unrecognisable foliage. Claydon felt sorry for the children, as the house was very much in need of repair. He couldn't imagine a mother's despair as she dropped her child off, unable to afford to feed or clothe the child herself. Acker nodded and picked up his black walking stick with a silver wolf attached to the top. He leapt from the carriage and waited for Claydon to join him. They both stood out from the bleak mansion with their crisp black suits and matching bowler hats. Wealth oozed from them, and it made Claydon feel uncomfortable having to see how well off they were compared to the orphans with no hope for their future.

"Stay here and wait for us," Acker called to the coachman.

The coachman tipped his hat towards Acker and smiled. "As you wish, sir."

The two brothers headed towards the large, peeling blue door. Claydon was about to pull the bell when a woman opened the door, surprising both of them. Her faded black maid's uniform with a stained white apron attached to the front looked too large for her thin frame. Her hair had been neatly pinned back into a bun and topped with a small white servant's bonnet. She eyed the brothers up and down, anticipating their reaction. "May I assist you, gentlemen?"

Both Acker and Claydon revealed their police identification cards to her. "Police, madam, and you are?"

Her brows lifted in surprise as she tried to block the entrance to prevent them from entering. "Edith, sir. What is this referring to?"

"We'd like to speak with the master of the house; please step aside and let us in," Acker said sternly, approaching her.

"Why do you need to see my master? He's very busy right now," she stuttered, her hand firmly pressed against the door to prevent them from opening it.

"This is about your missing children, madam; if you don't let us in, I'll be forced to come back with a search warrant."

Acker's stern tone startled Edith, and she quickly stepped back, allowing them entry. "I-I'm sorry, sir. Please, come in," she stammered, her eyes darting nervously between Acker and Claydon. "I was the one who contacted you about the children, but my master doesn't know."

As they entered the workhouse, Acker glanced around the dimly lit foyer, taking in the worn wooden floors and peeling wallpaper. "Why were you the one to contact us?"

Acker's question caught Edith off guard, and she stumbled slightly before regaining her composure. "I-I found out about your reputation, sir, and I thought you might be able to help us.

We've tried everything we can to find the missing children, but they've just... disappeared," she explained, her voice trembling with a mixture of fear and desperation.

Acker nodded, understanding her desperation. "Thank you for reaching out to us, Edith. We'll do everything we can to find them." He glanced up at the stairs, noticing two malnourished children peering down at them through the broken bannister. "How many children reside here?"

Edith sighed. "I have the necessary documentation in the master's office, but from the top of my head, I think there's around a couple of hundred children."

Out of a door in the corner of the foyer stepped three orphan lads. They stopped and fixed their gaze on Acker and Claydon, wondering who they were. Their hair was dishevelled and oily, and their clothes did not suit them well. They appeared less like workhouse boys and more like tramps. Among the boys stood Billy, the paperboy, his lean form looming over them as he watched the brothers with a look of fear on his face.

Edith grabbed Billy and shoved him toward the stairs. "Go get your master, boy."

Billy appeared terrified but did as he was told and ran off to find the master of the house. The other boys continued, whispering to one another as they passed through another door. Edith gulped, terrified of the two men. She scanned the foyer until her gaze was drawn to a pair of rotting double doors. "Gentlemen, you won't be disturbed here."

Acker and Claydon exchanged a look before nodding at Edith. "Thank you," Acker said, his voice soft but resolute. "We appreciate your help."

Edith hurried off, leaving the two detectives alone in the dimly lit foyer. Acker approached the rotting double doors cautiously, his hand resting on the worn handle. With a firm push, he pushed the doors open, revealing a large hall.

Claydon followed closely behind, his footsteps echoing on the creaky floorboards. "Let's see what secrets this place holds," he muttered under his breath, his senses on high alert as they ventured deeper into the workhouse.

Acker and Claydon looked around at the large hall filled with old tables and benches neatly lined up. Small bowls and wooden spoons had been carefully placed on the tables ready for dinner. Claydon reached for his handkerchief, recoiling from the smell of the orphans' lunch emitting from the kitchen's open doors.

Acker slapped his handkerchief away from his nose. "Remain respectable, sergeant."

Claydon groaned before slipping his handkerchief back into his pocket. "That smell can't be their lunch, surely?"

Acker shrugged and took a seat. "As I said, sergeant, remain respectable," he hissed at Claydon.

Acker wrinkled his nose while sniffing the air. "Poor boys, having to put up with this."

Claydon nodded. "I'm not surprised the children are going missing. Most of these windows are broken. Anyone could get in and take them, and no one would ever know."

Abruptly, the door opened and they both turned to see a podgy-looking man walk in. The buttons of his dark purple silk suit were straining against the girth of his protruding stomach. His patterned waistcoat held a gold pocket watch loosely, and a little handkerchief matching the colour of his suit stuck out of his side pocket. His shoes shone in the low light, the silver buckle nicely tucked under his freshly ironed pants. He was obviously wealthy, and his presence in the dilapidated hall made him stick out like a sore thumb. He saw the two brothers staring at his fancy suit and gave them a haughty smirk. "I'm Mr. Bodmin, the owner of this workhouse."

Acker and Claydon exchanged a quick glance before getting up to greet Mr. Bodmin. Acker extended his hand, offering a polite but firm handshake. "Inspector Acker, and this is Sergeant Claydon. We're here to inquire about the recent disappearances among the children in your care."

Bodmin's smile faltered slightly at the mention of the disappearances, but he quickly regained his composure. "Ah, yes, of course," he replied, his voice smooth and polished. "Terrible business, that. But rest assured, Inspector, we're doing everything in our power to assist the authorities in their investigation."

Acker raised an eyebrow sceptically, his gaze narrowing on

Bodmin. "We'll need full cooperation from you and your staff, Mr. Bodmin. Any information you can provide will be crucial in solving this case."

Bodmin nodded, his smile strained. "Of course, Inspector. Anything to ensure the safety and well-being of the children under our care." But as he spoke, there was a flicker of unease in his eyes, unnoticed by anyone but Acker, who made a mental note to keep a close eye on Bodmin's actions.

Billy stood beside the man, looking bleak and miserable. He had a large red mark across his cheek that wasn't there before, and Acker could tell the boy had been crying. Mr. Bodmin turned towards Billy and shoved him toward the door. "Be gone with ya, lad."

Billy cantered away quietly, still snivelling, until Claydon called out to him, forcing him to turn around. "Before you leave, you might be useful to us; I'd like you to stay."

Billy hesitated, looking uncertain, but Claydon's authoritative tone compelled him to obey. He shuffled back toward Acker and Claydon, wiping his tears with the back of his hand. "Y-yes, sir?"

Acker stood next to Billy, his expression softened with concern. "Billy, we need your help. Can you tell us anything about the children who have gone missing from the workhouse?"

Billy sniffled and nodded, casting a wary glance at Mr. Bodmin, who stood nearby with a scowl on his face. "I... I don't know much, sirs. But I heard whispers... strange noises at night. And... and sometimes, I see things... shadows moving where they shouldn't be."

Mr. Bodmin looked at Claydon, disgruntled. "What's this about, gentlemen? The boy knows nothing."

"Let us be the judge of that, sir," Acker said as he observed Billy shrink away from his master in fear.

Mr. Bodmin took a seat across from Acker. "Yes, of course."

The two brothers pulled out identical notepads, ready for Mr. Bodmin to begin speaking.

"Could you please tell us when this started, how it happened, and any other details you believe are relevant to our case?" Claydon questioned.

Mr. Bodmin shifted uncomfortably in his chair, growing

nervous with Acker's dark eyes staring at him. "Well, I don't know how it happens. They are usually taken during the night. At first, I thought that they were just running away. You know what orphans can be like?"

Claydon raised his head from his notes with a questioning look on his face. "And no one checks on the kids while they're sleeping?"

Mr. Bodmin sighed, mockingly concerned. "We have limited resources here, sir, and we cannot monitor every child who walks these halls."

Acker interrupted Claydon before he could finish. "And you weren't the one to report them missing?"

Mr. Bodmin cleared his throat, becoming tenser by the second. "No, I wasn't. I'm not sure who informed the police. I'm assuming it was Edith."

Acker's gaze drew to Mr. Bodmin's brow, where dribbles of sweat began to drip down his hairline. Before continuing, he scribbled something in his notebook. "Why didn't you inform us yourself?"

"I wouldn't get anything done here if I reported every missing child from this orphanage; children run away all the time."

Acker leant in close to Mr. Bodmin. "It is your responsibility, Mr. Bodmin, to keep these children safe; after all, you are the master of the house, are you not?"

His cheeks flushed, and he moved his gaze away nervously. "I am, indeed."

Claydon and Acker exchanged glances before focusing on Billy. "You, child, come here."

Billy's hands began to tremble as he walked over to stand beside his master. Acker gave him a quick once over, noticing that the boy appeared terrified of Mr. Bodmin. "Did you know the children well?"

The boy nodded slowly. "Yes, sir, I did. They were my friends."

Claydon gave Billy a warm smile, attempting to reassure him. "Is there anything else that you need to tell us?"

Billy cast a nervous glance at Mr. Bodmin to see if he could speak, but the man stared at the ground, avoiding everyone's gaze. "Well, there has been a man seen coming here."

Claydon and Acker sat up, suddenly more interested in Billy than the sulking Mr. Bodmin next to him. Mr. Bodmin glared at Billy. "That's enough now, boy."

Acker slammed his hand down on the table. "No, I will say when it's enough, Mr. Bodmin. Carry on, Billy. Say what you need to say."

Mr. Bodmin recoiled at Acker's sudden outburst, his expression a mix of surprise and indignation. He opened his mouth to protest, but Acker's steely gaze silenced him. Reluctantly, he kept his mouth shut, allowing Billy to continue.

Billy swallowed nervously, his eyes darting between Acker, Claydon, and Mr. Bodmin. "The man wears a dark cloak and has been seen staring in through the windows at night."

"Have you seen him?" Claydon asked.

Billy nodded again, this time with more certainty. "I have, and by the morning after he's been seen, there's another empty bed."

Mr. Bodmin, who was now looking down at the ground again, avoided Acker's accusing stares. "Did you inform Mr. Bodmin about this?"

"Yes, sir."

Acker turned his attention to a red-faced Mr. Bodmin. "Mr. Bodmin, why did you not report this to us sooner?"

The man waved his hands around the gloomy hall. "I didn't think it was necessary to report it because we have a lot of people prowling around here at night, stealing."

"That's a lie!" Billy exclaimed. Before Mr. Bodmin could slap him, he jumped back. "Aside from us kids, there's nothing worth stealing from here. You saw the prowler yourself, and you spoke to him! I saw you, as did the other children!"

Mr. Bodmin gave Billy a menacing look. "That's enough out of you!"

Acker leaned forward, his voice commanding. "Enough, Mr. Bodmin. It seems your guilt is showing more than you'd like." He turned to Billy, his expression softening. "Tell us everything you know, Billy. Your testimony might be the key to bringing justice to those who have been wronged."

"I saw him, exchanging something with the cloaked prowler a

few nights back when my friend was stolen from his bed," Billy explained.

Acker stood up, with his brother following his movements, knowing exactly what he was about to do. He had seen it so many times before. "Mr. Bodmin, I'm arresting you in connection with the missing children."

Mr. Bodmin's face twisted with shock and outrage as Acker spoke those words. He stood up, his hands trembling with fury. "You have no right! This is preposterous! I demand to see your evidence!"

Acker remained steadfast, his gaze unwavering. "We have enough evidence to detain you for questioning, Mr. Bodmin. You will come with us willingly, or we will use necessary force."

Claydon stepped forward, his hand resting on his holster as a silent warning. "It's in your best interest to cooperate, Mr. Bodmin."

Mr. Bodmin glared at them, his face flushed with anger and frustration. But after a moment of tense silence, he begrudgingly nodded, realising he had no choice but to comply. With a reluctant sigh, he held out his hands, ready to be handcuffed.

As Acker moved to restrain him, the door burst open, and a group of workhouse staff stormed into the room, their expressions a mix of shock and disbelief. A woman at the front, her eyes wide with panic, cried out, "What is the meaning of this? You can't arrest Mr. Bodmin!"

Acker turned to face the newcomers, his voice firm. "I'm Inspector Acker of the Bristol Police, and Mr. Bodmin is being detained in connection with the disappearance of several children from this workhouse. Stand aside and let us do our duty."

The workhouse staff exchanged uneasy glances, their initial shock giving way to apprehension. But the woman at the front, presumably one of Mr. Bodmin's allies, stepped forward defiantly.

"You have no right to barge in here and accuse Mr. Bodmin of such heinous crimes!" she exclaimed, her tone laced with indignation.

"Madam, stand aside and allow us to do our duty." Acker's

command echoed through the hall, cutting through the tension like a knife.

The woman hesitated, her expression torn between loyalty to Mr. Bodmin and the realisation that the situation was more serious than she had initially believed. After a tense moment, she reluctantly nodded, signalling to the others to clear a path.

Acker wasted no time, motioning for Claydon to escort Mr. Bodmin out of the room while he addressed the rest of the gathered individuals. "We will need your cooperation in this matter. Anyone with information regarding the missing children should come forward immediately."

As Acker and Claydon led Mr. Bodmin away, the rest of the workhouse staff and officials watched in stunned silence.

Acker turned to his brother as they made their way through the dingy foyer. "Claydon, I need a police officer here at night to capture this cloaked prowler."

Mr. Bodmin began to thrash around in Claydon's grip, attempting to free himself. "You need evidence to arrest someone like me! I'm not one of your tramps you can pick up off the street with no evidence!"

Claydon tightened his grip on Mr. Bodmin's arm, his expression unyielding. "We have enough evidence to detain you, Mr. Bodmin. You'll have your chance to defend yourself in court."

Claydon dragged Mr. Bodmin through the foyer toward the front door, where Edith had been quietly waiting for them. Her gaze shifted from her master to Billy, who skulked silently behind them, head bowed, staring at the floor. "What's going on here? Where are you taking Mr. Bodmin?"

"To the station, Madam, where he will be questioned until he tells us what he's hiding," Claydon huffed as he struggled to keep Mr. Bodmin still.

Acker approached Edith with a reassuring demeanour. "We are taking Mr. Bodmin into custody for questioning regarding the disappearance of several children from this workhouse. It's imperative that we gather all the necessary information to ensure justice is served." He glanced at Billy, offering him a sympathetic smile before turning back to Edith. "Rest assured, we will do everything in our power to bring those responsible to justice."

"This is an outrage! You cannot do this!" Mr. Bodmin screamed, his veins bulging in anger.

His raging shouts began to attract the orphans as they appeared one by one on the staircase, silently staring at their master being dragged away.

Acker quickly grabbed Billy's arm before he could escape. "You will join us too, Billy. You will tell us as much as you know, down at the station."

Acker's grip on Billy's arm was firm but gentle, a silent assurance that he was there to help. "We need your cooperation, Billy. Your testimony could be crucial in bringing justice for the missing children." He glanced at the other orphans gathered on the staircase. "All of you should come forward if you have any information. It's time to put an end to this."

The orphans retreated in fear, staring directly at their master thrashing around in Claydon's arms. Acker noticed the fear in the orphans' eyes and sighed inwardly. He knew it would take time to earn their trust, especially after witnessing their master's arrest. "Don't worry, children. You're safe now. We'll make sure justice is served," he assured them, his voice gentle yet authoritative.

They shook their heads and scarpered back up the stairs, away from the scene unfolding in the foyer below. Acker watched them go, feeling a pang of sadness for the children caught in such a situation. He turned his attention back to the task at hand, focusing on getting Mr. Bodmin and Billy to the station for questioning. With Claydon's help, they escorted the two suspects out of the workhouse and into the waiting carriage, determined to uncover the truth behind the missing children.

Edith's emotions seemed conflicted as she witnessed Mr. Bodmin being taken away. She couldn't help but feel relieved that the children might be safer now, but she also felt a pang of worry about what might happen next. With a heavy heart, she turned back toward the workhouse, knowing that there was much to be done to ensure the well-being of the remaining children and to uncover the truth behind the disappearances. She had a sense that her master was involved with the disappearances of her beloved children, and she was glad that the inspector thought so too.

"Come, Billy, you'll be safe with us."

Acker's reassuring words seemed to ease Billy's nerves slightly as they made their way to the carriage. The boy hesitated for a moment before nodding silently and climbing into the carriage beside Acker. The door closed behind them, and the carriage set off toward the police station, leaving the workhouse and its secrets behind.

## CHAPTER EIGHT

# The Bristol Dock

Apart from a few engineers in the distance, the docks were mostly deserted. It was crammed with crates and barrels full of goods waiting to be shipped, deserted by the earlier workmen, eager to get home after a long day of hauling. Chapman emerged from an alleyway, dressed in his brown bowler hat and grey suit. He looked to be a police officer attempting to pass himself off as a gentleman. The workers glanced over at him, knowing who he was by the way he was dressed. They became anxious by his presence and gradually shifted their workload to the other side of the docks.

Chapman continued his brisk walk along the docks, his eyes scanning the area for any signs of suspicious activity. Despite the workers' wary glances, he remained focused on his mission. He knew that this was a crucial part of the investigation into the murder of Lady Penelope, and he couldn't afford to be deterred by anyone's opinion of him.

He checked his pocket watch as he looked out at the horizon, watching the sun set slowly over the water. The hairs on the back of his neck began to tingle, and he cast a glance over his shoulder, hoping to see Bella. Although no one was there and the dock was deserted, he sensed that someone was watching him. The feeling of being watched sent a chill down Chapman's spine, but he tried to shake it off, attributing it to the tense atmosphere of the docks. However, the sensation persisted, growing stronger with each passing moment. With a quick glance around, Chapman couldn't spot anyone nearby, but the feeling lingered, unsettling him. Determined to find Bella, he squared his shoulders and continued his surveillance of the area, keeping a vigilant eye out for any potential clues or suspicious activity or where she might be waiting.

With the quiet evening fast approaching, the gentle lapping of water against the docks echoed softly, creating a soothing rhythm amidst the fading light. Seagulls circled overhead, their cries blending with the distant sounds of the city as it settled into the night. As the last rays of sunlight danced upon the rippling waves, a sense of calm washed over the deserted dock, a fleeting moment of serenity before night enveloped the city in its embrace.

Lost in contemplation, Chapman's gaze lingered on the rhythmic dance of the waves, their gentle ebb and flow a mesmerising sight against the backdrop of the setting sun. Despite the tranquil scene before him, his mind buzzed with thoughts of the day's events, the mysteries yet unsolved, and the challenges that lay ahead. As he stood on the deserted dock, Chapman found a moment of solace, a brief respite from the chaos of the world.

Feeling the chill of the evening air creeping in, Chapman snapped back to the present. The fading light signalled the end of his solitary contemplation on the dock. With a deep breath, he straightened his posture and turned to leave, his mind now focused on the tasks awaiting him. As he walked away from the water's edge, the echoes of the day's events lingered in his thoughts, driving him forward into the gathering dusk. He checked his pocket watch once more, frustrated by Bella's tardiness. He looked around one last time before returning the way he came, kicking an empty can along the way.

As Chapman retraced his steps, the feeling of being watched

continued to nag at him. He quickened his pace, hoping to leave the eerie sensation behind, but it seemed to follow him like a shadow. With each step, he felt the weight of anticipation building within him, a sense of unease gnawing at his insides. As he reached the end of the alleyway, he paused, glancing over his shoulder once more before stepping out onto the bustling street beyond.

A hooded figure stood in one of the alleyways leading to the dock, watching Chapman storm away. As Chapman faded from view, the person smiled beneath the hood, revealing only half of their face in the light. They peered down at Bella's slumped body on the floor and checked her pulse to make sure she was dead. Bella was face down in the alleyway with a huge, bloody gash on the top of her head. Her long jacket was filthy and stained red, partially concealing her maid's uniform. There was no one else around as the hooded figure began to stroke Bella's mangled hair away from her face. "You will stay forever beautiful now."

The hooded figure's words sent an excited chill down their spine as they continued to gaze at Bella's lifeless form. With a sense of eerie calm, they straightened up and glanced around the deserted alleyway, ensuring that no one else was present. Satisfied with their solitude, they leaned down and carefully covered Bella's body with an old piece of dirty material from nearby, obscuring her from view. Then, with a final lingering look, they disappeared into the darkness, leaving behind only the echoing silence of the empty alleyway.

# CHAPTER NINE

## Police Station

Acker and Claydon sat at a large desk, looking over a pile of paper and newspaper clippings strewn across it. The room looked dark and dingy, with only an outside lamp shining in to light it. The darkness encircled them, taunting them that time was running out. The room was barren aside from a neatly hung row of certificates with Acker's name on them. Chapman entered, irritated. He hung his coat on the rack before sagging into the chair next to Claydon, looking defeated.

Acker glanced up from the papers, his expression grave. "What's the situation, Chapman?" he asked, noting the frustration evident in Chapman's demeanour.

Chapman sighed heavily, running a hand through his hair. "It's not good, Inspector. Despite our efforts, we're no closer to finding the killer or unravelling the mystery of the missing children."

Claydon leaned forward, his brow furrowed in concern. "What about Bodmin? Did he give anything away during questioning?"

Chapman shook his head, his frustration palpable. "Not a thing. He's stubborn as a mule and denies any involvement in the disappearances."

Acker sighed, rubbing his temples wearily. "We need a breakthrough, something to turn this case around before it's too late."

Claydon nodded in agreement, his gaze fixed on the pile of papers before them. "We'll just have to keep digging. There's got to be something we've missed."

"What happened at Mr. Sheldon's?" Acker asked, clearly eager to find out what had happened.

"I have a little bit of information, but not enough to go on just yet."

Acker leant forward, his elbows resting on the desk. "What took place?"

Chapman began to rattle on, barely taking a breath. "Shelton basically threw me out of his house, and I wasn't allowed to question any of his servants, but one of them did give me some information. Her name is Bella, and she told me that Lady Penelope was not a nice person with a dark past. I was supposed to meet Bella at the docks to continue our conversation, but she never showed up."

Acker leaned forward, his interest piqued. "Did you find out anything else about this Bella? And why did she want to meet you at the docks?"

Chapman shook his head, his frustration evident. "I didn't have the chance to learn much more about her. But as for why she wanted to meet at the docks, that was my idea."

Claydon frowned, mulling over the information. "Could Bella have been onto something? Perhaps she knew something crucial about Lady Penelope's past that could shed light on the case."

Acker nodded thoughtfully. "It's worth investigating further. We need to find out what Bella knew and why she never made it to the docks."

Acker reclined in his chair and folded his arms, observing Chapman's expression. He wanted to make sure Chapman was telling the truth, and judging by his frustrated expression, he was. He let out a long sigh, unsure of what to do. He fell silent for a while before he clicked his fingers, thinking of a plan. "We must then return to Lady Penelope's residence and inquire as to why Shelton does not want us to speak with his servants. We'll do it first thing tomorrow morning."

"And what about Mr. Bodmin and the paperboy?" Claydon pressed.

Acker's face flashed with anger before settling into a solemn expression. "He can rot in his cell for one night. It won't hurt him. As for little Billy, give him a bed here and let him rest. He may be the only witness we have."

Claydon nodded in agreement. "Right, I'll see to it that Billy is taken care of. We can't afford to lose any potential leads."

Acker dismissed Claydon and Chapman with a wave of his hand. They left the room silently while he poured himself a large glass of whisky. As the fiery liquid seared his throat, Acker leaned back in his chair, the events of the day weighing heavily on his mind. He stared blankly at the dimly lit room, the shadows dancing around him, mirroring the turmoil within.

His thoughts raced, each one intertwining with the next, forming a complex web of unanswered questions and unresolved mysteries. The whisky provided a brief respite, dulling the edges of his thoughts and momentarily easing the burden of responsibility resting upon his shoulders.

But even as he sought solace in the amber liquid, Acker knew that there would be no rest for him tonight. The investigation demanded his full attention, and he was determined to see it through to the end, no matter the cost. With a heavy heart and another weary sigh, he set down the empty glass and prepared himself for the long night ahead.

## CHAPTER TEN

# The Cheesemongers

A fire crackled noisily in the corner of the room above the cheesemonger's shop. The sky outside was growing darker by the minute, and the fire projected a stunning orange glow across the floor. After years of disuse, the ornaments that adorned the shelves and bookcases had begun to gather dust. The floor was bare and creaking which had been hastily covered over with an ill-fitting, multicoloured rug. Betty looked comfortable as she nestled into one of the worn-out red armchairs, and although the room looked bare and had little furniture, it had a cosy vibe. Robert sat quietly next to the fire, smoking a pipe in one hand and reading the newspaper in the other.

Betty glanced up from her knitting, her fingers deftly moving the needles as she worked on a scarf. She watched Robert over the rim of her glasses, a small smile playing at the corners of her lips. Despite the worn furniture and dusty shelves, she found solace in the warmth of the room and for once, her husband looked happy.

As the fire crackled and popped, casting flickering shadows across the walls, Betty felt a sense of contentment wash over her. She took a deep breath, inhaling the familiar scent of tobacco and wood smoke, and let out a soft sigh of satisfaction. In moments like these, surrounded by the comforting embrace of home and her content husband, she felt truly at peace.

"Tea?" Betty asked, breaking the silence between them. She stood up and waddled over to a stove in one corner of the room to brew a cup of tea. A table beside the stove was cluttered with an expensive-looking China tea set that had already been set up for Robert.

Robert tilted his chair back and smiled at Betty. "Not right now, my dear. I'm about to leave."

Betty shot a look at him, dissatisfied with his response. "Now? For what?"

Robert got up, ignoring Betty's hurt expression, and folded his newspaper, neatly laying it on the armchair. "My darling, I'm going to the pub. That's what men do. We enjoy socialising."

Betty continued to pour tea into a large teapot. "We've discussed this before, Robert. You spend far too much time in that dreaded pub."

Robert's face instantly flushed with rage as he rushed towards Betty and kicked over the table that held Betty's special teacups.

Betty recoiled in shock as the table crashed to the floor, the delicate china teacups shattering into pieces. She stared at Robert, her eyes wide with fear and disbelief. "Robert, what's gotten into you?"

Robert's chest heaved with anger, his fists clenched at his sides. "I'll spend my time wherever I please, woman! You have no right to dictate to me!"

Betty's lower lip trembled, tears welling up in her eyes. "But Robert, we're supposed to be partners. We're supposed to support each other. Why do you always choose the pub over me?"

"No woman tells me what to do! You're nothing!" he screamed, kicking the boiling kettle to the floor.

Betty gasped in horror as the boiling kettle crashed to the

floor, scalding hot water splashing everywhere. She stumbled backward, narrowly avoiding the scalding liquid as it splattered across the room. Her heart pounded in her chest as she watched Robert's rage consume him.

"Robert, stop!" she cried, her voice shaking with fear and desperation.

But Robert seemed blinded by his anger, his face contorted with fury. He advanced toward Betty, his fists clenched, his eyes wild as he threw her across the room. "You dare question me? You dare challenge my authority?" he roared, his voice echoing off the walls.

Betty trembled with fear as Robert loomed over her, his cruel words slicing through her like a knife. She scrambled to her feet, her body aching from where Robert had thrown her, but she refused to show him any weakness.

As Robert strode toward the door, Betty forced herself to stand tall, despite the tears streaming down her cheeks. "You're a coward, Robert," she whispered, her voice trembling with anger and defiance. "A coward who can't face his own demons, so he drowns them in alcohol."

Robert paused, his hand on the door handle, his face twisted with fury. "How dare you," he growled, his voice low and menacing.

But Betty refused to back down. "You're a disgrace," she spat, her voice rising with every word. "A disgrace to yourself, to me, and to everyone who's ever loved you."

With that, Robert flung open the door and stormed out of the room, leaving Betty alone in the wreckage he had caused. She sank to her knees, tears streaming down her face, as she realised that she couldn't keep living like this. Something had to change, and she knew that change had to start with her.

## CHAPTER ELEVEN

# The Rummer Pub

Light from the pub on the corner spilled out across the cobblestone street, mixing in with the gas lamps on either side. The warm glow of the pub beckoned to Robert, promising solace from the raging thoughts of his home life. With each step he took, the sounds of laughter and music grew louder, drowning out the nagging voice of guilt in his mind. As he pushed open the door and stepped inside, the familiar scent of ale and tobacco enveloped him like an old friend, offering a temporary escape from his troubles.

He scanned the room, taking in the sight of jovial patrons gathered around tables strewn with empty glasses. The air buzzed with laughter and conversation, punctuated by the clinking of mugs and the occasional burst of hearty singing. He made his way to the bar, eager to lose himself in the comforting haze of alcohol and camaraderie.

Robert's usual facade of joviality was nowhere to be found. Instead, a simmering anger brewed beneath the surface, ready to erupt at any moment. He leaned against the bar, clenching his fists, his mind consumed by thoughts of his altercation with Betty.

He tapped the side of the bar, his anger pulsing through him, a turbulent storm raging within. Each tap echoed his frustration, reverberating through the noise of the pub. With a final glance around the room, he turned on his heel and stormed out into the night, his thoughts swirling in a tempest of fury.

He pulled his down cap over his face and scuttled away from the pub to a nearby alleyway where a group of women gathered outside a red door watching him warily. He walked towards them, reaching for his satchel of coins.

As he approached the women, their wary glances didn't deter him. His hand clenched around the coins in his satchel, his mind clouded with anger and frustration. He eyed the women with a mix of lust and desperation, hoping that their company would offer him some respite from his troubled thoughts. The sight of their smiles as they noticed the coins only fuelled his desires further, pushing him deeper into the darkness of his own emotions.

One of the women flashed him a toothless grin. "Back again, are we?"

"I am." Robert said, handing the money to the woman.

She eagerly snatched the coins and stuffed them into her small cloth bag attached to her dirty attire before tugging on his hand. "Same again?"

While the rest of them watched in annoyance that they weren't picked, Robert nodded and allowed the woman to lead him further down the alley. She pulled out a key, unlocked a door on the alley's side, and dragged a gleeful-looking Robert in after her.

## CHAPTER TWELVE

# Thornton's Secret

Two streets down from the pub, Thornton stepped out into the brisk night air from his shop and inhaled deeply with a smile on his face. He huddled into a dark cloak, pulling the hood up to hide his face.

Thornton's steps were light as he moved through the dimly lit streets, the cloak billowing around him as he kept to the shadows. His smile hinted at a secret satisfaction, his hands tucked securely into his pockets as he navigated the night with ease. Despite the darkness, there was a confident spring in his step, a sense of purpose driving him forward. He remained vigilant, casting quick glances around to ensure he remained unseen, his senses keenly attuned to the world around him.

From an alleyway nearby, Bailey observed Thornton hurrying suspiciously towards the docks. His past soldier instincts kicked in, and he quickly followed Thornton through the maze of alleyways to the dock, where the man stopped and looked around. Bailey stepped into the shadows, ducking behind a large crate of liquor to avoid being seen. Thornton could be heard quietly whistling as he pulled out a key to a large, broken-down warehouse opposite the river. He cast a quick glance behind him before disappearing into the derelict building, his cloak flapping in the breeze. Bailey stepped out from the shadows and rushed to the door before it closed completely. He slowly pushed the door open, taking care not to make a sound, and followed Thornton into an empty room with old worktops full of debris and tools. As Thornton unlocked a hatch in the middle of the floor, the moonlight shone through the dusty window, casting a silvery hue on his twisted smile.

Bailey's heart raced when he heard children crying for help emanating from the open hatch. He crouched lower, ensuring he remained hidden as he watched Thornton's every move with growing apprehension. The moonlight cast eerie shadows across the room, adding to the sense of foreboding. Thornton's smile sent a chill down Bailey's spine, his suspicions about the man deepening with each passing moment. With bated breath, Bailey waited, ready to uncover the truth behind Thornton's sinister actions.

Thornton stood for a moment, staring into the hatch with a thoughtful expression on his face. He then reached in and pulled a young girl out by her arm. She looked filthy, with long, scraggly blonde hair and a faded workhouse dress on. Thornton threw a bag of food into the pit, before slamming the hatch shut, immediately locking it. "Shut it, girl, or I'll give you something to cry about!" he hissed at her.

Bailey's blood ran cold as he witnessed Thornton's callous treatment of the young girl. Anger and disgust surged within him, but he knew he had to remain hidden for now, gathering evidence to bring Thornton to justice. He watched intently, committing every detail to memory, determined to uncover the full extent of Thornton's crimes. As the hatch slammed shut and the lock clicked into place, Bailey's resolve hardened. Thornton's cruelty would not go unpunished.

The girl suddenly stopped crying, petrified of Thornton, allowing him to lead her outside to the docks, where a man awaited them. When the man heard the little girl whimpering, he turned, and a broad smile appeared on his face. "Thornton," he said in a gruff tone, tipping his hat to him.

"Creed," Thornton smiled back and dragged the girl toward the man.

Bailey snuck through the door and hid behind a stack of barrels to watch Thornton hand the girl over to Creed. He watched from his hiding spot, his heart pounding in his chest as he observed the exchange between Thornton and the mysterious man. His instincts told him that this meeting was significant, and he strained to hear every word exchanged between them. He held his breath, waiting to see what would unfold next in this clandestine meeting on the docks.

"I have a lady looking for a girl. She'll do well as a maid. Well done, Thornton," Creed smirked as he looked down at the terrified girl, revealing a large scar on the side of his left cheek.

"I'll have another one for you tomorrow," Thornton said, counting a wad of notes received from Creed.

"Make certain you do. Business is booming right now, and we don't want anything to slow it down, do we?" Creed looked down at the whimpering girl and rolled his eyes. He reached into his pocket for a small piece of candy to silence her. "There you go, little lady. Now, keep quiet." He tipped his hat once more to Thornton before walking off into the darkness with the little girl. He chatted to her while she calmed down, slowly chewing on the candy and relishing its flavour.

Bailey stood and stretched his legs, inadvertently knocking over an empty bottle. The bottle clanged and rolled across the docks, echoing.

Thornton's head turned toward the noise, "Who goes there?"

Bailey's heart thudded loudly in his chest as he tiptoed away from the dock, trying to keep to the shadows. He cursed silently to himself as he tried to move quickly and quietly away from the dock, but the sound of his footsteps seemed to echo in the silence of the night. He kept his eyes fixed on Thornton, hoping he hadn't spotted him.

Thornton sprang into action, following the sound of footsteps. "Stop!"

Bailey retreated and darted into the alleyway, hoping to avoid being seen by Thornton, but it was too late. Thornton chased him down the street, his long, athletic legs quickly catching up. Bailey didn't have time to think as he darted in and out of the lamplight, revealing his identity to Thornton as he moved through another set of alleyways and onto another dark street. He could hear Thornton's footsteps slowing and eventually stopping to catch his breath. Bailey scurried into an open door and quietly closed it, listening intently for the sound of Thornton's footsteps to run past.

His heart pounded in his chest as he pressed his back against the closed door, trying to quiet his breathing. He strained his ears, listening for any sign of Thornton's pursuit. Seconds passed like hours in the darkness of the abandoned building as Bailey waited, trying to steady his nerves.

"I know who you are!" Thornton's voice echoed up the dark and dingy. "I'll track you down. If not today, then certainly soon! I'm not going to stop until I do!"

Thornton's footsteps faded into the darkness, leaving Bailey shaking inside the building. Everyone knew who he was, and it wouldn't be long before Thornton caught him. But there was one thing he was particularly adept at, and that was hiding.

## CHAPTER THIRTEEN

# Bella

The morning sunshine beamed through the windows of the police station. Officer Symons enjoyed the calm before the storm that usually descended upon the station as the day progressed. Sipping his coffee, he glanced out the window, watching as people bustled about their morning routines. The aroma of baked goods added a pleasant touch to the atmosphere, making the station feel more welcoming despite the serious nature of its work. He took a moment to appreciate the simple joys of a peaceful morning before diving back into his duties.

As he did so, a young police officer rushed through the doors of the station in a frenzy. He barged past the others and ran breathlessly towards the desk, where Symons sat quietly reading his paper. He stopped and peered over his drooping spectacles at the boy. "What's this about Hooper?"

The boy, red-faced and breathless, squeaked, "Symons, I must see the inspector. Where is he?"

Symons glanced up from his paperwork, his brow furrowing

in concern at the urgency in the young officer's voice. "He's in his office. What's happened, Hooper? You look like you've seen a ghost," Symons gestured towards a door at the end of the room, indicating Acker's office. "Go on, he's in there."

Hooper raced off to Acker's office. He knocked loudly and entered to see Acker slumped over his desk, snoring. "Sir, you must wake."

Startled, Inspector Acker jolted awake, blinking rapidly to regain his bearings. "Hooper, what's the urgency?" he asked, rubbing his eyes and straightening up in his chair.

Hooper turned away, embarrassed, once he noticed a half-drunk bottle of whisky on Acker's desk. "There has been another murder, sir."

Acker's expression shifted from grogginess to alertness in an instant. "Where? When?" he demanded, pushing himself up from his chair.

Another knock at the door interrupted Hooper before he could continue, Chapman and Claydon entering, fresh-faced and ready to start the day.

"What's the news today, sir?" Chapman asked, his gaze drawn to a flustered-looking Hooper.

Acker gave them a tired look, before turning back to face Hooper. "I would have found out what Hooper was trying to tell me if you hadn't just barged in here. Now, keep quiet and let the boy speak."

The men stared at Hooper, waiting for him to speak. "We've discovered another body, sir. They're bringing her in right now."

Acker quickly grabbed his stick and hastened to the door, with Chapman and Claydon close behind. As they approached the police station's front door, two officers appeared, carrying a body covered with a blanket on a stretcher.

Acker's heart sank as he recognized the grim sight. "Who is it?" he asked, already dreading the answer.

"There was no identification on her, sir, just a bloodied handkerchief," one of the officers said.

Acker's hand hesitated over the blanket before gently pulling it down. Chapman gasped loudly behind him, recognising the body immediately. Although the face was ghostly-white and the hair matted with dried blood, Chapman could tell it was the servant girl, Bella.

As he replaced the blanket over Bella's grimly pale face, Acker gave him a curious look. "You know this girl, Chapman?"

Chapman turned away from Acker, trying to compose his infuriated reaction. "Yes. That's Bella, the maid I was supposed to meet on the docks yesterday evening who never showed up."

Acker's expression hardened as he surveyed the scene, taking in the details of Bella's injuries. "This is grim," he muttered, his voice thick with emotion. "We need to find out who did this, and fast."

"At least we know she didn't just stand you up. She was offed before she could speak to you, so what does that mean?" Claydon said, staring down at Bella's covered face.

"It means she had evidence or knew something about Lady Penelope that could have aided us in our investigation," Chapman muttered.

Chapman's guilt weighed heavily on him as he stared at Bella's lifeless body. He couldn't shake the feeling that he could have done something to prevent this tragedy. Acker noticed Chapman's distress and placed a reassuring hand on his shoulder.

"We'll get to the bottom of this, Chapman," he said firmly. "But right now, we need to focus on finding justice for Bella."

"She was killed for a reason. We need to find out what it was," Claydon said.

Acker nodded solemnly, his mind racing with possibilities. "Put her in the back of the Black Maria and transport her to the hospital's mortuary for examination," he instructed the officers. Then, turning to Chapman and Claydon, he said, "We must return to Shelton's and find out what is really going on. Two deaths in one household raise an eyebrow, don't you think?"

Chapman watched as the officers took Bella's body to the morgue. "Quite right, sir. I want this killer found."

Acker placed a comforting hand on Chapman's shoulder and smiled reassuringly. "All in good time, Chapman. We first need to collect evidence to support our case."

Chapman nodded. "Then what are we waiting for? Let's go."

## CHAPTER FOURTEEN

# The Night of Bella's Death

Mist had quickly settled over the dark, empty street. It spread over the city, nestling comfortably over the buildings' rooftops. A warm, comforting light shone through Shelton's downstairs window as he peered out into the street, puffing on his pipe. He craned his neck, hearing light, quick footsteps scurrying across the street. He caught a glimpse of Evelyn, huddled in a big, dark cloak, running toward the front door. She glanced up at the window where Shelton stood looking at her and waved. The crimson blood on her hand glinted in the light of the streetlamp and he stepped back in surprise at her stupidity.

Shelton's heart quickened as Evelyn approached, her figure shrouded in the mist. He couldn't shake the feeling of unease that settled in the pit of his stomach, especially when he thought of the blood on her hands.

The butler opened the door and looked at her, puzzled.

"Where have you been? You're meant to be working." He raised a brow, noticing the stains on her hand. "Evelyn, what have you done?"

Despite Shelton's apprehension, he forced a smile and stepped into the foyer to greet her, the warmth of his home beckoning her closer.

She ignored the butler and headed straight to Shelton, where he took her arm and led her into the lounge. "I'll take it from here." He motioned to the butler to leave before shutting the lounge door. "Is it done?" he asked Evelyn as soon as he heard the butler's footsteps fade away.

She smiled gleefully. "Yes, it's done."

"Did anyone see you?"

She shook her head. "Not a soul."

"Good." Shelton puffed on his pipe while deep in thought. "It won't be long until the police find her and assume that she was also murdered by my wife's murderer."

"What if they come to us first?"

"Oh, they will, but we need to remain calm and keep to our story."

Evelyn pointed a shaky finger towards the door. "But what about him out there? He saw me."

Shelton smirked. "He won't talk. He's as loyal as a dog." He glanced down at Evelyn's hands again and tutted. "Wash your hands. We cannot leave any trace of evidence behind."

Evelyn nodded, but before leaving the room, she leaned in and kissed Shelton on the lips.

His heart raced as Evelyn kissed him, a mix of desire and suspicion swirling within him. He reciprocated the kiss with fervour, his mind clouded with conflicting emotions. But as quickly as the moment began, he abruptly pushed her away, his expression hardening as he gestured towards the door. "Go," he commanded, his voice tinged with both longing and urgency.

Without another word, Evelyn left, smiling slyly to herself.

## CHAPTER FIFTEEN

# The Hospital Mortuary - Present Day

The hospital mortuary was quiet and eerie. The imposing wooden doors of the mortuary did not look welcoming in the slightest and Acker found himself enveloped in a realm of muted hues and solemn whispers as he and Claydon marched through the corridor. The air carried the faint scent of antiseptic mingled with the earthy undertones of aged wood, creating an atmosphere heavy with reverence and gravity. Acker hated the clinical smell of hospitals and the sense of death they carried.

They walked through the wooden doors into the heart of the mortuary, straight into the preparation chamber, a space stinking of chemicals and death. There, under the soft glow of gas lamps suspended from the vaulted ceiling, the embalming tables stood like silent sentinels, awaiting their sombre duties. Polished marble countertops gleamed dully in the dim light, adorned with rows of shiny surgical instruments meticulously arranged in anticipation of their macabre choreography.

Against the walls, towering refrigerated chambers stood tall and proud, their iron doors etched with intricate patterns of wrought iron, guarding the slumbering forms within. Within those frigid confines, the departed repose in silent serenity, cocooned in a gentle embrace of frost and shadow.

Acker looked beyond the preparation chamber which held a hushed sanctuary reserved for the final farewells of grieving families. There, ornate mahogany pews lined the walls, their plush upholstery worn with the weight of countless mourners who had sought solace within those solemn bounds. Soft candlelight flickered in tarnished brass sconces, casting dancing shadows upon the walls adorned with doleful tapestries depicting scenes of eternal rest.

In the corner, a solitary desk stood vigil, its surface strewn with weathered ledgers and quill pens poised in silent contemplation.

Acker and Claydon's footsteps echoed softly against the polished marble floors as they approached the desk, where a solitary figure sat hunched over a weathered ledger, its pages yellowed with age.

The custodian of the mortuary, a stoic figure clad in a threadbare waistcoat with spectacles perched precariously on the bridge of his nose, glanced up from his task as Acker and Claydon drew near. His weary eyes, tinged with the weight of countless sorrows, met theirs with a silent acknowledgment, betraying a depth of wisdom forged in the crucible of loss.

"Good morning, gentlemen," he murmured, his voice a low, gravelly rumble that seemed to resonate with the echoes of ages past. "How may I be of service to you?"

Acker, with a gaze as steely as his resolve, stepped forward, his brow furrowed in quiet determination. "We seek information from the doctor regarding a recent arrival," he replied, his words measured and precise. "The body of Lady Penelope, and another recent body of a servant girl."

Claydon, with a hint of uncertainty flickering behind his steady gaze, nodded in silent agreement. "We believe the servant girl may be connected to an ongoing investigation," he added.

The custodian regarded them both with a solemn nod, his

expression betraying no hint of surprise or curiosity. With a deliberate motion, he reached for the ledger before him, its leather-bound cover worn smooth with age. Flipping through its pages with a practised hand, he paused, his fingers tracing the faded ink of a recent entry.

"A tragic affair indeed," he murmured. "The doctor is with the victims now."

As he spoke, he withdrew a small brass key from the depths of his waistcoat pocket, its surface tarnished with the patina of time. He unlocked a drawer in his desk and pulled out two documents.

"The doctor has written these up for you." He handed the documents to Acker and with a silent gesture, he beckoned Acker and Claydon to follow, leading them further into the depths of the mortuary.

The custodian led them into another, smaller, room. Two mortuary tables were located in the centre, each with a funnel attached underneath it, spilling bodily fluids into buckets. A tray filled with heavy-duty medical instruments had been neatly lined up next to the bodies, waiting to be used. Two bodies lay on the mortuary tables, covered with white sheets.

As Acker and Claydon followed the custodian, the air grew heavier with the scent of antiseptic and the unmistakable tang of mortality. Gas lamps flickered weakly against the whitewashed walls, casting an eerie presence over the room.

The custodian gestured towards the two tables, the crisp white sheets fluttering softly in the still air. A hushed reverence settled over the room as Acker and Claydon approached, their footsteps muffled against the cold stone floor.

The custodian drew back the sheet from the nearest table, revealing the pale form of Lady Penelope, her features frozen in an eternal respite. Acker's gaze softened as he regarded the lifeless figure before him, a silent acknowledgment of the tragedy that had befallen her.

Claydon's eyes widened in silent recognition as he turned his attention to the second table, where the servant girl Bella lay in similar quietude. Her features were drawn with an expression of serenity, her hands folded neatly across her chest in a gesture of quiet reflection.

Suddenly, the door to the left flung open, and a doctor dressed in a white shirt covered with a long apron burst in, trailed by the mortuary attendant carrying a doctor's bag. "Ah, Inspector. I've been waiting for your arrival."

Acker shook the doctor's hand. "Banes, good to see you. Can you tell us what you've found about Lady Penelope?"

Banes nodded and got right to work, examining the body while the mortuary attendant watched. "I'm afraid, not much. She had been slashed from ear to ear and struck on the back of the head with a blunt object." He leant in close and pointed to the purple gash on her neck. "As you can see, the cut is deep, indicating that whoever did it was either extremely strong or extremely angry."

"What else can we learn from the cut?" Claydon asked, drawing nearer to the body.

"The jagged edge suggests that this was not done by a doctor, butcher, or anyone else who deals with cutting or slicing. Whoever had done this wasn't very good with a knife." He then carefully pulled back the sheet further to reveal purple and black leg markings. "Which brings us to this. These markings were inflicted around the time of her death."

Acker inspected the markings, scrutinising each one. "So, what does all of this mean?"

"Normally, these bruises would indicate foul play, but I checked, and this is not the case," Banes responded matter-of-factly.

"So, you're saying she either knew her murderer or these markings occurred shortly before she was murdered?" Claydon pondered.

Banes shook his head. "I'm not implying anything, Sergeant, but these markings are most emphatically not the result of foul play. They're markings often indicative of rough intercourse. There is no forced entry around the vulva, which indicates that this woman was prone to having rough sex."

Acker pulled the sheet back over. "Mr. Shelton had told us that he hadn't seen his wife all day. And if what he said was true, it could only mean one thing: she was seeing other men behind his back."

"Which could be a motive for him?" Claydon asked eagerly.

"Exactly, Claydon. The puzzle pieces are starting to fit together."

The sudden cough shattered the heavy atmosphere, drawing the attention of the three men towards the morgue attendant for the first time. His presence, previously overlooked in the shadowy corners of the room, now commanded their full attention as he stood with a slight stoop, his features somewhat obscured by the flickering light of the gas lamps.

The morgue attendant cleared his throat, his voice a raspy whisper that seemed to carry the weight of untold secrets. "Forgive me for interrupting," he murmured, his gaze darting nervously between the assembled figures. "But there is something you ought to know."

Acker's brow furrowed in silent curiosity as he regarded the attendant with a probing gaze. "Speak," he commanded, his voice a low rumble that reverberated through the stillness of the room.

The attendant hesitated for a moment, his hands trembling slightly at his sides. "I... I couldn't help but notice earlier," he began, his words hesitant and halting. "About the body of Lady Penelope."

Claydon's eyes narrowed in suspicion as he exchanged a wary glance with Acker. "And what of it?" he demanded.

The morgue attendant swallowed hard, his throat dry and constricted. "It's just... there's something odd about the markings on Lady Penelope's legs," he confessed, his voice barely above a whisper. "A body of a woman came through here around a fortnight back with the same markings on her legs."

The revelation hung in the air like a dense fog, casting a pall of unease over those in the mortuary. Acker's brow furrowed in concern as he exchanged a glance with Claydon, the gravity of the morgue attendant's words weighing heavily upon them.

"The same markings?" Claydon echoed, his voice tinged with disbelief. "Are you certain?"

The morgue attendant nodded, his eyes wide with apprehension. "They were the same type of markings," he replied, his voice trembling with uncertainty. "The woman was around the same age as Lady Penelope."

"What did the woman die of?" Acker asked.

The morgue attendant hesitated for a moment, his gaze shifting uneasily between Acker and Claydon as he wrestled with the weight of his revelation. "The woman's cause of death was by drowning," he began. "There were no outward signs of trauma or injury. The postmortem indicated that she was drunk at the time of her death. Her death was ruled accidental due to the amount of alcohol in her system. She was a well-known prostitute."

Acker's brow furrowed in silent contemplation as he absorbed the attendant's words. "And the markings on her legs, are you sure they're the same as Lady Penelope's?" he pressed, his tone measured and deliberate.

The attendant swallowed hard, his throat dry with apprehension. "I can't be sure of it, but they look very similar," he confessed, his voice barely above a whisper. "Intricate patterns, possibly done by the same person."

Claydon's eyes narrowed in suspicion as he exchanged a wary glance with Acker. "Could it have been foul play?" he ventured.

The morgue attendant shook his head, his features drawn with a solemn resignation. "No indication to say foul play," he replied. "Dr Banes made sure of it."

Banes nodded. "I saw no sign of foul play on the prostitute's body. The markings do look very similar to Lady Penelope's, but without the body here, I cannot say for certain."

Acker regarded Banes with a thoughtful expression, his mind racing with the weight of their discoveries. "Where is the body now?"

"Buried in a pauper's grave in Bristol cemetery, Inspector. No family came forward to claim her," Banes replied.

Acker's jaw clenched with a mixture of sorrow and determination as he absorbed the news of the prostitute's lonely fate.

"No family..." he murmured. "No one to mourn her passing."

Claydon cleared his throat, bringing the attention to him. "If any more bodies with the same markings come through here, notify us immediately."

The custodian and mortuary assistant nodded solemnly.

"You have my word," Banes replied. "I will keep a vigilant

watch over the mortuary, and should any more bodies with similar markings arrive, you will be the first to know."

Acker and Claydon exchanged a silent glance, their minds ablaze with the urgency of their investigation. "Thank you," Acker said, his voice tinged with gratitude. "Your assistance in this matter is greatly appreciated."

With a shared nod of agreement, the morgue attendant and the custodian turned to leave the mortuary, their footsteps echoing softly against the cold stone floor, leaving the doctor, inspector, and sergeant alone.

"That's Harvard," Banes said, breaking the silence between them. "He's my assistant and also the embalmer. James is the custodian of the mortuary."

Acker nodded in acknowledgement, returning his attention to the body. "Is there anything else we need to know about Lady Penelope?"

"That's all I've got for now; I'll keep working on her, and James has given you the documents of my findings so far."

The door opened, and Chapman entered with a cigarette dangling from his mouth. "My apologies, I overslept."

"I was about to send out a search party," Acker said sarcastically as Chapman joined them.

Chapman gave him a sidelong glance. "Well, sir, I'm here now."

Acker gestured with his fingers for them to join him at the table with Bella's body. "How about this lady?"

"She died as a result of blunt force trauma to the head," Banes pointed to the area of the wound.

"Is it possible that it's the same weapon?" Acker asked, examining the wound closer.

"Quite possibly, but I'm not sure. The markings differ slightly, but they are very similar," Banes explained.

"Is there anything else?" Claydon asked.

Banes nodded and pulled down the sheet. "There is, in fact, one. Bella has foul-play marks, but the wounds are not fresh. She also has a lot of markings on her arms and back that indicate the use of a whip."

Chapman withdrew his gaze from Bella's body, filled with

guilt. "I saw those on her arm when I last saw her. She tried hiding them from me. I should have just taken her to the station instead of leaving her there."

"So, the markings don't have anything to do with her death?" Claydon asked, steering the attention back to the body.

"No. These were done a while ago, but there are a lot of them, so it happened at least few times. To me, it appears that this had been going on for some time," Banes elaborated.

Acker looked at Banes, puzzled. "Doctor, you're telling me that little Bella here was mistreated on multiple occasions?"

Banes nodded glumly. "That's how it appears to me. Some of the markings are new, while others are older."

Before heading out the door, Acker patted the doctor on the back. "Thank you very much, doctor. Continue your excellent work." He dragged Claydon and Chapman along with him, leaving the doctor alone to work. "It's time to pay a visit to Shelton."

## CHAPTER SIXTEEN

### The Morning After Robert's Disappearance

Betty's mind drifted, her thoughts swirling with the events of the night before, of her conversation with Robert. Despite her best efforts to focus on her work, her attention kept slipping, causing her to make small mistakes like miscounting change or forgetting to offer certain items to customers.

As the never-ending line of customers persisted, Betty struggled to maintain her usual efficiency. She found herself lost in a cycle of worry and frustration, her mind replaying the argument with Robert and wondering how they would resolve their differences.

With each passing customer, Betty's inner turmoil grew, her movements becoming more mechanical as she went through the motions of serving them. She forced a smile onto her face, trying to hide her distraction from the customers, but inside, she was struggling to keep it together.

Her movements behind the counter were swift, a testament to her years of experience in customer service. No one would have known the distress she was going through as she greeted each customer with a warm smile, quickly taking their orders and ensuring they were promptly served. She deftly juggled multiple tasks, effortlessly multitasking as she fulfilled orders, handled payments, and restocked the counter when needed.

As the early morning rush subsided, Betty finally found herself with a moment of respite. With the last customer gone, she took a deep breath, grateful for the temporary lull in activity. She glanced around the now-empty shop, the quiet allowing her thoughts to once again drift back to her conversation with Robert.

Betty leaned against the counter, replaying their argument in her head, analysing every word and gesture, searching for a solution to their ongoing struggle. She knew that their relationship was at a crossroads, and she couldn't shake the feeling of uncertainty that hung over her like a dark cloud.

Lost in her thoughts, Betty barely noticed the mingling shopper who approached the counter. She snapped back to reality as he placed his order, forcing a smile onto her face as she attended to his needs. Once the transaction was complete, the customer left, leaving Betty alone once again with her thoughts.

Robert, looking dishevelled from his evening's engagement, barged through the door with a smug expression on his face. Betty didn't bother looking up from the counter as she spoke to him angrily. "Robert, where have you been all night?"

Robert gleefully looked at her sad expression, knowing that she knew what he'd been up to all night. "It's a wife's duty not to ask such silly questions, Betty."

She glanced up slowly, hesitating before focusing her gaze on his smug smile. "I'm only concerned about you, Robert, because there's a murderer on the loose."

He chuckled as he placed a cold hand on top of hers. "Oh, my dear Betty, don't worry about it; I'm sure he won't go after an old man like me."

Betty's expression hardened as Robert's words sank in. She withdrew her hand from beneath his cold touch, her concern turning to suspicion. "Robert, that's not funny," she said sternly, her voice tinged with worry.

But Robert's smug smile only widened, his eyes gleaming with mischief. "Oh, come now, Betty. You know I have a knack for getting out of sticky situations," he teased, oblivious to her growing unease.

Betty's mind raced with a mix of fear and frustration. She couldn't understand why Robert would make light of such a serious situation, especially with a murderer on the loose in their town. She knew she had to confront him about his reckless behaviour, but a part of her feared what she might uncover.

Deep down, she loved him but hated the way he treated her. He was the only man she had ever known. He was mostly kind and tender to her needs, but as he grew older, his loving care dwindled, leaving a miserable and grumpy old fool who thought he knew better than anyone else. His arrogance was toxic to the ears, and she knew he'd been at it again when she saw his red, rosy cheeks and gleaming smile. She was terrified for herself, but she couldn't stop the words that started tumbling out of her mouth. "Yes, Robert. You are an old man now, so I suggest you start acting like one rather than prowling around the streets at night looking for other women; the police may question you."

Betty's words hung in the air, heavy with both frustration and fear. She watched as Robert's smug expression faltered, his rosy cheeks paling slightly at her accusation. For a moment, there was silence between them, broken only by the faint sound of idle chatter outside the shop.

Robert's initial shock gave way to indignation, his brows furrowing as he bristled at Betty's accusation. "How dare you insinuate such a thing, Betty?" he retorted, his voice laced with defensiveness. "I may have my flaws, but I would never betray you like that."

But Betty remained unmoved, her own resolve unwavering. "Actions speak louder than words, Robert," she said. "I've seen the way you look at other women when you think I'm not watching. I've heard the rumours whispered behind our backs."

Robert's gaze flickered, guilt briefly flashing in his eyes before he quickly masked it with anger. "Rumours are just that—rumours," he snapped, his tone sharp. "You should know better than to listen to idle gossip."

But Betty shook her head, her heart heavy with disappointment. "I wish I could believe you, Robert. I truly do," she said softly, her voice tinged with sorrow. "But I can't ignore what's right in front of me. I've seen you late at night up to no good."

He glowered at her, his lip curling into a snarl. "You've been following me?"

She began wiping down the counter, ignoring his accusing stares. "I have my ways."

He lunged over the counter, inches away from her face. "How dare you!" he screamed, pushing her hard and watching her stumble back in surprise. Her foot slipped, and she fell through the open hatch into the cellar.

Robert's anger turned to shock as he watched Betty stumble down into the cellar. His heart pounded in his chest as he listened to the sounds of her descent, each thud and crack echoing painfully in the silence that followed.

Horror washed over him as he realised what had just happened. He staggered forward, his trembling hand reaching out to grasp the edge of the hatch. He peered down into the darkness below, his mind reeling with disbelief and fear.

"Betty!" he called out, his voice filled with panic. But there was no response, only the eerie silence of the cellar.

With a shaky breath, Robert's mind raced as he struggled to process the gravity of the situation. Guilt gnawed at him as he realised the consequences of his actions, the weight of his anger and resentment crashing down upon him.

"Betty?" his voice trailed off as he stared into the darkness, only to be met with an eerie silence. "Betty?" he called out again, this time louder, but there was still no response. He dashed down the stairs, almost colliding with Betty's crumpled body at the bottom. His hands shook as he stared down at Betty's crumpled form, horror washing over him at the sight of the red liquid pooling beneath her head. His mind raced with guilt and fear, grappling with the reality of what had just transpired.

With trembling hands, he reached out to shake her, desperate for any sign of life. "Betty, please," he pleaded, his voice choked with emotion. But there was no response, only the haunting silence of the cellar.

His heart pounded in his chest as he recoiled at the sight of the blood, the weight of his actions crashing down upon him. "What have I done?" he whispered, his voice barely audible over the thoughts racing through his mind.

But his frantic attempts to wake Betty were interrupted by the sound of the shop door opening above. His blood ran cold as he realised he was no longer alone, his terror mounting at the thought of being discovered.

Thornton's voice echoed down into the cellar, calling out to him and Betty. Panic seized Robert as he realised the gravity of the situation, his mind racing with the fear of being caught.

With a heavy heart, he turned away from Betty's still form, his hands trembling as he braced himself to face Thornton's questions.

Robert rushed up the creaky wooden steps to prevent Thornton from going down and slammed the hatch shut with force, causing the entire counter to rattle.

Thornton stared puzzled at Robert, watching the beads of sweat dripping from his brow. "Are you okay, Robert? You appear a little flustered."

Robert tried to compose himself by forcing a grin. "I'm fine; I was just cutting up some cheese to display; getting older does take a toll on your body, you know?"

Thornton smirked as he looked Robert up and down, his gaze resting on his huge, bulging stomach. "If you get that way just by cutting up cheese, you need to walk more."

"What can I do for you, Thornton?" He asked through gritted teeth, ignoring his remark.

"Not much, really; I heard a commotion from outside and came in."

Robert's phoney smile fades. "Commotion?"

Thornton leant over the counter with a sly grin on his face and looked down at the hatch. "It was quite loud; I'm surprised no one else heard it from outside. How is Mrs. Rowe?"

Robert gave him a stern look and stepped on the hatch. "She's fine; she's downstairs cutting up some cheese."

Thornton chuckled, giving him a sly wink. "Sure, she is."

Robert's heart raced as he tried to maintain his composure in front of Thornton, his mind racing with the fear of being discovered. He forced a strained grin, attempting to play off Thornton's questions and divert suspicion away from the cellar.

But Thornton's sharp gaze didn't falter, his smirk betraying a hint of scepticism as he eyed Robert up and down. Robert's stomach churned with unease under Thornton's scrutiny, his attempts to deflect attention growing more desperate by the second.

As Thornton continued to press him with questions, Robert felt the weight of his guilt bearing down on him. He knew he had to tread carefully, to somehow keep Thornton from discovering the truth about Betty's condition.

Summoning all his willpower, Robert feigned nonchalance, trying to steer the conversation away from the cellar and back to more mundane topics. But Thornton was relentless, his probing questions leaving Robert feeling exposed and vulnerable.

With a sinking feeling in his chest, Robert realised that he was running out of excuses. He knew he had to act fast to prevent Thornton from uncovering the truth, even if it meant resorting to drastic measures.

He began tapping his foot, frustrated with Thornton's little game. "Look, Thornton, if you're not going to buy anything, then can you please leave? I have work to do."

"As you wish. I'm sure we'll bump into each other again very soon. Good day to you, sir," Thornton said over his shoulder as he left the shop.

Robert breathed out a loud sigh of relief, before quickly heading back into the cellar, closing the hatch behind him.

## CHAPTER SEVENTEEN

# Inspector Acker's Office

In the heart of the bustling police station, nestled within the labyrinthine corridors and interview rooms, sat the inspector's office.

A massive oak desk, weathered by time and countless deliberations, sat in the centre of the room, strewn with parchments, inkwells, and an assortment of investigative tools – magnifying glasses, fingerprint kits, and meticulously organised case files bound in frayed leather.

Bookshelves lined the walls, sagging under the weight of leather-bound volumes and dusty manuscripts, their spines bearing witness to a lifetime of the inspector's relentless pursuit of justice. The air was alive with the soft rustle of pages turning and the occasional whisper of a breeze slipping through the cracked window panes, carrying with it the distant chatter of the bustling city beyond.

The scent of aged leather and musty tomes hung in the air, mingling with the faint aroma of pipe smoke, a perennial companion to the inspector's ruminations. The room was bathed in the warm glow of sunlight, streaming over the mahogany-panelled walls adorned with curious artefacts and maps of the city's intricate streets.

Behind the desk sat Acker himself, his piercing gaze mulling over the latest photographs of Lady Penelope's crime scene while Claydon and Chapman sat silently watching him. Acker leant his elbows on the desk, his face screwed up in concentration. He began rummaging through the scrawny-looking notes on his desk, attempting to piece together the puzzle.

After a few minutes, Acker cleared his throat, looking at the other two. "So, what we know so far is that Lady Penelope wasn't very loyal to her husband, and the servant girl, Bella, was involved in something that we're unsure of at this point in time."

Claydon nodded thoughtfully, his brow furrowed in contemplation. "That's correct; and it seems that there may have been tensions brewing between Lady Penelope and her husband for some time."

Chapman chimed in, his voice laced with curiosity. "Yes, it appears that Lady Penelope's indiscretions were no secret among the household staff. Bella's involvement adds another layer of complexity to the situation."

Acker shuffled through the papers on his desk, his expression grave. "This investigation just keeps getting more complicated as the days go on."

Chapman examined the photographs of Bella and the crime scene, trying to mask his guilt as he stared down at the pictures. "Do you believe Shelton is involved? Banes stated that Bella had multiple wounds, which could indicate that she was abused by someone in the home."

Acker nodded thoughtfully. "It's a possibility, Chapman, but we can't just storm in and question him; we need to be cautious."

"Do we need to question the servants again?" Claydon pondered.

Chapman sighed loudly as he carefully replaced Bella's photo on the table. "I'm particularly interested in Evelyn, one of the servant girls who appeared to be hiding something when I was last there."

Acker gathered the evidence and neatly stacked it on the side of his desk. "Chapman, I want you to go back to Mr. Shelton's townhouse and question the servants again; if you have any problems with Mr. Shelton, you come and get me."

Chapman looked at him, perplexed. "I thought we were all going down there. What about you? What are your plans?"

"You can handle Shelton for the time being, Chapman. I'm going to question Mr. Bodmin, who I'm sure has changed his tune by now."

"What about the kid Billy?"

Acker got to his feet and wriggled into his coat. "We'll deal with him later." He held the door open and waited for them to leave before locking the office behind him. He slipped the key into his pocket, eyeing Chapman as he left the station.

Claydon glanced warily at Acker. "Can Chapman deal with Shelton? He's still shaken from the servant girl, Acker."

"He's the best man to deal with Shelton. He's angry, which I'm sure he'll use to get information. He'll be fine, Claydon. Come on, we have work to do. Let's go see our friend Mr. Bodmin."

As Acker and Claydon descended the worn stone steps into the dimly lit cellar cells, the air grew heavy with the weight of impending confrontation. Each footfall echoed in the narrow corridor, reverberating off the damp walls like a sombre prelude to the impending interrogation.

Acker, with his simmering anger barely contained beneath the surface, moved with purpose, his steps infused with a sense of determination bordering on ferocity. His eyes gleamed with a steely resolve as he looked ahead, his eyes blazing. The image of a smug-looking Mr. Bodmin in his mind only fuelled his anger.

Claydon trailed behind, his manner subdued, a silent witness to the tempest brewing within his brother's soul. He knew all too well the toll that Acker's righteous fury could exact, the inevitable clash of wills that awaited them in the depths of the underground cells.

As they reached the end of the corridor, Acker's mischievous smile, tinged with a hint of menace, spoke volumes of the impending confrontation. Claydon's heart sank, knowing that the delicate dance of interrogation would soon descend into a brutal symphony of violence, his fists serving as instruments of justice in the absence of more civilised discourse.

With a heavy sigh and a silent prayer for restraint, Claydon steeled himself for the ordeal ahead, knowing that in the shadowy realm of the cellar cells, the line between right and wrong blurred, and justice exacted its toll in blood and bone.

As they rounded the corner, Claydon's heart lurched as he caught sight of Mr. Bodmin, a pitiable figure huddled in the corner of the dank, mould-ridden cell. The man's dishevelled appearance spoke volumes of the ordeal he had endured, his clothes tattered and torn, his bruised visage a testament to the violence that had been inflicted upon him already.

A pang of guilt gnawed at Claydon's conscience as he averted his gaze, unable to meet Mr. Bodmin's eyes, knowing full well the role his brother had played in the man's suffering. The sight of those black and blue bruises etched upon Mr. Bodmin's face served as a stark reminder of the brutality that often accompanied Acker's relentless pursuit of justice.

"Are you ready to talk yet?" Acker demanded as he stopped outside the cell.

Mr. Bodmin's eyes filled with terror as he glanced from Claydon to Acker. "I've already told you that I have no idea who is taking the orphans, and that is the truth!"

Acker grabbed the cell bars, his knuckles turning white from the sheer aggression. "How come I don't believe you?"

In frustration, he raised his arms into the air, revealing more bruises on his arms. "I don't know!"

"Mr. Bodmin, I suggest you start telling us the truth, or my little brother, Claydon, will have to beat it out of you instead."

Claydon began rolling up his sleeves in preparation for entering the cell. Mr. Bodmin shrank away from the bars, fearful of the man's tensed knuckles. "If I knew who it was, I would have told you by now!" He cowered into the corner as Claydon reached out to open the door.

As Acker and Claydon stood on the precipice of confrontation, their intentions laid bare before the fearful figure of Mr. Bodmin, they were abruptly stopped by the ominous intrusion of a deep, gravelly voice that reverberated through the dimly lit corridor like a thunderclap in the still of the night.

"Acker."

Acker's blood ran cold as he turned to face the source of the voice, his heart pounding in his chest as he beheld the imposing figure that loomed in the shadows behind them. There, framed by the flickering lamplight, stood a man whose very presence commanded respect, his ruthless gaze piercing through the darkness with an intensity that sent a chill down Acker's spine.

"Sir," Acker stammered, his voice betraying a hint of trepidation as he struggled to maintain his composure in the face of this unexpected encounter. He knew all too well the consequences of crossing paths with this formidable adversary, a man whose reputation preceded him like a spectre haunting the streets of the city.

The man's eyes narrowed, his expression inscrutable as he regarded Acker with a mixture of disdain and curiosity, his gaze flickering briefly to Claydon, whose clenched fists betrayed his readiness for conflict. In that moment, the tension hung heavy in the air, the steely figure knowing exactly what was about to happen.

"Acker," the man repeated, his voice a low rumble that echoed off the cold stone walls, sending shivers down Acker's spine. "I trust you have a good reason for this?"

Acker swallowed hard, his mind racing as he searched for an explanation that would satisfy this formidable adversary. For in the presence of this enigmatic figure, Acker knew that his every word and action would be scrutinised with a keenness that left no room for error.

As Superintendent Landrake stepped into the flickering light of the gas lamp, his imposing figure cast in sharp relief against the shadows, Claydon couldn't help but feel a twinge of envy stir within him. His gaze lingered on the superintendent's impeccable attire – the gleam of his gold pocket watch nestled within the folds of his silk waistcoat, the mark of a man accustomed to the finer things in life.

Claydon's admiration for Landrake's stature, both literal and figurative, was palpable as he observed the way the superintendent carried himself with an air of authority and dignity that commanded respect. There was a certain allure to Landrake's presence, a magnetic charisma that drew others to him like moths to a flame.

A smirk tugged at the corner of Claydon's lips as he watched Acker's sullen expression come under the scrutiny of the superintendent's piercing gaze. In that moment, Claydon couldn't help but revel in the subtle shift of power dynamics, relishing the opportunity to witness his brother receive a lecture from the very man he aspired to emulate.

Superintendent Landrake's white, wispy hair framed his weathered features, the lines etched upon his brow a testament to the years spent navigating the treacherous waters of Bristol's criminal underworld. And yet, despite the severity of his countenance, there was a warmth in Landrake's eyes that spoke of a deeper understanding, a compassion tempered by the harsh realities of life on the streets.

As Claydon continued to watch in silent admiration, he couldn't help but harbour dreams of one day following in Superintendent Landrake's footsteps, of embodying the same blend of strength and integrity that defined the man before him.

"Superintendent, what brings you here this morning?" Acker asked, keeping his voice as steady as he could.

Landrake scowled at him. "I was called in by our chief superintendent because he had heard rumours about Mr. Bodmin being incarcerated here, and what do I find? That his assumptions are correct; if you want to stay on this case, I suggest you let him go."

Acker shook his head, refusing to obey. "But, sir, he's one of our suspects."

Landrake glared questioningly at him. "On what grounds?"

Mr. Bodmin looked smugly at Acker's flustered face, while Acker glanced nervously at Claydon. "We have information that Mr. Bodmin is involved with the disappearances of the orphans. We have a witness."

Landrake raised a brow. "A witness?"

"Yes, sir. A boy who resides at the orphanage."

Landrake scoffed at the mention of the boy. "So, you're telling me that a boy had witnessed Mr. Bodmin handing over a government-supported child? Why would he do that when he's paid to have the child?"

Acker ran his hand through his hair, flustered. "I don't know the necessary details yet from the witness, but he has stated that he's witnessed Mr. Bodmin in cahoots with the abductor."

"You cannot arrest someone with as little evidence as this, Acker. A boy for a witness? He probably wants his master gone, so he can do as he pleases. You should have questioned the boy before you arrested Mr. Bodmin; I suggest you tread more carefully in the future." He motioned for Mr. Bodmin's cell to be opened. "Please accept our apologies, Mr. Bodmin; you will be returned to your home, and I hope you understand that this was a terrible mistake on our part."

Mr. Bodmin glared angrily at Landrake, his eyeballs nearly popping out of their sockets. "Mistake?! My clothes are ruined because I was beaten and punched all night. I expect to be compensated."

"And you will, sir, I promise. This will not happen again, will it, Acker?" he asked Acker bitterly, giving him a stern look to shut him up.

As Superintendent Landrake's authoritative voice resonated through the cells, a palpable sense of chastisement hung in the air, casting a shadow over Acker's earlier fervour. With a curt nod of acquiescence, Acker begrudgingly acknowledged the superintendent's admonition, his expression a mixture of contrition and defiance.

Claydon watched in silence as Mr. Bodmin's cell was opened, his heart heavy with a mixture of relief and regret. The injustice inflicted upon Mr. Bodmin weighed heavily upon his conscience, a stark reminder of the collateral damage that often accompanied the pursuit of truth in the unforgiving streets of Bristol.

As Mr. Bodmin emerged from the confines of his cell, his anger palpable in the glare he levelled at Landrake, Claydon couldn't help but feel a pang of sympathy for the man's plight. The outrage of his ordeal was writ large upon his dishevelled appearance, an antithesis to the polished veneer of authority that surrounded

Landrake.

With a weary sigh, Landrake extended his apologies once more to Mr. Bodmin, his words laced with sincerity as he acknowledged the grievous error that had been made. Although Mr. Bodmin's resentment simmered just beneath the surface, Claydon sensed a begrudging acceptance in his demeanour.

As Landrake turned his gaze upon Acker, his tone tinged with bitterness, Claydon could see the weight of responsibility bearing down upon his brother's shoulders. With a stern look that brooked no argument, Landrake silenced Acker's protestations, reminding him of the consequences of his actions in no uncertain terms.

Acker stood still, his silence a palpable testament to his simmering frustration. He couldn't help but seethe with indignation as Mr. Bodmin passed by, his smug sneer a bitter reminder of the humiliation Acker had endured. Every fibre of his being yearned to wipe the arrogant grin from Bodmin's face, to unleash the fury that burned within him, but the weight of Landrake's disapproving gaze bore down upon him like a leaden mantle, quelling the urge to act on his impulses.

With a resigned sigh, Acker begrudgingly stepped aside, swallowing his pride as Mr. Bodmin sauntered past, the pompous satisfaction radiating from him like a noxious cloud. The temptation to lash out, to give in to the primal urge for retribution, gnawed at Acker's resolve, but the fear of jeopardising his livelihood held him in check, a silent sentinel guarding against the recklessness of his anger.

Claydon hovered in the background, a silent observer to the tension that crackled in the air like static electricity. As Landrake's gaze settled upon him, Claydon felt a shiver of apprehension course through his veins, his heart hammering in his chest as he braced himself for the inevitable reprimand that awaited him.

"Hail a cab for Mr. Bodmin and make sure he's comfortable."

Claydon nodded and followed Mr. Bodmin up the stairs, attempting to keep the peace by making small talk with him. Landrake observed them leaving before turning his attention to Acker. "Let me remind you, Acker, that you were almost reprimanded the last time something like this happened," he hissed quietly.

"But I was right, and he was guilty and hung for it. Just because someone is high up doesn't stop them from going against the law." Acker's defiance rang clear in his casual shrug. To him, the ends justifies the means, and no amount of bureaucratic red tape could deter him from his mission to root out corruption and wrongdoing in a city plagued by vice and villainy.

But as Superintendent Landrake's exasperated sigh filled the air, a tangible sense of resignation settled over him like a heavy cloak. He knew all too well the futility of trying to rein in Acker's impulsive nature, his penchant for bending – and sometimes outright breaking – the rules in pursuit of his own brand of justice.

"You're a good detective, Acker," Landrake conceded, his voice tinged with a weary resignation born of years spent navigating the city of Bristol. "But you have to tread carefully and employ different strategies when dealing with these types of people. You can't arrest them unless you have evidence."

The words hung in the air like a solemn decree, a reminder of the immutable truths that governed their profession. In the face of Acker's stubborn determination, Landrake knew that reason and logic would only go so far. But still, he harboured a sliver of hope that Acker would heed his counsel, that perhaps, with time and experience, he would learn to navigate the complexities of their world with greater finesse.

"I'm going with my gut instinct. I know he's somehow connected to the disappearances of the orphan children. He'll make a mistake and, before you know it, he'll be back in that cell," Acker said, honestly.

"A gut instinct is not enough! You need evidence. Don't make me remind you again. I've had enough of having to bail you out all the time."

"I'm just curious to know who informed the chief."

"Mr. Bodmin has friends in very high places. You have now made this investigation very difficult for both of us. There are eyes everywhere, Acker; remember that." Landrake gave him a warning look.

Acker looked away to avoid the superintendent's displeased look. "I'm just doing my job, sir."

"Then follow the rules and stop inventing your own." He dismissed Acker with a wave of his hand and walked away from him, effectively ending their argument.

Acker groaned as he stared meanly at the now-empty cell. "I almost had him," he muttered to himself as he closed the cell door.

Claydon appeared beside him with a sullen look on his face. "What should we do with the boy?"

Acker was deep in thought as he stared at the empty cell. Billy might be the only one who could stand up to Bodmin and help him get locked up for good, or even better, sent to the gallows. "We need to keep him safe. Bodmin would do anything to keep that boy quiet to avoid being arrested, but if he doesn't know where he is, then he can't get to him."

"Where should we take him? He can't stay here. Is there anywhere who'd take him in?" Claydon asked.

"We have to be sneaky about this. We need to take him somewhere where Bodmin wouldn't know where to look. If the boy is right and Bodmin is involved somehow, then he's in a lot of danger. Bodmin now thinks he has won by using his status as a means to get out of jail, but at the moment, we have the upper hand. Only you and I can know where Billy is. We'll have to take him to someone we can trust." Acker thought for a moment, racking his brain of where to take the witness. He couldn't really trust anyone on the police force in case the superintendent finds out. He needed to tread carefully, and that meant giving the boy to someone he could truly trust.

Acker's mind buzzed with the urgency of their situation as he contemplated their next move in the dim confines of the cellar. The realisation that Mr. Bodmin's release had only emboldened him fuelled Acker's resolve to protect young Billy at all costs. The boy's safety was paramount, and Acker knew he had to act swiftly and decisively to keep him out of harm's way.

With a heavy heart, Acker made the difficult decision to involve his wife in their clandestine operation. Though the thought of exposing her to the dangers that lurked in the shadows of their world filled him with trepidation, he knew deep down that she was the only one he could truly trust to keep Billy safe from harm. "He'll be safe with my wife."

Claydon raised his brow, alarmed by his brother's response. "You want your wife involved in this?"

"We have no choice, Claydon. I know he'll be safe there. Get a carriage ready for him and make sure no one sees him. I can't have this getting out."

With a nod of reluctant acquiescence, Claydon departed to make the necessary arrangements, leaving Acker alone with his thoughts in the oppressive silence of the jail cells. The weight of their predicament bore down upon him like a leaden weight, each moment ticking by with agonising slowness.

In the stillness of the jail cells, Acker's mind churned with a singular purpose: to bring Mr. Bodmin to justice for his heinous crimes. Though the evidence remained elusive, Acker's gut instinct told him that Bodmin was the key to unravelling the mystery of the missing children. And as he plotted his next move in the shadows, Acker vowed to remain vigilant, waiting for the moment when Bodmin would make his fatal mistake and justice would finally be served.

He straightened his coat and followed after Claydon, where he found him at the entrance of the station staring out the window at Mr. Bodmin getting into a carriage. Bodmin turned and grinned slyly at the police station before getting in.

"Just ignore him, Claydon. He's doing it on purpose," Acker muttered as he watched the carriage pull away. "Go and get Billy, then meet me outside. Make sure no one sees him."

Claydon nodded and headed into a small room beside the desk that sat at the front of the station's foyer. Acker put on his hat and headed to the next carriage that pulled up outside. An elderly gentleman got out and held the door open for Acker. Acker tipped his hat towards the man and smiled. "Thank you, sir."

Claydon appeared, accompanied by a terrified-looking Billy. Claydon had given him a cloak to wear as well as an oversized hood to cover his head. Acker motioned for Billy to enter while the elderly gentleman looked at Acker and Claydon strangely.

They both climbed in after Billy, and the carriage pulled away from the police station toward the roadside food stalls, leading to Acker's residence.

## CHAPTER EIGHTEEN

# The Night of Robert's Mistake

In the heart of Bristol City, shrouded by tendrils of mist and whispering shadows, lay the silent kingdom of the departed: a large graveyard, nestled amidst ancient oaks and weeping willows, its entrance marked by ornate iron gates that creaked mournfully in the breeze.

Robert stepped beyond the threshold of the gates, greeted by a symphony of whispers, the soft rustle of leaves underfoot, and the distant tolling of church bells. Marble angels stood sentinel before him, their stoic faces weathered by time, their outstretched wings casting long shadows upon the mossy earth.

He walked past the rows of weather-beaten tombstones, adorned with intricate carvings and faded epitaphs, holding a sack over his shoulder, large enough to fit a body inside. Ivy and wildflowers weaved a tapestry of life amongst the graves, their vibrant hues a stark contrast to the sombre tones of stone and shadow. Shafts of ethereal moonlight pierced through the canopy of trees, illuminating forgotten mausoleums and crumbling crypts with an otherworldly glow. Robert glanced around, terrified that someone could be watching him.

A grave digger stood at the far end of the cemetery, next to a shallow pit, wearing filthy old worker's clothes. Robert's heart hammered in his chest as he approached the solitary figure amidst the eerie stillness of the graveyard. The grave digger, a weathered man with dirt-stained hands and a face etched with the lines of hard labour, leaned casually on his spade, the glint of curiosity in his eyes betraying his otherwise stoic stature.

Hand trembling, Robert extended the satchel of coins towards the gravedigger, the weight of his secret heavy upon him. With a practised nonchalance, the gravedigger accepted the payment, the clinking of metal against metal punctuating the silence like a dirge. "You keep your mouth shut about this, you hear?"

Carefully, Robert lowered Betty's lifeless form into the shallow pit, his movements furtive, as if afraid of the very air itself carrying his sins to the heavens. His gaze darted nervously to the gravedigger, a silent plea for discretion hanging in the air like a whispered prayer.

A cloud of tobacco smoke wafted lazily from the gravedigger's lips as he regarded Robert with a knowing gaze, the corners of his mouth curling into a wry smile. With a slow nod, he spoke, his voice a gravelly whisper that seemed to echo with the weight of the ages.

"Say no more, sir. My lips are sealed."

Robert nodded, satisfied with the man's response. "Good. She's a nobody. No one's going to miss her being around, and if you are asked any questions, then report to me first. Got it?"

The grave digger nodded. "As you wish, sir. I'll keep my word."

Robert looked down into the pit and noticed how shallow it was. "Don't you think it's a little shallow?"

The man shrugged as he investigated the pit. "That's the best I could do with the little time you'd given me, but don't worry, I'll make it look like the soil hasn't been disturbed."

"I can't have anyone finding her, do you hear?"

"As I said, I'm a grave digger, and this is my job. I ask no questions. I just dig and get paid. She won't be found, and if she ever is found, then her body will look unrecognisable, so no need to worry, sir."

"Alright then, I'll leave you in peace to get on with it. But remember this: if you are asked any questions at all, then you come to me first. Understand?"

The grave digger nodded once more before returning the mud back into the pit, covering Betty's body with dirt.

## CHAPTER NINETEEN

# Acker's Residence

Nestled amongst a row of elegant Victorian townhouses on Royal York Crescent overlooking the harbour, its façade adorned with intricate wrought iron balconies and ornate bay windows, stood a stately red-bricked house that blended in with the others.

Twin gas lamps flanked the heavy wooden door, their soft glow casting a warm welcome upon the cobblestone pathway that wound its way to the entrance. Above, a gabled roof stretched skyward, its slate tiles weathered to a mottled grey by the relentless march of time.

Through the tall, narrow open windows, lace curtains billowed gently in the breeze, offering glimpses of a world within that seemed to exist in a realm untouched by the chaos of the city streets beyond.

Acker stood on the doorstep of his house, with Claydon

standing beside him. He motioned for Claydon to press the bell while holding Billy's shoulders to prevent him from escaping. With the exception of a few shoppers, the street was mostly deserted. They stared at the boy as they walked past, disgusted by his attire. The boy was barely dressed, and he could feel the inspector's cold hands seeping through the rags on his shoulders.

The door opened and in the threshold of the house, framed by the intricate carvings of the door frame, stood a woman whose presence seemed to command the very essence of elegance and poise. Clad in layers of sumptuous fabric that draped gracefully around her form, she exuded an aura of refined dignity.

She looked at them, shocked to see her husband standing on the doorstep with a young boy. "I wasn't expecting you until after dark."

Claydon blushed as she turned her attention to him and smiled. She welcomed them in, curious as to why her husband had turned up with a straggly-looking boy.

In the streaming sunlight, she moved with the grace of a waltz, her silhouette a study in elegance against the backdrop of velvet draperies and ornate furnishings. She exuded an air of refined poise that spoke volumes of her upbringing. Her hair, a cascade of chestnut curls adorned with delicate ribbons and pearls, framed a face that seemed untouched by the passage of time. Dark lashes fluttered like butterfly wings against porcelain skin, her eyes like pools of deep sapphire that held a hint of mystery within their depths.

Behind her, a small girl with a cherub face and the same chestnut curls leapt into Acker's arms. "Lizzie!" he exclaimed, squeezing her little chubby cheeks.

There was a striking resemblance between her and Acker's wife, with beautiful sapphire eyes and an oval-shaped face. Her hair was the same style as her mother's, pinned back into a neat bun, with a bow on top.

"I've missed you!" Lizzie hugged Acker, squeezing him tightly.

Acker's hand gently caressed Lizzie's cheek, a tender smile playing at the corners of his lips. "I've missed you as well, Lizzie," he murmured, his voice tinged with warmth and affection.

Leaning in, he placed a gentle kiss upon her cheek before turning to face Billy, who stood nearby.

With a gracious gesture, Acker introduced Billy to his wife, Mary, the lines of concern etching themselves into her brow as she regarded the unexpected guest. Mary's gaze flickered between Acker and Billy, a silent question lingering in the air.

"Why is he here?" Mary inquired, her tone laced with apprehension as she sought clarification from her husband.

Claydon responded to Mary's query with calm resolve. "He's going to be staying here for a while," he explained, his words carrying the weight of a decision already made.

Mary's expression shifted to one of puzzlement, her eyes searching Claydon's face for further explanation. "He's here to stay?" she repeated, her disbelief palpable.

A nod from Claydon affirmed the truth of his statement. "Yes, ma'am," he confirmed, his tone steady and unwavering as he met Mary's quizzical gaze.

Acker's frustration boiled over, his voice edged with anger as he demanded access to his wife. "Goddamn it, man, let me speak to my wife," he growled, his tone laced with irritation.

Sensing the intensity of Acker's emotions, Claydon acquiesced, stepping back to grant him passage. With a silent nod, he allowed Acker to lead Mary into the sanctuary of the lounge, his grip firm yet gentle as he held her hand. In the quiet intimacy of the lounge, Acker and Mary found themselves enveloped in a cocoon of privacy, shielded from prying eyes and unwanted intrusion. Acker's hand tightened around Mary's, a silent reassurance of his presence.

Mary's voice trembled with a mix of confusion and apprehension as she confronted Acker, her gaze searching his face for answers. "What's going on? Why do I have to take in that boy?" she questioned, her tone tinged with uncertainty.

Acker met Mary's eyes with empathy, understanding the weight of her concerns yet steadfast in his decision. Taking a deep breath, he gently squeezed her hand.

"Mary, I know this is unexpected, but we need to protect Billy," Acker began, his voice gentle yet firm as he sought to explain the situation. "His circumstances are difficult, and he's a witness to a case. I need him safe, and I trust you with my life. I know you'll keep him safe here."

Mary listened intently, her brow furrowed with worry as she tried to make sense of the sudden upheaval in their lives. "But why us? Can't he be taken to another orphanage?" she pressed, her voice tinged with frustration. "Why must we bear this burden?"

Acker's expression softened as he reached out to brush a stray lock of hair from Mary's face. "Because if he goes to another orphanage, he may be found, Mary," he replied, his voice steady. "He needs to be protected and I know you will do that. Please, just do this one thing for me. Keep the boy safe. Don't let anyone know he's here, and if there's any danger, alert me or the station immediately."

In that moment, Mary understood the magnitude of the task before her, the weight of Acker's trust resting heavily upon her shoulders. Silently, she vowed to protect the boy with every fibre of her being, drawing strength from Acker's unwavering faith in her ability to safeguard their newfound charge.

As Claydon eavesdropped on the conversation between the inspector and his wife from behind the closed door, a sense of relief washed over him. He knew that Acker had swayed Mary, ensuring Billy's safety within the confines of their home. Billy would be protected, and they could carry on seeking evidence on Mr. Bodmin without fear of someone finding the boy.

Approaching Billy with a reassuring smile, Claydon stooped to his level, his gaze meeting the boy's. "Billy, you'll be safe here," he assured him, his voice firm yet gentle.

But fear lingered in Billy's eyes as he glanced nervously around the opulent foyer, the stark contrast between the grandeur of his surroundings and the harsh reality of his past threatening to overwhelm him. "But if Mr. Bodmin finds out, he'll undoubtedly whip me," Billy whispered, his voice trembling.

Claydon placed a comforting hand on Billy's shoulder, his touch a steadying presence amidst the boy's uncertainty. "He won't find out, Billy," Claydon insisted, his tone resolute. "You just keep your head down and behave yourself. We'll make sure you're protected. And don't go back to your paper round job, not until we say you can."

Lizzie's eyes sparkled with excitement as she processed the new dynamic unfolding before her. "Does that mean I get a big brother?" she exclaimed, her voice bubbling with uncontainable joy.

Claydon couldn't help but smile at Lizzie's exuberance, her innocence a welcome respite from the weight of their adult concerns. "Yes, Lizzie," he replied, his tone infused with warmth and affection. "Billy will be like your big brother now."

Acker's return drew the attention of the trio, Mary trailing behind him with a pout on her lips. Lizzie's smile greeted them warmly, her eyes alight with excitement as she bounded forward to embrace Billy in a spontaneous hug.

Billy, momentarily taken aback by the unexpected gesture, hesitated for a moment before returning the embrace, his heart warmed by the genuine affection in Lizzie's gesture. As her arms encircled him, he felt a sense of belonging wash over him, a newfound connection forged in the unlikeliest of circumstances.

Lizzie's delighted squeal filled the foyer, her joy contagious as she declared, "I've made a new friend with whom to play!" Her enthusiasm was infectious, bringing smiles to the faces of those around her and dispelling the lingering tension that had weighed heavily upon them only moments before.

"Mary, can you make sure our guest room is ready for Billy? I'm sure that he's going to want to freshen up before dinner," Acker requested.

Billy glanced between Acker and Mary, uncertainty flickering in his eyes. "Freshen up?" he echoed, his confusion evident.

Acker offered a reassuring nod, his expression kind as he explained, "Yes, Billy. There will be a bowl of water waiting for you in your room for you to wash your hands and face with."

Mary, ever the gracious hostess, took Billy's hand and led him up the grand staircase to the guest room. Lizzie, her excitement palpable, trailed behind them, her eager anticipation bubbling over as she jumped up and down with glee. As they ascended the stairs together, Billy couldn't help but feel a glimmer of gratitude for the kindness and hospitality extended to him by the inspector, and he was glad that he had spoken up about what he had witnessed to get him where he was now.

Acker paused at the stairwell, his gaze lingering on Mary as he called out to her, "I have to return to the station, but hopefully I'll be back before nightfall!"

"I'm not holding my breath!"

Mary's retort echoed back to him, her voice tinged with frustration, but Acker's expression remained stoic, masking the guilt that threatened to consume him.

Quickly regaining his composure, Acker turned his attention to Claydon, his resolve unwavering as he gestured towards the door. "Let's get back to the station. This evening, we will visit Shelton and question him. I'm sure Chapman would have gotten something out of the servants by now," he declared, his voice tinged with determination.

Stepping outside, Acker pulled his hat firmly onto his head and took a deep breath of the crisp morning air, the weight of responsibility settling upon his shoulders once more. With a sense of purpose driving him forward, he climbed back into the waiting carriage, Claydon following suit.

As they rode back to the station, the exhaustion of their morning work washed over them like a tidal wave, leaving them drained and weary. Acker rapped his cane against the roof of the carriage, signalling to the coachman to pick up the pace, while Claydon settled back into his seat, his eyelids growing heavy with fatigue.

In the dim light of the carriage, they fell into a comfortable silence, the rhythmic clatter of hooves against cobblestone lulling them into a state of drowsy tranquillity. And as the sounds of the city faded into the distance, Acker and Claydon drifted off to sleep.

## CHAPTER TWENTY

# An Arrest

The setting sun cast long shadows across the darkening streets of Bristol, lending an ominous air to the scene. A lamplighter from across the road scurried from one gas lamp to the next, illuminating the street as darkness began to approach. Claydon huddled deeper into his coat, the chill of the evening seeping into his bones as he waited impatiently for Shelton to answer the door. Chapman stood on the street, unwilling to go in. He had been there once already that day, questioning the servants, and once Shelton saw him again, he would surely not allow them in.

Acker's frustration boiled over, his voice echoing through the quiet street as he pounded angrily on the door, his words sharp and commanding. "Open up, Shelton. We know you're in there!" he shouted.

Claydon watched nervously as Acker's outburst echoed

through the empty street, a knot of apprehension forming in the pit of his stomach. "Sir, I don't think he'll let us in if you keep acting like that," he ventured cautiously, his words tinged with concern as he scanned the deserted surroundings for any signs of movement.

But Acker's glare silenced him, his steely gaze locking onto Claydon with unyielding intensity. "Silence, Claydon; I know what I'm doing," he snapped, his tone brooking no argument as he turned back to face the door, his resolve unshaken by Claydon's caution.

Claydon couldn't help but roll his eyes as Shelton's head peered out from the window above, his smug demeanour only adding to the frustration of their encounter. "Don't you think it's a little late to make inquiries, gentlemen? I've already had one of you here today. Twice in one day is a bit extreme. Return tomorrow. I'm getting ready to go to bed," Shelton's voice drifted down to them, accompanied by the telltale sound of the window sliding shut.

But Chapman's sudden revelation halted Shelton's retreat. "At the docks, we discovered one of your servants, sir. She's been murdered," Chapman's voice rang out, cutting through the night air like a knife.

The window stopped in its tracks, and Shelton's head reappeared, curiosity etched into his features. "At the docks? What on earth was she doing there and why hadn't you told me this earlier when you were here?" he asked, his tone shifting from concern to annoyance.

"That's what we're curious to find out," Acker interjected, his voice tight with restrained frustration as he struggled to maintain his composure in the face of Shelton's dismissive demeanour.

With an exasperated sigh, Shelton relented, albeit begrudgingly. "I'll just be a moment. My butler will let you in," he conceded, disappearing back into the darkness of his room.

The door swung open, revealing the stern figure of Shelton's butler, his disapproving glare a silent warning. "Make this quick, gentlemen," he hissed, stepping aside to allow them entry.

Acker's patience wore thin with each passing second, his

irritation palpable as he strode past the butler and into the foyer. "This will take as long as it takes," he growled, his voice a low rumble of frustration as he prepared to confront Shelton with the grim reality of their investigation.

The butler's swift ushering into the lounge left Acker and his companions with little choice but to follow, the heavy door slamming shut behind them like a final punctuation mark on their intrusion. Acker's gaze bore into Chapman and Claydon, his voice a low growl as he issued his command. "We won't leave until we have something to go on. Got it?"

Chapman and Claydon nodded in silent agreement, settling onto one of the plush leather sofas beside the crackling fire. Claydon eagerly welcomed the warmth, raising his hands toward the flickering flames in a futile attempt to banish the chill that lingered in his bones.

The door creaked open once more, and Shelton emerged, his appearance dishevelled and his irritation palpable. "How can I assist you?" he asked curtly, making a beeline for his drink cabinet without bothering to acknowledge his unexpected guests.

Acker wasted no time in getting to the heart of the matter, his words measured and deliberate as he addressed Shelton. "We have reason to believe that your maid's death was caused by someone in this house. We'd like to ask you a few questions, as well as your servants."

Shelton's response was a thin smile and a sip of his drink, the liquid amber glinting in the firelight as he settled into one of the plush chairs, his pipe already lit and billowing smoke into the room. "Why me?" he questioned, the smoke curling around him like a shroud of defiance. "I have nothing to do with it. Besides, I have been away on business."

Acker waved his hand in a futile attempt to disperse the smoke, his frustration mounting with each passing moment. "Because she's your maid, sir, and you might be able to tell us something that will help us with our investigation," he replied, his voice a terse reminder of the gravity of the situation.

Shelton's laughter echoed through the room, a bitter edge to the sound as he entertained the grim notion of a connection between the two murders. "Don't you think she was murdered by the same person who murdered my wife? In less than a week, there have been two murders. They must be linked in some way," he mused, his voice tinged with a hint of unease.

Acker's gaze bore into Shelton with unwavering intensity, his suspicion evident in the narrowing of his eyes. "Quite possibly, the murderer may be residing in this house," he stated bluntly, his words hanging heavy in the air.

Shelton shifted uncomfortably in his seat, the weight of Acker's accusation bearing down on him like a leaden cloak. "Well, I was away on business, so it can't be me. I have witnesses who know my whereabouts," he protested, his tone defensive.

Chapman's fury erupted like a volcano, his outburst a torrent of rage and curses directed at Shelton. Acker intervened swiftly, placing a calming hand on Chapman's shoulder and urging him to sit. "Calm down, Chapman. We'll find out," he whispered into his ear, his voice a soothing reassurance amidst the storm of emotions.

As Acker and Shelton engaged in a tense standoff, an awkward silence settled over the room, broken only by the sound of Shelton's loud exhale of smoke. "I will send my servants to your police station for questioning first thing tomorrow morning," Shelton announced, his tone defiant. "But I can assure you, gentlemen, that you will find nothing. I am very proud of my servants, and I carefully select who I hire. I'm sure I'll know if there's a murderer among them."

Chapman leaned in, his proximity a deliberate attempt to unsettle Shelton as he broached the sensitive topic. "I see you have a lot of women working here," he remarked, his voice low and probing.

Shelton's response was laced with a cruel smile, his words dripping with disdain. "They are far more obedient than men," he stated matter-of-factly.

Chapman's sarcasm cut through the air like a knife. "What? So, you can whip and beat them to get them to obey you because they are the weaker sex?" he retorted, his words a calculated jab aimed at Shelton.

Shelton winced visibly at Chapman's barb, his discomfort

evident as he shifted in his seat. "What exactly does this mean? You can't just walk in and start accusing me of all sorts in my own home!" Shelton protested.

Acker moved swiftly to defuse the tension, pulling Chapman away from Shelton and positioning him by his side. "My apologies, Mr. Shelton. My colleague is currently overcome with emotion. It won't happen again, will it, Chapman?" Acker stated firmly, his gaze fixing Chapman with a warning glare.

Chapman nodded begrudgingly, the fire in his eyes tempered by Acker's admonition. "As I previously stated, the purpose of our visit this evening is to ask you a few questions and to question your servants," Acker continued, his tone businesslike as he retrieved a notebook from his pocket.

Shelton's patience wore thin as Acker began his questioning, his responses terse and guarded. "Where were you yesterday and the night before?" Acker inquired, his pen poised to record Shelton's answers.

"I was here. My butler, as well as my servants, can vouch for me," Shelton replied bluntly, his gaze fixed on the dwindling contents of his glass.

"Are your servants and butler your only witnesses?" Acker pressed, his tone insistent.

"Yes," Shelton confirmed tersely, a hint of irritation creeping into his voice. "Are you interrogating me or accusing me of both murders?"

Chapman seized on Shelton's inconsistency, his smirk evident as he prodded further. "Wait a second. You said before that you were away on business. So, which one is it? Were you here or away?"

Caught off guard, Shelton stumbled over his words, his frustration evident. "I was away, and then I came back," he stuttered, his composure slipping. "Anyway, that's beside the point. You're already accusing me of murdering my own wife and servant. Do I have to remind you that the person you should be looking for is probably out on the streets right now, while you're right here accusing me in my own home?"

Acker remained unmoved by Shelton's outburst, his gaze unwavering. "It's just a few questions right now, sir, and before we leave, we'll ask your servants who saw you and who didn't on those nights," he stated calmly.

But Shelton's patience had worn thin, his frustration boiling over into anger as he lashed out at Acker. "You're not going to ask them right now. It's too late in the evening for this. They'll be at the police station tomorrow morning," he retorted, his voice dripping with disdain.

"Shelton, it's not too late. Are you concerned that your version of events will conflict with those of your servants?" Chapman snapped.

Chapman's behaviour only served to stoke Shelton's ire, his face flushing red with rage. "I suggest you zip your mutt's mouth shut before I have him chucked out of this house, Inspector," he snapped, his eyes blazing with fury.

Acker's swift action silenced Chapman's outburst, the sharp smack on the back of his head serving as a stark reminder to maintain decorum. "Chapman, behave yourself, and Mr. Shelton, please gather your servants. We'd like to confirm that what you're saying is correct," Acker instructed, his tone firm and authoritative.

Shelton's face contorted with barely-contained rage, but he begrudgingly complied with Acker's request, striding over to the wall where a call bell hung. With a sharp ring, he summoned his servants, who appeared promptly, their expressions a mixture of confusion and apprehension.

The majority of the servants had already retired for the evening, clad in their nightgowns, while others remained in their uniforms, caught off guard by the unexpected summons. They formed a line before the officers, their eyes wide with trepidation as they awaited further instructions.

With practised ease, Shelton began to pace along the line of servants, his hands clasped behind his back as he addressed them. Before the officers could intervene, he shot them a sneering glance, silently warning them to keep silent. "The inspector would like to ask you a few questions, and you will be taken to the police station tomorrow morning to answer a few more," he announced, his tone laced with thinly veiled contempt.

The servants exchanged uneasy glances, their fear palpable as they struggled to comprehend the gravity of the situation. But Shelton's assurance did little to assuage their concerns, their minds racing with thoughts of what awaited them at the police station.

"Ladies, there is no need to be afraid. I shall wait in here to make sure they don't hound you," Shelton added, his words dripping with false reassurance as he motioned for the servants to maintain their silence.

Acker's gaze swept over the assembled servants, his expression one of quiet determination as he addressed them. "Sorry for bothering you at this late hour, but I need to know if any of you saw your master last night or the night before. It is critical that you tell the truth," he implored, his voice calm yet firm.

The room remained silent, the weight of Acker's words hanging heavy in the air. "Anyone?" he prompted again as he scanned the faces before him, searching for any sign of acknowledgment.

Chapman and Claydon kept a vigilant watch on Shelton, their suspicions heightened by his nervous demeanour. Their attention was drawn to Evelyn, who stood at the end of the line, her restless movements betraying her uncertainty.

Shelton's silent plea for Evelyn to step forward did not go unnoticed by Acker. He averted his gaze from the inspector, his cheeks flushing with embarrassment. But as Evelyn finally spoke up, Acker turned his attention on her face, searching for any hint of deception.

"I did, sir," Evelyn whispered, her voice barely audible above the hushed murmurs of the room.

Acker nodded, his expression serious as he pressed for further details. "Did you? When and where?" he asked, his tone gentle yet insistent as he sought to uncover the truth hidden beneath the surface of Evelyn's hesitant confession.

Acker's smirk grew wider as he observed Shelton's furious reaction to Evelyn's admission. The tension in the room was palpable, each passing moment fraught with anticipation as Acker continued his interrogation.

"Madam, how long has this been going on?" Acker inquired, his gaze unwavering as he watched Shelton's face contort with rage.

Evelyn's eyes darted nervously between Acker and Shelton, her fear palpable as she hesitated before replying, "Not for very long."

Acker's tone remained steady, his eyes boring into Evelyn's as he pressed for more details. "Look at me, not at your master. I'm looking for the truth from you. How long has this been happening, before or after your mistress's murder?" he questioned, his voice insistent.

Evelyn's gaze dropped once more to the ground, her fingers twisting nervously as she struggled to find the words. "I'm not certain," she whispered, her voice barely above a murmur.

Acker's expression hardened, his patience wearing thin as he prodded for a definitive answer. "Are you sure?" he pressed, his voice firm with authority.

"Yes, sir. I'm not certain."

Acker's sarcasm cut through the tension, his words laced with suspicion as he fixed Evelyn with a piercing gaze. "You're deceiving me. Do you want to come with us to the station?" he quizzed.

But before Evelyn could respond, Shelton's voice interrupted from behind Acker. "She's not going anywhere, Inspector," he stated, his tone defiant.

Acker turned to face Shelton, his smirk still playing on his lips. "Mr. Shelton, she is now a part of our investigation, as well as you. If you want to join her at the station, then I suggest that you carry on talking, or if you want to stay in the comfort of your own home, you can shut that hole in your face," he retorted, his voice dripping with sarcasm.

Shelton's jaw clenched with anger, his frustration growing evident as he ground out his next words. "It's not against the law to sleep with someone else," he stated through gritted teeth.

Acker remained unfazed by Shelton's deflection, his attention turning back to Evelyn. "At this point, there could be a motive for murder. Your servant could be our killer," he stated bluntly.

"What is your name?" Acker asked, addressing Evelyn directly.

"Evelyn," she responded, her voice trembling with fear and uncertainty.

Acker nodded, his expression grave as he made his decision.

"All right, Evelyn, you must accompany us to the station," he declared, motioning for Chapman and Claydon to approach.

Evelyn's eyes widened with panic as Chapman and Claydon rose from their seats, ready to take her into custody. "They're taking me away, Shelton. Please help me! What should I tell them?" she pleaded, her voice filled with desperation.

Shelton turned away from Evelyn, his guilt and fear palpable in the air. He watched as Chapman and Claydon escorted her to the door, his heart pounding with apprehension. "She can't leave like that. She'll perish from the cold. Allow her to change and show some empathy," he implored.

"Of course, she can, but you'll have to wait here," Acker insisted, jabbing his finger into Shelton's shoulder to emphasise his point.

As Shelton walked away to sit by the fire, his gaze briefly met the butler's, a silent communication passing between them. The butler, with a steely resolve, took charge of Evelyn from Chapman and Claydon, leading her away with a firm grip on her arm. With a swift exit, he left the room, closing the door behind him.

Acker's attention shifted to the remaining servants, his voice cutting through the tense silence. "I'll see you all at the station first thing tomorrow morning. You may now leave and return to your beds," he announced.

The servants hurriedly departed, their hushed whispers echoing in the quiet room as they retreated to their respective quarters. The lounge fell into a heavy silence, broken only by the crackling of the fire as Shelton absentmindedly poked at it with a stick, sending ash dancing into the air.

"I'm sure that we'll be back very soon, Mr. Shelton," Acker remarked, his voice cutting through the quiet.

Shelton's response was curt, his attention still fixed on the fire. "I'm sure you will," he muttered, his tone tinged with bitterness. Acker turned to leave, intent on joining Chapman and Claydon in the foyer, when Shelton's voice stopped him in his tracks. "Just be gentle with her, please. Her mind is not all there," Shelton called out, his words a surprising plea.

Intrigued by Shelton's cryptic statement, Acker paused and turned back to face him. "What do you mean?" he questioned, his curiosity piqued.

As Shelton revealed Evelyn's past, Acker listened with a hint of sympathy in his eyes. "She had an accident when she was a little girl. According to her mother, she hasn't been the same since," Shelton explained, his voice tinged with a mixture of sadness and resignation.

Acker nodded understandingly, his expression softened. "I'm sure she'll be fine, sir," he replied, offering what reassurance he could.

But Shelton persisted, his concern evident as he added, "She gets things mixed up, and she says things she doesn't mean. Just bear that in mind, Inspector."

Acker gave a slight nod, acknowledging Shelton's warning before a sudden commotion in the foyer drew his attention away. Without another word, he excused himself and made his way to investigate the disturbance, leaving Shelton alone in the dimly lit lounge.

In the foyer, chaos ensued as Evelyn struggled against Chapman and Claydon, her desperation evident as she attempted to break free from their grasp. Dressed in her servant's uniform and a long coat, she fought against them with all her might, her screams echoing through the house.

"Enough of that, Evelyn!" Acker's voice boomed angrily, cutting through the tumultuous scene.

"I don't want to go! I don't want to go!" Evelyn screeched, her voice filled with desperation as she continued to struggle.

"You're coming with us whether you like it or not. Now, get out!" Acker commanded as he pushed her back into the grip of Chapman and Claydon.

With great effort, Chapman and Claydon managed to restrain Evelyn and guide her outside to the waiting carriage. Despite her resistance, they succeeded in getting her inside, her screams fading into the night as the carriage pulled away from the house.

Acker followed them out, closing the door behind him and casting one last glance through the lounge window at Shelton. The butler stood in the doorway, watching with concern before disappearing back into the house to find his master.

And as the carriage disappeared into the darkness, carrying Evelyn away to the station, Acker couldn't shake the uneasy feeling that lingered in the air. The mystery surrounding Bella's murder and now Evelyn's involvement weighed heavily on his mind, and he knew that they were only just scratching the surface of the truth hidden within Shelton's seemingly respectable home.

## CHAPTER TWENTY-ONE

## Bristol Cemetery – Night

The mist hung thick in the air, swirling and curling around the graveyard's headstones as if reluctant to reveal the secrets hidden within. The descending night brought with it an unsettling silence, broken only by the occasional rustle of leaves and the distant hoot of an owl. Eerie, ghostly shadows danced across the wet, dewy grass, casting macabre patterns upon the ground.

The trees that encircled the graveyard seemed to loom ominously, their gnarled and twisted branches reaching out like skeletal fingers. They swayed in the breeze, shedding their leaves in a sombre dance over the small mounds of earth, each large enough to hold a body. The tombstones stood sentinel, their weathered faces bearing the names and dates of those long gone, their heads perfectly aligned as if in silent conversation.

In the midst of this eerie scene, a scratching sound broke through the stillness, growing louder and more insistent as it moved closer. Something, or someone, was passing through the earth, disturbing the peace of the graveyard. At first, the disturbance was subtle, like wriggling worms emerging through the soaked mud.

But upon closer inspection, the truth was far more chilling. The muddy earth of Betty's shallow resting place was disturbed, and through the wet soil, fingers clawed their way upwards with a desperate urgency. They grasped at the air, their nails caked with dirt, as if their owner sought escape from a nightmare buried deep within the earth.

The scene was a haunting tableau, a macabre dance of the undead as the fingers struggled and writhed, yearning for freedom from their earthen prison. The mist enveloped this ghastly sight, shrouding it in an otherworldly haze, as if nature itself recoiled from the horror unfolding.

Betty's emergence from the muddy pit was a gruesome sight, her arm slick with blood and muck as it reached out to grasp anything solid for support. Her head followed, a wild look in her bloodshot eyes as she gasped for air, trying to wipe the dirt from her face. With a desperate strength born of survival instinct, she pulled herself from the shallow grave, her body trembling with the effort.

As she stood, her ragged breaths filled the silent cemetery, her cry of desperation echoing among the headstones. Blood and mud dripped from her dishevelled hair, and she spat a mixture of soil and crimson from her mouth, her chest heaving with the effort to breathe.

Betty's gaze fell upon her surroundings, the realisation of where she was and what her husband had done to her crashing down like a wave. Anger ignited within her, a fiery fury that burned away any fear. *How could he do this to me, to his own wife?*

Her legs felt weak beneath her, but determination fuelled her steps as she stumbled along the gravely path towards the exit. Each movement was an effort, the mud clinging to her clothes and dragging at her like unseen hands pulling her back into the earth. But she pressed on, driven by the need to get somewhere safe, to escape the nightmare that had become her reality.

Betty's mind raced with thoughts of what she needed to do. She needed to tell someone, anyone, the truth about her husband.

She needed to reveal the monster he truly was before he could do this to her again, or worse, to someone else.

As she reached the iron gates of the cemetery, she paused for a moment, catching her breath and looking back at the graveyard behind her. The mist continued to swirled around the headstones, moonlight casting an eerie glow from above. But there was no time to dwell on the haunting scene. With a determined set to her jaw, Betty pushed open the gates and stepped out into the cool night air, her heart pounding with adrenaline and fear.

She would find help. She would make sure that her husband paid for what he had done. And as she disappeared into the darkness, leaving behind the graveyard and its secrets, the echo of her cry lingered in the night, a haunting reminder of the horrors that lurked in the shadows.

## CHAPTER TWENTY-TWO

# The Missing Orphan

Edith burst into Mr. Bodmin's office, her face flushed with worry, panic evident in her trembling hands. "Sir, another child has gone missing! The girl, Samantha, I can't find her anywhere! Her bed is empty!" she blurted out, her voice quivering with distress.

Mr. Bodmin, seated at his desk, appeared unfazed as he continued to peruse his paperwork without looking up. "Have you searched for her?" he asked nonchalantly, his tone betraying little concern.

Edith nodded vigorously, her distress growing more palpable by the second. "Yes, I have! But she's nowhere to be found! Should I notify the detective?" she asked, desperation creeping into her voice.

Bodmin finally raised his head from the papers, irritation flashing in his eyes. "No, there's no need to involve them. I'm sure she's just playing outside," he replied dismissively, as if the disappearance of a child was a mere triviality.

Edith's frustration boiled over, and she slammed her hand down on the desk, her voice rising in anger. "I don't think you quite understand, Mr. Bodmin! The girl in question is due to be picked up this afternoon by Lady Elspeth for adoption!" she exclaimed, her eyes brimming with tears.

Bodmin's face paled, fear and realisation dawning on him as he bolted from his chair, his heart pounding with dread. "Why didn't you tell me?" he demanded, his voice trembling with anxiety as he grabbed her by the arm and hurried towards the door.

Edith struggled to keep up with him, her sobs echoing through the office. "I tried to tell you, but you weren't interested!" she cried, her words a mix of anger and despair as she followed him out of the office and into the corridor.

Edith winced as Bodmin's grip tightened on her arms, his fingers digging into her flesh painfully. "Stop your crying, wench, and tell me where she was last seen," he growled, his voice filled with anger and impatience.

Before Edith could respond, a small voice piped up from behind them. "She was taken from her bed," the child said timidly, stepping forward.

Bodmin whipped around to face the child, his eyes blazing with fury. "Don't lie to me, boy! She's probably just run away," he spat, his voice dripping with disdain.

But the child stood firm, taking a step back to avoid Bodmin's outstretched hand. "It's the truth. I saw it," he insisted, his eyes wide with fear.

Edith, her heart pounding with dread, stepped forward, pulling her arm away from him. "I'm going to inform the police, Mr. Bodmin. Too many children have gone missing from here, and it needs to stop," she said, her voice trembling.

But Bodmin was not about to let her go so easily. He grabbed her arm again, his grip like a vise, and yanked her back towards him. "Let me go. You're hurting me!" Edith cried out, struggling against his hold.

Bodmin's cruel smile sent shivers down her spine. "I suggest you look around again before contacting those idiots," he sneered, his voice low and menacing. "Go now, and don't return to my office until you have something to go on, rather than these ridiculous fabrications concocted by a small child with nothing better to do. Now, beat it!"

With that, he released her, causing Edith to stumble backward and nearly fall against the stairwell. She scrambled to her feet, her heart racing, and hurried away with the boy close behind her, fear gnawing at her insides.

Meanwhile, Bodmin's face was grim as he rushed back to his office, ignoring Edith's loud blubbering. He hastily scribbled a note on a blank piece of paper, nearly upsetting his ink pot in the process. Retrieving an envelope from his desk drawer, he stuffed the note inside and dashed for the front door.

Outside, the large overgrown garden stretched out before him. Bodmin's eyes scanned the surroundings until they landed on three children playing with a pile of sticks near the gate. "You, boy, come here!" he bellowed, his voice echoing across the fields.

The children froze and looked over, their faces pale with fear as they recognized Bodmin. With hurried steps, they approached him and lined up, their hands clasped behind their backs.

Bodmin grabbed the tallest boy and thrust the envelope into his hand. "I need you to call upon Mr. Thornton as quickly as you can. That letter needs to reach him before nightfall," he commanded, his voice urgent.

The boy nodded, his eyes wide with apprehension. "I'm not sure who that is, sir," he said timidly.

Bodmin's patience was wearing thin, and he glared at the boy. "He's the man who brings the pies here every week; you know who he is. Take my carriage and hurry about it!"

With that, he pushed the boy towards the iron gates, watching as he ran off with the letter flapping in his hand. Bodmin checked his pocket watch, his expression tense. "He should hurry up," he muttered to himself before dismissing the other children with a wave of his hand. "Do not tell the mistress about this; otherwise, there'll be consequences for your actions," he warned them sternly as they scurried off into the darkness.

Edith observed him from the upper window, absorbing every word. Wiping away her tears, she collected her thoughts. Revealing she had overheard him was out of the question; his retribution would be swift.

Pieces of the puzzle clicked into place, especially his unease when she mentioned the detective. It dawned on her why he was so nervous. She knew she had to inform the authorities about what she had uncovered. As she paced the room, a plan crystallised in her mind. A police officer was due back in the evening to monitor the house. That was her signal to notify him and guide him to seek assistance. Clapping her hands with determination, she knew she would be alright. Despite her loyalty to her master, she had no choice. She couldn't stand by while more children vanished. Even though these children weren't related by blood, she felt a duty to shield them. She shuddered at the thought of why Mr. Bodmin was taking the children and to whom he was giving them.

"What are you doing in here?" a harsh, disdainful voice interrupted her thoughts.

Her blood turned to ice as she slowly faced her master. "I am searching for Samantha, as you instructed, sir," she murmured, struggling to keep her composure.

His eyes fell on her trembling form, and he sneered, meeting her fearful gaze. "She won't be here. She's likely playing outside. When Lady Elspeth arrives, inform her that the girl has run off, and we are searching. She'll probably turn up before nightfall."

"I hope so, for all our sakes," she replied, her voice faltering slightly, trying to hold back tears. He rolled his eyes at her.

"What do you mean by that?" he snapped.

"If the police discover another missing child, they will return," she said meekly.

"She'll return, I'm certain of it. Now, go downstairs and prepare the hall for lunch," Bodmin commanded.

She nodded and left the room without another word, her mind racing. Taking the stairs quickly, she wanted to put as much distance between them as possible. He now disgusted her. It was hard to believe he was behind the disappearances, and she dreaded what his next move might be.

As she reached the lower floor, someone grabbed her hand from behind, and she jumped in fright. Turning, she realised it was the little boy from earlier. His rosy cheeks were red from the cold, and his hand was icy. "I'm telling the truth, miss. I really did see someone take Samantha."

Edith's heart went out to the boy, his ill-fitting clothes and unkempt appearance tugging at her heartstrings. Kneeling beside him, she gently stroked his cheek, feeling the roughness of neglect. "I know. We'll fix this, I promise," she whispered softly, making sure her voice didn't carry to where Bodmin could hear.

The boy nodded, a weak smile crossing his malnourished face, hunger evident in his eyes. "I was too scared to stop them from taking her. Am I going to be in trouble?"

"No, no, my dear child, you did nothing wrong. We'll bring her back, I promise," she reassured him, squeezing his hand before standing up. A loud knock interrupted their moment, echoing through the foyer.

"You go on now. I'll answer the door," Edith said, watching the boy scamper off before hurrying to open the door.

On the porch stood a tall woman, flanked by two identically dressed men in black suits. The woman's cheeks were rosy, and her eyes sparkled with something that made Edith uneasy. Her once vibrant red hair had faded to a soft silver, styled in an elaborate coiffure adorned with pearls and lace. The scent of lavender and aged paper lingered around her. Her pale blue eyes, sharp and discerning, peered out from behind delicate spectacles perched on the bridge of her patrician nose. Every wrinkle on her face told a story, each line earned through years of wisdom and experience in navigating the complex social hierarchy of Victorian society.

The woman was dressed in a gown of rich, dark velvet the colour of midnight adorned with intricate lace and elegant embroidery. Her slender fingers, adorned with antique rings and jewelled brooches, delicately held a silver encrusted walking stick as she stared at the awe on Edith's face.

"Good day, Edith," the woman chimed, pushing past Edith to enter. The two men followed, their expressions stoic as they glanced around with disdain. The woman wrinkled her nose at the smell in the air, and Edith flushed with embarrassment.

"Lady Elspeth, welcome. Shall I inform Mr. Bodmin of your arrival?" Edith offered, ready to leave to find him.

"There's no need, my dear. I'll find him myself. Is he in his office?" Lady Elspeth asked, her hand on Edith's shoulder.

Edith nodded, indicating the stairwell. "First door on the left."

The woman smiled, her silk-gloved hand warm on Edith's shoulder. "I hope Samantha is prepared for her new journey. I'm eager to show her my home. I'm sure she'll love it!" she exclaimed before ascending the stairs, her footsteps echoing through the empty hall.

Edith felt the weight of guilt settle heavily on her shoulders as she turned away from the two imposing men standing against the wall, their scrutiny like a physical presence. One of them caught her guilty expression and arched an eyebrow, his voice cutting through the tense air. "What's with that look?"

"You'll find out soon enough," Edith muttered under her breath, bracing herself for the inevitable uproar that would follow upstairs.

It didn't take long for chaos to erupt. A piercing shriek echoed down the staircase, followed by a flurry of hurried footsteps. Lady Elspeth stormed down the stairs, her face a mask of fury as she fixed her gaze on Edith. "What happened to her? Where is my little girl? I paid dearly for her!"

Mr. Bodmin appeared behind her, flustered and trying to placate the enraged woman. "Please, Lady Elspeth, allow me a moment to explain."

Edith wanted nothing more than to reveal the truth, to scream at Lady Elspeth that her precious Samantha had been kidnapped and sold by the man standing beside her. But she bit her tongue, knowing the consequences of such a revelation.

With a heavy heart, she stepped back from the stairwell to let them pass. Lady Elspeth, her voice filled with anger and desperation, demanded answers. "Where has she gone? What have you done?"

The air was thick with accusation and fear. Edith stood by, her hands clenched at her sides, wrestling with her conscience. She knew she had to do the right thing, no matter the cost. But for now, all she could do was wait and watch as the truth unravelled before them.

The tension in the room was terrible as Mr. Bodmin tried to calm the incensed Lady Elspeth. "We're actively searching for her, and I assure you, if you give us a little time, she'll be back in your care by tomorrow morning," he implored, his voice strained.

But the veins on Lady Elspeth's forehead stood out prominently as she glared at Bodmin. "How could you let this happen? Why would she try to escape when she knows I'm coming to take her to what she described as a castle? I don't blame her for wanting to leave these... these shambles!" her gestures emphasising the state of disrepair around them.

Bodmin raised his hands defensively. "I understand your frustration, Lady Elspeth, but please, there's no need for yelling. She will be back tomorrow. Just give us until then."

"If my little girl is not here by tomorrow morning, I will shut this place down," Lady Elspeth warned, her voice firm.

"What do you mean by that?" Bodmin asked, taken aback by her threat.

"Don't think I haven't noticed your lavish lifestyle or the condition of this building. I paid you a substantial amount, and it seems you've spent it on yourself," she snapped, her finger pointing at Bodmin accusingly.

Edith, who had been quietly observing, couldn't help but crack a small smile as she saw Bodmin's expression falter. "That's not true!" he protested, growing increasingly flustered.

"Once I have my little girl, I will return in exactly one month to see if there's been any improvement. If not, I'll be shutting this place down. These children deserve more than this," Lady Elspeth declared firmly, her gaze unwavering.

"Lady Elspeth, I don't agree with your accusations, and I won't stand for being disrespected in my own home," Bodmin retorted, his voice strained.

But Lady Elspeth paid him no heed, turning her attention to Edith, who had been lingering near the staircase. "I'll be back first thing tomorrow morning, Edith. Ensure the girl is here, or I'll have to take further action against this establishment."

Edith nodded earnestly. "Yes, ma'am. I'll do everything in my power to find her."

"See that you do," Lady Elspeth said sternly, before making her way to the door. She paused, casting a warning look at Bodmin. "I must warn you, sir, I'm not one to be trifled with; you don't want to make an enemy of me."

With that, she swept out of the foyer, her two men following silently behind. Bodmin let out a long sigh, the weight of the situation evident on his face. "Prepare for the girl's return," he instructed Edith, his voice weary.

Edith nodded, her determination renewed. She would do everything in her power to bring Samantha back, no matter the obstacles in her way.

\* \* \* \*

The hours dragged on, each minute feeling like an eternity as Edith anxiously waited by the window. Her eyes scanned the darkening path outside, her stomach twisting with hunger, yet she resisted the urge to eat. The boy Bodmin had sent off earlier had not returned, and she knew she had to be patient.

As dusk settled, casting long shadows through the orphanage, a carriage arrived quietly, its wheels creaking softly against the worn gravel. Edith's heart skipped a beat as she recognized the figure of Thornton stepping out, cloaked and hidden. He was accompanied by the boy, who seemed both nervous and resigned.

Silently, Edith crept down the stairs, keeping to the shadows, her heart pounding in her chest. A faint glow emanated from the hallway as Mr. Bodmin hurried with a candle towards the door. With a swift motion, he pulled it open, ushering Thornton and the boy inside.

"Where is she?" Bodmin's voice was urgent, tinged with desperation.

"She's in the carriage," Thornton replied bluntly, his tone devoid of sympathy. "But I need to replace her with someone else. Otherwise, I won't have anyone to sell, and you'll be left empty-handed."

"I can't just give you another child!" Bodmin protested, panic creeping into his voice. "Edith is already suspicious. If she discovers another child missing, she'll surely involve the police again."

"That's your problem, not mine," Thornton retorted coldly. "I need another child, preferably a girl, or I'll be taking the one in the carriage back with me. The police are swarming this place as it is. There's already one outside, snooping around."

Edith's heart pounded in her chest as she listened, hidden in the darkness. The realisation of what was happening sent a chill down her spine.

Bodmin's anger was palpable, his voice a low, menacing growl. "I cannot provide you with another child until next month, Thornton!" His eyes flickered to the trembling boy standing behind Thornton. "Go to bed, boy," he barked, pointing a finger towards the staircase. "And if you dare breathe a word of this to anyone, you'll regret it. I promise you, you'll end up in a shallow grave!"

Terrified, the boy scampered past Edith, who stood hidden in the shadows, and dashed up the stairs to his room, his footsteps echoing through the silent orphanage.

Turning back to Thornton, Bodmin's expression softened slightly, though the malice in his eyes remained. "You'll have to find a child on the streets. There are plenty around. I'm sure you'll manage."

Thornton let out a frustrated groan. "Fine, but I want something in return, Bodmin. Go fetch the girl, and I'll wait here."

Thornton stood at the door, watching the flickering shadows of Bodmin's retreating figure disappearing into the night. The sense of danger lingered in the air, heightened by the events of the evening. His ears pricked at the sound of a soft noise coming from the stairs, like a mouse scurrying.

Turning swiftly, Thornton's eyes adjusted to the darkness, catching sight of a figure attempting to sneak up the stairs. Without hesitation, he raced up the steps, closing the distance in a few strides. With a quick, deft movement, he grabbed the intruder from behind, their startled squeal echoing in the dimly lit hall.

"Let me go!" the voice cried out, and Thornton's grip tightened, recognising Edith's voice.

The commotion alerted Bodmin outside, who hurried back in, the sleeping girl still cradled in his arms. His face fell when he saw Edith pinned by Thornton. "What did you hear, Edith?" he demanded, his voice tinged with a mixture of anger and fear.

Edith, now caught, stopped struggling against Thornton's hold. "Everything," she admitted quietly, her voice trembling.

Thornton and Bodmin exchanged worried glances, the weight of their secret heavy in the air. Thornton's grip on Edith tightened, nearly causing an old painting of the orphanage to fall from the wall. "We can't let her live. She's seen too much," he growled, his cold stare fixed on Edith.

Edith's heart raced in her chest as she pleaded for her life, the fear evident in her eyes. "I won't say anything, I promise. Please, just let me go. You're hurting me," she gasped, struggling to breathe under Thornton's relentless grip.

Thornton's expression remained impassive, unmoved by her pleas. "What should we do with her?" he asked Bodmin, the weight of the decision heavy on both of them.

Bodmin's face reflected a mix of sadness and regret, the reality of the situation sinking in. "If you kill her, Thornton, I won't have a maid to keep the children in line. Someone needs to run this house," he said quietly, placing a hand on Thornton's arm to prevent him from squeezing any tighter. "She won't talk," Bodmin continued, his voice pleading. "Let her go."

Thornton released his grip on Edith, his glare burning into her petrified face. "If I can't get rid of her, then I suggest you lock her up somewhere, Bodmin," he sneered, his voice dripping with malice. "This place is already under police scrutiny. She could escape and alert them to our activities."

"She won't," Bodmin asserted, gently pushing Thornton away from Edith. "I guarantee it. Edith, go to your room upstairs. I'll come to speak with you shortly."

Edith didn't need to be told twice. With trembling legs, she rushed up the stairs, the echo of her footsteps mingling with the racing of her heart. She didn't dare look back at Thornton's menacing figure as she disappeared into the safety of her room, slamming the door shut behind her.

Meanwhile, Bodmin remained in the darkened hall, facing Thornton's seething form. "If we dispose of her, the police will undoubtedly suspect me," Bodmin murmured, his voice strained with worry.

"We're already in a precarious position," Thornton snapped back, frustration evident in his tone. "But mark my words, she'll sing like a bird if given the chance."

"She won't if she knows what's good for her," Bodmin retorted, turning to gaze out of the window towards the approaching dawn. "You need to leave. The first light of morning is upon us, and I don't want anyone to see you here. I'll take care of Samantha's return. Will the girl talk?" he asked, turning back to face Thornton.

Thornton shook his head, a cold certainty in his voice. "She won't remember a thing."

"Alright then, don't forget to pull your hood up before you leave," Bodmin whispered as he began the task of carrying the sleeping girl upstairs to her bed. He glanced back at Thornton, a twisted smile playing on his lips. "I'm sure you'll have no trouble finding another girl to take her place. Keep your eyes open on the streets; there's always someone in need."

Thornton remained silent, his mind already plotting his next move. With a nod to Bodmin, he turned and made his way out of the orphanage, pulling his hood up to conceal his features from any prying eyes.

As he stepped into the waiting carriage, the chill of the night air enveloped him, and he let out a sigh. The coachman emerged from the shadows and took his seat, waiting for instructions.

"Take me back," Thornton instructed quietly, his mind already drifting to the task ahead. The carriage rumbled to life, the sound of hooves on the gravel echoing through the night.

As they travelled away from the orphanage, Thornton watched the familiar building grow smaller in the distance, disappearing from view as they followed the winding road out of the estate. Thoughts of where to find another child swirled in his tired mind, but frustration mounted as no clear plan formed.

With a heavy sigh, Thornton let his thoughts drift away, exhaustion setting in. He settled back into the comfortable seat of the carriage, the rhythmic motion lulling him into a fitful doze. The events of the night weighed heavily on his mind, but for now, sleep beckoned, offering a temporary respite from the darkness of his deeds.

## CHAPTER TWENTY-THREE

# Royal York Crescent

Under the cloak of night, Acker's residence stood like a silent sentinel, its grandeur softened by the darkness. The moon cast a silvery glow upon its towering spires and ornate turrets, lending an ethereal quality to its imposing facade. A wrought-iron gate creaked softly in the cold breeze, a haunting melody that echoed through the deserted streets of Bristol.

Through the tall, arched windows, a dim light flickered, casting long shadows that danced across the rich tapestries and velvet drapes within. The glow of candlelight illuminated the intricate woodwork of the grand staircase, its bannisters polished to a gleaming sheen. Alone, Lizzie moved through the dimly lit hallways, her footsteps muffled by the thick carpets that lined the floors.

In the stillness of the Victorian house, the only sound that dared to break the silence was the mournful whistle of the wind as it slipped down the chimney. The darkness seemed to creep in from every corner, swallowing the grandeur of the ornate furnishings and casting long, menacing shadows.

Her heart fluttered nervously in her chest, the sense of unease palpable as the hairs on the back of her neck prickled with a cold shiver. The oppressive weight of the night pressed down on her, suffocating her in its embrace. She despised the darkness, its ominous presence a constant reminder of her fears.

This night was no exception. Her father was absent, as he so often was, lost in the pursuit of work that seemed to consume him entirely. She could almost hear his distant voice, promising to come home early, to spend time with his family. But those promises were always broken, leaving her mother to weep quietly in her room, alone and afraid.

Little Lizzie's heart swelled with joy when her father brought Billy home to live with them. In a house that often echoed with emptiness, Billy became her beacon of light, her source of laughter and companionship in the long, lonely days. He was a lively presence, always eager to play games and help with chores around the house.

Despite their age difference, Lizzie took on the role of teacher with enthusiasm, patiently guiding Billy through the world of letters and words. His eyes would light up with excitement whenever they sat down together to practise reading and writing, his eagerness infectious.

But beneath Billy's cheerful exterior, Lizzie sensed a hidden sorrow, a weight that seemed to linger in his eyes. There were moments when she caught him staring off into the distance, lost in his own thoughts, and she couldn't help but wonder what troubled him so deeply.

It gnawed at her, this unspoken secret that seemed to hang between them like a heavy curtain. She longed to ask him, to ease the burden he carried, but she feared that prying too much would drive him away. So, she kept her questions locked inside, her curiosity a silent ache that she carried with her.

As she tiptoed through the foyer towards the kitchen, Lizzie's mind was consumed with thoughts of Billy. She navigated the familiar floorboards with care, avoiding the ones that groaned and protested beneath her weight. These were the small details she had come to know well, the quirks of their old house that she had learned with ease.

As Lizzie made her way through the shadowed foyer, a sudden movement jolted her, nearly knocking her off balance. A gasp escaped her lips, her heart hammering wildly in her chest. Before she could even register what had happened, terror gripped her throat, rendering her unable to scream.

Something had emerged from the darkness, a looming figure that seemed to materialise out of thin air. Panic surged through her veins, her whole body trembling with fear. The small candle she clutched in her hand slipped from her sweaty fingers, extinguishing the flickering light that had guided her.

The foyer plunged into near-complete darkness, leaving Lizzie disoriented and vulnerable. She could feel the figure's presence looming ominously before her, its intentions unknown. But despite the darkness, she knew the layout of the house like the back of her hand. With a surge of adrenaline-fueled terror, she bolted towards the front door, her bare feet pounding against the cold, hard floor.

With trembling hands, she yanked the heavy door open, the hinges creaking in protest. Moonlight flooded into the foyer, casting long shadows that danced and swayed with her frantic movements. Her heart raced even faster as she took a desperate breath of the cool night air, her lungs burning with exertion.

"Lizzie, wait! It's me! Billy!" a voice called out from the darkness behind her, but she was too consumed by fear to process the words. Every instinct screamed at her to run, to escape the looming threat that seemed to follow her.

An orange glow suddenly illuminated the foyer from near the kitchen door, casting eerie shadows on the walls. Lizzie caught a glimpse of a dark figure frantically stomping something out on the ground, the acrid smell of smoke filling the air.

Without hesitation, Lizzie turned and fled into the street, her feet pounding against the cold cobblestones. Her nightdress fluttered around her legs, becoming damp from the moisture of the night. She shivered violently, the chill seeping into her bones as she ran, her heart pounding in her ears.

As she raced through the unfamiliar streets, her mind raced with horrible thoughts and images. Fear clutched at her chest like icy fingers, threatening to suffocate her. She didn't know where she was going, only that she had to escape, to put as much distance between herself and the darkness that lurked behind her.

The night seemed endless as she ran, her breath coming in ragged gasps. Tears streamed down her cheeks, mixing with the cold rain that began to fall from the sky. But still, she ran, driven by fear and the primal need to survive.

Eventually, her legs could carry her no further, and she slowed to a stumbling walk. She looked around, her surroundings unfamiliar and foreboding in the dim light of the moon. Her heart pounded in her chest as she tried to gather her bearings, her mind reeling with terror and confusion.

Alone and lost in the darkness, Lizzie hugged herself tightly, the damp night air chilling her to the bone. She was far from safety, and the night stretched out before her like an endless abyss.

Lizzie's heart raced as she looked up, her eyes falling upon a large sign above a nearby shop window that read, 'Thornton's Pork.' The name meant nothing to her, but she hurried into the shelter of the shop's small archway, seeking refuge from the biting wind that whipped through the empty streets.

The relief was palpable as a carriage appeared around the corner, its wheels clattering against the cobbled pavement before coming to a stop just outside the shop. A man emerged from the carriage, his form cloaked in darkness, and Lizzie felt a glimmer of hope.

But as he approached, his shock at finding her there quickly gave way to a twisted smile that sent a chill down her spine. "Who are you, and what are you doing here?" he inquired, his voice smooth yet filled with an unsettling edge.

"I'm lost," Lizzie replied, her voice trembling with fear and uncertainty.

For a moment, Thornton seemed taken aback by her simple answer, but then his smile widened, revealing a hint of malice.

"Don't worry, my dear child; I'll help you find your way," he said, his tone dripping with false kindness.

As the carriage pulled away without a second glance, leaving them alone in the dimly lit street, Thornton swiftly removed his cloak and draped it around Lizzie's shoulders. She clutched the soft, velvety fabric to her chest, grateful for the warmth it provided against the biting cold.

"Thank you very much, sir," she murmured, her voice barely above a whisper.

"Come inside," Thornton offered, taking her hand in his and unlocking the door to the shop. The warmth of the shop beckoned invitingly from within, and Lizzie followed him inside, her heart pounding with a mixture of fear and relief.

He guided her to a small fireplace, where he began to light the logs, the flames casting a flickering glow across the dimly lit room. Lizzie settled herself beside the fire, the warmth seeping into her chilled bones, and she let out a sigh of comfort.

"How do I address you?" Thornton asked, his eyes watching her intently as he tended to the fire.

"My mother calls me Lizzie," she replied, her voice soft but steady as she basked in the newfound warmth of the shop. The crackling of the fire filled the silence that followed, casting dancing shadows on the walls as the log began to burn steadily.

Despite the relief of the fire's warmth, Lizzie couldn't shake the unease that settled in the pit of her stomach. She was alone with a stranger, and something about Thornton's demeanour set her on edge. But for now, she pushed aside her fears, focusing instead on the comforting glow of the fire and the hope that she would find her way home soon.

"You've stumbled upon the perfect spot, Lizzie. I specialise in reuniting young ones with their families," he chuckled, thoroughly entertained by his own fabrication.

Eyes twinkling with delight, she responded, "You do? I live nearby, but mummy never lets me wander, so I've no clue how to find my way back."

"Fret not, little one. I'll escort you right to your doorstep. Once you've warmed up a bit," he assured her.

"Thank you ever so much, sir. You're terribly kind. What

might your name be?" she asked.

He hesitated briefly, contemplating whether to disclose his true identity. After a moment's thought, he replied, "Jeremy Bodmin is my name, and the quest for lost children is my game," punctuated by a chuckle at his own jest, which elicited a grin from Lizzie, revealing her missing teeth.

"It seems your grown-up teeth will be arriving soon," he remarked with a smile.

"Yes, mummy says they're on their way, and I can hardly wait! I'll be all grown up," she beamed.

He nodded, tending to the fire with a stick. "Are you feeling warm enough?"

"Oh, yes, I'm eager to go home," she confirmed.

Rising, he vanished into the adjoining room, returning with another coat. "Here, try this one. It's much cosier," he suggested. She shed his cloak, which he promptly donned, pulling up the hood. "Before we head home, I've got something quite thrilling to show you."

"Like what?" she inquired.

"Think of it as a Lizzie adventure!" he proclaimed.

Clapping her hands in glee, she rose to her feet, following him into the night. Taking her tiny, angelic hand, he guided her towards the Bristol docks. Perhaps luck was on his side tonight, he mused, as the docks loomed into view.

## CHAPTER TWENTY-FOUR

# Corn Street - Day Time

In the heart of Corn Street, amidst the ornate architecture and cobblestone roads, lay the enchanting spectacle of the market. The air was alive with a symphony of sounds—vendors' calls mingling with the chatter of eager shoppers, the clip-clop of horses' hooves on the cobbled paths, and the occasional clang of pots and pans from a nearby stall.

Amidst the hubbub, the market held a sense of camaraderie. Vendors greeted regulars by name, exchanging tales and news of the day. The market was not just a place of commerce but a community gathering, where stories were shared over steaming cups of tea and the day's catch was haggled over with good-natured banter.

As the sun arched higher in the sky, casting dappled patterns of light through the canopy of awnings, the market buzzed with a lively energy. It was a place where time seemed to slow, allowing visitors to lose themselves in the sensory tapestry of Victorian life, if only for a moment, amidst the charming chaos of the daytime market.

Betty entered the marketplace and was greeted by a kaleidoscope of colours and scents. Awning-covered stalls lined the narrow lanes, their wooden frames adorned with garlands of fresh flowers and ribbons fluttering in the breeze. The market was a patchwork of goods—a feast for the senses. But it wasn't for Betty, not today.

A stall filled with shimmering silks and velvets, cascading in rich hues caught her eye as she passed by. Nearby, the scent of freshly baked bread wafted from a bakery stand, where golden loaves nestled next to rows of pastries glistening with sugar, rumbled her stomach.

As she went further along, the metallic glint of intricate jewellery dazzled under the sunlight, enticing passersby with its delicate craftsmanship. They ignored the stumbling figure of Betty weaving her way through the crowd of shoppers as their beady eyes glazed over the stalls. Across the way, a stall overflowed with exotic spices and teas, their fragrant aromas mingling with the earthy scent of herbs from a neighbouring apothecary. That was Betty's favourite stall, but as she passed by, the smell made bile rise within her throat.

Betty stumbled through the bustling crowd, her head swimming with pain and confusion. Her trembling hands clutched at her aching skull, the sticky warmth of blood mingling with the dirt that still clung to her clothes. Passing shoppers cast curious glances at the dishevelled woman, their gazes lingering uncomfortably on the mud-caked fabric.

Desperate to avoid any interaction, Betty kept her gaze fixed on the ground, hoping to disappear into the throng of people. But the world around her spun and swirled, refusing to stay steady. With each unsteady step, her resolve wavered until finally, her strength gave out.

Collapsing to the ground, she sank into the hard cobblestones, her breath ragged and shallow. Above her, the sky seemed to swirl with blurry shapes, indistinct and hazy. Shadows loomed over her, their concerned murmurs blending into the cacophony of the market.

"Are you alright, miss?" a voice broke through the haze, cutting through the chaos around her. Betty blinked up at the fuzzy figure hovering above, struggling to focus on the face that peered down with genuine concern.

She tried to speak, but her parched throat only managed a hoarse whisper. "I... I don't know," she managed, her voice barely audible over the din of the crowd.

A gentle hand reached out to support her, helping her into a sitting position. As her vision slowly cleared, Betty found herself staring into the eyes of a kind stranger, their features slowly coming into focus.

"Let's get you some help," the voice said softly, offering a steadying arm.

"Isn't that Robert's wife?" another voice queried amidst the growing concern.

"It is indeed. Covered in all this mud, she's hardly recognizable. Look at her head, it's bleeding! She needs a doctor. Someone must hurry and inform the cheesemonger!" The urgency in the second voice cut through the clamour of the market.

The mention of Robert's name sent a jolt of fear through Betty's battered body. She shook her head vehemently, trying desperately to communicate without words, not wanting Robert to know she was alive. Before she could make her plea, strong hands gripped her arms, pulling her unsteadily to her feet. A dizzying wave swept over her, and she stumbled, falling into the embrace of someone behind her, their coat feeling familiarly masculine.

"Miss, we must get you to a doctor. Can you manage to walk?" The man's voice was earnest, but Betty could only stare back at him, her mind muddled with pain and confusion. Tears mingled with the grime on her cheeks as she tried to form words, only managing a pained groan.

"She needs a cab!" Another voice rang out from the crowd, urgency rising.

A carriage appeared, screeching to a halt beside them. The door flew open, and Robert emerged, his face a mask of false concern as he rushed towards her.

"Betty! What in heaven's name happened? I've been beside myself with worry." His arms enveloped her, squeezing tightly in a gesture that felt more like a threat than comfort. "If you breathe a word of this to anyone, I'll ensure you're buried for good this time," he hissed into her ear, the menace chilling her to the core.

She stared ahead, bewildered, as he pulled away, his expression still twisted in feigned concern. "Who did this to you, my dear?" his voice was honeyed deceit, and Betty found herself unable to form a coherent response, her heart pounding with a mix of fear and betrayal.

Betty's throat felt constricted with the weight of unspoken words, her attempts to shout or plead with Robert stifled into a mere croak. Fear gripped her anew, replacing the exhaustion in her limbs with a trembling dread. As she tried to push him away, his grip only tightened, his nails biting into her arm like claws.

"Let's get you to a doctor and then to Detective Acker. We need to file a report. Whoever did this to you must be held accountable," Robert's voice cut through the chaos, his words a sharp contrast to the cruelty in his actions. With a strength borne of desperation, he pulled her away from the crowd, his determination overpowering her weakened state.

From the shadows, Bailey watched in silent horror as Betty's struggles seemed futile against her husband's grasp. Her limbs flailed, her cries muffled by the chaos around them. Bailey couldn't understand why the onlookers did nothing, but he dared not reveal himself, not with Thornton approaching with that sly grin.

"You look as though you've risen from the grave, Betty," Thornton's chuckle was as chilling as his wink.

Robert's eyes widened at Thornton's arrival, a mix of fear and suspicion clouding his features. Betty continued to sob, her attempts to break free growing more frantic with each passing moment. Robert's attention shifted to Thornton, wondering if he knew about his misdeeds.

*Had the gravedigger spoken?* Anger surged within him, fuelled by the realisation that his secrets might not be as secure as he'd thought.

"Did you follow me last night?" Robert's voice was a low,

menacing hiss as he lunged towards Thornton.

"I don't know what you're talking about," Thornton's innocent facade crumbled for a moment, replaced by a sly smile as he yanked his arm away, slipping out of Robert's reach. With a shrug, he walked off, leaving Robert stunned and Betty still struggling in his grasp.

The crowd had thinned now, their attention drawn away by the spectacle. Bailey observed from his hidden vantage point as Robert forced Betty into the waiting carriage, the slam of the door echoing with finality. The carriage lurched into motion, disappearing into the crowded streets, leaving Bailey alone with the weight of what he had witnessed.

## CHAPTER TWENTY-FIVE

# Lost & Found

Samantha perched uneasily on the rickety, worn bench beside the foyer's staircase, her heart fluttering with anxiety. She was waiting for her new family to arrive, yet her mind was a jumble of confusion, unable to piece together the events of the night before. Fragments of memories danced at the edges of her consciousness, elusive and fleeting.

Earlier, when Mr. Bodmin had questioned her about that fateful night, she had drawn a blank. His stern expression had left her feeling uneasy, his nervous yet assertive demeanour adding to her growing apprehension. He had pressed her to tell Lady Elspeth that she had managed to escape, but Samantha knew deep down that it wasn't the truth. The fear of what Mr. Bodmin might do if she revealed the real story hung heavy over her.

As the clock on the wall ticked away the moments, Samantha couldn't help but fidget with her clammy hands. Beside her sat an old cloth bag, its contents a collection of cherished mementos from her time at the orphanage. She hadn't seen Edith, her closest friend, in days, and worry gnawed at her as she wondered where she might be.

A sudden, loud knock at the front door shattered the silence, causing Samantha to startle so violently that she nearly toppled off the bench. Mr. Bodmin emerged from the kitchen door, his face flushed and flustered, casting a wary glance in Samantha's direction.

"Remember, child," his voice was low and urgent, "be careful with your words. The consequences will be severe if you are not."

Samantha nodded, her heart pounding in her chest as she watched Mr. Bodmin hurriedly make his way to the door. The weight of his warning settled heavily on her shoulders, mingling with the uncertainty of her situation. Her heart raced as Lady Elspeth swept into the foyer, a vision in her ruby-red gown and matching hat. The grandeur of her entrance was a stark contrast to Samantha's own nervous presence, clutching her cloth bag tightly to her chest.

"Darling! There you are!" Lady Elspeth's voice was filled with warmth and concern as she hurried towards Samantha, arms outstretched for an embrace. But Samantha's response was not what she expected. With a mixture of guilt and apprehension, Samantha squirmed out of the hug, unable to meet Lady Elspeth's gaze.

"Why did you run away?" Lady Elspeth's question hung heavy in the air, her eyes searching Samantha's face for answers.

Samantha's gaze shifted to Mr. Bodmin, unsure of what to say. "I'm not sure," she mumbled softly, her voice barely above a whisper.

Lady Elspeth noticed Samantha's reluctance to meet her eyes and turned her attention to Mr. Bodmin, her expression demanding an explanation. Mr. Bodmin met her gaze with a sly smile playing on his lips.

"We found her hiding nearby," he stated matter-of-factly, his tone masking any hint of deceit.

"I don't believe it for a minute, Mr. Bodmin," Lady Elspeth's voice was firm, her eyes flashing with determination. "You'd better start telling the truth to me or else-"

"Or else what, madam?" Mr. Bodmin's retort was sharp, a hint of defiance in his tone.

Lady Elspeth's eyes narrowed into determined slits as she stepped closer to him, her ruby-red gown swishing with purpose. "Or else, Mr. Bodmin, I'll have my men turn this place over. I'm sure they'll find something amiss hidden in that murky office of yours."

A flicker of fear passed over Mr. Bodmin's face at the threat, his bravado momentarily faltering. "You have no need to do that," he protested weakly. "Samantha is speaking the truth. She was terrified and fled. Moving to a new home can be quite daunting for a child her age."

"Most children would be eager to leave this place, and Samantha should be no exception," Lady Elspeth countered, her voice steely with resolve. "Something is not right here, Mr. Bodmin, and I intend to find out what it is."

Mr. Bodmin's attempt to maintain composure was palpable, his shrug a feeble facade of confidence. "Then look around, madam. I guarantee you won't find anything," he insisted, his voice strained.

Lady Elspeth's eyes swept the foyer, her keen gaze noticing the absence of Edith's usual presence. "Where is Edith?" she asked, her tone sharp with suspicion.

"She took ill and retired to bed yesterday evening," Mr. Bodmin replied smoothly, a practised lie slipping effortlessly from his lips.

Samantha's heart clenched with the weight of another falsehood. Edith hadn't been seen since her return, and the realisation sent shivers of fear down Samantha's spine. As she stared into Mr. Bodmin's cold, calculating eyes, she found herself shaking uncontrollably.

Summoning her courage, Samantha spoke up, knowing that Mr. Bodmin's facade would crumble in the presence of Lady Elspeth. "I haven't seen her since I returned," she confessed, her voice trembling but resolute.

Lady Elspeth's gaze hardened as she turned her full attention to Mr. Bodmin. "Where is she?" she demanded, her tone sharp with anger.

A bead of sweat dripped down Mr. Bodmin's brow, his eyes darting nervously towards the staircase. "I'll go fetch her, but she's quite unwell, Lady Elspeth. She won't be pleased at being disturbed," he muttered, his unease evident.

Lady Elspeth's patience wore thin as she snapped her fingers, her voice firm. "Go find her," she commanded.

With a resigned sigh, Mr. Bodmin stomped up the stairs, disappearing from sight. Left alone with Samantha, Lady Elspeth turned her piercing gaze towards the girl, her frustration evident. "I need to know the truth, Samantha. What happened to you? I don't believe you simply escaped. I know you wouldn't do such a thing."

Samantha's eyes remained fixed on the floor, unable to meet Lady Elspeth's intense stare. "I have no recollection of anything. It's like the entire day vanished from my mind, and I can't seem to grasp it," she confessed quietly.

"What do you remember?" Lady Elspeth asked gently, taking a seat beside Samantha on the bench.

"I remember a man in a cloak, but his face was obscured. I was terrified of him. And... I remember a carriage," Samantha recounted, her voice barely audible as she tried to keep their conversation private.

"Do you recall Mr. Bodmin? What was he doing at the time?" Lady Elspeth pressed.

"I'm sorry, Lady Elspeth, but I can't remember much of anything. It's all a haze," Samantha admitted, her fear and confusion evident in her eyes.

A loud cough from above shattered the tense moment, and they both turned to see Mr. Bodmin glaring down at them from the bannister. "She's on her way," he announced curtly, his tone laced with irritation.

Edith descended the stairs in a flurry, her cheeks flushed with embarrassment as she rushed to Lady Elspeth's side, an apologetic expression on her face.

"Please accept my apologies, Lady Elspeth. These past few days have been... challenging," Edith murmured, her eyes downcast.

"You appear to be in good health, Edith," Lady Elspeth observed, noting the young woman's flushed complexion.

Edith's embarrassment deepened, her cheeks turning an even deeper shade of red. "Mr. Bodmin was kind enough to grant me a few days off to rest and recover," she explained, her voice barely above a whisper.

Lady Elspeth's brow furrowed with concern as she studied Edith. There was something in the maid's eyes—fear, perhaps, or guilt—that troubled her deeply. She glanced between Edith and Mr. Bodmin, noticing the way Edith kept stealing nervous glances at the man, and the close proximity between them raised a red flag in her mind.

"Mr. Bodmin," Lady Elspeth addressed him, her voice firm, "could you please leave us? I'd like to speak with Edith alone."

Bodmin's stubbornness was evident as he shook his head defiantly, his proximity to Edith growing even closer. "No, I'm not going anywhere. You can speak with Edith in front of me if you need to. This is my property, and I am free to go wherever I want," he declared, his voice tinged with arrogance.

Lady Elspeth's mind raced as she searched for a way to separate Edith from Bodmin. She needed to ensure they could speak freely without his interference. An idea sparked in her mind, and she turned her attention back to Edith.

"Okay, Edith," Lady Elspeth began, her tone measured and composed. "I have a proposition for you. How would you like to come and work for me? You'll be well compensated, and I can offer you a position as a maid in my household."

Edith's eyes widened in surprise, a glimmer of hope flickering in her expression. "Work for you, Lady Elspeth?" she echoed, her voice uncertain.

"Yes," Lady Elspeth nodded, seizing the opportunity. "I see how hard you work here, and I believe you deserve better. You'll have a comfortable place to stay and a fair wage."

Edith hesitated, torn between loyalty to the children she cared for and the chance for a better life. "I... I'm sorry, Lady Elspeth, but the children here need me. If I leave, there will be no one to look after them," she explained, her voice filled with concern.

Lady Elspeth nodded understandingly, her mind working quickly to find a solution. "I understand your dedication, Edith. How about this? You can work as a maid for me one day a week. I'll send a carriage to pick you up and take you back. In the meantime, I'll arrange for one of my maids to substitute for you here for the day. That way, you can continue to care for the children here, but also have the opportunity for a change of scenery and a bit of extra income."

Edith's eyes widened with surprise and gratitude. The prospect of working for Lady Elspeth, even part-time, was a dream come true. "Oh, Lady Elspeth, that would be wonderful! Thank you so much," she exclaimed, a smile spreading across her face.

The veins on Bodmin's forehead bulged with anger, his voice rising in protest. "I will not allow this. She is my maid, and you cannot just take her from me," he declared.

Lady Elspeth's expression remained composed, though a glint of steel flashed in her eyes. "Should I remind you who you're speaking to, Mr. Bodmin?" she countered, her voice firm. "Is Edith under contract with you?"

"No, but—" Bodmin started, but Lady Elspeth cut him off with a raised hand.

"Then my response is simple and clear," she interrupted, her tone unwavering. "She is free to come and go as she pleases. I've offered her a better job with a higher salary, and she will continue to work here for the rest of the week. I fail to see why you're so opposed to it, unless..." Lady Elspeth trailed off, her gaze sharp as she levelled a pointed look at Bodmin. She expected an explanation, but none came. Bodmin remained silent, his jaw clenched in frustration.

With a final glance of disdain at Bodmin, Lady Elspeth turned her attention to Edith, who stood by nervously. "Come, Edith," she said gently, reaching out to take the maid's hand. "Let's speak in private about your new position."

Edith's eyes widened with gratitude as she followed Lady Elspeth, leaving Bodmin fuming in the foyer. As they moved out of earshot, Lady Elspeth could feel the weight of Bodmin's gaze on her back, his silent fury palpable.

Meanwhile, Bodmin knew he had to tread carefully. If word

got out about his secret business dealings, it could mean the end of everything he had built. He needed advice, someone who could help him navigate this precarious situation. And there was only one person he could think of — Thornton.

Thornton was a sly man, but he was also cunning and intelligent. If anyone could help him devise a plan to salvage his business and protect his secrets, it was Thornton. He knew he had to act fast before everything unravelled before him.

As Bodmin's mind whirled with schemes and plans, a dark determination settled over him. He was adamant that Lady Elspeth and Edith would never set foot inside his home again. If it meant getting rid of them both to cover his tracks and protect his secrets, then so be it.

## CHAPTER TWENTY-SIX

# The Interrogation

In the dim light of the interrogation room, grey shadows danced along the walls, cast by the flickering flames of oil lamps that hung precariously from the ceiling. The air was heavy with the scent of damp stone and musty parchment, suffused with an aura of impending dread. Worn wooden furniture stood stoically against the cold, plain walls, bearing the weight of countless interrogations past.

The most chilling feature of the room was the solitary window, its panes obscured by thick iron bars that cast stark shadows across the room. Through the narrow slits, only slivers of light dared to intrude, offering a glimpse of the world beyond to those trapped within. At the room's centre lay a sturdy oak table, its surface scarred with the marks of time.

Claydon, Acker, and Chapman sat stoically across from Evelyn, their expressions a mixture of scrutiny and determination.

The air in the room seemed to thicken with tension as Evelyn shifted uncomfortably in her seat, her eyes darting nervously between the detectives.

Her tear-streaked cheeks betrayed the fear within her, each sniffle a testament to her mounting anxiety. But despite her distress, she remained silent, her lips pressed tightly together in defiance and loyalty to her master. To Evelyn, the detectives were merely obstacles standing between her and the comfort of Shelton's embrace. She longed to escape this suffocating room, to return to the safety of his arms where she could find comfort and understanding. But Shelton's whispered assurances echoed in her mind, reminding her of the necessity of her actions. She harboured no remorse for the choices she had made, for in her eyes, they were made out of love for her master.

As the detectives pressed on with their questioning, Evelyn's thoughts drifted to the threat of discovery. She prayed silently that she had left no trace of her involvement behind, willing herself to believe that she had acted with impunity and loyalty.

"Miss Evelyn, I'm getting tired of your silent treatment. If you want to rot inside one of our cells, that's fine by me, but you're wasting our time," Acker warned.

Evelyn's breath caught in her throat as the detectives' words hung heavy in the dreadfully cold air of the interrogation room. The chill seemed to seep into her very bones, her body trembling uncontrollably as she fought against the oppressive atmosphere closing in around her.

Her gaze darted fearfully between the detectives, their faces etched with disdain and impatience. Acker's warning cut through her like a blade, his tone sharp and unforgiving. She felt the weight of their accusations pressing down upon her, threatening to crush her beneath their relentless scrutiny.

"She is refusing to speak with us, sir. Let's just lock her up and wait for her to scream for her release," Chapman said.

"Is the murderer still in cell number one? We can place her with him," Claydon scoffed.

The mention of the murderer in the nearby cell sent a shiver down Evelyn's spine, the thought of being locked away with such a notorious figure filling her with dread. The room seemed to spin around her, the walls closing in as if to suffocate her with their unyielding presence.

"What murderer?" she squeaked.

"Oh, so she can speak." Chapman chuckled.

Her heart raced erratically, the sound of blood rushing in her ears drowning out the detectives' words. She struggled to focus, to make sense of the accusations being hurled at her, but the ringing in her ears only grew louder, drowning out all else.

Acker pulled his pipe from his pocket and stuffed it with tobacco. "Well, if you don't talk to us, then you'll be spending the night with our famous inmate, who is due to be hung next week for murder."

As Acker leaned back in his chair, the flicker of his pipe casting eerie shadows across the room, Evelyn's eyes widened in terror. She felt as though she were teetering on the edge of a precipice, her very sanity hanging by a thread.

But amidst the fear, Evelyn's defiance remained unbroken. Clenching her fists tightly, she met the detectives' gaze. "I haven't done anything wrong," she muttered.

"You're hiding something from us. It's very obvious."

"It's not my fault that I'm in love with Shelton. When two souls connect, they are destined for each other."

"Do you want to know what your little lover boy told me before we took you away?" Acker asked, a sneer forming on the corners of his mouth.

Yet, as Acker's sneer widened, Evelyn couldn't help but feel a chill run down her spine. *What had Shelton revealed to them? What secrets lay hidden beneath the surface of their love?* Dread coiled in the pit of her stomach as she awaited the detectives' next move, her fate hanging precariously in the balance.

She nodded eagerly. "Yes."

"He told me that your mind isn't fully formed because of a childhood accident. He told me that you lie and are deceitful, and that the only reason he has you as a maid is out of sympathy for you. Evelyn, he does not adore you. He's just taking advantage of you. Do you really want to protect someone like that?"

Her mind raced, desperately trying to reconcile the image of

Shelton she had held so dear with the unsettling truths now laid bare before her. *Could it be true? Had I been nothing more than a pawn in his game all along?*

Claydon's sympathetic gaze offered a glimmer of solace amidst the storm of emotions raging within her. She felt her resolve falter as doubt gnawed at the edges of her certainty. *Was it possible that Shelton had deceived me so thoroughly?*

But even as her heart wavered, Evelyn's pride refused to let her surrender completely. She clung to the fragments of her shattered belief, clinging desperately to the notion of Shelton's love even as doubt crept insidiously into her thoughts.

"He'd never say that!" she screamed. "He claims to love me!"

"He would say that if he needed you to do something for him. Was there anything he wanted you to do that he didn't want to do himself for fear of being caught? Is there anything he has asked you to do recently?" Acker asked, blowing a ring of smoke into the room.

When Acker pressed her for answers, Evelyn's instinct was to retreat, to shield herself from the harsh reality bearing down upon her. But the truth was already written across her face, her attempts to hide her shock futile in the face of the detectives' scrutiny.

"I take that as a yes," said Chapman.

"I'm not going to talk to any of you. I'd like to speak with a woman," She demanded.

Acker looked at her, confused. "A woman?"

"Yes, a woman officer. I'm allowed that at least."

"We haven't got any women police officers, Evelyn."

Her demand for a woman officer was a feeble attempt to regain control, to find solace in the presence of someone who might understand her plight. But even that small comfort was denied to her, leaving her feeling more isolated and alone than ever before.

In that moment, Evelyn realised that she stood at a crossroads, her fate hanging in the balance. Would she continue to cling to the illusion of love, or would she dare to confront the harsh truths lurking in the shadows of her own heart? The choice was hers alone to make, but the consequences would be far-reaching and irreversible.

"Then I won't talk. It's that simple." She looked at them, daring them to argue back.

They exchanged bewildered glances, grappling with the unprecedented demand thrust upon them. The idea of a woman navigating the perilous realms of law enforcement clashed with their ingrained beliefs, rendering them speechless in the face of Evelyn's audacity.

"I'm not certain that's feasible, Evelyn," Acker confessed reluctantly, his tone betraying a hint of unease. "It's not the place for a woman, you see. Too precarious."

But Evelyn remained resolute, her eyes blazing with determination as she pressed her plea for empathy. She refused to be silenced by the patriarchal norms that sought to confine her worth to the confines of her gender.

"Then I won't talk. You have no idea what a woman goes through just to be noticed. I want a woman here who will understand me and, instead of accusing me, will support me," she explained.

Acker couldn't help but admire Evelyn's tenacity, recognising the untapped potential simmering beneath her composed facade. He saw an opportunity to harness her cunning intellect to unravel the intricate web of deceit spun by Shelton.

Before he could delve further into his strategy, a sudden upheaval disrupted the interrogation as a frantic officer burst into the room with news of Acker's distressed wife.

The sound of hysterical crying could be heard behind the officer, causing Acker to leap to his feet, nearly knocking over his chair. "What's the matter with her?"

The police officer shrugged. "Beats me. She only wants to talk to you."

As Acker rushed to comfort his distraught wife, a flurry of questions and concerns filled the air, leaving the detectives grappling with a new urgency.

Mary's frantic demeanour drew Acker's attention like a magnet, pulling him away from the intensity of the interrogation. He gently but firmly guided her aside, attempting to quell her rising panic amid the bustling activity of the police station.

"What's the matter, Mary? Can't you see I'm busy?" Acker's voice held a touch of impatience, tempered by concern for his wife's distress.

As Mary struggled to compose herself, her words tumbled out in a rush of anguish. "Lizzie... she's gone!" Her voice trembled with emotion, barely audible over her own sobs.

Acker's heart lurched at the revelation, his mind racing to comprehend the gravity of the situation. "What do you mean, 'she's gone'?" His voice betrayed a mix of shock and disbelief.

Mary's response came in gasping sobs, her words choked with tears. "I woke up this morning, and she was gone! The door was wide open, and there's no sign of her anywhere!"

The sudden commotion drew the attention of the other officers, their curious gazes fixed on Acker and Mary as they grappled with the unfolding crisis. Claydon, sensing the urgency in the air, appeared at Acker's side, his expression mirroring the shock reverberating through the room.

"Lizzie's missing," Acker explained tersely, his voice heavy with concern.

Claydon's eyes widened in shock, the gravity of the situation sinking in as he struggled to process the sudden turn of events. "When did this happen?" he asked.

"Last night," Acker returned his focus to Mary. "Where is Billy? Has he seen her?"

Mary took out a handkerchief and blew her nose. "I asked him, and he says he has no idea where she is."

Acker's brow furrowed with worry as he surveyed the sombre faces of his fellow officers, his voice steady despite the tumult of emotions swirling within him. With a deep breath, he called for their undivided attention.

"Listen up, everyone," his voice rang out, commanding the station's focus. "As of last night, my daughter has vanished. I need each and every one of you to mobilise immediately and join the search."

The officers ceased their tasks, their expressions shifting from routine duty to earnest concern as they absorbed Acker's words. He continued, his tone measured but urgent, "Some of you are already familiar with her appearance, but for those who aren't, I'll provide a photograph. She's likely still in her nightclothes and may be frightened, so approach with caution."

A hushed murmur swept through the station's foyer as the officers processed the gravity of the situation. Acker's daughter, vulnerable and alone, had become the focus of their collective mission. He pressed on, his voice firm with resolve, "She's unfamiliar with the outside world, and time is of the essence. We need to find her, no matter the cost."

The shared concern among the officers cast a pall over the station, each face etched with worry as they grappled with the chilling realisation that a child kidnapper may be at large. Acker's heart ached at the thought of his own daughter's disappearance, his mind racing with the grim possibilities that loomed before them.

Beside him, Mary's sobs punctuated the heavy silence, her tear-stained face pleading for solace in the midst of the chaos. "I just need to find my little girl," she whispered, her voice trembling with anguish.

A voice broke through the tension, its question hanging heavy in the air. "Do you believe this is related to the missing children case, sir?"

Acker's gaze snapped to the officer, surprise flickering in his eyes at the unexpected insight. It was a possibility he hadn't dared to entertain, his thoughts consumed by the immediate urgency of finding Lizzie. But as the implications sank in, he realised that it could be true.

"It's possible," he admitted. Turning to Mary, he saw the desperation mirrored in her tear-filled eyes, a silent plea for reassurance.

"Mary, I need you to do something for me," Acker began, his tone gentle yet firm.

Raising her eyes from the floor, Mary met his gaze, her expression a mix of hope and fear. "What is it?" she asked.

With resolve hardening his features, he leaned in closer to Mary, his voice carrying a quiet determination. "I need you to trust me, Mary. We'll find Lizzie, I promise. But I need your help. I need you to talk to a girl on my behalf while I go look for our daughter. She won't speak with a man; she wants to speak with a woman, and we don't have any female officers."

"Why me? I'm not sure how to question someone," she said, sniffling loudly.

"Because you are kind and understanding, Mary. She is terrified and has become involved with a dangerous man. I'm looking for information from her. Besides, it will distract you for a while."

"Will I be alone?"

"I'll leave Chapman with you, and he'll remain outside. Here-" he pulled out a notebook and pencil from his pocket. "Take this; you'll need to jot down notes as she speaks."

"Okay, I'll do it, but please keep me updated on Lizzie. I'm worried sick."

Acker nodded. "Of course I will, my darling. I'll leave you in the capable hands of Chapman," He gently lifted her chin to his face. "Mary, I'll find her. I promise."

She kissed his lips and watched as he grabbed his hat and coat. "Gentlemen, let us proceed. Investigate every nook and cranny of this city. Leave no alleyway unexplored. I want my daughter found."

He left with a group of willing officers, leaving Mary with Claydon. "Come along with me. I'll explain everything to Chapman before joining the search." Claydon took her hand in his and led her away.

## CHAPTER TWENTY-SEVEN

# Robert's Cover Up

Betty sat silently in one of the armchairs in their living room, her mind still clouded and bewildered, yet now recalling the events that had transpired. Her heart raced as she heard the heavy footfalls of Robert approaching up the stairs. She knew she needed to distance herself from him, but she felt trapped without a clear escape plan or access to funds. He controlled their finances, leaving her with no financial autonomy.

Fear snaked through her veins, coiling around her heart with icy tendrils. Every beat sent a shiver down her spine, a whispered warning of impending danger. Her breaths came shallow and rapid, as if the very air around her had turned hostile, suffocating her with its malevolence.

Just as Robert entered, bearing a glass of water, she brushed more mud from her dress. "Here, drink this," he offered, and she accepted gratefully, her trembling fingers wrapping around the cool, smooth glass. "Do you remember anything?" he asked anxiously.

She took a sip and shook her head, feigning ignorance. "No, I can't recall anything. I just remember waking up struggling to breathe."

Relief washed over him, evident in his smile. "At least you're safe now. I won't let you out of my sight again."

His words sent a chill down her spine. "Thank you, but I'm fine. I just need to freshen up." Rising from her seat, she placed the half-empty glass on the table, her mind racing to devise a plan to break free from his control. "Should I consider seeking medical attention? My head is throbbing."

Fear flickered in his eyes. "There's no need for that. I'll assist you in cleaning up."

Defeated, her shoulders slumped. "But whoever harmed me could still be out there. I need to inform someone, Robert."

His grip tightened on her arm as anger flashed across his face, dragging her forcefully towards the wash basin. "Betty, you'll stay here and rest. If there's a threat lurking, I won't allow you to venture out. It's safer for you here."

"Can you tell me what happened to me?" she murmured softly, her voice tinged with apprehension, wary of provoking further anger.

He paused in washing her hands, his gaze piercing as he examined her. "You were out purchasing supplies for the shop, and then you vanished."

"So, the authorities are aware of my disappearance? Maybe I should inform them of the situation so they can search for the culprit."

"Betty, no. The police are oblivious. There's no reason to involve them because it won't occur again. You'll remain here where a wife belongs," he asserted firmly.

She detected the fury simmering in his eyes as he vigorously scrubbed her hands. Choosing silence, she resolved to bide her time until he granted her freedom in a few days. It would be her sole opportunity for escape. He couldn't evade accountability for his actions. Despite his outward appearance—his large, bushy beard and rosy cheeks—she knew deep within that he was a vile, deceitful man devoid of compassion. She refused to let him inflict harm on anyone else. He deserved imprisonment, and she was determined to see it through. Over the next few days, she would strategize a method to rid herself of him, even if it meant employing the same tactics he had used against her. At the very least, she would liberate herself from his malevolence, reclaiming ownership of the shop that rightfully belonged to her from the outset.

## CHAPTER TWENTY-EIGHT

## Shelton

Shelton reclined in his chair, his gaze fixed on his servants who stood before him, their expressions a mix of concern and confusion. Across the room, the butler watched them closely, noting their reactions to Shelton's domineering attitude.

Standing up, Shelton paced the room, his hands clasped behind his back as he addressed them with unwavering seriousness. "When you're questioned at the station, you will not utter a word that could incriminate me or anyone else in this household, regardless of what you may have witnessed. You may discuss matters concerning our late mistress, but my personal history is off-limits. Is that understood by all?"

In unison, they nodded, their hopes pinned on the conclusion of this unsettling conversation. As they exchanged glances, the butler scrutinised them, attempting to decipher if any of them grasped the implications behind their master's words. Yet unbeknownst to them, he alone held the knowledge of every clandestine detail within the household. Every whisper, every hidden truth was his domain, and if necessary, he would leverage it against his master. Among them, he stood as the sole entity capable of challenging Shelton's authority. Perhaps this was precisely why his master kept him in such close proximity.

"And if I discover that any of you have breathed a word to the authorities about me, there will be consequences for each and every one of you," Shelton warned sternly, his voice carrying a weight of undeniable threat. "You are dismissed."

With a wave of his hand, he signalled their departure, and they hastened out of the room, eager to escape the oppressive atmosphere that seemed to cling to their master like a sinister shroud. Each step away from him felt like a release from an invisible vice, yet the tension in the air only seemed to thicken in their wake.

As they hurried through the foyer, whispers circulated among them, the low murmurs reflecting their shared unease. Shelton's demeanour, more ominous than ever, cast a shadow of suspicion over the household, exacerbating the lingering sense of dread that had settled among them since the tragic demise of his wife. They recalled the days when he prowled the corridors in solitude, confiding only in the butler, and now, his ominous warnings only powered their apprehension.

Silent and sombre, they retrieved their coats and ventured out onto the street, each step heavy with the burden of uncertainty. Fear clung to them like a second skin, suffocating in its intensity, and the overwhelming weight of dread threatened to crush their resolve. They longed to extricate themselves from the web of intrigue that ensnared them, yearning for nothing more than to fulfil their duties and fade into the background. With heavy hearts and troubled minds, they trudged onward toward the station, the burden of Shelton's threats bearing down upon them like an unrelenting storm.

## CHAPTER TWENTY-NINE

## Thornton's Mistake

Thornton leant casually against the counter, engrossed in the morning newspaper. The creak of the door drew his attention, and he glanced up to find Mr. Bodmin storming in, brandishing a crumpled newspaper bearing the alarming headline, 'Detective's Daughter Snatched from Her Bed.' With a scowl, Bodmin flung the paper across the counter, fixing Thornton with an accusing glare. "Please tell me this wasn't you."

Thornton chuckled dismissively, barely bothering to lift his gaze from the newspaper. "You've crossed town just to show me a newspaper headline?"

Bodmin's frustration boiled over as he slammed his fist onto the counter. "Do you understand the gravity of this situation? The entire city is in an uproar searching for that girl! Where is she?"

"I fetched a handsome sum for her," Thornton replied nonchalantly.

"You've already sold her?"

Thornton nodded with a smirk. "Last night."

"I can't believe you, Thornton. What possessed you to do such a thing? You've jeopardised everything!" Bodmin's voice trembled with anger.

"Relax, Bodmin. No one will ever trace it back to us. Besides, I didn't pluck her from her bed; she was already wandering the streets when I stumbled upon her." Thornton retrieved a coin pouch from beneath the counter and tossed it to Bodmin. "Here's your share for the girl."

Bodmin opened the pouch, his eyes widening at the sight of the coins within. "This is all from selling her?"

Thornton chuckled. "Indeed."

"What makes her so valuable?"

"Because she's the detective's daughter. Though Creed didn't realise her identity when he took her from me; someone else footed the bill. She's likely serving as a maid in some affluent woman's household, oblivious to the valuable asset in her employ," Thornton explained.

Bodmin regarded him warily. "But what if they track her down, Thornton? She could unravel everything we've worked so hard to build."

"You worry too much. She's vanished without a trace. She's probably halfway across the country by now. Creed's not as inept as you think." Thornton returned to his newspaper, a wry grin playing on his lips as he perused the article detailing Acker's missing daughter. "We've made headlines."

"Thornton, this isn't a joke. If you persist with this reckless behaviour, you'll land us in big trouble," Bodmin cautioned.

"I've taken precautions. If you're so concerned, ensure you've done the same."

Bodmin furrowed his brow, anger boiling within. "And what precautions have you taken?"

As Bodmin took a seat on one of the stools, Thornton's expression darkened, a glint of secrecy gleaming in his eyes. A faint smirk played across Thornton's lips as he reminisced about the encounter with the young girl. He remembered the alias he had used, Jeremy Bodmin, ensuring that if she were discovered, the blame would fall on Bodmin, not himself. "Let's just say, I have my methods," he remarked cryptically, flipping the page of the newspaper with a casual air.

The sight of Thornton's smug expression unsettled Bodmin deeply. He sensed that Thornton was hiding something, and a wave of nausea washed over him at the thought. Rising to his feet, he pointed an accusatory finger at Thornton. "If I discover you've entangled me in this mess, Thornton, you'll pay dearly. I refuse to take the fall for your actions."

Thornton barely glanced up from the newspaper, seemingly unfazed by Bodmin's threats. "Do as you wish, sir, but if you leave now, you'll forfeit your payment, and your precious orphanage will crumble without my financial support." With a decisive snap, he closed the newspaper, locking eyes with Bodmin. "You'd do well to proceed with caution. Lady Elspeth has taken an interest in you, and she's not one to relent until she uncovers the truth."

Bodmin recoiled slightly at Thornton's words, taken aback by the sudden mention of Lady Elspeth. "How do you know about Lady Elspeth?" he demanded, his hands shaking.

"Sir, my reach extends far and wide. There's nothing you can keep hidden from me. I warned you about your little maid Edith, but you refused to heed my advice, and now we're facing the consequences," Thornton stated grimly.

"B-but Edith would never betray me. She's been a loyal servant for years," Bodmin protested, his voice trembling with uncertainty.

"I've witnessed her devotion to those children. She'll do anything to protect them, even if it means exposing your secrets to the authorities. You must act swiftly to eliminate the threat," Thornton insisted, placing the paper down on the counter.

"I can't just dispose of her like that. She's been with me for nearly a decade. Finding someone as dedicated as her would be impossible," Bodmin countered, his loyalty wavering.

"In that case, I'll have to handle it myself," Thornton declared coldly, his eyes turning cold and condescending.

Bodmin met Thornton's unwavering gaze, stunned by the callousness in his words. Thornton's eyes, normally mischievous, now seemed devoid of emotion, sending a chill down Bodmin's spine. "I won't allow it," Bodmin asserted firmly.

"Then be prepared to face the consequences. You can't run from this. It's your problem, and I've provided you with a solution. Deal with it, Bodmin," Thornton retorted.

"What happened to you? What turned you into such a heartless person?" Bodmin pressed, desperation creeping into his voice.

"That's none of your concern," Thornton replied dismissively, looking away from Bodmin.

"There must be a reason you're so emotionless, especially when it comes to children and women. Thornton, you're cold, ruthless... I want to know why," Bodmin persisted.

With a surge of anger, Thornton advanced towards Bodmin, his face contorted with fury as he unleashed his pent-up emotions. "Because everything I held dear was ripped away from me!" he roared.

Bodmin took a step back, shocked by Thornton's outburst. "How so?"

Thornton sighed heavily, the weight of his past burdens evident in his attitude. "I once had a son, a baby boy. His mother, a despicable woman, took him away from me, and I haven't laid eyes on him since. She was wicked, with no concern for anyone but herself."

"I'm truly sorry to hear that, Thornton. It must have been a devastating ordeal," Bodmin offered sympathetically, his mind filling with more questions.

"I have no idea where he is, or even if he's still alive. But one thing is certain: she got what was coming to her," Thornton continued, his voice laced with bitterness.

"Who are you referring to?" Bodmin asked.

"Lady Penelope," Thornton stated bluntly, looking angrily out of the shop window at the market on the street.

Bodmin recoiled, astonished by Thornton's revelation. "You... you killed her?"

Thornton scoffed. "I wish I had the chance. But someone beat me to it."

"So, Lady Penelope's child is your son?" Bodmin deduced.

Thornton nodded grimly. "Yes, she bore him in secret and

then cast him aside before I could even hold him."

"But wasn't she married to a man named Shelton?" Bodmin questioned.

"Lady Penelope had many lovers, Bodmin. Don't act so surprised. She was a vile creature who only cared for herself. Shelton likely had no inkling of her true nature."

"Well, I suppose you have a point. He must have suspected something was amiss. Perhaps he was the one who ended her life?" Bodmin speculated.

"It's possible. All I know is, good riddance," Thornton remarked coldly.

"And you have no idea what your son looks like?" Bodmin pressed.

"No, only that he had a prominent birthmark on the lower side of his thigh on his right leg. I've searched for him tirelessly, but to no avail. Lady Penelope likely disposed of him long ago. She was hardly the maternal type," Thornton explained bitterly.

"But why did you involve yourself with her if she was so callous?" Bodmin queried, wanting to know more about Thornton's mysterious past.

"Because she was the most enchanting woman I'd ever encountered, and I was powerless to resist her allure," Thornton admitted with a wry chuckle.

A spark of excitement flickered in Bodmin's eyes as an idea struck him. "I've just had a stroke of brilliance, Thornton."

Thornton raised an eyebrow, intrigued. "And what might that be?"

"If we can prove that Lady Penelope's child is also yours, he would be entitled to a substantial portion of her estate, effectively making it yours," Bodmin proposed eagerly.

Thornton stared at Bodmin, dumbfounded. "How is that possible?"

"With Lady Penelope and Shelton having no children of their own, her estate would lack an heir. It's imperative that we locate that child," Bodmin explained determinedly.

"Bodmin, do you think I've been idle all these years? She's covered her tracks quite thoroughly," Thornton replied with a hint of resignation.

"Then I'll begin scouring the archives for records from the orphanage, and you can do the same for the nearby workhouses. How old would the child be now?" Bodmin suggested, eager to take action.

Thornton shrugged. "Somewhere between thirteen and fifteen, I reckon. But why the sudden eagerness to help me, Bodmin? What's in it for you?"

"If I locate your son, I expect 15% of the estate as my share. It's only fair," Bodmin declared, his excitement palpable. "That money could greatly benefit the orphanage and ensure I'm not left empty-handed. And Lady Elspeth, that dreadful woman, won't have a leg to stand on."

Thornton nodded in agreement. "Very well, if that's your condition."

However, Thornton harboured ulterior motives. He had no intention of sharing the inheritance with Bodmin, especially if the man couldn't even dispose of a mere servant. Instead, he resolved to keep Edith's demise a secret, using her to frame Bodmin for treason. With Bodmin out of the picture, Thornton could secure the fortune and reunite with his son without interference. All he needed to do was wait for Edith to incriminate Bodmin, then ensure her silence permanently.

"Excellent," Bodmin exclaimed, donning his hat and retrieving his cane from the counter. "I'll commence my search immediately. And in the meantime, Thornton, try to avoid any trouble."

Thornton met Bodmin's gaze with a stern expression. "I assure you, I'll do just that."

Despite Bodmin's eagerness, there lingered a sense of unease in his heart. He feared Thornton's calculating nature but remained motivated by the prospect of financial gain. This plan offered a way out of trouble without resorting to violence, provided he could win Edith's cooperation.

"I'll be in touch. Good day, sir," Bodmin bid farewell, exiting the shop with a resounding slam of the door.

Left alone, Thornton sat in contemplative silence, plotting his next move. He needed a foolproof strategy that would implicate Bodmin while absolving himself of any blame. As the crackling of the fire filled the room, a wicked grin spread across Thornton's face, his eyes gleaming with mischief. His plan was flawless, and nothing would stand in his way now.

## CHAPTER THIRTY

# Mary's Hand

Mary sat across from Evelyn, observing her tear-streaked face with sympathy. Meanwhile, Chapman, growing increasingly impatient, silently urged Mary to begin the interrogation. His frustration mounted as Mary seemed hesitant to proceed.

Feeling out of her depth, Mary struggled to find her footing in this unfamiliar role. She was accustomed to baking treats and fulfilling domestic duties, not conducting interrogations. Yet, she knew she had to push past her discomfort for the sake of uncovering the truth for her husband.

Summoning her courage, Mary gently placed a hand on Evelyn's trembling one. "Evelyn, can you tell me why you're here?" she asked softly.

Through her tears, Evelyn managed a feeble smile. "I... I made a mistake. I said things I shouldn't have, and now my master is furious with me," she confessed.

"Why is your master so angry? What did you say to upset him?" Mary pressed gently, observing the expression on Evelyn's face.

"I... I told the police about our relationship, a secret we were meant to keep. If I go back now, he'll... he'll hurt me," Evelyn whimpered, her fear palpable.

Mary's heart ached for the frightened girl before her. "How long have you been involved with your master, Evelyn? Was it before or after your mistress's death?" she inquired, her tone gentle but insistent.

"Before," Evelyn admitted, wiping her nose with a dirty handkerchief. "I had nothing to do with my mistress's death. My master was with me that night, so he couldn't have done it," she insisted, her voice quivering.

"Is your master prone to violence?" Mary asked.

Evelyn glanced nervously at Chapman. Mary looked at him, prompting him to exit the room discreetly. Once alone, she confided, "He can be... persuasive. I've seen him harm other servants, but I don't believe he's capable of murder. He loved her," she insisted, though uncertainty lingered in her voice.

Mary listened intently, her mind racing with questions. "Did he ever leave your side that night without your knowledge?" she probed gently.

"It's possible, but... but I don't think he would. He loved her too much," Evelyn murmured, her gaze downcast.

Mary reassured her, "You're safe here, Evelyn. The police will protect you. But I need you to tell me everything you know."

Evelyn hesitated, the fear which she was feeling becoming unbearable. "Can you promise that I'll be safe?" she implored urgently.

Mary nodded solemnly. "I promise, Evelyn. You're safe with us."

With a trembling sigh, Evelyn confessed, "I don't believe my master killed his wife, but... but I know he murdered one of our fellow servants, Bella. He made me do it."

Mary's eyes widened in shock. "Are you certain?"

Evelyn nodded tearfully. "Yes. He's a powerful man, Miss Mary. I had no choice but to obey him."

As Mary scribbled notes furiously, she murmured, "You're in

a difficult position, Evelyn."

"What will happen to me, Miss Mary?" Evelyn asked, her voice laced with fear.

Mary offered her a reassuring smile. "I'll ensure you're taken care of. You won't come to harm here."

Before Mary could offer further reassurance, Chapman entered the room, interrupting their conversation. "Apologies, ladies, but we need this room for the servants from Mr. Shelton's house."

Reluctantly, Mary stood, but not before ensuring Evelyn's comfort. "You'll be safer in Acker's office," she suggested, leading Evelyn to the more hospitable space.

As Mary departed to fetch food for Evelyn, Chapman approached her, eager for information. Mary divulged Evelyn's revelation about Bella's murder, prompting Chapman's anger to flare.

"She knew all along and said nothing!" he exclaimed furiously.

Mary recoiled, realising she may have overstepped. "Calm yourself, Chapman. Let the detective handle this." As Chapman struggled to rein in his emotions, Mary urged him gently, "Proceed with caution, Chapman. They're likely scared and won't talk easily."

With a deep breath, Chapman nodded, his mind swirling with unanswered questions. He knew he needed to tread carefully, even if it meant pushing Evelyn to her limits to extract the truth.

## CHAPTER THIRTY-ONE

# The Streets of Bristol

The streets teemed with police officers, their eyes scanning the crowds for any clue that might lead them to Acker's missing daughter. Claydon stood on the sidewalk, his gaze sharp as he watched the passersby, hoping for a break in the case.

Hours had slipped away in their search, yielding nothing. It was as if the girl had evaporated into thin air. Frustration brewed among the officers as they faced a wall of silence from the bustling pedestrians.

Acker sidled up to Claydon, his anxiety palpable. "Any progress?"

Claydon shook his head, his tone heavy with disappointment. "No luck so far, sir. It's like everyone's a ghost out here."

Acker's frustration boiled over, and he grabbed an elderly passerby, desperation evident in his grip. "Do you know anything about my daughter?" he demanded, his voice quivering with emotion.

The man recoiled, fear etched on his face. "I... I don't know anything!" he stammered, trying to break free from Acker's grasp.

Claydon intervened, gently prying Acker's hands from the man's shoulders. "Acker, calm down. This isn't helping anyone."

But Acker brushed him off, his agitation evident. "Leave me alone, Claydon."

Claydon sighed, knowing he had to defuse the situation. "You need rest, Acker. Let me take you home."

Acker relented, exhaustion washing over him as he leaned heavily against Claydon. "You're right. I need to clear my head."

Claydon signalled to two nearby officers, directing them to escort Acker home. With a solemn promise to find his daughter, he watched them lead Acker away, a sense of determination settling in his heart.

Alone now, Claydon turned his attention to a familiar figure among the crowd: Bailey, the local tramp. He approached him, determination etched on his face.

"You were out that night. You must have seen something," Claydon pressed, his voice firm as he stood directly in front of him.

Bailey's eyes darted nervously, stroking his unkempt beard. *What can I say without putting myself in danger?*

Claydon knelt beside him, his gaze unwavering. "I can see it in your eyes. You know something. Please, tell me."

Bailey hesitated, torn between fear and a desire to help. With a heavy sigh, he knew he had no choice but to speak.

"I've seen nothing, sir."

"Why are you deceiving me?"

Bailey spoke quietly so that only Claydon could hear him. "I'll be in danger if I tell you anything." He then looked up and spotted Thornton approaching them through the crowd. His eyes grew wide with terror as he pushed Claydon out of the way to escape. He stumbled a little, nearly falling over, but quickly managed to lose them in the crowd.

As Bailey slipped away into the bustling crowd, Claydon's frustration simmered. He knew the tramp was withholding crucial information, and his sudden flight only deepened the mystery.

"Go after him!" Claydon barked at the officers, his voice urgent as he brushed dirt from his trousers.

The officers sprang into action, darting through the throng of people in pursuit of Bailey. But the tramp proved elusive, disappearing into the labyrinthine streets of the city.

Claydon scanned the crowd, his mind racing with questions. *What could have terrified Bailey so much that he would risk assaulting an officer and fleeing?*

Despite the apparent normalcy of the scene, Claydon sensed an undercurrent of danger. Someone had instilled such fear in Bailey that he was willing to risk everything to escape.

With determination burning in his chest, Claydon rallied the nearby officers, his voice commanding attention. "Gather round!"

The officers converged, eager for direction as Claydon laid out his plan. "That man knows something, and we need to find him before someone else does. Search every nook and cranny, from abandoned buildings to alleyways to the docks. He can't have vanished completely. We'll track him down, no matter what it takes."

Unbeknownst to Claydon, Thornton lurked nearby, eavesdropping on his orders. Panic gnawed at Thornton's insides as he realised the urgency of the situation. If Bailey spilled the truth to the police, his carefully constructed facade could crumble, spelling disaster for him and his plans. Time was running out.

## CHAPTER THIRTY-TWO

# Lady Elspeth's House

The opulent lounge exuded an air of refinement, every corner adorned with exquisite details. Vases brimming with exotic blooms added a splash of colour, while the grand mirror above the mantelpiece reflected the room's splendour. Edith couldn't help but admire Lady Elspeth's impeccable taste, longing for a life of luxury instead of servitude.

As she meticulously dusted each silver-framed portrait, the crackling fire cast a warm glow, painting her cheeks with a rosy hue. She hummed softly to herself, relishing the tranquillity of the moment. It was her first day in Lady Elspeth's service, and she hoped to make a favourable impression for future opportunities.

Samantha's arrival broke the serene atmosphere, her attire as charming as her demeanour. With a bundle of shiny Conkers in hand, she greeted Edith with a radiant smile, sparking a brief exchange of pleasantries. But the cheerful moment was interrupted when Samantha relayed Lady Elspeth's summons.

Edith's stomach dropped, and a sickly feeling rose within her. "I'll go to her right now." She then glanced at the fire and positioned the fireguard across it to prevent Samantha from approaching it. "Stay away from there. It'll burn you if you get too close."

Samantha nodded, hardly listening and continued to play with her Conkers while Edith quietly exited through the lounge door. She knew why Lady Elspeth wanted to speak with her, and she didn't want to lie to her, even if it meant getting her master into a lot of trouble. She had no choice but to tell the truth in order to protect the children.

As she descended the stairs to Lady Elspeth's study, her legs trembled. She gripped her feather duster tightly, nervously twiddling with it as she knocked on the door. Lady Elspeth called for her to enter, and Edith walked in slowly, hoping not to be bombarded with questions.

Inside, Lady Elspeth sat regally at her desk, her presence commanding yet inviting. After a polite exchange, she broached the topic of Edith's master's finances, brandishing a document that raised troubling questions. "I want to talk to you about your master's finances. I've been going over them, and they don't seem to add up."

Edith gulped loudly. "What would you like to know?"

"So, when I came to collect Samantha, I took this from his desk, which I'm sure he's desperately looking for now, and I can see on here that he seems to be getting quite a sum from an unknown source. Do you have any knowledge of this?" She displayed the paper for Edith's inspection. "It just doesn't make sense."

Caught off guard, Edith knew she couldn't conceal the truth any longer. With a deep breath, she confessed to witnessing something significant the night Samantha was found. But before she could elaborate, a sudden interruption shattered the moment.

A servant burst into the room, bearing urgent news that demanded Edith's immediate attention. "I'm sorry for intruding, Lady Elspeth, but Miss Edith is desperately needed. The servant you swapped for Miss Edith became ill unexpectedly and returned here. A carriage is waiting outside to take Miss Edith home. Her master requires her assistance."

Lady Elspeth, though visibly annoyed, reluctantly released her servant, instructing her to return the following week.

As Edith prepared to depart, Lady Elspeth seized the opportunity to express concern, her voice laced with genuine care. "Does your master pose a threat?"

With tears welling in her eyes, Edith reassured her mistress, touched by her unexpected kindness. Despite the uncertainties ahead, she found solace in Lady Elspeth's empathy, grateful for the brief respite from her worries.

Lady Elspeth's comforting gesture brought a sense of relief to Edith's troubled heart. "We'll pick up where we left off next week. And remember, if you ever need anything, don't hesitate to come to me. You and the children are under my protection now."

Touched by her words, Edith offered a final expression of gratitude before making her way to the waiting carriage. As she stepped inside, uncertainty lingered in her mind, but she found solace in the knowledge that Lady Elspeth's kindness would serve as a guiding light in the days to come.

## CHAPTER THIRTY-THREE

# Harvard's Secret

Harvard lingered by Bane's side, quietly observing as the doctor meticulously examined Bella's form on the mortuary table. The peculiar scent of death, distinct and heavy in the air, oddly brought him solace. He savoured these moments, relishing the silent company of the deceased, all the while careful not to attract undue attention from his superiors. The mortuary had become his sanctuary, a realm where he felt an inexplicable sense of belonging amidst the quietude of lifeless figures.

Bane's pencil danced across his notebook, capturing his observations. "These markings bear a striking resemblance to those on the lady in red. It's the same handiwork."

"Could it be the work of the killer?" Harvard interjected eagerly.

"I believe so, but there's a discrepancy with Bella's markings. They seem older," Bane remarked, noting another detail on

Bella's shoulder. "This one, for instance, predates the others. I must fetch the inspector; he needs to see this."

Harvard nodded, stepping aside as Bane made his exit. Alone with Bella, he allowed himself a moment of intimacy, leaning in to sniff her hair with a mixture of melancholy and admiration. "What a pity," he murmured, his touch gentle against her cold cheek. "You could have been something truly beautiful."

The abrupt voice behind him startled Harvard, causing him to turn and face Chapman's stern gaze. Caught off guard, he struggled to compose himself. "I was merely examining the mark on her shoulder," he explained, his nerves palpable.

Bane's return interrupted their exchange, offering a reprieve. "Ah, there you are," he addressed Harvard before turning to Chapman. "Have you encountered the inspector? I need to discuss something with him."

Chapman's scrutiny lingered as he approached Bella's body, prompting Harvard to retreat with an air of unease. As the tension between them thickened, Bane's suggestion for Harvard to depart felt like a merciful release from the mounting discomfort.

Relieved yet unsettled, Harvard complied, his departure marked by a lingering sense of displacement and a longing for the familiar embrace of the mortuary's quietude.

As Chapman observed Harvard's sombre demeanour while he gathered his belongings, a sense of unease crept over him. He couldn't shake the disquieting feeling that there was more to the embalmer than met the eye. The way Harvard regarded Bella's form with what seemed like affection sent a chill down Chapman's spine, prompting him to make a mental note to delve deeper into Harvard's background later.

Meanwhile, Harvard retreated with a heavy heart, his steps weighted with defeat. Being ousted from the mortuary, the one place he considered his haven, left him adrift and vulnerable. Despite having a place of his own nearby, it paled in comparison to the comforting embrace of the mortuary's cold confines. The allure of its stone-cold floor, the familiarity of its silent inhabitants—these were comforts he couldn't easily relinquish.

In his solitude, Harvard's connection to death felt almost palpable, akin to an insatiable addiction. While others may have recoiled from such intimacy with mortality, for Harvard, it was a consuming passion, a drug he couldn't resist. Misunderstood and isolated, he sought solace in the company of the departed, their silent presence offering a sense of belonging he found nowhere else.

Harvard slipped out of the bustling hospital, his cloak drawn tightly around him as if seeking refuge from the thronging crowd. With his hood pulled up, he sought anonymity amidst the chaos, his unease mounting with each passing moment. Large crowds were his bane, and the bustling streets only amplified his discomfort. He hurried back to his sanctuary, his steps quick and deliberate on the cobblestone path leading to his home above the cheesemonger's shop.

Ignoring the bustle below, Harvard hurried past Robert, engrossed in his dealings with customers, and ascended the creaking staircase with a sense of urgency. Yet, the sound of soft crying halted his rush, emanating from behind the closed door of Betty and Robert's home. His curiosity piqued, Harvard hesitated momentarily, his instincts urging him to intervene.

As Betty's desperate pleas reached his ears, Harvard's resolve faltered, torn between the desire to help and the fear of intruding. He remained silent, hoping to avoid detection, yet the anguish in Betty's voice tugged at his conscience.

When Robert's heavy footsteps echoed on the stairs, Harvard retreated into the shadows, his gaze fixed on the unfolding scene with a mixture of concern and intrigue. Robert's callous words only fuelled Harvard's unease, leaving him unsettled by the domestic turmoil he had unwittingly stumbled upon. As Robert's anger erupted into violence, Harvard's heart sank, haunted by the knowledge of the suffering concealed behind closed doors.

Harvard remained rooted in silence, his curiosity piqued by the tense exchange unfolding behind the closed door. He took a cautious step away from the wall, his footsteps light as he ascended the stairs with a mix of trepidation and intrigue.

The sound of Betty's desperate pleas tugged at Harvard's conscience, stirring a desire to intervene yet paralyzed by uncertainty. He lingered in the shadows, a silent observer to the unfolding drama.

As Robert's heavy footsteps sounded on the stairs, Harvard retreated further into the darkness, his breath caught in anticipation. The confrontation that followed unfolded before him, revealing glimpses of a troubled relationship fraught with pain and resentment.

Betty's cries pierced the air, echoing the anguish of a woman trapped in her own home, her pleas for freedom met with callous indifference. Harvard's heart ached for her plight, yet he remained frozen, a silent witness to her suffering.

When Robert's anger erupted into violence, Harvard recoiled, his stomach churning with a mix of horror and disbelief. The sight of Robert's aggression left him shaken, haunted by the realisation of the darkness lurking behind closed doors.

As Robert unlocked the door and stormed into the room, Harvard's heart sank, the emptiness within mirroring the hollow ache of Betty's absence. In that moment, he knew that the scars of their tumultuous relationship ran deep, leaving behind wounds that may never fully heal.

"Don't feed me that nonsense," Robert's voice echoed with raw emotion, laced with anger and frustration. "I can see it in your eyes, Betty. You remember. It's not my fault!" His words reverberated against the closed door, the weight of his accusation hanging heavily in the air.

Leaning heavily against the door, Robert's impatience grew palpable as he awaited Betty's response, but silence was her only reply. The absence of her voice only powered his mounting fury, his cheeks flushed with a burning intensity.

"BETTY!" Robert's voice thundered through the room, his frustration boiling over as he pounded against the door with a forceful kick. The sound reverberated through the cramped space, a stark reminder of the turmoil consuming their once-peaceful home.

With a trembling hand, Robert withdrew a rusty key from his pocket, its worn surface a testament to the turmoil within their home. Slowly, he inserted it into the lock, the metallic click of the tumblers falling into place echoing through the tense silence. As the door swung open, Robert's heart pounded in his chest, his breath catching in anticipation.

"Betty?" His voice trembled with a mixture of hope and dread as he peered into the dimly lit room, his eyes scanning the shadows for any sign of his wife. But the emptiness that greeted him sent a chill down his spine, his heart sinking in despair.

Meanwhile, hidden in the shadows beneath the staircase, Harvard strained to discern the chaos unfolding within the room. The sounds of crashing and raised voices reached his ears, a cacophony of discord that stirred a sense of unease within him. Knowing that he needed to escape before Robert discovered him, Harvard slipped past the door with silent precision, his steps light as he ascended the stairs to his sanctuary.

As he closed the door behind him, Harvard breathed a sigh of relief, the din of the argument below fading into the background. Alone in his room, he felt a sense of sanctuary wash over him, grateful to be spared from the turmoil raging within Robert and Betty's home. Safe behind closed doors, Harvard allowed himself a moment of respite, the chaos of the world outside momentarily forgotten.

Harvard's gaze drifted around the room until it settled on the life-sized doll nestled in the corner, a familiar sight that never failed to bring a smile to his lips. "Good day, darling," he whispered softly, his voice carrying a hint of affection as he approached the doll. With gentle care, he clasped the doll's stiff hand in his own, intertwining their fingers in a silent gesture of companionship. "Have you missed me?"

The doll's unyielding gaze remained fixed ahead as Harvard pressed a tender kiss to its cheek, his affectionate gesture met with an unresponsive stillness. As the doll's hand slipped from his grasp, causing it to tumble from its perch, Harvard's anxiety spiked, his quick movements to restore it to its former position betraying a sense of unease.

"I'm sorry, darling," he murmured apologetically, his smile returning as he straightened the doll's attire with meticulous care. "I didn't mean to do that." With a sense of satisfaction, he stepped back to admire his handiwork, his eyes tracing the contours of the doll's form with a hint of pride. "You are my crowning achievement."

Despite his fondness for the doll, Harvard couldn't ignore the faint scent of preserving chemicals that hung in the air, the telltale sign of his meticulous maintenance routine. It was a small price to pay to keep his cherished creation in pristine condition, a testament to his unwavering dedication.

As another crash reverberated from below, the disturbance below causing him to jump in his seat. "Wow, they're really going at it down there," he muttered to himself, his voice barely audible over the tumultuous sounds emanating from the floor below.

Seeking solace in his art, Harvard approached his cluttered dresser and retrieved a pad of paper and a slightly worn pencil. Flipping through the pages, his eyes settled on a half-finished drawing of his cherished doll, prompting him to take a seat and resume his work. With each stroke of his pencil, he meticulously captured the essence of his creation, his talent for depicting death evident in the hauntingly lifelike images that adorned his sketches.

Despite the oddity of his fascination with the deceased, Harvard found comfort in his solitary pursuits, his preference for seclusion shielding him from the judgmental gaze of others. He relished the silence of his own company, finding comfort in the macabre beauty of his chosen profession.

As the crashes from below subsided into an unsettling silence, Harvard's unease only grew, a sense of foreboding settling over him like a heavy shroud. Ignoring the nagging feeling in the pit of his stomach, he attempted to focus on his art, his pencil tracing delicate lines across the page.

But the eerie stillness that permeated the air only served to heighten Harvard's apprehension, his senses attuned to the faint scraping sound that echoed from beneath the floorboards. Despite his efforts to dismiss the unsettling sensation, Harvard found himself unable to shake the feeling of impending dread that lingered in the air.

With a heavy sigh, he reluctantly set aside his sketch pad, the allure of the mortuary beckoning to him with an irresistible pull.

After a while, he fell into a light sleep, awakened only by more noise from below. It was the early hours of the morning, and darkness was still upon the city.

Resigned to the fact that sleep would elude him in the wake of the unsettling events of the night, Harvard prepared to venture out into the early morning light, his hunger and thirst momentarily forgotten in the face of his insatiable yearning for the familiar embrace of his favourite place. As he slipped out the door, leaving it ajar in his haste, Harvard's mind was consumed by thoughts of the mortuary, the strange noises from the night before fading into the recesses of his mind.

The Bristol hospital loomed ahead, and he hastened towards it, the wind tousling his hair and flushing his cheeks. Clutching his bag tightly, he skirted around the building to reach the mortuary's rear entrance. He preferred arriving unnoticed, an instinct he couldn't quite explain but felt keenly.

With a jangle of keys, he unlocked the side door and slipped inside, greeted by the familiar musty scent of the mortuary. A wave of relief washed over him as he approached a table to set down his bag. Rooting through it, he unearthed a bruised apple, deeming it sufficient sustenance despite its imperfections.

As he chewed, a subtle sense of disquiet prickled the back of his mind, though he couldn't pinpoint its source. Meandering among the tables of bodies, he stumbled upon a cluttered table strewn with bloodied medical equipment, evidence of the doctor's recent activity post-Chapman's expulsion. Casting a glance at Bella's form, he noted a fresh incision adorning her torso, prompting him to cover her with a clean white sheet.

Before he could dwell further, the door behind him creaked open, admitting Inspector Acker and his retinue of officers bearing a body shrouded in white. "Place her there," the inspector commanded, indicating an empty table, "and rouse the doctor!"

"But he's asleep, sir," one officer interjected.

Acker fixed him with a stern gaze. "I don't care. Go and fetch him and inform him that there's been another one. I want him here within ten minutes!"

The officers hurried out, leaving Acker and Harvard alone. "What brings you here so early?" Acker inquired, without bothering to turn toward him.

"I've come to complete the preparations for his burial," Harvard stammered, gesturing toward a hefty man with a protruding belly lying on a nearby table.

Acker nodded, waving a dismissive hand. "Proceed with your tasks."

Harvard set about cleaning the soiled medical equipment, all the while keeping a wary eye on Acker's movements. His nerves were on edge, an uncomfortable sensation in his favourite environment. He surreptitiously watched as Acker uncovered the new body. A gasp escaped his lips, drawing Acker's attention. "Do you recognize her?"

Harvard couldn't conceal his shock as he shook his head, rendered momentarily speechless. He wasn't sure why he lied, but one thing was certain: Betty's lifeless form lay on the mortuary table, and Robert was likely responsible.

## CHAPTER THIRTY-FOUR

# The Docks

Creed lingered in the shadows, his patience stretched thin as he awaited Thornton's arrival. The moon cast its ethereal glow upon the river, painting its surface in shimmering silver. A chill wind swept through the air, prompting Creed to pull his coat tighter around himself. Despite the risk of being noticed, the urgency of his need to speak with Thornton kept him rooted in place. His attention snapped upward at the sound of approaching footsteps, prompting him to take cover behind a nearby barrel. As a cloaked figure emerged onto the dock, scanning the surroundings, Creed straightened, recognizing Thornton.

"I'm here," he called out. He could sense Thornton's concealed smirk as he closed the distance. It fuelled Creed's frustration. Thornton's actions had nearly cost him everything.

"I trust you grasp the significance of this meeting, Thornton," Creed uttered through gritted teeth, struggling to maintain composure.

Thornton revealed his face, wearing a knowing grin. "I'll venture a guess."

Creed's voice carried a simmering intensity, a blend of frustration and disbelief. Thornton's smirk remained steadfast, though his eyes hinted at a deeper, more sinister amusement.

"Why? What drives you to these reckless acts, Thornton?" Creed's words were laced with a restrained fury, his patience stretched thin.

Thornton's response was smooth, almost mocking. "Why, Creed, can't you appreciate the thrill of it all?"

Creed's grip on Thornton's hood tightened, his resolve palpable. "This isn't a game, Thornton. Lives are hanging in the balance because of your actions."

Thornton's grin widened, a glint of mischief dancing in his eyes. "But isn't that what makes it all the more exhilarating? The risk, the danger?"

Creed's frustration bubbled to the surface, his voice edged with exasperation. "You're playing with fire, Thornton, and one day, you'll get burned."

Thornton's expression softened momentarily, a flicker of something akin to remorse passing over his features before being replaced by his usual bravado. "Perhaps. But I couldn't pass it up," he chuckled. "Besides, it's created quite a stir among law enforcement officers. I enjoy watching them squirm."

Creed shoved him, his frustration evident. "You're a fool, Thornton. Selling her would risk her being recognized!"

"Then where is she?"

"Sleeping in the carriage. I had to ensure she wouldn't flee."

"Why bring her here?"

"Because you're returning her. I won't let this ruin us! Orphaned children are one thing, but she's the inspector's daughter!"

"I won't take her back, Creed. She's your responsibility now," Thornton retorted.

"Persist with this plan, and I'll find another business partner," Creed warned.

Thornton glanced nervously at the river. "You wouldn't dare, Creed."

"I will if you don't return her to the inspector," Creed insisted.

Exasperated, Thornton relented. "Fine! Bring her, and I'll find a way to deal with her."

"No, Thornton. She goes back safely," Creed insisted.

"You're getting soft in your old age," Thornton remarked, pushing Creed towards the alley. "Go get her."

Creed paused for a moment and studied Thornton's expression, wondering if he was going to keep his end of the bargain. With a flicker of a nod from Thornton, Creed felt satisfied with his response and rushed off into the alleyway that led to a sound-asleep Lizzie, tucked up comfortably in his carriage. Thornton's smirk bothered him, and he felt the man's eyes boring into the back of his head as he retrieved the girl. She felt warm and cosy beneath the blanket he had given her as he carried her from the carriage. He looked around to ensure that no one was watching him. That was the last thing he needed—to be watched by prying eyes that would tell on him without a second thought.

He retreated, keeping to the shadows as Thornton lingered, his penetrating gaze unsettling Creed. Doubt gnawed at Creed's mind. *Was entrusting the girl to Thornton a mistake?* Approaching cautiously, he locked eyes with Thornton. "Can you handle this?" he asked warily.

Thornton's response was swift and assured. "Give me the girl, and I'll ensure she's returned safely."

Handing over the sleeping child, Creed took a step back, his apprehension palpable. "If she's not home by morning, I'll find you. This must end, Thornton."

Thornton's disdainful sneer preceded his departure. "Your threats hold no sway over me, Creed. She'll be home safe, but I'm keeping the payment."

"Just ensure she's returned," Creed called after him as Thornton faded into the shadows. His unease lingered as he watched Thornton vanish with the child. Despite Thornton's business acumen, his unsettling aura left Creed uneasy. Doubts plagued him as he made his way back to his carriage, questioning the wisdom of his decision.

## CHAPTER THIRTY-FIVE

# Taken

The doorbell's chime sounded out through the grand foyer and into the lounge, where Shelton sat in silence, his pipe emitting wisps of smoke as he gazed into the flickering flames. A sinking feeling gripped his stomach as he realised that the late-hour visitor must be here to arrest him. It was a fear he had anticipated. Though Evelyn possessed strength, her youth and vulnerability made her susceptible to the probing of law enforcement, potentially revealing his darkest secrets. He had long foreseen the inevitable arrival of the police at his doorstep, and now that moment had arrived.

With unsteady feet, he rose from his seat and approached the front door. The absence of his usual retinue of servants left the house eerily quiet and empty. They were still detained at the station, undergoing interrogation regarding his whereabouts on the night of his wife's murder. While technically innocent, neither he nor Evelyn could claim innocence in the crime. Both faced the grim prospect of hanging, unless he could deftly shift the blame onto her shoulders and evade justice. Despite lacking evidence tying him to Bella's demise, Shelton had orchestrated the events from the comfort of his home, manipulating Evelyn into executing his sinister plan. Her swift compliance had once been a testament to her love, but now it served as a catalyst for his burgeoning contempt towards her, as she had single-handedly shattered their carefully constructed facade, leaving him to grapple with the consequences.

Claydon and Chapman engaged in a heated exchange as Shelton unlatched the door. Their argument abruptly stopped when they caught sight of him, their attention immediately diverted to the quivering figure before them. Without hesitation, they brandished their police identification and pushed past Shelton, entering the foyer with determination.

"Apologies, sir, but you're required to accompany us to the station," Claydon declared, his gaze sweeping the foyer in search of any potential witnesses.

Shelton's nerves tingled as he locked eyes with the officers, bracing himself for the inevitable click of handcuffs. "And what exactly is the basis for this request, gentlemen?"

"We need to pose a few inquiries regarding the information provided by Miss Evelyn," Claydon responded, noting Shelton's uneasy stance.

Even as Shelton complied, reaching for his coat from the nearby rack, he couldn't shake the simmering anger radiating from Chapman's glare. The absence of handcuffs confused him, sparking a glimmer of hope that he might not be implicated in a crime he didn't commit. Perhaps, he mused, Evelyn's affection had shielded him from suspicion. But he remained resolute in his determination not to be ensnared by anyone, prepared to shift blame onto her if necessary. After all, he refused to let himself be brought down, regardless of the cost.

"I'm ready. Lead the way," Shelton said, slipping into his coat with a nonchalant gesture. As the door slammed shut behind him, he relished the rush of fresh air enveloping him as they made their way towards the awaiting carriage.

Observing Shelton's compliance, Chapman couldn't shake off his sense of unease. It was out of character for Shelton to consent without resistance. This sudden change in behaviour left Chapman deeply disturbed. His suspicion heightened as he watched Shelton effortlessly open the carriage door with his silver cane and step inside. The absence of any discernible emotion on Shelton's face only fuelled Chapman's curiosity further.

As they embarked on their journey, Chapman couldn't help but wonder about the thoughts swirling within Shelton's mind. There was a palpable sense that Shelton was withholding something, and Chapman was determined to uncover the truth lurking beneath the surface.

## CHAPTER THIRTY-SIX

# Robert's Findings

Harvard lingered on the threshold of the shop, hesitant to go inside. The encroaching darkness cast elongated shadows over the dwindling shoppers, signalling the end of another bustling day. Despite the chill creeping through his bones, he hesitated to seek refuge indoors, fearing the looming presence of Robert. By now, Robert would have undoubtedly learned of Betty's fate, her lifeless form consigned to the cold confines of the mortuary.

The frost-coated windows obscured his view, rendering the interior of the shop an obscure silhouette against the wintry backdrop. Uncharacteristically early closure suggested an air of suspicion, a departure from Robert's relentless pursuit of profit. Harvard's unease intensified, a tangible tremor coursing through his veins as he grappled with his fear.

Yet, retreating to the safety of his home posed its own peril. If he failed to return promptly, Robert would surely discern his knowledge of the grim discovery, amplifying the danger lurking in the shadows. Caught between the devil he knew and the uncertainty of the night, Harvard stood paralyzed by the weight of his dilemma, each option fraught with its own risky consequences.

Drawing in a steadying breath, he crossed the threshold of the shop with caution. Each step was a whisper against the worn floorboards as he made his way towards the rear of the building, ascending the staircase with a cat-like grace. Pausing midway, he allowed his eyes to adjust to the enveloping darkness, attuning his senses to the eerie stillness that permeated the air.

His movements were fluid, calculated, as he navigated the narrow hallways with silent precision. Every creak of the floorboards was deftly avoided, his footsteps a mere whisper against the backdrop of silence. Harvard's senses prickled with fear, the hairs on the nape of his neck standing on end as he ascended the second flight of stairs. The absence of sound was deafening. After all, what else could occupy Robert's attention but the sanctity of his beloved shop? Not even a raging inferno could tear him away from its hallowed confines.

Pressing onwards, Harvard crossed the final stretch of stairs with bated breath, his trembling fingers fumbling for the keys to his sanctuary. Yet, as he reached the top, a sliver of light pierced the darkness, emanating from his slightly ajar door. A wave of disorientation washed over him, clouding his thoughts with uncertainty. Had he forgotten to secure his refuge before departing for work? The haze of his mind obscured his recollection as he pushed open the door, his hands trembling uncontrollably.

And there, seated upon his bed, was Robert, an ominous presence in the dimly lit room. His expression was inscrutable, his features etched with an unsettling rigidity as he cradled Harvard's cherished doll in his grasp.

"I've been waiting for your return," Robert uttered softly, his voice a mere whisper that seemed to echo through the room. Harvard felt the colour drain from his face, rendering him motionless in the doorway.

Maintaining his composure, Harvard remained rooted to the spot, his gaze fixed upon his treasured doll, a silent sentinel guarding against any harm inflicted by Robert's intrusion. "What brings you to my doorstep?" he asked, nervously.

A sly grin crept across Robert's lips, a silent acknowledgment of the unspoken truths lingering between them. "There's no need for denial, Harvard. You've seen her, haven't you? I can read it in your expression. She's already met her fate in the cold embrace of the mortuary."

Harvard's nod was slow, deliberate, a silent admission of the grim reality he faced. "Yes, I've seen her," he confessed, stammering.

Anticipation gleamed in Robert's eyes as he leaned forward, hungering for information. "Has her identity been unveiled?" he pressed, a definite eagerness underscoring his words.

With a solemn shake of his head, Harvard placed his coat upon the nearby table, his movements deliberate and measured. "Not yet, and I'm certain you understand why, Robert. You've taken measures to ensure her anonymity," he remarked, his words tinged with accusation.

Robert's chuckle echoed through the room, a discordant melody amidst the tension that hung in the air. "Indeed," he agreed, a sense of satisfaction colouring his tone.

Harvard's gaze darted nervously between Robert and the doll, his mind awash with unspoken questions and mounting dread. "I'll ask you once more, Robert. What is your purpose for being here?" he demanded.

Robert's gaze trailed to the life-sized doll, a contemptuous sneer twisting his lips. "So, this is your little secret," he remarked, his tone dripping with disdain. "Impressive work, Harvard. But who is she?"

"She's nobody," Harvard replied curtly, moving to retrieve the doll, only to have it snatched away by Robert's grasping hand. "Look, what do you want?" he demanded, edging towards the safety of the door.

"I'm here to ensure your silence," Robert stated matter-of-factly, toying with the doll's locks of hair. "And there's another matter I need your assistance with."

"What could that possibly be?" Harvard asked.

"As I walked up these stairs, I deliberated over whether to

dispose of you," Robert confessed with a chilling smile, showcasing the doll's eerily lifelike hand. "But now, having stumbled upon your little secret," he continued, pausing to gauge Harvard's reaction, "I believe we can come to an understanding."

Harvard's frustration simmered beneath the surface as he implored Robert to cut to the chase. "Just spit it out, Robert."

"I want you to retrieve my wife from the mortuary," Robert declared, his tone unwavering. "And then, I want you to do to her what you've done to this unfortunate woman here."

"Why?" Harvard's voice trembled with disbelief, his eyes locking onto Robert's with a mixture of fear and confusion.

"I need people to believe she's still alive," Robert explained, his tone laced with a chilling determination.

"And if I refuse?" Harvard countered, a flicker of defiance igniting within him.

"Then I'll expose your secrets to the authorities, leaving you bereft of your precious mortuary and your precious doll," Robert replied, his smile morphing into a menacing grin, knowing full well the stakes were weighted heavily against Harvard.

"But people will see through the charade if they lay eyes on her," Harvard argued, desperation creeping into his voice.

"She'll remain secluded upstairs, only making sporadic appearances near the windows," Robert countered coolly. "I've devised a cover story about Phossy Jaw, or some such ailment. It's foolproof."

"Robert, nobody will buy such a ludicrous tale," Harvard protested, his frustration mounting.

"That's your conjecture," Robert retorted sharply. "There's no proof to suggest otherwise."

"And what about visitors?" Harvard pressed, his mind racing with the implications of Robert's scheme.

"I'll simply claim she's contagious and off-limits," Robert replied dismissively. "Trust me, Harvard, I've thought of everything. Follow my instructions, and your secrets will remain buried."

"I can't risk tampering with a body, especially with a murder investigation underway," Harvard insisted.

Robert seized upon Harvard, his face inches from his own.

"You've done it before, and you'll do it again," he insisted, his voice dripping with menace.

"But this time, the stakes are higher. The detective suspects your wife's involvement in Lady Penelope's murder," Harvard protested.

"That's your concern, not mine," Robert shot back, his tone final as he pushed Harvard towards the bed where the doll lay inanimate.

"Please, don't do this," Harvard pleaded as Robert made his exit.

"You have no choice," Robert's words lingered in the air as he vanished down the stairs.

Harvard sank to his knees, the weight of Robert's demands bearing down on him like a suffocating shroud. His mind raced with the futility of the situation, knowing that compliance would only lead to further despair. In that darkened room, he realised the depth of the abyss into which he had been thrust, his fate entwined with the schemes of a man consumed by madness.

## CHAPTER THIRTY-SEVEN

# Bailey's The Hero

Bailey darted through the cold, deserted streets with the stealth of a hungry mouse, his eyes fixed on Thornton's every move. In his arms, he cradled a young girl, unmistakably the detective's daughter. Moving swiftly and soundlessly, Bailey shadowed Thornton, ensuring he remained unseen while maintaining close proximity. The thought of losing them filled him with dread, a gnawing fear that spurred him on; he couldn't bear the notion of any harm befalling the girl.

The girl's locks fluttered against Thornton's cloak as they ascended the steps to his shop. Bailey observed Thornton's nervous gestures as he fumbled with his keys, the urgency in his movements betraying his apprehension. With bated breath, Bailey waited, his senses attuned to every subtle detail as Thornton finally succeeded in unlocking the door.

"Hmm. So, he does possess emotions after all," Bailey muttered under his breath, a hint of surprise in his tone.

Thornton's sudden glance over his shoulder sent Bailey scrambling behind a nearby wall, his heart pounding erratically in his chest like a jar full of trapped butterflies. The ominous creak of the door closing spurred him into action, propelling him toward the fogged-up window of the shop. With the girl's fate hanging in the balance, Bailey knew he couldn't stand idly by and allow Thornton to carry out his sinister intentions.

Peering through the glass, Bailey observed Thornton laying the girl gently on the floor, his contemplative stance belying the danger lurking within. As the girl stirred and her eyes fluttered open to meet Thornton's gaze, a sharp squeal pierced the air, sounding out through the street and alerting a nearby dog to bark in response.

Seizing the opportunity, Bailey disregarded the weight of fear settling in his chest and sprung into action. With determination coursing through his veins, he flung open the shop door and launched himself onto Thornton's unsuspecting form. Thornton stumbled backward, caught off guard by Bailey's sudden assault, crashing to the ground under the force of Bailey's onslaught. As the girl scrambled to safety, Bailey relentlessly pummelled Thornton, each blow powered by a fierce resolve to protect the innocent.

"You!" Thornton's scream pierced the air as he forcefully kicked Bailey off his back.

The girl's cries intensified, echoing in the night air, while another dog joined in with its barking, adding to the chaotic noise. Sensing the urgency of the moment, Bailey knew he had to act swiftly. With determination blazing in his eyes, he lunged at Thornton once more, pinning him to the ground. "Go now, and don't look back!" he commanded, straining against Thornton's resistance.

With tears streaming down her face, the girl staggered to her feet and fled from the shop, her small form disappearing into the darkness. She raced blindly through the streets, guided only by the instinct to escape danger. Finally, she stumbled upon a brightly lit pub, where the boisterous laughter of patrons spilled out into the night.

Meanwhile, Bailey wasted no time in delivering a punishing blow to Thornton's gut before making his own escape from the shop. With his heart pounding in his chest, he dashed down a nearby alleyway, desperate to put as much distance as possible between himself and Thornton. The sound of Thornton's laboured footsteps echoed behind him, prompting Bailey to hide behind a stack of crates, holding his breath in silent anticipation.

As Lizzie approached the pub, her cries for help drew the attention of the patrons and passersby alike. A concerned woman rushed to her side. "Why are you out here, dear? Who are you running from?" she asked, her voice filled with maternal concern.

Meanwhile, an off-duty police officer emerged from the pub, his eyes widening in recognition as he spotted her. "Lizzie?" he exclaimed, reaching out to her with a mix of relief and concern.

With tear-filled eyes, Lizzie looked up at him, her exhaustion evident in every fibre of her being. Hungry and weary, she could only manage a weak nod in response to his inquiry, her fate now in the hands of those who had come to her rescue.

"Is that the inspector's daughter?" The woman stared at her, taken aback.

The officer disregarded the woman's question and pushed everyone aside to leave with the girl. "Everyone, please take a step back. Give the girl some room to breathe." He grabbed Lizzie's hand and pulled her away from the gathering throng of people. "I'll escort you back to your father," he assured, hailing a passing cab with a sharp whistle. "You'll be safe with me. I'm a police officer."

## CHAPTER THIRTY-EIGHT

## The Girl Is Found

Acker's ears pricked at the sound of his name echoing through the corridor, prompting him to peer out from his office. To his astonishment, a perspiring police officer dashed toward him, a triumphant grin lighting up his face. "Look what I've found!" he exclaimed, revealing a frightened Lizzie tucked behind him.

Acker's eyes widened in a blend of shock and relief as he rushed forward to envelop his daughter in a tight embrace. "Lizzie! Where on earth have you been?!" he exclaimed, his heart pounding with joy. With Lizzie safely in his arms, he hurried off to find Mary, leaving the officer standing alone in the hallway. "Mary! Lizzie's been found!"

As Acker whisked Lizzie away to reunite with her mother, the officer caught up with him, pulling him aside with a sense of urgency. Acker listened intently as the officer whispered into his ear, nodding in acknowledgment before ushering Lizzie into his office. "Stay here with Mummy, Lizzie. I'll be back shortly," he reassured her, closing the door behind him before turning his attention back to the officer. "Tell me everything, officer...?"

"Biggins, sir," the officer corrected respectfully. "I heard a commotion outside the pub and found your daughter in distress. I brought her straight here."

"And did she mention anything?" Acker asked, his brow furrowed with concern.

"It seems she's struggling to recall much, but she did mention trying to remember the name of the man who took her," Biggins replied earnestly, his gaze meeting Acker's with a sense of determination.

"A man took her...can she provide a description?" Acker asked.

"It's possible, but she's exhausted and famished. It would be wise to wait until she's had a chance to rest," Biggins advised, his tone reflecting a sense of compassion.

Acker nodded in agreement, his mind racing with possibilities. "Of course," he replied, lost in thought. Pacing the foyer with a hand stroking his chin, he formulated a plan. "I want every available officer to scour the streets and track down this individual. Meanwhile, I'll stay here and extract any information she can provide." With a firm nod, Biggins prepared to depart, but Acker halted him with a firm grip on his arm. "But exercise discretion, Biggins. The culprit may be lying low. Leave Claydon and Chapman here, but take the others."

"Understood, sir," Biggins acknowledged before leaving, offering Lizzie a reassuring smile as he gathered the officers to outline the strategy.

Turning his attention to Mary, Acker inquired about Billy's whereabouts. "He's at home with the maid, receiving lessons in reading and writing," Mary explained as she settled into a chair, cradling Lizzie in her lap. "What's your plan?"

A flicker of anger flashed across Acker's features as he gazed out the window into the darkened night sky. "I intend to hunt down the man responsible, Mary. Rest assured, justice will be served."

"Please refrain from speaking so harshly in front of the child. She's been through enough," Mary admonished, covering Lizzie's ears protectively.

"Of course, but I do need to ask her some questions. We must apprehend this man swiftly; he may attempt to flee the country," Acker explained, glancing at Lizzie before continuing. "Are you ready to talk, Lizzie?"

Lizzie nodded.

A warm smile graced Acker's lips as he addressed his daughter, striving to maintain a sense of calm and reassurance in his voice. "Lizzie, sweetheart, can you tell me what happened? Where were you taken from, what was the man's name, and where did he take you?"

Lizzie shifted uncomfortably, meeting her father's intense gaze with trepidation. She recognised that determined look in his eyes and felt the weight of his expectations. Fearing to disappoint him, she concentrated hard, struggling to recall the events of her escape. "A man with long hair helped me get away," she began slowly, her memory gradually surfacing as she recounted the details of her rescue.

"And there was another man?" Acker probed gently.

"Yes, he suddenly appeared and fought the man who took me. But there might have been another man too," Lizzie added, her brow furrowing in concentration. "He seemed nicer; he gave me candies."

"Can you describe these men?" Acker pressed.

"The man with the candies had a scar on his face, and the other man took me to a shop. It smelled like a bakery," Lizzie recalled, her words tumbling out as she struggled to piece together the fragments of her memory.

Acker sighed heavily, sinking back into his chair with a sense of frustration. "Lizzie, please try to remember. It's crucial."

"I'll try, but my mind gets foggy," Lizzie confessed, her gaze flickering nervously to her father. "But I do remember the first man's name."

Acker's eyes widened with anticipation as he leaned forward eagerly. "And what did he say his name was?"

"Mr. Bodmin, I think," Lizzie replied hesitantly.

Acker sprang to his feet, his chair clattering to the ground behind him. "Say that again?"

"He said his name was Mr. Bodmin," Lizzie repeated, her voice tinged with uncertainty.

Acker stood motionless for a moment, his mind racing as he absorbed the revelation. Without a word, he bolted from the office, his wife's questions falling on deaf ears. Bursting into the main area of the police station, he raised his voice, commanding the attention of everyone present. The officers halted their activities, their eyes widening in surprise as Acker addressed them with uncharacteristic urgency. Claydon and Chapman emerged from the interrogation room, exchanging puzzled glances.

Mary appeared, clutching a trembling Lizzie in her arms, her expression fraught with concern as she watched her husband pace the corridor like a man possessed. Waiting for silence to descend, Acker spoke with unwavering determination. "My daughter has identified her kidnapper, and we know him well. I want a cab waiting for me outside this entrance, and I expect each of you to join me in apprehending this man."

"Who is it?" Claydon asked, his gaze fixed on Lizzie.

"Mr. Bodmin," Acker pronounced the name with disdain, his eyes ablaze with fury. He observed the shock ripple through the room as everyone turned their attention to the young girl nestled in Mary's arms. "I want that man tracked down and brought back here. He could be anywhere by now. Gentlemen, I want every corner of the streets combed, and every person questioned about his whereabouts."

"Are you absolutely certain it was him who abducted your daughter?" Chapman interjected, his tone tinged with scepticism.

"Without a shred of doubt. I want you and Claydon by my side. The rest of you, fan out and locate him. I'll begin at the orphanage," Acker declared, snatching his coat from the nearby rack. Turning to Mary, he instructed, "Stay here and keep her safe."

Mary nodded solemnly and retreated into the office with Lizzie. Acker donned his hat and stormed outside, where a waiting cab stood at the front entrance. Claydon and Chapman trailed after him, exchanging uneasy glances. They were keenly aware of the inspector's volatile mood. Acker's anger was palpable, and they knew from experience that in such moments, he was prone to disregarding protocol and acting on impulse.

Acker was teetering on the brink of jeopardising his career, but

Claydon and Chapman couldn't fault him. They understood the depth of his rage following his daughter's abduction. With the identity of the kidnapper now known, they feared their inspector might lose control and take matters into his own hands. Their priority was to ensure Acker maintained his composure, lest they all find themselves in dire straits.

## CHAPTER THIRTY-NINE

# The Mortuary

In the dusky recesses of the mortuary, where shadows pirouetted with the wavering glow of a solitary candle, Harvard stood shrouded in the cloak of darkness. Draped in his worn coat and leather apron, once vibrant but now weathered to the hue of ancient parchments, Harvard moved with a hushed reverence past the table bearing Bella's form. His gaze lingered upon her pallid skin and nails, his touch tender as he caressed them with gentle care.

Lost in contemplation, Harvard remained unaware of the doctor's silent ingress, his focus solely on the task at hand - applying preservatives to Betty's body to preserve her as much as possible. Startled, he whirled around at the sound of Banes' voice, his nerves betraying him as he almost dropped the vessel of fluid, only just managing to save it from shattering upon the unforgiving floor.

"I apologise, sir. I'm just concluding my work here," Harvard stammered, his heart racing with fear as he sidled away from Betty's lifeless form.

Banes' scrutinising gaze bore into Harvard's own, suspicion lingering in the air like a haunting spectre. "Why do I find you here at such an hour, Harvard?"

Summoning every ounce of composure, Harvard faltered, weaving a web of falsehoods in hopes of concealing his true intentions. "I was merely following the inspector's orders, sir, to prepare her for her final rest."

The doctor's eyes narrowed, their scrutiny piercing through Harvard's facade as they drifted to Betty's body, now adorned with the glimmering traces of preservation fluid. "Is that so? I hadn't realised the inspector had issued such a directive."

"Yes, sir. That's what he wants."

With a heavy sigh, Banes replaced the white sheet over Bella's head, whispering silent prayers into the stillness of the mortuary. "We're still in the dark about her identity," he lamented, his confusion noticeable. "She deserves more than anonymity."

"I'll consult the inspector come morning," Harvard offered, his words tinged with a hint of unease.

Banes regarded him with a puzzled expression. "But didn't you say he ordered her burial?"

"Yes, but..." Harvard hesitated, his mind churning with unspoken apprehensions.

"But what, Harvard?" Banes pressed, stepping closer, his gaze piercing through the veil of Harvard's facade.

Harvard's hand instinctively found the cool metal of a scalpel hidden behind his back. He clutched it tightly, hoping that he wouldn't have to use it. "I'm simply following orders, sir," he replied, his voice strained with tension.

The doctor's features softened momentarily, exhaustion etched into the lines of his face. "Forgive me, I'm just overworked. I'm going to get some rest." With a tired yawn, he shuffled towards the door, leaving Harvard alone with his thoughts.

As the echoes of Banes' departure faded into the night, Harvard's mind raced, grappling with the implications of his actions. He couldn't afford to arouse suspicion, not when his carefully laid plans hung in the balance. With determination, he turned his attention back to Betty's lifeless form, steeling himself for the arduous task ahead.

## CHAPTER FORTY

## Shelton's Interrogation

Seated across from a police officer in the stark interrogation room, Shelton's mind buzzed with uncertainty. *Where is the inspector,* he wondered, *along with his loyal hounds who had unceremoniously yanked me from the comfort of my home?*

His servants, recently released, had borne witness to his forced entry into the same room they had occupied mere moments earlier. Their anxious stares had weighed heavily upon him, now morphing into a gnawing sense of irritation and frustration as he awaited the inspector's arrival.

Restlessness coursed through him, amplified by the officer's silent scrutiny from across the table. Shelton's legs trembled beneath the weight of anticipation, his hands betraying his impatience with nervous fidgeting. The creak of the door drew his attention, a flicker of hope extinguished as a man's head poked in with news of the inspector's absence, diverted instead to apprehending Mr. Bodmin.

The officer signalled for the door's closure, resigning himself to the task at hand. "Well, Shelton, it appears I'll be conducting the questioning in the inspector's stead. My name is Constable Trent, and I'm the station's psychologist. I studied in Leipzig, Germany, at the university for five years before returning here. Just to let you know, I'll be using some of my techniques as I question you today."

Shelton let out a resigned sigh, his eyes rolling in exasperation as the young officer began to recite inquiries from a worn notebook. He obliged each query with unwavering honesty, though beneath his compliance simmered a growing frustration. Constable Trent's inquiries, lacking depth and insight, painted a portrait of naivety that grated against Shelton's patience. It seemed this interrogation would yield little more than superficial probing, leaving Shelton to ponder the gravity of his predicament in the absence of true scrutiny.

Constable Trent furrowed his brow as he diligently transcribed Shelton's responses. Shelton, for a fleeting moment, entertained the hope of imminent freedom, until Trent's voice pierced the silence once more, his tone betraying a sense of gravity that sent a chill down Shelton's spine.

"Can you elucidate why Bella's body bore scars akin to those found on your late wife and several other servants we've interrogated?" The question hung heavy in the air, its implications like daggers piercing through Shelton's facade of composure.

A weight settled in Shelton's chest, suffocating any pretence of denial. He knew the query bore Evelyn's mark, her silence now a damning accusation echoing through the interrogation room. With resignation seeping into his voice, Shelton confessed, "I suppose I fancied maintaining control over my servants and my late wife."

Trent's gaze hardened, his youthful features contorting with a mixture of disbelief and disgust. "And why exclusively target women?" he pressed, his voice tinged with indignation.

"Because they pose no resistance," Shelton replied callously, his words dripping with the venom of entitlement. "A woman's duty is to gratify her master."

"Are you suggesting you derive pleasure from inflicting harm upon women?" Trent's voice trembled with a mixture of outrage and incredulity.

Shelton's retort came swift and cold, devoid of remorse. "I inflict pain solely to assert dominance, nothing more."

Trent's scrutiny intensified, probing the depths of Shelton's depravity. "Then why is Evelyn devoid of any such markings?" he asked, his suspicion palpable.

"There was no need," Shelton replied with a calculated calmness. "Her submission was already assured."

"And yet she accuses you of your servant's demise," Trent persisted, his voice laced with scepticism.

Shelton's facade wavered, replaced by a simmering anger. "That, I cannot fathom. I have witnesses who can attest to my presence at home that evening."

Returning to his notebook, Trent continued his interrogation, each question a damning indictment of Shelton's character. "Were the markings on your wife's body inflicted prior to her demise?" he inquired, casting a scrutinising gaze upon Shelton's countenance.

"How would I know?" Shelton spat with venomous fury. "I learned of her death from the police at my door, not a moment sooner." His words hung in the air, a bitter testament to the darkness that lurked within the confines of his soul.

"The markings on her body indicate that some of them were done after she died, leading us to believe that you were the one who caused them. You've already admitted to being the one who made those markings previously."

The interrogation room crackled with tension as the young officer levelled his accusation at Shelton, the weight of his words hanging heavy in the air like a guillotine poised to strike. Shelton's jaw clenched in defiance as he rose from his seat, looming over the table with a fierce intensity that belied his desperation.

"I never laid a hand on her!" Shelton's voice reverberated through the room, his words a vehement denial of the damning allegations.

The officer remained unfazed, a paragon of calm amidst the storm of Shelton's fury. "Please, sir, lower your voice," he implored, his tone measured and steady. "Let's get to the bottom of this."

Shelton seethed with frustration, his resolve faltering under the weight of the officer's unwavering gaze. Unable to meet his accuser's eyes, he turned his gaze to the blank expanse of the wall behind the officer, his thoughts racing with a futile attempt to decipher the young man's true intentions.

But the officer's next words shattered Shelton's illusion of control, revealing a cunning intellect lurking beneath his youthful facade. A smirk danced across the officer's lips as he exposed the ruse, laying bare the deception that had ensnared Shelton in its web.

Realisation dawned like a thunderbolt, illuminating the depths of Shelton's naivety. He had underestimated the officer's intellect, his arrogance a fatal flaw that now sealed his fate.

"I already warned you that I have studied psychology," Trent said, his voice tinged with satisfaction. "And you, Mr. Shelton, exhibit every sign of deception." He turned his attention to the door and shouted, "Jennings, get in here! I need you to escort Mr. Shelton to a cell."

Panic surged through Shelton's veins like wildfire. With a swift motion, Jennings rushed in and restrained him, but Shelton fought back with desperate fury, his instinct for self-preservation overriding all reason.

In a blur of motion, Shelton broke free from the officers' grasp, his heart pounding with the urgency of escape. With adrenaline coursing through his veins, he bolted from the interrogation room, heedless of the chaos erupting in his wake.

"Don't let him get away!" Trent's voice echoed through the station, a futile cry lost in the tumult of pursuit. But Shelton was already gone, disappearing into the labyrinthine streets beyond the station's walls, a fugitive fleeing the spectre of justice before anyone could stop him.

Alone in the darkness, Shelton's breath came in ragged gasps, his mind consumed by the bitter taste of betrayal. He had evaded capture, but the shadow of suspicion lingered like a phantom, haunting his every step as he vanished into the night, a man untethered from the chains of his past, but shackled by the weight of his sins.

## CHAPTER FORTY-ONE

# Murdered Who?

As the creaking door of the shop swung open, Thornton crumpled to the ground, his chest heaving with exhaustion and anxiety after his search for Bailey. A sharp pang of frustration pierced through him, mingling with the gnawing fear that gripped his heart like a vice. "God help me," he muttered under his breath, his voice a strained whisper in the dimly lit room.

With a frustrated grunt, Thornton tore off his cloak and flung it over the counter, his movements betraying the anger raging within him. He ran a hand through his dishevelled hair, his mind racing with frantic calculations as he sought a solution to his predicament. He couldn't afford to let Bailey slip through his fingers; the consequences would be dire.

Despite the chaos swirling around him, Thornton's thoughts remained razor-sharp, his keen intellect a shield against the dangers that lurked in the shadows. It was this same intellect that had kept him one step ahead of the law for so long, his cunning schemes cloaked in a veil of calculated deception.

To Thornton, morality was a luxury he couldn't afford. In a world rife with cruelty and betrayal, he knew that survival meant seizing whatever opportunities presented themselves, regardless of the collateral damage left in their wake. If someone stood in his path, they were expendable—a sacrifice to his own ambitions.

Though the prospect of surrendering Bodmin to the authorities weighed heavily on his conscience, Thornton knew it was a necessary evil to ensure his own safety. He would find another pawn to play his game; there were always willing participants eager to dance to his tune.

But it was Bailey who posed the greatest threat, a loose end that threatened to unravel all of Thornton's carefully laid plans. With determination, Thornton vowed to eliminate this obstacle by any means necessary, for in the unforgiving world he inhabited, there was no room for sentimentality. Survival was the only law that mattered, and Thornton intended to abide by it at any cost.

With urgency coursing through his veins, he knew time was of the essence. The thought of his child weighed heavily on his mind, a silent plea echoing in the recesses of his heart. Thornton could only hope that Bodmin had gleaned some crucial information before his inevitable arrest.

Determined to locate Bailey before the long arm of the law could snatch him away, Thornton's mind whirled with potential strategies. Grabbing a sturdy chopping knife from its resting place behind the counter, he steeled himself for the frigid night air that awaited him outside.

The chill bit at his skin, seeping into his bones and sending shivers cascading down his spine. But Thornton paid it no mind as he retraced his steps to the last place he had seen Bailey. The weight of the knife pressed reassuringly against his thigh, a silent reminder of the task at hand.

As he ventured into the darkness, Thornton's thoughts turned to the enigmatic figure of the old tramp. He had heard whispers of the man's past, rumours of a life once lived in service to his country. A survivor by nature, the tramp possessed skills honed in the crucible of adversity, a resourcefulness that set him apart from the masses.

Drawing upon this knowledge, Thornton resolved to adopt the tramp's perspective, to see the world through eyes attuned to the nuances of survival. It was a daunting task, but one he embraced with grim determination. For in the pursuit of Bailey, there could be no room for hesitation or doubt.

Locating the man proved to be a challenge, but Thornton wasn't overly concerned about the police catching Bailey. He knew Bodmin had connections within law enforcement, capable of disposing of Bailey if necessary. However, Thornton was determined to find him first. He wanted Bailey to suffer for his actions; allowing him to live would jeopardise Thornton's illicit endeavours.

Quietly slipping into the alley, Thornton sifted through discarded crates and refuse, finding nothing but decaying rat carcasses. Frustrated, he longed to stumble upon Bailey's body instead. But luck wasn't on his side. He stepped back, covering his nose from the stench, and noticed a slightly ajar side door, suspecting it was Bailey's previous hiding spot.

Entering the dilapidated building, Thornton paused to let his eyes adjust to the darkness. Cobwebs adorned the filthy walls, and old newspapers littered the damp floor. He meticulously searched every corner, hoping Bailey hadn't left yet and was perhaps asleep somewhere inside.

Stealthily ascending the decrepit staircase, Thornton deftly avoided the worn-out sections, his senses heightened with each step. Entering the first room, he found only dilapidated furniture, ravaged by rodent teeth. Not lingering, he proceeded to the next door, his sense of urgency palpable.

In the darkness of the room, a dusty heap of blankets concealed what seemed to be Bailey. Thornton discerned a faint grunting and the outline of a hand protruding from the covers. Approaching with caution, he aimed to maintain silence. A floorboard betrayed him with a creak, causing the tramp to stir. Thornton halted, anticipating resumption of the snoring, yet silence ensued.

Drawing a knife from his pocket, he pounced onto the bed,

thrusting the blade into the blankets until the stirring ceased. Hastily retreating, he left the weapon by the motionless form, his mind consumed with the deed. Descending the stairs, confusion clouded his thoughts; the absence of resistance felt unnerving.

With the biting cold gnawing at him and fatigue weighing heavy, he opted to delay inspection until morning, rationalising the stability of the scene. Slinking back to his abode, he cleansed his hands of blood before settling into the warmth of his bed, cloaked in a shroud of unease.

## CHAPTER FORTY-TWO

# Betty Returns

As Robert prepared to flip the sign on his shop door to 'closed', he stole a moment to peer through the window. The sun was sinking behind Bristol's rooftops, casting a warm glow that gently faded into twilight. The once-bustling street lay deserted, residents tucked away in their cosy homes, awaiting the dawn. A delicate mist unfurled like a silken veil, draping over the cobblestones and creeping towards Robert's shop.

Standing by the window, hands clasped behind his back, Robert surveyed the eerie tranquillity. The mist enveloped every corner, shrouding the crumbling buildings in a ghostly embrace. Even the moon, obscured by wisps of fog, cast an otherworldly silver light upon the scene. Shadows danced across the cobbled street, emanating from dark alleyways like tendrils of darkness.

Robert found solace in the solitude of the night, relieved that the usual raucousness of the pub's patrons was absent. Only a gathering of crows perched on a nearby rooftop provided company, their jarring calls punctuating the stillness.

Yet, beneath his outward calm, Robert's nerves buzzed with

agitation. He paced the shop floor, anxious for Harvard's return. Betty's disappearance weighed heavily on his mind, each passing moment increasing the risk of discovery. He hastily tidied the countertop, disposing of remnants with shaky hands, his thoughts consumed by the urgency of the situation.

As the fire consumed the last of the discarded cheese, Robert settled into a chair, glancing at his pocket watch. "Almost time," he muttered, steeling himself for the inevitable reckoning.

Beneath his jacket, he trembled, the warmth of the roaring fire unable to penetrate the icy grip of grief. Since Betty's passing, even the stove upstairs, once her cherished domain, failed to bring comfort. Last night's mishap with the scalding water went unnoticed until he set the pan down, the searing pain delayed, now manifesting in a raw, angry wound on his palm. *Strange*, he mused, *to feel the pain only after the fact*. It was as if Betty's spirit lingered, accusing him. He wouldn't blame her; he deserved her haunting presence. The shop, once alive with her laughter and warmth, now echoed with emptiness, amplifying his loneliness and regret.

"I should visit the alleyway ladies after Harvard returns," Robert contemplated, seeking solace in distraction.

As if summoned by his thoughts, the door creaked open, Harvard stumbling in with a solemn burden draped over his shoulder. Robert's heart raced as Harvard locked the door behind him, his eyes fixed on the ominous black bag.

"Will you lend a hand?" Harvard gasped, his breath laboured.

"Did anyone see you?" Robert's voice was tense, his suspicion palpable.

"Would I be here if they did?" Harvard retorted, his irritation evident. "Quit with the questions and help me."

Without further questioning, Robert rose to assist, though a chill gripped him as he reached for the bag. He couldn't bear the thought of facing Betty again. Harvard, sensing his hesitation, urged him forward, reminding him of their grim task.

Wordlessly, Robert gripped the cold, unyielding bag, its contents devoid of life's warmth. Together, they ascended the creaking stairs, burdened not just by the weight of the body, but by the weight of their shared guilt. It felt like carrying a statue, devoid of emotion or humanity.

Anxiety laced Robert's voice as he asked, "How long did it take?"

"All day. The inspector's still clueless about her identity. I staged a mortuary break-in to divert suspicion and fingers being pointed at us," Harvard replied, a hint of defiance in his tone.

"You mean pointed at you?" Robert retorted, his scepticism evident.

"If I go down, you're coming with me, Robert. We're in this together," Harvard shot back, his gaze unwavering.

Betty's weight strained Robert's muscles, her form precarious in his grasp. They barely managed to manoeuvre her into the living room, each passing moment feeling like an eternity. As Harvard unveiled the lifelike doll, Robert stood transfixed, awe mingling with discomfort.

"Help me dress her," Harvard commanded, pulling the body from the sack.

Robert hesitated, recoiling from the surreal task. "I can't. It's too bizarre."

Harvard's patience waned, irritation flashing in his eyes. "Then I'll return her, and you'll face murder charges."

After a moment's hesitation, Robert relented, his movements hesitant as he touched the doll's cold, clammy skin. With each adjustment, he fought the urge to recoil, his discomfort visible. Harvard, in contrast, seemed at ease, his deft hands manoeuvring the doll with practised precision.

"There you go, my lovely," Harvard cooed, a smirk playing on his lips as he admired his handiwork.

As hours slipped by unnoticed, the sun's gentle ascent over Bristol's rooftops finally roused Robert from his daze. Exhausted and sleep-deprived, he and Harvard had toiled through the night, labouring over the doll until she was ready to be displayed. Harvard carefully positioned her by the window, ensuring she was visible yet shielded behind the netted curtain from prying eyes.

"She feels heavier. What did you do?" Robert's voice trembled with unease.

Harvard, standing beside the doll, admired his handiwork. "I had to fill her, prevent decay."

Robert suppressed a shudder, unwilling to delve into the details. His gaze lingered on Betty's vacant stare, drawn into the void of her glassy eyes. They weren't the same colour as before. Harvard had used different glass eyes. It wasn't until Harvard's interruption that he snapped back to reality, realising he had been lost in contemplation.

"Beautiful, isn't she?" Harvard chuckled, oblivious to Robert's inner turmoil. "One of my finest creations."

But to Robert, the doll seated in his wife's cherished chair was a grotesque mockery. Despite her resemblance, she lacked Betty's warmth, her essence. A wave of regret and self-loathing washed over him, threatening to consume him whole. He fought back tears, unwilling to show weakness before Harvard.

"You can go now," Robert muttered, his gaze fixed on the lifeless doll.

With a nod, Harvard departed, leaving Robert alone with his torment. As the shop door closed behind him, Robert's anguish erupted, a choked scream escaping his lips. He sank to his knees, tears flowing freely as he cradled the doll, his heart heavy with remorse.

"My love, what have I done?" he sobbed, his tears mingling with the faint scent of Betty's clothes, tainted by the chemical odour of the doll's waxy skin.

## CHAPTER FORTY-THREE

# Where Have They Gone?

Acker's fury blazed as he stared out the carriage window, the orphanage looming ahead like a foreboding shadow. Claydon and Chapman exchanged tense glances, bracing themselves for the confrontation with Mr. Bodmin.

They couldn't afford a repeat of their previous encounter, not with a witness this time. Claydon clenched his fists, feeling the reassuring weight of his knuckle dusters in his pocket, a silent reminder of their readiness for whatever lay ahead.

With a sharp command from Acker, the carriage halted at the orphanage's entrance. Claydon caught sight of a curious child peering from behind a curtain and offered a reassuring smile, hoping to dispel any fear their presence might evoke.

Acker wasted no time, leaping from the carriage and storming up the steps. Instead of politely ringing the doorbell, he pounded on the wood with furious determination. "Bodmin, open up! It's the police!"

The echo of his words reverberated through the stillness, a stark contrast to the quiet facade of the orphanage. Inside, the air crackled with tension, anticipation hanging heavy as they awaited Bodmin's response.

Chapman's attention was drawn to another twitching curtain, where a frightened boy peered out, his eyes wide with fear.

"Sir, please," Chapman interjected, his voice firm yet gentle as he restrained Acker. "We need to approach this calmly. We're frightening the children." Acker paused, his anger tempered by the sight of the trembling child.

Claydon stepped forward, offering a reassuring gesture to the boy. "We're here to help. Could you open the door for us? We're from the police," he explained, displaying his badge for the child's reassurance.

The boy vanished from the window, and after a moment, the door creaked open. Standing before them, the child nervously relayed that their master had left with Edith.

Acker's frustration flared, propelling him into the dusty foyer. "Where did he go?" he demanded, his voice sharp with impatience.

The boy shrugged, his small frame trembling with uncertainty. "He left in his carriage. Edith went with him."

Concern etched Chapman's features as he knelt before the child. "Are you alone here? Is there anyone else to care for you?"

"There's a cook," the boy replied, gesturing towards the dining hall's twin doors.

Chapman took the boy's hand, leading him towards the kitchen. As they entered, the pungent aroma assaulted their senses. Claydon's impulse to speak was quashed by Acker's sharp reprimand, urging him to maintain composure.

The air thickened with the scent as they approached the kitchen. Acker's eyes stung as he beheld the dishevelled cook, her figure hunched over a bubbling pan, the smell of her concoction nearly overwhelming.

Meredith's heart raced as she turned, the wooden spoon slipping from her grasp at the sight of the imposing figures in their polished uniforms. She instinctively raised her hands, anticipating arrest, but the boy's reassurance gave her pause. Tentatively, she lowered her hands, eyeing Acker's stern expression warily.

Claydon's gentle voice broke the tension. "How should we address you?"

"Meredith Barns, sir," she replied, her voice trembling slightly.

Acker wasted no time. "We need to know where your master is, Miss Barns."

"He left this morning with Miss Edith," Meredith explained, her voice quivering. "He didn't say where he was going, just rushed out."

Chapman scribbled notes in his notebook. "Is this out of character for him?"

Meredith nodded, her gaze flickering between the officers. "Yes, it is. Normally, he informs me of his whereabouts, especially when Edith isn't here. But this time, he left without a word. And Edith... She seemed reluctant to go with him."

"What do you mean?" Chapman prompted, his pencil poised.

"Well, she was struggling to break free as he escorted her to his carriage."

"Why didn't you intervene?" Acker questioned.

"I prefer not to involve myself in their disputes, sir," Meredith replied carefully. "Their relationship has been tense lately, so it wasn't unusual to witness such moments. His forcefulness with her has become somewhat routine."

Meredith hesitated, weighing the risks of divulging more to the police. She couldn't afford to lose her job, but the memory of Edith's fearful eyes as she was dragged away nagged at her conscience. With a heavy sigh, she continued, hoping her words wouldn't incriminate her. "There is something, although I'm not certain if it's relevant to why you're here."

"Go on," Acker urged eagerly.

"I overheard Edith and Mr. Bodmin arguing a few nights ago," Meredith recounted. "She was accusing him of something related to the missing children from the orphanage. She sounded upset, mentioning another man's involvement, though I can't recall his name."

"You must try to remember," Acker insisted. "It could be crucial to our case. You might have witnessed a kidnapping."

Meredith's eyes widened at the implication. "All I know is that Mr. Bodmin might be connected to the children's disappearances. I don't have any more information."

Acker turned to Chapman. "Stay with Meredith. See if she remembers anything else. Claydon and I will search Mr. Bodmin's office for evidence."

Chapman nodded, while Meredith's mind raced with the weight of her revelation.

Claydon trailed behind Acker as they navigated the hallway, stopping in the foyer where Acker addressed him with solemn urgency. "Claydon, we must find something. This man is cunning and dangerous, and he won't stop until he's caught. It's our duty to protect these innocent children."

Claydon nodded firmly. "Yes, sir. There has to be evidence here that will bring him to justice."

Their conversation continued as they ascended the stairs, each step a resolute stride towards Bodmin's office. With a forceful kick, Claydon shattered the lock, the door crashing to the floor with a deafening thud that echoed through the hallway. Inside, chaos greeted them—papers scattered, drawers overturned, and the remnants of a fire still smouldering in the hearth.

Acker surveyed the scene with a sinking heart. "He attempted to cover his tracks," he muttered, lifting a charred document with his cane. "But there must be something left."

Claydon knelt by the fireplace, sifting through the ashes for salvageable clues. "It seems he fled in haste, neglecting to ensure the destruction of these papers," he observed, holding up a singed fragment with a triumphant grin. "He's attempted to obliterate his financial records."

Acker approached, his brow furrowing as he examined the scorched remnants. "These contain the names of the missing orphans, and look here." He pointed to the last entry on the list. "It's my daughter's name." His shock turned to fury as he deciphered the chilling truth. "He's been trafficking children for profit."

Claydon sifted through the charred remnants until his fingers landed on another document. Holding it up to the light, he examined it closely. "Here's another list of names and prices. It seems Bodmin has been at this for quite some time." He pointed to a signature at the bottom, adjacent to Bodmin's handwriting. "Meredith was right. There's another party involved."

"Can you decipher the signature?" Acker asked.

"Regrettably, no. It's illegible, a jumble of squiggles," Claydon replied, frustration evident in his voice. "But this could be the key evidence to bring Bodmin down."

"Retrieve everything. I want every file, every scrap of paper, even the burnt ones, to be analysed at the station. We need to uncover this accomplice," Acker commanded.

## CHAPTER FORTY-FOUR

# The Wrong Man

Hours dragged on, each passing minute weighing heavily on Thornton's mind. Despite the steady stream of customers flowing in and out of the shop, he couldn't shake the image of the body in the abandoned building. With a forced smile, he attended to their needs, serving pies and exchanging pleasantries, but the spectre of the previous night loomed over him.

His thoughts swirled with doubt and dread. Had he truly killed Bailey, or was it an innocent soul caught in the crossfire of his desperate actions? The distinction mattered little to Thornton; all he cared about was removing the witness to his dark deeds. The possibility of failure gnawed at him, threatening to unravel his carefully constructed facade.

As night descended once more, Thornton seized the opportunity to slip away from the shop. Shrouded in a cloak, he ventured back to the alleyway, the cold biting into his skin. The door stood wide open, a foreboding omen that sent a chill down his spine. Could the body have been discovered already?

His heart pounded in his chest as he ascended the creaky staircase, the echoes of his footsteps reverberating through the empty building. Each creak and scuttle of vermin sent shivers down his spine, but he pressed on, determined to confront the truth. With a surge of adrenaline, he raced towards the room where the body lay, his pulse pounding in his ears.

As Thornton's eyes adjusted to the dimness, he barely registered the mound of blankets atop the bed. With a sense of relief, he spotted the hand protruding from the covers, still intact. Without hesitation, he tore the sheets away, revealing the motionless figure beneath.

To his dismay, it wasn't Bailey. The man lying before him was dressed in finery, a stark contrast to the rough exterior of the tramp. Thornton's eyes lingered on the glint of a gold pocket watch, a valuable prize for the taking. Swiftly, he liberated the watch, already envisioning the profit it would fetch on the market.

Turning the body over, Thornton's stomach churned at the sight of a dark stain on the mattress, accompanied by the metallic tang of blood. Recognition flickered in his mind as he struggled to recall the man's identity. Then it hit him - Shelton, Lady Penelope's husband, a man of wealth and influence.

Fear gripped Thornton as realisation dawned upon him. If this wasn't Bailey, then the tramp had likely gone to the authorities. With a sense of urgency, he scrambled to his feet, his mind racing with the implications of his mistake. Bailey had a head start, and Thornton knew he had to act quickly to protect himself from the consequences of his actions.

Backing away from the blood-soaked scene, Thornton's legs trembled with fear, his mind reeling at the thought of Bailey still at large. He had thought it was all over, that he could finally breathe easy, but now his thoughts were a tangled mess, impossible to unravel. The metallic scent of blood hung heavy in the air, driving him to flee down the broken staircase.

His cloak snagged on a jutting hook, sending him tumbling to the floor below. Pain shot through his leg as he landed, his vision swimming with images of impending doom. He staggered out of the forsaken building, his mind consumed by dread, ignoring the searing pain in his thigh.

As he limped back to the shop, he spotted two figures outside, pounding on the door. Ducking behind a wall, he observed from a distance, his heart pounding with fear. Closer now, he recognised the faces of Bodmin and Edith. Stepping into the dim glow of the gas lamps, he exhaled a shaky breath, puzzled by their unexpected presence and limped toward them.

Bodmin's expression was a mask of anger and fear as he demanded entrance. Thornton met their gaze head-on, his own eyes probing theirs for answers. They seemed like bottomless pits, devoid of feeling, yet tinged with apprehension. "What have you done?" Thornton's voice was steady, though suspicion lingered in his tone.

Examining them closely, Thornton sensed their unease, like a scent hanging in the air. Bodmin squirmed under his gaze, avoiding eye contact as if fearing Thornton could read his thoughts. Thornton had a reputation for unravelling secrets, peeling back the layers of a person's mind until their innermost truths lay bare.

"The police have finally caught wind of your little side hustle, haven't they?" Thornton's tone dripped with disdain. Bodmin's cheeks flushed crimson as he nodded, unable to find his voice. "And now you come crawling here for shelter, am I right?"

Another hesitant nod from Bodmin confirmed Thornton's assumption. Edith watched the exchange, her surprise mingling with concern. She had never witnessed her master so vulnerable, yet there was a glimmer of satisfaction in seeing him humbled. Still, she couldn't shake the apprehension of what Thornton might do next.

"What's she doing here?" Thornton gestured towards Edith with a dismissive flick of his finger. "Didn't I tell you to get rid of her?"

Bodmin's gaze shifted uncomfortably to Edith. "She's an excellent maid. Takes good care of me."

Thornton rolled his eyes. "You're too soft, Bodmin. I'll deal with her if you won't."

Bodmin's jaw clenched, his frustration bubbling to the surface.

"I won't let you."

Thornton's demeanour darkened as he turned his focus to Edith. "Then you leave me no choice." His hand reached out, but Bodmin stepped in, shielding Edith from Thornton's grasp. "Bodmin, don't be foolish. You want to survive this, don't you?" He edged closer to Edith. "If she lives, she'll bring about your downfall, and you know it."

Though Bodmin knew Thornton spoke the truth, he couldn't bring himself to harm Edith in any way. "She won't say a word."

Thornton narrowed his eyes at Edith, sensing her fear. "Oh, she will. I can see it in her eyes. She'd run if she had the chance."

"Let's go inside and discuss this," Bodmin pleaded, still holding tightly to Edith's trembling hand.

Thornton stood there, his mind racing with options. The pain in his leg was unbearable, and he knew he needed to tend to it soon. Stitches were necessary, and Edith was his only hope. "Fine, Bodmin, have it your way," he relented with a heavy sigh. He ushered Bodmin and Edith inside, the door creaking open to reveal the warmth of the shop. "But you both must stay out of sight upstairs. I can't have my customers getting curious."

Bodmin nodded in agreement, eager for the respite from the cold. He shrugged off his coat, narrowly missing the display of Thornton's knives. Thornton shot him a stern glance before pointing to the coat rack in the corner. "Hang it over there." Then, he leaned over the counter and retrieved a dusty wooden box. Blowing off the dust, he handed it to Edith. "This has needles and thread. I need you to stitch up my wound."

Edith looked at him, confused until he gestured to the deep gash on his thigh. Though she was adept at sewing, the prospect of stitching a wound was daunting. "I'm not sure I can," she admitted, the metallic smell of blood making her stomach churn.

Thornton gripped her wrist firmly, pulling her toward a chair by the fireplace. "Do you want to survive?" he demanded, pushing her down onto the floor. "You'll do as I say."

Her hands trembled as she retrieved the needle and thread from the box, carefully threading it through the eye. "Shouldn't we sterilise the needle first?"

"There's a pan of water on the stove upstairs, Bodmin. Fetch it quickly!" Thornton barked, his impatience fuelled by the throbbing pain in his leg.

The room fell into an uneasy silence, amplifying Edith's sense of apprehension. She desperately searched for something to say, realising that her survival depended on Thornton's approval. "How did you injure your leg?" she ventured timidly.

His expression darkened, a scowl etching across his face. "That's none of your concern," he snapped, his voice laced with irritation.

Edith lapsed into silence once more, the passing moments dragging like heavy chains. Thornton's intense gaze bore into her, dissecting her with an unsettling scrutiny. When his hand brushed against her shoulder, a shiver ran down her spine. Suppressing the urge to recoil, she endured his touch, knowing defiance would only lead to her death.

Bodmin's return interrupted the tense atmosphere, though his gaze lingered disapprovingly on Thornton's hand in Edith's hair. "I brought the water," he announced quietly, averting his eyes to conceal his irritation.

Thornton grinned smugly. "Good. Bring it here, and let your little maid handle the needle."

Bodmin placed the pot on the floor, his apologetic glance directed at Edith. She met his gaze with a silent plea, understanding the gravity of their predicament. With trembling hands, she submerged the needles into the water, trying to compose herself despite the fear raging within her.

Abruptly, Thornton's question shattered the fragile calm. "Have you found my son yet?"

Edith's shock was palpable, her disbelief evident in her widened eyes. How could such a vile man have a child? The incongruity of it all left her speechless.

Bodmin cleared his throat, visibly unsettled by the abrupt change of topic. "No, I haven't found him yet. But I'm searching diligently. I'll recognise him by the birthmark; it shouldn't be too challenging."

Thornton scoffed, his tone dripping with disdain. "Seems like quite a challenge for you, Bodmin. My son's inheritance is at stake. With Shelton gone, the money rightfully belongs to him."

Edith's eyes widened in disbelief. "Your son?"

"Silence, woman!" Thornton snapped, his gaze sharp and commanding.

"How do you know Shelton is dead?" Bodmin pressed, his brow furrowing with concern.

"I found his body earlier tonight," Thornton replied curtly.

"Where?" Bodmin asked urgently.

"That's not important. What matters is finding my son," Thornton insisted.

"But with the authorities on my tail, it's nearly impossible for me to search," Bodmin protested.

"You'll find a way. You always do," Thornton retorted dismissively.

As Edith spotted a needle on the floor, an idea began to form in her mind. She swiftly retrieved it, concealing her intentions from the men. Pretending to select a clean needle from the pot, she deftly replaced it with the dirty one. If Thornton intended to treat her like dirt, she would sew his wound with a contaminated needle, ensuring infection. Suppressing a smirk, she prepared the needle and thread. "It's ready."

Thornton eyed her suspiciously. "That was rather quick, don't you think? Shouldn't it soak longer?"

"It's been in the water long enough. Let's get that wound stitched," Edith replied smoothly, concealing her satisfaction.

## CHAPTER FORTY-FIVE

# Lady Elspeth

As the night draped its shadow over the moors surrounding her estate, Lady Elspeth's unease deepened. She had been anticipating Edith's return all day, but as darkness fell once more, her apprehension grew. Edith was not one to vanish without cause. Lady Elspeth regarded her as a capable woman, sharp-witted and reliable. So, where could she be?

Turning away from the window, Lady Elspeth settled into a chair by the crackling fire, her furrowed brows betraying her concern. Should she venture to the orphanage to uncover the mystery of Edith's absence? Perhaps Mr. Bodmin, despicable as he was, had confined Edith against her will. Lady Elspeth had observed the rogue's lingering glances at her maid, detecting an unsettling lust beneath his facade.

Restlessness seized her, prompting her to pace the room. Her legs trembled, her heart raced, and her thoughts raced even faster. She knew she couldn't delay any longer. Her instincts clamoured, insisting that something was wrong, and Lady Elspeth had always trusted her intuition. Edith needed her.

With determination, Lady Elspeth stormed into the foyer, heedless of her butler's astonished gaze. Seizing her coat from the rack by the front door, she declared, "Prepare my carriage. I'm going to the orphanage."

"Now, Miss Elspeth? But it's dark out there, and bandits are known to roam," the butler voiced his concern, his worry etched on his features.

She gave him a look that brooked no argument, and he bowed, acquiescing to her wishes. Departing without further protest, he returned moments later to find her waiting impatiently by the door. "If you're determined to venture out into the night's perils, then I shall accompany you," he declared, reaching for his coat.

Grateful for his company, she smiled. "I appreciate it."

Unlocking the door, he guided her down the stone steps to the carriage, assisting her inside with a gentle hand. "There you are, my lady," he said, his voice warm with care. Once settled, he knocked on the carriage, signalling to the coachman that they were ready. Nestling into the corner, he glanced at her. "What's the urgency?"

"I have a sense that something is amiss," she confessed, her apprehension mounting as darkness descended over the fog-shrouded moors. "Edith failed to appear today, and it's unlike her to miss a day's work."

He nodded, sharing her concern, his gaze following hers as she peered out the window at the passing landscape. He noticed her legs trembling beneath her dress. "What do you suspect has occurred?"

"I cannot say for certain, but I suspect Mr. Bodmin is involved," she confided, her voice tinged with anxiety. "During my last visit to the orphanage, I sensed he was hiding something. When I pressed him about his finances, his reaction was one of fear and defensiveness."

"What about the children? Could they know something?"

Geoffrey ventured.

"Perhaps, but they're too frightened to speak up," Lady Elspeth replied.

As she retreated into her thoughts, a heavy silence enveloped the carriage. Geoffrey peered out the window, observing the mist swirling from the moors. The rhythmic galloping of the horses echoed as they raced towards the orphanage. When they arrived, darkness cloaked the building, intensifying Lady Elspeth's concerns. Another carriage obstructed their path, prompting their carriage to screech to a halt. Lady Elspeth wasted no time waiting for Geoffrey to open her door; she leaped out and dashed towards the open front door of the building.

As she neared, a glint of silver caught her eye. "Don't move!" a voice commanded. Lady Elspeth froze, her heart racing, as a figure emerged, wielding a gun. It was Chapman. "Who are you?"

Lady Elspeth and Geoffrey raised their hands in a gesture of peace. "I'm Lady Elspeth, and this is my butler, Geoffrey."

"What brings you here?" Chapman questioned, his grip on the gun steady, his police badge gleaming in the dim light.

A chill ran down Lady Elspeth's spine. "Oh, dear. What's happened to Edith?"

"Answer my question, Madam," Chapman pressed, his tone firm. "What are you doing here?"

"Edith failed to appear today, so I've come to ensure her well-being," Lady Elspeth explained.

Chapman lowered his revolver, realising they were not suspects. Stepping aside, he gestured for them to enter. Acker and Claydon hurried down the stairs, clutching charred documents. Acker's expression fell as he realised they were not the suspects he anticipated. "Lady Elspeth, what brings you here at this hour?"

Meredith emerged from the hallway, a child grasping her hand. "I thought I recognised your voice, madam."

Lady Elspeth's eyes, wide with fear, searched the room until they settled on Meredith. Recognition flashed across her face. "I demand to know what's happening. Where's Edith?"

"Mr. Bodmin left with her earlier. The police are here investigating him as a suspect," Meredith calmly explained. "Would you care for a drink, madam? You seem like you could use one."

Geoffrey approached Lady Elspeth; his touch gentle on her shoulder before turning his attention to the inspector. "What's going on?"

"I suggest you both return home. This doesn't concern you, and I'm pressed for time," Acker insisted.

"It does concern me, sir. Edith is my maid, and I demand to know her whereabouts!"

"I don't know where she is! She left with Mr. Bodmin. They could be anywhere by now, and I have no time to waste talking to you," Acker retorted.

"Sir, what about the children?" Claydon interjected.

Acker rubbed his tired eyes, sighing heavily. "What can we do with them? We can't take them with us, Claydon."

"Shouldn't we find them other homes? There's no one here to care for them."

"Every orphanage and workhouse is already overcrowded. They can't take any more in."

"I'll take them in," Lady Elspeth offered. She turned to Geoffrey. "Return to the manor and gather every available carriage from the stables. The children cannot stay here alone; it's not acceptable. Take some of them now and place them in the carriage. Explain the situation to the staff. They'll understand."

"Yes, madam, as you wish," Geoffrey said before heading upstairs. He signalled for Meredith's assistance. "You can come and help me."

"Well, that's a generous offer, Lady Elspeth. Thank you for your kindness, but we must leave," Acker stated, undeterred by her compassion toward the children.

She grasped his arm before he could pass her. "Just tell me what this man has done, Acker. I can offer assistance."

"He kidnapped my daughter and attempted to sell her," Acker revealed bluntly.

Her jaw dropped in shock. "How do you know this?"

"My daughter provided his name. We've also found evidence of his involvement. Please, madam, step aside so I can apprehend this criminal."

She released his arm and stepped back, praying that Edith

wasn't involved. "Is Edith implicated?"

"She didn't willingly go with him. I believe she's somehow entangled in this mess, but I don't think she's actively involved," Acker remarked as he headed out. Claydon and Chapman trailed after him to the carriage, leaving Lady Elspeth to ponder alone.

## CHAPTER FORTY-SIX

# Evelyn

Evelyn sat in her cell, her gaze fixed on a droplet poised to fall from the ceiling. A streak of rust snaked down the stone wall, filling the air with the scent of decay. Across from her, two men slumbered in their cell, while a guard hummed softly outside. The cells were dim and filthy, with only a narrow window at the back offering a glimpse of light. Time seemed to stretch endlessly; hunger gnawed at her stomach, a reminder of the missed dinner. Sleep eluded her, the cold stone bench offering little comfort. She longed for the warmth and security of Shelton's home, but since her arrest, she hadn't seen him. She hoped he would understand, but she refused to take the fall for his schemes.

She had been led to the cells amidst Shelton's protests, Mary's flushed cheeks betraying her discomfort. Promises of return hung in the air, but as hours passed, Evelyn's anxiety grew. She needed answers, yearning to escape the confines of her grim cell. The door creaked open, and Mary's voice broke the silence, signalling her release. Evelyn scrambled to her feet, her muscles protesting after hours of confinement. With Mary's help, she navigated the stairs, her heart pounding with anticipation. Mary's demeanour offered no clues, her gaze inscrutable as they hurried back to Acker's office. Evelyn held her breath, hoping for clarity about Shelton's fate.

"We have a problem," Mary announced, her voice barely above a whisper as she closed the door behind her. Evelyn's tension eased slightly, but anticipation still gripped her as she awaited Mary's explanation. "Biggins will fill you in while I attend to Billy and my daughter. My husband is on his way back with Mr. Bodmin."

Evelyn's eyes widened in disbelief. "Is the inspector arresting Mr. Bodmin?"

Mary hesitated, meeting Evelyn's gaze with a steady look. "Have you ever met Mr. Bodmin?"

"He's visited Shelton a few times. Sometimes alone, sometimes with a man named Creed," Evelyn replied.

Mary's curiosity flared. "Could you elaborate on those visits?"

Evelyn sighed. "I prefer not to pry into my master's affairs. What he does is his own business."

"You might reconsider after hearing what Biggins has to say. Your master, Shelton, has tried to pin everything on you. He's escaped and could be looking for you," Mary revealed before leaving the room.

Evelyn's remorse mingled with fear, knowing Biggins would exploit her vulnerability to extract more information about Shelton's dealings.

As Biggins took a seat across from her, Evelyn's legs trembled nervously, her fingers clutching the seat cushion. "Now that you're updated, do you know where Shelton might hide?"

She racked her brain, but nothing surfaced. "I'm not sure. Maybe somewhere remote, where he won't be found."

"You need to think harder, Evelyn. We must locate Shelton and uncover details about Bodmin and Creed's meetings. It's crucial," Biggins pressed.

"The person you need to ask is Shelton's butler. He knows everything. And as for where my master could be hiding, the only place I can think of is the old building next to the pie shop in the city. His father owned a shop there before he died, but Shelton allowed the place to fall into ruin. It's now abandoned."

Biggins leant back, satisfied. "That's the only place you can think of?"

"I know he won't leave the city. He'd stay near his home, waiting for the right moment to collect his things before fleeing properly. No one goes to his father's derelict shop. It would be the perfect hiding place for him."

"Thank you. This will help." He returned his pencil to his pocket and got up to leave. "I'll be back shortly."

"Can I at least have a blanket and some company?" She asked.

Biggins smiled warmly. "Of course, you can. I'll send Billy in. He has nothing to do at the moment." He flipped his notebook shut and left the room, closing the door quietly on Evelyn. He immediately spotted Billy sitting in the corner of the station. "Billy! Make yourself useful and keep Miss Evelyn company for a while."

Billy glanced at him with an annoyed look in his eyes. "Do I have to?"

Biggins grabbed him by the scruff of the neck and pushed him towards Acker's office. "Do as I say, boy."

Billy sighed loudly but did as he was told, scraping his already-broken shoes across the floor towards the office. He had put his old shoes back on to reminisce about his true roots and where he came from. He missed his friends terribly, and being sat in this strange place, bored and with nothing to do, made him miss them even more.

"Biggins!" A hostile voice yelled from behind him.

He jumped at the sound of the voice, knowing who it was right away. "What a pleasant surprise, superintendent."

"Where has Acker gone? I need to see him right away." The man insisted, pushing by Biggins on his way to the office. He stormed into the room and came to a halt when he noticed Billy and Evelyn. "Who in the name of God are you?"

Biggins grabbed the superintendent by the arm and led him out of the office. "Sir, a great deal has happened in both cases since your last leave. I assure you that everything is under control."

"Well, I can see that, Biggins. Who are those two in there?" He pointed to the office.

"They're witnesses to the cases, sir. The inspector is bringing a suspect in now."

"And who might that be?"

"Mr. Bodmin."

Rage filled the man's eyes. "I've already spoken to him about this!"

Biggins grabbed his shoulders and ushered him to sit down. "Sir, before you get angry, there have been developments in the missing orphan case. We have a witness, Acker's daughter. She said the man who kidnapped her was called Mr. Bodmin. The inspector is at the orphanage now to arrest him."

The superintendent observed in silence, a mix of anger and sympathy crossing his features as he exchanged glances with Biggins, plotting his next move. "And Lizzie is certain of this?"

Biggins affirmed with a nod. "The man revealed his name to her. She managed to escape when another man with long hair intervened at the shop to protect her."

"Shop?" Landrake's brow furrowed in confusion.

"She couldn't identify the exact shop, but she described the scent of pastries. We're actively searching for both the man and the shop. It will take some time, sir, but we're on it. The inspector is fully committed to resolving this."

"And what about Lady Penelope's murder?" He scratched his chin in contemplation, frustrated with himself for overlooking crucial details. He knew Acker would bask in the media limelight once the case was cracked. It should be him receiving accolades; after all, he held the highest reputation as superintendent.

"The investigation is ongoing, but we have a lead and a potential confession in Bella's murder—the servant girl. You just met her in the office. We're ensuring her safety here as Shelton has escaped and gone into hiding." As the superintendent jotted notes in his book, Biggins outlined the next steps in their inquiry. His pen moved swiftly, capturing every detail. He marvelled at Acker's swift progress while seething at Mr. Bodmin's betrayal. He had vouched for him, only to be made a fool in front of his colleagues. He yearned for Bodmin's capture, eager to enact justice for the exploited orphans sold into a life of slavery. The thought churned his anger even further. He anticipated Bodmin's arrival at the station, eager to confront him and ensure he faced the consequences of his despicable actions. "I want Bodmin brought in as soon as possible, and I intend to be present when he arrives."

Biggins was taken aback. "Sir, I implore you not to act hastily. We must handle this by the book, as you always advocate."

"That man has humiliated me!" His outburst drew the attention of fellow officers. "I shielded him, only to discover he orchestrated everything! He's made me a laughingstock!"

"Sir, please, take a moment to compose yourself. I understand your frustration, and he will face consequences, but we must proceed with caution. There's more to this than meets the eye."

Landrake snapped his notebook shut, intrigued by Biggins' words. "Explain."

"Lizzie mentioned another individual involved. We must locate him, and Bodmin holds the key."

"Then we hunt him down and bring him to justice. Additionally, we need to find Shelton. I want you to arrange for a wanted poster of Shelton. I want his face plastered across the city, so he cannot evade us!"

"Of course, sir." Biggins fidgeted nervously, knowing he had to divulge another murder or risk the superintendent's wrath. "Also, there's been another killing. The victim remains unidentified, and no one has come forward. She might be connected to Lady Penelope's murder, but as of now, it's a dead end."

Landrake remained frozen, absorbing Biggins' revelation. He couldn't believe Acker had managed to keep these events under wraps. After a moment, he responded, "So, three murders in a month, and we're still clueless? Biggins, we can't afford a repeat of last year's chaos! London was gripped by fear. If this escalates, the city will descend into madness!"

"The city's already on edge, sir. Some believe Jack the Ripper has returned, but localised to here, Bristol. Have you seen the headlines? Rumours abound. We're doing our utmost, but these murders defy explanation. They appear unrelated."

"Find the connection, Biggins. We need closure swiftly."

Before further discussion, the door burst open, revealing a furious Acker, trailed by Claydon and Chapman. Acker scanned the room, locking eyes with the superintendent.

Anger tinged Landrake's voice as he rushed over. "Where's Bodmin?"

Acker stepped back, raising his hands. "Sir, we're still searching. Someone tipped him off, and he's gone."

The superintendent narrowed his gaze. "A leak from here? Are you certain?"

"He'd already fled with his accomplice when we arrived. Lady Elspeth's taken in the children, but we're still on Bodmin's trail."

"And the unidentified victim?"

Acker shot a glance at Biggins before returning his attention. "I'll take you to the hospital mortuary now. But be warned, the killer's made identification almost impossible."

The superintendent felt a chill down his spine as images of Ripper's victims entered his mind. "Lead the way, Acker."

## CHAPTER FORTY-SEVEN

# Caught

Harvard left the cheesemongers thoroughly pleased with his craftsmanship. His restoration of Betty, especially her face, was nothing short of brilliant. Despite a twinge of envy towards Robert, who now had her, he hoped this would pacify him. The lingering scent of chemicals and the faint residue of dried blood on his hands mattered little; he'd cleanse himself at the mortuary, erasing any trace.

Skipping down the deserted street, he basked in the early light, chimney smoke swirling in the air, accompanied by the lively chorus of morning birds. The chill didn't faze him; it was a splendid morning, despite the sleepless night. Walking to his abode, the mortuary, he relished the anticipation of the day ahead.

But as he neared the police station a few streets down from the hospital mortuary, an unusual sight greeted him. Normally quiet at this hour, it buzzed with activity. A raucous crowd swarmed the entrance, waving banners and accusing, "The ripper is here!"

The strain on the officers was evident as they struggled to

contain the crowd, their apprehension plain on their faces, much to Harvard's amusement. Journalists from all around the city swarmed, weaving through the throng, stoking the frenzy of the banner-wavers. Everywhere he looked, panic reigned, fuelled by exaggerated tales spun in the papers. Yet Harvard knew the truth. Jack the Ripper wasn't haunting this city; it was a fevered lie, blown out of proportion. Betty, now a masterpiece resting below his abode, stood testament to his skill. The police, chasing shadows, only fed the hysteria, lost in a maze of rumours.

The thought of being the linchpin in solving the puzzle brought a wicked grin to Harvard's lips. He could almost taste the fame that awaited him. Amidst the chaos, a lone figure caught his eye—a tramp, seemingly inconspicuous but for the telltale signs of blood. Harvard pondered the man's potential involvement, sensing his fear, his guilt.

Shrugging off the distraction, Harvard made his way across the streets to the safety of the mortuary's rear entrance, away from prying eyes. But before he could revel in the familiar scent of decay, strong arms seized him, wrenching him into the room's centre, where Acker, Chapman, Claydon, and the superintendent awaited.

Harvard's heart plummeted as he realised his oversight from the night before. His throat tightened audibly as he took in the sight of the imposing figures before him, all dressed in matching, intimidating black suits with pristine white collars. Acker, in particular, exuded authority, leaning casually on his gleaming black cane topped with a snarling wolf, a weapon in disguise. Gripping his hat with a fierce intensity, Acker's eyes blazed with fury, signalling trouble for Harvard if he didn't cooperate.

As they ushered him into a chair, Harvard's nerves frayed. "What's happened here? Why is everything in disarray?" His voice wavered like that of a frightened child. The room fell silent as they scrutinised the dried blood on his hands, a damning clue he failed to conceal in time.

Acker's cane struck his hand with a sharp crack, eliciting a pained cry from Harvard. "Explain the blood, Harvard."

Shrinking back, Harvard stammered, "It's from yesterday. I haven't had a chance to clean up yet." Trembling, he massaged his throbbing hand.

The superintendent cut to the chase. "Do you know anything about what happened here or the whereabouts of the third body?"

All eyes bore into him, awaiting his response, but Harvard could only falter. "I... I don't know."

Acker's voice dripped with contempt. "Look around, Harvard. This wasn't a break-in; it was staged. Care to explain why we should believe otherwise?"

Sweat trickled down Harvard's brow as Acker closed in, his accusation hanging heavy in the air. "Why, Harvard, would someone stage a break-in with both doors locked tight and no broken windows?"

Harvard's gaze dropped guiltily to the floor. "It was me."

"Indeed," Acker said, the stick poised menacingly above Harvard's head. "What became of the body, Harvard? Speak!"

"I swear, I've done nothing!" Harvard's voice cracked with fear, dreading the imminent blow from the walking stick. "I'm innocent, I tell you!"

"Speak the truth, or face the consequences." Acker's threat hung in the air as he brandished the stick dangerously close to Harvard's head.

"I swear, it wasn't me!"

"Tell us why you've taken her!" Acker's voice thundered, stick poised to strike.

Harvard's eyes widened in terror as the silver wolf atop the stick gleamed ominously. "I didn't take Betty, I swear!"

As the room fell into an eerie silence, the superintendent intervened, lowering Acker's arm. "Who is Betty?" he demanded, breaking the tension.

Harvard sighed, realising his mistake. "She's Robert's wife, the cheesemonger."

"And where is she now?" Claydon asked calmly.

"At their shop. Robert has her upstairs," Harvard admitted, stealing a glance at Acker, who seemed more shocked than enraged. "And I didn't kill her. I preserved her for Robert. He's the one who did it."

The superintendent's anger flared. "You knew and said

nothing, obstructing our investigation?" His voice boomed, nearly toppling Harvard from his seat.

Acker's stick struck the chair with a sharp crack, making Harvard flinch. "You'd best start talking, Harvard, or face the hangman's noose!"

Harvard recoiled from the intensity of their scrutiny, palms raised in a feeble attempt to ward off their judgement. "Fine, fine, let me explain." He cleared his throat, avoiding their piercing gazes. "Betty's killer is her husband, Robert. He's the proprietor of the finest cheesemonger in town, and I happen to reside above it. That's how I know him. The day Betty died, they had a colossal row. I could hear the commotion from my room—bangs, crashes. The next day, her body turns up at the mortuary. I recognised her by a distinctive ring she wore, a gem Robert had gifted her not long ago."

Chapman's scepticism was palpable as he folded his arms. "And where is she now?"

Harvard sighed, knowing his next words would only deepen their suspicion. "Robert wanted me to preserve Betty's body, to make it seem like she's still among the living. So, I obliged. She's back at their place now, seated in her favourite chair. I must say, I did quite a remarkable job, ensuring she looked lifelike and concealing any injuries."

Acker averted his gaze from Harvard's smug demeanour, resisting the urge to lash out. "I couldn't care less about your craftsmanship, Harvard. What you've done is disturbing, to say the least." He struggled to comprehend Harvard's lack of remorse, a sickening realisation settling in. They had a madman in their midst, a revelation that wouldn't sit well with higher-ups. "What compelled you to commit such a deed?"

"That's none of your concern, sir."

"It's very much our concern, and you will tell me. What leverage did Robert have over you to commit such a heinous act?"

"Preserving a body isn't a crime. Egyptians have been doing it for centuries."

Acker leaned in, his hands gripping the chair's armrests. "Stealing evidence is a felony," he growled. "You'll tell us, or we'll bring your friend in here and question him. I doubt he'd appreciate you turning him over to the police. We might even leave you alone in a room with him. Who knows what he'd do."

Harvard blanched, his hands quivering violently. "That's illegal. You can't do that."

"We can, and we will," Acker asserted. "If you don't start speaking truth, we'll have no choice but to leave you tied to that chair."

A knock interrupted their tense exchange, and Banes peeked into the room. "Am I interrupting?"

Acker backed away from Harvard. "No, you're not. But you might want to know that your assistant here has absconded with a victim from the mortuary."

Banes arched an eyebrow at Harvard. "Excuse me?" Harvard pleaded silently as Banes cautiously entered, clutching his bag. "I don't understand."

"Apparently, Harvard has a peculiar hobby of pilfering bodies from the mortuary and turning them into dolls," Chapman explained, having surmised Harvard's illicit activities.

The superintendent halted Banes's impending questions. "Before you inquire further, know that Harvard is under arrest and will face the consequences." He turned back to Harvard, his tone firm. "You'll be placed in a cell. Any resistance will result in severe consequences. Do you understand?"

Harvard swallowed hard, resigned to his fate. The thought of spending even a night in those bleak cells filled him with dread. As visions of the noose clouded his mind, panic coursed through his veins, rendering him powerless. He didn't want to die; he wanted to live. "How can I avoid the death penalty?" he muttered nervously to Acker.

Acker exchanged a glance with Landrake, caught off guard by the request. Such a query was unprecedented. "I'll leave that to you, Superintendent Landrake."

The superintendent paused, equally surprised. "You can start by divulging everything you know about the victims. Every detail, no matter how trivial it may seem to you."

Suddenly, Hooper and Biggins barged into the mortuary, panic evident on their faces. Breathless, they struggled to speak. Biggins pulled Landrake aside, whispering urgently into his ear, while Hooper lingered awkwardly by the door, cheeks flushed.

The superintendent's expression turned grave. "Are you certain of this, Biggins?"

Biggins nodded solemnly. "Unfortunately, sir. We're discreetly bringing the body in as we speak. Evelyn, the servant girl, tipped us off."

Landrake's shock was palpable as he stared into the distance. "Good heavens. We're on the brink of a riot," he muttered under his breath.

"What's going on?" Acker demanded, growing increasingly impatient with the secrecy.

The superintendent turned to the sergeants. "Take Harvard to the cells, Chapman, and station a guard outside at all times. Claydon, brief Banes on the situation and gather as much information on the victim's injuries as possible. Banes, another body will be arriving shortly. I want a detailed report on my desk as soon as possible." He then addressed Acker. "Come with me."

Biggins and Hooper followed, their expressions reflecting the sombre gravity of the situation. Meanwhile, Chapman, Claydon, and Banes took charge of Harvard. As the group made their way back through the hospital, Acker felt his heart pound with increasing intensity. "Sir, please, what's happening?"

Landrake pulled Acker aside, his own emotions evident in the furrow of his brow. "A body has been discovered, Acker."

"And?"

"It's Shelton. He's been murdered."

## CHAPTER FORTY-EIGHT

# Bailey's Confession

Bailey surveyed the unruly crowd outside the police station, their anger palpable as they hurled bottles at the windows in a frenzy. It was now or never to quell the chaos; if action wasn't taken soon, peace would elude the city indefinitely.

Pushing through the throng of intoxicated labourers and anxious onlookers, Bailey winced at the cacophony assaulting his ears. Ever since his altercation with Thornton, his head throbbed incessantly, the dried blood from his brow wound tightening with each passing moment. He knew he should have sought stitches, but time was against him now. Death loomed ominously, his body drained and weary from the blood loss inflicted during the fight. The gash on his stomach still seeped blood, a grim reminder of his mortality.

Clinging to the handrail for support, Bailey ascended the station steps, pounding on the door in urgency. The officer who cracked it open eyed him warily. "What's the matter?"

"I need to see the inspector," Bailey gasped, hand still pressed against his wounded side.

Recognising Bailey, the officer hastily ushered him inside, bolting the door behind them. "We've been searching for you."

Bailey nodded weakly. "I know. I have crucial information for the inspector about Shelton and the missing children." His legs gave way beneath him, and he grasped the officer's shoulder for support.

"We need to get you to a doctor," the officer insisted, leading Bailey to a chair. "Wait here while I fetch someone."

Bailey seized the officer's arm, urgency flashing in his eyes. "There's no time for that. Trust me, I know what's happening. Go find the inspector and tell him to bring his notebook." He gestured toward Acker's office.

The officer dashed down the corridor, skirting past the office where Banes and Acker were speaking quietly. "Sir, please, come quickly!"

Acker turned, urgency etched on his features. "Not now; this is urgent."

"No, sir, we've located the tramp. He's here and eager to speak, but he's in dire shape," the officer reported.

Acker's eyes widened in astonishment, and he hurriedly departed, gesturing for Banes to carry on. "Banes, you know what needs to be done."

The officer firmly gripped Banes's shoulder, urging him toward the door while snatching Banes's medical bag on the way. "Sir, we need your assistance too. The man's condition is critical. He may not have much time."

They converged around Bailey, who was drenched in sweat, his breaths laboured. Acker knelt beside him, notebook in hand. "What brings you here?" he asked softly.

Bailey met his gaze through tears, managing a feeble smile. "Sir, I'm on my last legs. There's nothing more they can do to me."

"Who?" Acker pressed eagerly.

"You were on the right track, but there are two more. Bodmin didn't take your daughter; it was a man named Thornton. He's the one who did this to me," Bailey gasped, coughing up blood. He grimaced in pain, pleading with Banes for assistance. "Just give me enough time to see those men hang for their crimes."

Banes nodded, swiftly attending to Bailey's wounds with a collection of tools and vials. "Stay as still as possible," he instructed.

"What about this man?" Acker inquired.

Banes carefully cleaned Bailey's wounds, causing him to wince. "He runs Thornton's Pie Shop across the street. He also killed a man named Shelton, mistaking him for me. I've been evading him ever since."

"Do you have any information about Lady Penelope's murder?" Acker probed further.

Bailey nodded slowly, pushing through the pain. "I saw her arguing with someone in the alley. It looked like a man, but I can't be certain."

"And what was the argument about?" Acker asked, pen poised over his notebook.

"It was about abandoning a baby boy at an orphanage. The first man left in a rage, then another man arrived. He seemed important, rich even, from his attire," Bailey recounted.

"Did you witness her death?" Acker pressed.

"No, unfortunately. But she was acquainted with both men. There might have been someone else there too, but it was too dark to discern," Bailey explained.

Acker jotted down notes swiftly. "And who is this other man working with Bodmin and Thornton?"

"His name is Creed," Bailey replied, wincing as Banes prodded at his wound.

"Creed?" Biggins interjected. "Evelyn mentioned a man named Creed visiting Shelton's house."

Acker rose, flipping over his notes. "Biggins, interrogate Evelyn again. We need the truth. And question Shelton's butler, by force if necessary." He gestured to the others. "Prepare yourselves. Bodmin and his servant may be holed up at Thornton's pie shop. Half of you come with me, the other half bring Robert here and arrest him. Ensure Betty's body is returned to the mortuary." He turned to Bailey and Banes. "Take care of him, Banes. He stays here." With that, he closed his notebook and stowed it away.

"What are we waiting for? Let's move!" he barked at the officers.

## CHAPTER FORTY-NINE

# Creed

Bodmin and Edith sat opposite the window, a serene scene against the backdrop of passing clouds. Between them, a dish of water with potatoes awaited Edith's careful peeling. Her voice hummed softly to a tune only she could hear. Earlier, she had glimpsed Thornton's limping descent down the stairs, her hope pinned on the success of her clandestine scheme, her needle's dirty deed.

Outside, the market's buzz mingled with the clatter of stall preparations, a symphony of morning routines. Bodmin's composure wavered at the commotion outside, prompting him to leap from his seat, drawn to the window's edge.

"Step away. You'll draw attention," Edith hissed, clutching his arm.

He shrugged her off. "What if Thornton has run to the authorities? He should have returned by now."

"He's fetching Creed, just as you instructed. Stop fretting." Her thoughts drifted to the orphanage. Images of the children's faces flashed through her mind, stirring a wave of anguish. She prayed they found refuge, cared for and safe. Her heart ached for them, longing for their company once more. Among them, Billy held a special place. When he was left at the orphanage's doorstep, she had felt an immediate bond, naming him as her own. Memories of their playful moments warmed her soul, yet his return that fateful night bore scars and secrets she couldn't unravel. He was like a son to her, and his absence left a void she couldn't bear. If she faced the gallows, her final plea would be for one last glimpse of him.

Dread washed over her at the thought of Lady Elspeth. What did her mistress think of her now? She never intended to be entangled in this chaos, yet here she was, a fugitive alongside her master. Across the room, she fixed her gaze on Bodmin's back, a silent testament to her disdain. He stiffened, sensing her silent reproach. "They've returned," he announced, turning to meet her gaze. "I can see them."

The shop's bell chimed, heralding the arrival of heavy footsteps on the stairs. The door swung open, revealing a stranger to Edith, his grin wide and unsettling. "Well, well, Bodmin, seems we've landed ourselves in a bit of trouble, haven't we?" His laughter carried as he shed his coat and hat, revealing a long scar etched along his cheek.

Bodmin shot him a wary glance. "We're all in this together."

Creed's grin widened. "Not all of us have the police on our tail. So, no, we're not all in this together." His gaze then fell upon Edith. "And who might this charming lady be?"

"Edith, sir," she replied courteously.

Thornton arrived with a cup of tea. "Well, Creed, what's the plan?"

Creed sighed. "If you don't fancy dancing at the end of a rope, I suggest you both vanish and never return."

"And what about our livelihood?" Bodmin interjected, irritation evident in his voice.

"Our business is kaput, thanks to you, Bodmin. You'll have to find another hustle. Perhaps Edith here could fetch a tidy sum," he mused, his laughter tinged with malice.

A sudden crash outside jolted them, prompting Bodmin to rush to the window. His face drained of colour as he beheld the chaos below. "We've been discovered," he muttered, his voice barely audible over the shouting from outside.

Thornton shoved him aside, spilling his tea in the process. "What do you mean?" Panic gripped him as he peered out the window, clinging to Bodmin for support. "What have you done, Creed?"

All eyes turned to Creed, his once confident attitude now replaced by a pallor akin to death. "I swear, I had nothing to do with this!"

## CHAPTER FIFTY

# The Plan

Mary sat across from Lizzie at the kitchen table, watching her daughter quietly sketching away. She took a serene sip of her tea, then carefully set the cup back on its saucer, not wanting to break Lizzie's focus. Yet, the hundreds of questions about her daughter's recent disappearance bubbled in her mind, and she couldn't hold back any longer. "Do you remember anything else from that night?"

Lizzie paused her drawing, a perplexed frown knitting her brows. "Mummy, I've told you already. A man came and rescued me from the shop. He looked like a tramp and smelled like one, too. Everything else is a blur."

Mary nodded, her scepticism still lingering. "I'm glad he saved you, darling. I just hoped you might recall more." She took another sip, her gaze drifting to the grandfather clock against the wall. "I wonder where Billy's got to. It's getting late." She changed the subject, not wanting to unsettle her daughter further. Lizzie had been through enough.

As dusk crept in, casting eerie shadows, Mary rose to light the gas lamps, feeling the constriction of her bodice. She made a mental note to loosen it next time. She disliked the tight dresses, a preference imposed by her husband, Acker, who believed they epitomised femininity. It was just another example of women's voices being stifled. Mary yearned to engage in politics, to challenge societal norms that held women back. She resented the societal confines that allowed men freedom while women were expected to tend to the home. Mary loved her husband, but her frustration simmered, threatening to boil over. Their marriage teetered on the brink of collapse.

A sharp knock jarred Mary as she settled back down, nearly toppling her tea. "Come in," she called, steadying the cup.

Billy entered looking dishevelled, the typical demeanour of a teenager. Yet, clad in the clothes Mary had selected, he appeared more presentable. He pulled out a chair and sat, his gaze distant, lost in thought.

Mary reached for his hand, sensing his unease. "Are you alright, Billy?"

Billy offered a shaky smile, averting his gaze. "Yeah, I'm fine. Just a long day at the station." He sighed deeply, picking at the table with his soiled nails. "I miss my friends. When can I see them?"

Mary reclined in her chair, taken aback. She hadn't anticipated Billy longing for the dilapidated hovel he called home. "Well, Lady Elspeth has kindly taken the children in for now until arrangements are made for them," she informed him.

Billy's eyes lit up with excitement. "I like Lady Elspeth. Can we visit them?"

"I don't see why not. I'll arrange for a carriage to pick us up first thing tomorrow morning," Mary said, formulating a plan. A visit to Lady Elspeth's would offer her a chance to converse with another woman, a welcome change from the children's constant company. She nodded affirmatively. "Yes, we'll visit her tomorrow."

Lizzie glanced up from her drawing to see Billy grinning. "Can I come too?"

Billy eagerly nodded. "Absolutely, little sister."

A wave of warmth washed over Mary as she observed Billy interacting with her daughter. Initially unsure about him, she now watched him across the table, her heart melting. With her guidance, he had transformed into a neat young man, almost ready to face the world.

She sat in silence, appreciating the tender moment between Billy and Lizzie, her mind racing. Perhaps it was time to broach the subject of his origins, to inquire about his biological parents. Uncertain whether to ask, she took a deep breath. "May I ask you something, Billy?" Billy nodded, continuing to tousle Lizzie's hair. Mary paused, wary of upsetting him, then continued. "Do you remember anything about your past? Where might your real parents be?"

Billy's hand stilled, his shoulders tensing. "I don't remember my parents," he murmured. A flicker of fear crossed his face before vanishing.

"Have you ever wondered about them?" Mary asked, her voice gentle.

Avoiding Mary's gaze, Billy seemed uncomfortable. "I asked Miss Edith once when I was younger. She only told me a little."

"What did she say?"

"She found me as a baby on the orphanage doorstep. There was a woman in a red dress riding away on a horse, but she didn't turn back. Miss Edith doesn't know anything else," Billy explained, a hint of sadness in his voice. "I miss Edith. Where could she be?"

Mary refrained from mentioning that Edith was now a fugitive along with Mr. Bodmin. "I'm not sure, Billy, but I'm certain she's thinking of you. You two had a strong bond."

"We did. She was like a mother to me."

Suspecting Billy was withholding something, Mary observed his clenched fists. She opted not to press him further, concluding their conversation. Rising from her seat after depositing her teacup in the sink, she addressed the children. "Time to get ready for bed."

Billy pushed his chair back and departed quietly, saying nothing to either of them. He retreated into his shell, his fear and nerves apparent. It was her fault entirely. She should have remained silent. She could only hope he would return to his cheerful self by morning.

## CHAPTER FIFTY-ONE

# A Knock at The Door

A sudden thud against the window jolted Robert from his slumber, the echo reverberating through the room like a warning from the depths of the night. Blinking away the fog of sleep, he squinted at the clock, its hands barely visible in the dim light, and pondered the source of the disturbance. Another heavy thump rattled the wooden frame, sending tremors coursing through his bones, and he cast a wary glance toward the armchair where Betty's lifeless form sat, a silent sentinel in the gloom. Her glassy eyes seemed to bore into his soul, haunting him with their frozen gaze.

"Stop staring," Robert muttered, his voice a hoarse whisper, as he slid off the bed, his movements cautious and deliberate. The rhythmic pounding from outside intensified, each impact a palpable pulse of fear that set his nerves alight. Creeping toward the window, he peered into the darkness, the void beyond swallowing the feeble light of the street lamps, leaving only a yawning abyss in its wake.

"Perhaps it's a storm," he murmured, the words dissipating into the stillness of the room. "That would explain the banging."

He roused from his drowsiness, limbs stretching languidly as he rubbed at the tousled mop of hair atop his head. An inexplicable unease prickled at his senses, a phantom whisper of warning that danced just beyond the reach of his consciousness. With each resounding thud echoing from the floor below, the atmosphere grew heavier, the air thick with anticipation and foreboding. "What in blazes is that racket?" he muttered, his gaze drifting toward the window where the night enveloped the world in a cloak of impenetrable darkness.

A shiver coursed down his spine as his eyes fell upon the figure of the life-sized doll, its form cast in eerie silhouette against the dim light filtering through the glass. "You're not my Betty," he murmured, a chill settling in the pit of his stomach, urging him to put distance between himself and the unsettling sight. Descending the staircase to the shop below, he abandoned all hope of returning to the solace of sleep amidst the banging that besieged his home.

A flicker of movement caught his eye, drawing his attention to the window's edge, where a shadowy figure prowled in the inky blackness. Gripping a cheese knife in one hand, he reached for the key protruding from the lock, the metal cool against his clammy palm as he prepared for the unknown threat lurking beyond the threshold. With bated breath, he twisted the key, the mechanism yielding to his touch, just as the door lurched open with violent force, admitting a flood of uniformed figures into the room.

Before he could react, strong arms seized him, wrenching him from his sanctuary and hurling him to the ground with a force that stole his breath. "Curse you, coppers! What in blazes is the meaning of this?" He cried out, struggling against his captors with futile desperation.

Biggins stood before him, an unwavering pillar amidst the chaos. "You're under arrest for the murder of your wife, sir," he declared, his voice a solemn indictment that vibrated through the air like a death knell.

Robert's heart clenched in his chest, the weight of accusation bearing down upon him with suffocating intensity. He cast a knowing glance toward Biggins, the pieces of the puzzle falling into place with chilling clarity. "I suppose Harvard's had a word with you, then?"

Biggins' lips curled into a smirk, a flicker of triumph dancing in his eyes. "Consider your words duly noted, sir," he purred, his voice dripping with satisfaction. With a curt nod to the officers, he assumed control of the situation, his attitude radiating an aura of unwavering authority. "Take him into custody, gentlemen. I'll manage proceedings from here."

The officers complied without hesitation, their grip firm as they dragged a protesting Robert from the shop, his desperate cries echoing through the night air. "I demand my rights! I demand legal representation!"

"The only rights you'll be exercising are the ones read to you at the gallows!" Biggins retorted, his voice a thunderous condemnation that echoed through the street. He watched impassively as Robert was thrust unceremoniously into the waiting carriage, the harsh reality of his impending fate sinking in with each passing moment.

A fleeting expression of shock crossed Robert's features before fury consumed him, his accusations ringing out like a battle cry. "Harvard's the one you want! He's the murderer, not me!"

As the carriage rumbled away into the night, leaving behind a trail of dust, Biggins was left alone with his thoughts. Clad in his nightclothes, Robert's figure appeared pitiable against the backdrop of the dimly lit street. Yet, amidst the mayhem and confusion, his final words lingered in Biggins' mind, a nagging doubt gnawing at the edges of his consciousness. What if they had apprehended the wrong man? What if Harvard's web of lies extended far beyond their grasp?

## CHAPTER FIFTY-TWO

# The Butler

The station bustled with the urgency of a beehive, a symphony of footsteps and murmured conversations echoing off the walls. The crowd outside grew larger by the hour, and it was only a matter of time before they smashed through the doors to demand justice for the murders of Bristol. Each passing second seemed to quicken the pace, the weight of unresolved cases pressing down on the officers like a relentless force. Claydon navigated the corridors, his steps purposeful as he approached the interrogation room. With his notebook in hand, he prepared to coax the truth from Shelton's enigmatic butler.

Pushing open the door, Claydon entered the room, his presence commanding attention. The butler, Jeeves, rose respectfully at his entrance, a silent acknowledgment of authority. "Please, take a seat," Claydon offered, gesturing to a chair opposite him.

"And Jeeves, if I may address you as such, let's dispense with formalities. We're here to understand, not to uphold the barriers of status."

Jeeves nodded, a flicker of gratitude in his eyes as he settled back into his seat. "Very well, sir."

Claydon wasted no time in delivering the grim news, his tone solemn yet resolute. As the weight of Shelton's demise sank in, Jeeves' facade of stoicism crumbled, replaced by a torrent of disbelief and grief. "Murdered, you say?" His voice trembled with emotion, his world shaken to its core by the revelation.

"The abandoned dwelling above his father's shop," Claydon confirmed, his gaze unwavering. "Now, Jeeves, if you could shed some light on the events leading up to this tragedy, it could prove invaluable in our pursuit of justice."

A shadow passed over Jeeves' features, a mixture of sorrow and resolve. "Lady Penelope was a master of manipulation, sir," he began, his voice heavy with remorse. "She and Mr. Shelton engaged in a twisted dance of deception, fuelled by secrets and betrayal."

Claydon leaned in, his pencil poised to capture every word. "And Evelyn? How did she come to learn of these secrets?"

"Many years ago, before she died, her mother was also a servant in my master's household. She had revealed all of Lady Penelope's secrets and transgressions to Evelyn."

Claydon nodded, quickly scribbling down notes. "So, what happened once your master discovered that?"

"He demanded to know where the child was, but Lady Penelope refused. She did, however, tell him who the father was—a man named Thornton."

"Thornton? We've just brought him in for questioning."

"Everything changed at that point. Shelton decided to befriend Thornton and a man named Creed, becoming involved in the abduction of orphan children to sell them as slaves. Thornton remained in the shadows, while Creed did his dirty work for him. They would meet with Mr. Bodmin late at night. But my master had a different plan. He was looking for his wife's child to dispose of it, and then Mr. Thornton. Unfortunately, he was never able to locate the youngster. Only I am capable of identifying the boy by a birthmark on his leg." Jeeves turned away from Claydon, avoiding his inquisitive stare. "I never notified my master because I didn't want that poor innocent child tangled up in this mess, and having the blood of that on my hands was something I couldn't do."

Jeeves's revelations unfolded like chapters from a gripping tale of intrigue and betrayal. Claydon listened intently, his pen dancing across the pages of his notebook as he captured each word with precision. The air crackled with tension as Jeeves recounted the clandestine dealings that had unfolded within the walls of his master's estate.

"So, Lady Penelope's secrets were passed down through Evelyn's mother," Claydon remarked, his voice a steady anchor amidst the storm of revelations. "And when your master learned the truth, he embarked on a dangerous path of vengeance."

Jeeves nodded gravely, his gaze fixed on some distant point beyond the confines of the room. "Indeed, sir. But his quest for retribution led him down a dark path, one intertwined with the sinister machinations of Thornton and Creed."

Claydon leaned forward, his brow furrowed in concentration. "And this child, the heir to Lady Penelope's estate—do you believe he still lives?"

Jeeves's expression softened, a flicker of sorrow clouding his features. "If he does, sir, he remains hidden from the world, his true identity shrouded in secrecy."

"And the birthmark on his leg," Claydon pressed, his curiosity piqued by the prospect of such a distinctive identifier. "You're confident you could recognise it if you saw it again?"

A solemn nod was Jeeves's only response as he rose from his seat, his movements measured and deliberate. With a gesture, he indicated the spot on his leg where the birthmark had once been. "A mark of fate, sir, etched into the fabric of his being."

Claydon absorbed this information, his mind racing with possibilities. "If this child is indeed alive, he holds the key to unlocking the mysteries of Lady Penelope's past."

Jeeves nodded in agreement, his gaze steady as he met Claydon's probing stare. "But whether he knows his own truth, sir, remains to be seen."

As the weight of their conversation settled like a heavy cloak upon their shoulders, Claydon's thoughts turned to the enigma of Lady Penelope's pregnancy. "How did she manage to conceal such a secret, Jeeves? And where did she give birth, if not within the confines of her own home?"

Jeeves chuckled softly, a glimmer of mischief in his eyes. "Ah, Lady Penelope, a woman of secrets and intrigue, she was. A delicate figure, she concealed her condition beneath the tight confines of her corset. Her dalliances were many, sir, but one among them stood out—a doctor by the name of Banes. He sheltered her in his abode as she neared her time."

"Banes?!" Claydon's exclamation pierced the air, halting Jeeves's from talking.

A puzzled expression flickered across Jeeves's features. "You are acquainted with the gentleman?"

Claydon waved a hand wearily, urging Jeeves to continue. The flood of information threatened to overwhelm him, and he struggled to maintain his composure.

"That's the crux of it, sir. The fate of Lady Penelope's offspring remains shrouded in mystery."

"What of Robert, the cheesemonger? Is he implicated in this affair?"

"Lady Penelope mentioned him fleetingly, sir. She implied he provided financial assistance in exchange for her hospitality. Beyond that, I cannot say."

"And Evelyn? Was she the one responsible for Bella's demise?"

"Indeed, sir. Pressured by my master's demands, she carried out the deed. Yet, her attitude upon her return was...unsettling. She displayed a curious excitement, scarcely bothering to cleanse her hands of the bloodstains until prompted by Mr. Shelton. Her innocence is but a facade, I fear."

Claydon rose from his seat, joints protesting with every movement. "I believe that concludes our discussion for now. Please remain here until the inspector's return." With a tired sigh, he closed his notebook and exited the room, his weariness weighing heavily upon him. The clamour of his thoughts echoed in his mind, urging him to seek respite before exhaustion claimed him entirely.

As Claydon strode past the front desk, Banes caught a glimpse of him through the office window, where he was attending to Bailey. A chill ran down Banes's spine at the sight of Claydon's tense expression. He couldn't shake the feeling that Claydon was onto something, and fear gnawed at him, dreading that his past would come back to haunt him. It had been years since those dark days, and he prayed that Jeeves had long forgotten. He couldn't afford to let his sordid history resurface.

Once consumed by a madness born of an unhealthy obsession with Lady Penelope, his former flame, Banes had lost himself in a whirlwind of delusion and desire. But he had fought tooth and nail to rebuild his life and career, and he refused to let it all unravel now. The thought of Jeeves potentially exposing his secrets sent shivers down his spine. If sins could stain the skin, his hands would be crimson. The impending resolution of the case hung heavy in the air, and Banes knew he had to vanish, disappear back into the anonymity of London before the truth caught up with him, before he found himself among the ranks of the accused.

# CHAPTER FIFTY-THREE

# Cuffed

Amidst the sound of smashing and banging, fear gripped them all, paralysing them in place. Even Creed, typically unflinching, wore a mask of anguish as he retrieved a revolver from his pocket. If he were to go down, he'd take a few of those blue-uniformed pests with him. Edith's eyes widened at the sight of the weapon. "You can't shoot them!"

"Why not, little lady?" Creed retorted, a smirk playing on his lips.

"Because I'm innocent! I don't want to die!" Edith's voice rose above the noise as the door splintered under the assault. She darted past Creed, determination propelling her forward. "I'm leaving. You can stay here and die if you want, but I'm going to live!"

Meanwhile, Thornton slouched in his chair, his face draining of colour as he inspected his wound, a putrid stench wafting from it. He recoiled, retching at the sight, hastily pulling his trousers back down.

"You witch! This is your doing!" Thornton accused, his voice tinged with madness. "Creed, end her!"

Creed's grin widened as he aimed the revolver at Edith's head. "As you wish, Thornton."

But before he could pull the trigger, Bodmin intervened, diverting the shot to Edith's shoulder. She cried out in pain, clutching her wounded arm as she fled down the stairs.

"Leave her be!" Bodmin roared, grappling for the gun. But Creed shoved him aside, pursuing Edith with lethal intent, leaving Thornton alone in the room, laughter turning to silence.

Downstairs, gunfire erupted, mingled with Edith's anguished cries. Bodmin rushed to her aid, leaving Thornton to stew in his pain. Sweat beaded on his brow, his wound throbbing relentlessly, causing him to retch in agony.

"You're not looking too good," a voice observed from the doorway. Thornton lifted his gaze to see Chapman, a stern expression on his face. "You'd better tend to that leg, or you'll lose it."

Thornton scoffed. "Leave me be, you meddling blue bottle."

Chapman strode purposefully into the room, seizing Thornton by the arm with authority. "I'm afraid I can't let you off the hook. You're under arrest."

Thornton jerked his arm away, a twisted grin spreading across his face at the notion of finally facing consequences. "And what exactly am I being arrested for?"

"Harbouring fugitives, sir. That's a serious offence." Chapman moved to grab Thornton again, but the man stumbled, his legs buckling beneath him, the room spinning.

The ringing in Thornton's ears drowned out Chapman's commands. Vomit surged from his mouth, pooling at Chapman's feet. "I need backup in here!" Chapman yelled, struggling to keep Thornton upright. Another officer rushed in, strong arms hoisting Thornton to his feet.

"Put him in the back of the carriage. And what of the other one? Is he alive?" Chapman inquired, brushing himself off.

Thornton, tears streaming down his face, interjected, "Alive?

Who?"

But the officer ignored him, shaking his head in response to Chapman. "No, sir."

With a sigh, Chapman ordered, "Transfer the body to the mortuary. It could be crucial evidence."

As Thornton was dragged from the room, he felt weightless, his body limp and unresponsive. His mind swam with fog, unable to focus. He stumbled into the officer's grasp, marvelling at the man's strength as he was carried downstairs. The officer handled him like a feather, effortlessly navigating the steps.

In the light, Thornton caught sight of a slumped figure by the door, blood pooling beneath it. A scar etched across the cheek confirmed the worst: Creed was dead. "Creed!" Thornton screamed, struggling against the officer's grip. "Let me go, I need to—"

But his plea was drowned out as the officer's grip tightened, crushing Thornton's ribs. "Please," he gasped, "I can't breathe!"

Thornton's feeble protests fell on deaf ears as the officer unceremoniously tossed him into the carriage. "Quit your whining, or you'll have bigger problems than broken ribs," the officer threatened, slamming the door shut, enveloping Thornton in darkness.

Outside, a throng of curious onlookers clustered around the shop, their anxious voices blending with the chaotic flutter of startled birds taking flight from nearby rooftops. The police struggled to contain the crowd, urging them to step back.

Chapman's voice cut through the clamour, attempting to reassure the restless crowd. "Please, everyone, remain calm. All will be revealed in due time. Rest assured, the streets are now safe."

The crowd erupted in relieved applause, a ripple of gratitude spreading through their ranks as Chapman hurried back to the carriage. Meanwhile, Edith found herself sandwiched between two officers, her mind racing with uncertainty. She glanced nervously at them, attempting to strike up a conversation in the stifling silence, but her efforts were met with stony silence.

As the carriage rattled away, Thornton stole a glance at Bodmin's hunched form in the dim light. Relief washed over him; the burden of secrets and lies lifted from his shoulders. With nothing left to lose, he harboured thoughts of dragging everyone down with him, even contemplating falsehoods to implicate Edith. But a flicker of compassion stayed in his head—she, at least, deserved a fighting chance.

Yet, as the carriage trundled on, Thornton's resolve wavered. The weight of impending doom pressed down upon him, driving him to entertain darker thoughts. She had tried to kill him with a dirty needle. But as the shadows lengthened within the carriage, he couldn't shake the nagging feeling that, in the end, the truth would out, no matter the cost.

## CHAPTER FIFTY-FOUR

# A Secret Uncovered

The carriage ride to Lady Elspeth's mansion stretched on, a dreary journey through the mist-shrouded moors. The fog draped over the land like a heavy cloak, veiling the treacherous bogs that lurked ominously below. Each step of the horses was cautious, as if they too sensed the peril lurking beneath the murky waters.

Inside the carriage, Mary, Lizzie, and Billy sat in a sombre silence, their gazes fixed on the monotonous expanse of grey outside. The scent of damp moss and earth seeped into the cabin, mingling with the bone-chilling cold that permeated the air. Through the mist, the skeletal silhouettes of trees loomed, ghostly sentinels in the empty landscape.

Mary couldn't help but feel a pang of sympathy for the coachman, his haggard figure barely visible through the fog as he struggled to navigate the perilous terrain. Each cough and splutter echoed the hardships of their journey, a reminder of the harshness of their surroundings.

Guilt gnawed at Mary as she imagined the warmth and comfort awaiting them at Lady Elspeth's mansion. The crackling fire, the plush seats, the steaming cup of tea—such luxuries seemed like a distant dream amidst the bleakness of the moors.

Turning her gaze to Billy, Mary observed his jittery leg and unreadable expression. "Are you excited to see your friends, Billy?" she asked, her voice soft.

He didn't look her in the eye. Instead, he stared out the window, listening to the galloping hooves of the horses. "Yes," he said bluntly, his face remaining expressionless.

"I'm thrilled! New friends sound marvellous," Lizzie exclaimed, her joy palpable as she clapped her hands together.

Mary offered a tight-lipped smile, a twinge of elitism clouding her thoughts momentarily as she hesitated about her daughter mingling with the orphaned children. Quickly pushing aside such uncharitable musings, she focused on Lizzie's excitement. "How many friends do you think you'll make?"

"Lots and lots! I want as many friends like Billy," Lizzie exclaimed, her laughter bubbling forth like a brook.

Billy grinned crookedly at Lizzie, his affection for her evident as he tousled her curls. "There's only one Billy, but I'll be your friend," he said warmly.

The mansion's spires emerged from the mist, a reassuring sight for Mary, who silently thanked Providence for their safe arrival. If the weather persisted, she doubted her resolve to return home, unwilling to endanger the children. Perhaps a stay at Lady Elspeth's until the weather cleared would be prudent. Mary edged closer to the carriage door, anticipation mounting as they neared their destination.

A welcoming glow spilled from the mansion's windows, casting a warm aura that contrasted with the chill of the fog. The distant sounds of children's laughter reached them, stirring a tender maternal feeling in Mary's heart. She longed for the pitter-patter of more little feet, though she knew her husband would object. Still, she cherished Billy as her own, nurturing hopes of watching him blossom into adulthood.

The coachman's opening of the door snapped Mary out of her reverie, and she gratefully accepted his offered hand. Billy, less patient, bounded out of the carriage, nearly stumbling on the gravel path. Meanwhile, Lizzie darted ahead, her excitement propelling her towards the mansion's welcoming embrace, disappearing into the mist like a sprite drawn to its haven. A bright orange lamp on each side of the porch lit their way down the path.

"Be cautious, miss. At this time of year, the moors are treacherous," the coachman spoke quickly, his voice raspy and solemn. "I don't think I'll be returning to pick you up if the weather stays like this today, but if you like, I can fetch you tomorrow morning."

"Of course, whatever you believe to be best. Good day to you, sir." Mary reached into her purse and tipped him before turning to walk with Billy.

As they approached, the door swung open, revealing Lady Elspeth beaming at Billy. "My goodness, Billy, you look positively dapper!" she exclaimed.

Billy blushed at the compliment. "Thank you, Lady Elspeth."

With a warm gesture, she ushered them inside and closed the door behind them with a decisive thud. "Little Lizzie has already dashed off to join the other children. Billy, you're welcome to join them while I have a chat with Mary."

Billy nodded and made his way towards the sounds of laughter emanating from the hall. Mary and Lady Elspeth followed his departure with fond gazes before Lady Elspeth led Mary into the cosy lounge. A crackling fire greeted them, its warmth chasing away the chill of the outside world. They settled into plush chairs before the hearth, eager to thaw their cold fingers.

"It's dreadful weather out there. How was your journey?" Lady Elspeth inquired, smoothing her dress with practised grace.

"It was quite chilling, to be honest," Mary admitted, still trying to shake off the cold.

Keeping an eye on her guest, Lady Elspeth pulled a bell rope to summon a maid. A soft chime rang out, and a maid appeared promptly in the doorway. "Tea, please," Lady Elspeth requested with a nod.

The maid curtsied. "Right away, madam."

Turning her attention back to Mary, Lady Elspeth leaned in, her curiosity evident. "Any developments in the case?"

Mary nodded. "Progress is being made. Several arrests have been made in connection with the murders and the missing children."

Lady Elspeth's eyes sparkled with interest. "What of the missing children themselves? Have they been found?"

Mary's expression saddened. "Not yet, but I have hope. Bodmin, Thornton, and a man named Creed have been apprehended. There's also talk of a secret lovechild of Lady Penelope's."

Lady Elspeth leaned forward eagerly. "Do they know who the child is?"

Mary shook her head. "Not yet. But Shelton's butler may hold the key. He claims the child has a distinct birthmark on his right leg. However, it's been fifteen years. The child may be long gone. You of all people knew what Lady Penelope was like."

Lady Elspeth's countenance twisted with fury as she gazed into the crackling flames. "That woman was a scourge upon this earth. I rejoice in her death. She stole my husband, then discarded him like refuse. Her presence brought nothing but sorrow and ruin wherever she went. I thank Providence daily that she can no longer poison my life with her avarice and malice."

As Mary observed the fire reflecting in Lady Elspeth's eyes, a chill crept over her. Despite the warmth of the room, the bitterness in Lady Elspeth's words sent shivers down her spine. There was a darkness about the woman, a palpable aura of hostility that seemed to seep into the very air, corrupting everything it touched. Mary sensed that beneath Lady Elspeth's refined exterior lurked a profound bitterness, transforming her into something altogether more sinister—a creature consumed by hatred.

Before Lady Elspeth could continue, a gentle rap sounded at the door, and her demeanour shifted in an instant, the rage dissipating like mist in the sun. "Please, enter!"

The servant girl glided into the room, bearing a tray adorned with delicate porcelain. Wisps of steam curled from the teapot, filling the air with the soothing scent of herbs. Mary's anticipation grew as she watched the girl set the tray down with practised grace, her stomach fluttering at the sight of the exquisite tea set.

"Thank you," Mary said with a grateful smile as the servant poured, filling the room with the comforting aroma of freshly brewed tea. With deft movements, the girl attended to the room, straightening cushions and tidying with effortless efficiency. As she departed, she cast a discreet glance around the room, her departure leaving behind the faint fragrance of roses lingering in the air.

A bolt of lightning crackled outside the mansion, illuminating the room with a sudden flash, causing Mary to jump in her seat and nearly spill her teacup. Lady Elspeth chuckled softly. "Just a storm, my dear. Nothing to fear." Together, they watched as the tempest raged outside, rain pelting down on the gravel path. "Perhaps it would be wise for you and the children to stay the night. I wouldn't want you caught in this downpour."

The idea of spending the night in Lady Elspeth's grand estate had seemed appealing, but now, Mary's mind raced with uncertainty. She couldn't shake the feeling of unease that had settled over her since their arrival. Yet, the thought of venturing out into the storm with her children in tow was equally daunting. With a hesitant nod, she agreed. "Thank you, Lady Elspeth. I'm sure the children will be thrilled."

"My servants will prepare chambers for you in the east wing. It's rarely used since it belonged to my late husband," Lady Elspeth explained. Mary's spine tingled at the mention of Lady Elspeth's husband, who had vanished amidst the scandal surrounding Lady Penelope. Lady Elspeth caught Mary's apprehensive expression. "If he were alive, he would have returned by now. I believe he's passed," she added with a hint of resignation.

A piercing scream shattered the air, sending Mary and Lady Elspeth racing towards the commotion. Mary's heart pounded with dread as she feared for Lizzie's safety. Bursting through the doors into the hall, they found a group of servants gathered around a fallen figure. Mary pushed through the crowd, her motherly instincts kicking into overdrive. "What's happened?" she demanded.

As the crowd parted, Lady Elspeth joined Mary at the scene. It was Billy, writhing in pain on the floor, his leg scalded and blistered. Shattered crockery lay scattered around him. "Take him upstairs at once!" Lady Elspeth commanded.

Two servants swiftly lifted Billy and carried him up the staircase, Mary following close behind. In Lady Elspeth's room, they laid Billy on the bed, where Lady Elspeth wasted no time in tending to his injury. Mary watched, her heart heavy with worry, as Lady Elspeth inspected Billy's leg. Suddenly, she froze, her gaze fixed on a mark beneath the burn.

"What is it?" Mary asked, her voice trembling.

Lady Elspeth gently lifted Billy's thigh, revealing a peculiar birthmark, dark and distinctive against his pale skin. Mary's breath caught in her throat as she realised the significance of what she was seeing.

## CHAPTER FIFTY-FIVE

# Banes

In the dimly lit mortuary, Banes darted about with frantic urgency, stuffing his medical tools into his bag with haste. Every movement was laced with the fear of being discovered by Claydon. The sight of Jeeves earlier, with his telltale relief, sent shivers down Banes' spine. The butler had undoubtedly spilled the secrets of their shared past with Lady Penelope. Suspicion coiled around Banes like a tightening noose, driving him to a state of jittery paranoia as he scrambled to gather his belongings. If he didn't act fast, Claydon would connect the dots, and Banes would be left holding the blame. Silencing Jeeves was no longer an option; he needed an escape plan, and fast. He had managed to sneak out from the station and back to the hospital without anyone seeing him.

The mortuary's cold air gnawed at Banes, visible puffs of breath escaping his lips as he scurried about. Gurneys cluttered the space, hindering his movements as he navigated the cramped room. On the embalming tables lay new arrivals, their faces etched with frozen terror, their skin eerily pallid and artificial, like macabre wax sculptures.

Amidst the mayhem, one body seized Banes' attention—a woman's torso, bloated and slick with moisture, a grim testament to the horrors of mortality. His pulse quickened as realisation dawned. "They've found her," he muttered, the weight of his words hanging heavy in the frigid air.

He hadn't intended to snuff out her life, yet the rush of cutting off her breath overwhelmed him, pushing him past the point of no return. Accidental as it was, her death unleashed something primal within him, coursing through his veins like a potent poison. It stirred memories long dormant, a surge of adrenaline he hadn't felt since his youth. The thrill of domination mingled with remorse, a tumultuous cocktail of conflicting emotions. He thought he'd sworn off such violence, yet here he was, succumbing to its allure once more.

After covering his tracks as best he could, he had fled, scattering her remains across the city, erasing any trace of her identity. She was but a nameless wanderer of the night, seeking easy coin, eager to please until her unfortunate encounter with him turned fatal. Lady Penelope was the sole confidante of his tormented past, a past he'd bared to her in moments of intimacy, finding solace in her acceptance of his darker desires. With her gone, the floodgates of his suppressed urges burst open, unleashing a torrent he struggled to contain.

His brow beaded with sweat, his pulse thundering in his ears, he cast furtive glances at the door, fearing discovery. There was no plausible excuse for his erratic behaviour, no desire to justify himself to anyone. All he craved was escape, to vanish from prying eyes into the shadows.

A sound outside the door jolted him, his heart leaping into his throat as he clutched his bag close. Praying it wasn't Claydon, he braced himself as the door creaked open, revealing a wide-eyed Harvard. "Sir, are you here?"

Perplexed and startled, Banes rose from his hiding spot, setting his bag down on the table with a thud. "I thought you were still in custody."

Relief flooded Harvard's face as he gently shut the door behind him. "I managed to slip away. The guard nodded off and dropped the keys." His eyes flickered to Banes's bulging medical bag. "Leaving the city?"

"That's not your concern, Harvard. My business here is concluded, and it's time for me to move on. Back to London, to broaden my medical horizons," Banes replied, every word a fabrication.

Harvard's gaze sharpened with suspicion. "I've heard whispers from the police station. The walls in that place have ears. Every secret echoes through them."

Banes trembled as his eyes darted toward the mortuary's rear exit. "I need to leave."

"Take me with you. Please," Harvard pleaded, gripping Banes's arm. "If you don't, I'll have no choice but to reveal your destination. They'll hunt you down, sir. Let me assist you, protect you. You're not as spry as you once were."

Reluctantly, Banes relented. His ageing body was beginning to betray him, and he knew he needed assistance. "Fine, but we must hurry. Let's go."

"Where are we headed?" Harvard asked, trailing behind Banes.

Banes pressed a finger to his lips, urging silence as he grabbed his medical bag before slipping out the door. The storm outside had intensified, the air thick and oppressive. They darted through alleyways, avoiding the prying eyes of passersby, seeking refuge from the impending deluge. But the city was abuzz with talk of Lady Penelope's murder, making escape near impossible.

As they darted through the shadows, a police officer's whistle pierced the air. Banes yanked Harvard into a hiding spot, their hearts pounding in sync with the drumming rain. They watched as officers corralled suspects into awaiting carriages, their faces obscured by dark sacks.

"They've apprehended someone," Banes remarked, a smirk playing on his lips as he observed the scene.

"We need to go. They may have noticed our absence. And we have to pass by the police station to get to the docks," Harvard urged, his voice tinged with worry.

They melted into the throng, but Banes's nerves betrayed him, and he collided with a passerby. Claydon's shout rang through the air, pointing straight at a panicked Harvard.

"They're there!"

With a decisive grip, Harvard seized Banes by the shoulders, propelling him through the bustling throng like a master puppeteer. Leaving Banes behind was out of the question; he was the sole individual who had ever treated Harvard as an equal.

"Don't let them get away!"

The urgency in Claydon's voice spurred Harvard on, igniting a surge of adrenaline coursing through his veins. Without hesitation, he scooped up Banes, his own legs carrying them swiftly through the maze of alleyways to safety.

## CHAPTER FIFTY-SIX

# The Cells

In the cramped confines of the jail, inmates awaited their grim fate, their execution looming ever closer. Iron bars separated them, mere barriers between them and their inevitable fate. The air was thick with a putrid stench, invading every corner of the cellblock with its foul presence. Lightning flashed sporadically, casting brief illumination on the desolate cells before plunging them back into darkness. Etchings on the walls bore witness to the desperate attempts of past prisoners to escape, their claw marks a haunting reminder of their futile struggles.

Ignoring Acker's gaze, Bodmin's sanity teetered on the brink as he surveyed the grim surroundings, his resolve waning with each passing moment. Acker, positioned before the row of cells, observed his charges with a critical eye, his hands clasped behind his back. The guard responsible for Harvard's escape had been swiftly dismissed, Acker refusing to tolerate any more incompetence among his ranks. With a court appearance looming, Acker sought redemption, replacing the negligent guard with a more focused successor.

Across the room, the new guard maintained a vigilant watch over the inmates, his sharp eyes tracking their every move. Satisfied with his choice, Acker turned his attention to Thornton, whose pallid complexion and profuse sweating betrayed the infection on his leg. Thornton's feeble attempts to garner sympathy did little to sway Acker's determination. Casting a glance at Bodmin, who rocked back and forth on his stool, Acker's thoughts momentarily turned to Edith. Her soft sobs echoed through the cellblock, eliciting a twinge of guilt in Acker's conscience.

"Madam, enough of that racket," Acker snapped, his irritation visible as Edith's sniffles persisted. Wrestling with his conscience, Acker relented, unlocking Edith's cell door with a heavy heart. "Get out of here."

Edith silently complied as Acker guided her out of the cell, her gaze fixed firmly on the ground to avoid the lecherous remarks of her fellow inmates. With a heavy heart, she followed Acker up the station steps, bracing herself for the impending interrogation. "I have some questions for you," Acker informed her tersely.

"Please, sir, believe me. I was compelled to accompany my master. I had no part in his actions," she pleaded, tears welling in her eyes once more.

Pushed into the interrogation room, Edith's distress turned to horror as she noticed Jeeves slumped in his chair, a medical instrument protruding from his chest. She recoiled in shock, collapsing into Acker's arms in a mix of terror and despair.

"I need assistance!" Acker called out, his voice betraying his shock rather than anger.

Chapman hurried to the scene, his brow furrowed in concern as he took in the grisly sight. Acker gently lowered Edith to the ground, his mind racing with the need to shield her from further trauma. "Take her to my office," he instructed a passing officer. "Give her something to calm her nerves."

Chapman hesitated, voicing his concern. "But, sir, what about the investigation? Shouldn't we keep her under observation?"

"I believe she's innocent," Acker asserted. With a nod to the officer, Edith was whisked away, leaving Acker to confront the grim reality before him.

Acker knelt beside Jeeves, his fingers seeking a pulse he knew would not be there. "He should have been guarded," he muttered to himself, a pang of guilt gnawing at his conscience. Surveying the room, his eyes fell upon Claydon's pencil, a clue to the mystery unfolding before him. "Fetch Claydon," Acker ordered Chapman.

Chapman's words hit Acker like a blow to the chest. "Claydon's after Banes and Harvard," he repeated, his voice edged with concern as he watched Acker scour the room for clues.

"Banes?" Acker's eyes widened in disbelief.

Chapman could feel a cold sweat breaking out on his forehead as he relayed the unsettling news. "Yes, sir. Banes escaped earlier with Harvard. Jeeves mentioned that Banes might have been involved in Lady Penelope's childbirth."

Acker's agitation was palpable as he pinched the bridge of his nose. "So, you're telling me our own medical expert could be implicated in the very crime we've been investigating?"

Chapman nodded solemnly, bracing for Acker's inevitable eruption. "Yes, sir. It seems that way."

A wave of frustration washed over Acker as he processed the implications. "So, all the evidence provided by Banes could be tainted because he might be the culprit?" He clenched his jaw, struggling to contain his rising anger. He had placed his trust in Banes, and now it seemed that trust had been misplaced. Paranoia gnawed at him as he realised there might be no safe haven within the station.

With Bailey's safety in mind, Acker stormed out of the room, ignoring Chapman's questioning gaze as he headed toward the office where he had last seen Banes tending to him.

"Where are you going?" Chapman's voice echoed after him.

Ignoring the question, Acker burst into the office, his heart pounding in his chest as he found Bailey lying in a chair, his complexion drained of colour. "Bailey!"

Acker gently tapped Bailey's clammy cheeks, hoping to rouse him from the brink of death, but it was futile. Desperation gnawed at him; Bailey's time was slipping away, and Acker felt powerless to stop it. The urgency of the situation weighed heavy on his shoulders; there was no time to find another doctor, no time to save Bailey.

The realisation hit Acker like a ton of bricks—he had failed, and the consequences would be dire. Panic surged through him as he contemplated the legal fallout. Losing his job seemed inevitable now, a bitter pill to swallow.

Chapman hovered behind him, his own distress mirroring Acker's. "Oh no," he murmured, his voice heavy with regret. The sight of Bailey's fading breaths filled them both with a profound sense of shame. "He's not going to make it, is he?"

As Bailey's pulse faded, guilt etched itself across Acker's features. "No, he isn't, and we're to blame." The weight of responsibility bore down on him as Bailey drew his final breath.

Acker recoiled from the body, grappling with the enormity of their failure. "I can't believe it. Two witnesses dead," he muttered, his voice laced with guilt. Turning to Chapman, he faced the grim reality ahead. "We'll be held accountable for this. There will be an inquest, and we'll likely lose our jobs."

Chapman struggled to comprehend the magnitude of their predicament. "But how were we supposed to know about Banes's connection to Lady Penelope?"

Acker shook his head wearily. "It doesn't matter now. We'll be blamed regardless."

For the first time, Chapman saw vulnerability in Acker's eyes, a stark departure from his usual stoicism. He wanted to offer comfort, but they were both ensnared in the same web of incompetence.

Acker sank into a chair beside Bailey's lifeless form, his mind racing with desperate thoughts. "For now, we keep this under wraps. We see this case through to the end before they strip me of my position," he instructed Chapman. "Find my brother. Tell no one else. Lock up the interrogation room. I'll wait here."

Chapman nodded, his heart heavy with resignation. As he left the room, a sense of foreboding settled over him. The road ahead was fraught with uncertainty, but he was determined to see the case through, no matter the cost.

## CHAPTER FIFTY-SEVEN

## Claydon

The city's alleyways loomed dark and forbidding as Claydon raced through them, each turn leading to yet another dead end. Piles of debris cluttered the paths, and women draped in finery lurked in the shadows, beckoning with coy gestures. Claydon paid them no mind; he had neither the time nor the inclination for such distractions. Raised in opulence alongside his brother, he couldn't fathom the desperate existence of these women, their threadbare garments a stark contrast to his own privileged upbringing.

Grateful for his affluent background, Claydon couldn't imagine enduring the squalor that surrounded him. He glanced at the women, noting the grime that marred their skin and the tattered state of their attire. Their desperate circumstances painted a grim picture, a world away from his own.

Approaching cautiously, Claydon held up a hand to forestall

their propositions. "Ladies, we're here on official business, not to engage in your services. We need to ask you a few questions."

"It'll cost you," one replied, her Cockney accent thick with defiance.

Rolling his eyes, Claydon tossed her a coin. "Will you answer our questions now?"

"A penny for each," she demanded, a smirk playing at her lips.

Sighing, Claydon produced a silver coin from his pocket. "Fine," he conceded, eager to be done with the exchange. "Have you seen two men pass through here in the last hour?"

Accepting the coin with a grin, she pointed down the alley. "Two men dashed that way, leaping over the wall. One carried a large bag."

"Thank you, ladies," Claydon replied, retreating from their solicitation. "You've been most helpful."

"Are you sure you don't want some company for the night?" she called after him.

"No, thank you, madam," Claydon replied, hastening toward the wall where Banes and Harvard had fled. "Biggins, give me a boost."

Claydon clambered onto Biggins' back as the man knelt in the filth, using him as a boost to scale the wall. Gripping the edge, Claydon hauled himself up and then extended a hand to assist Biggins. "The rest of you, circle around to the rear. We need to trap them," he commanded.

"Where do you reckon they're headed, sir?" Biggins asked after leaping across.

Balanced on the wall, Claydon surveyed the surroundings. Buildings hemmed them in, with a glimpse of Bristol's dock visible between two derelict factories. A sly smirk touched his lips as he glanced down at Biggins. "I've got a hunch. Follow me!" With a bound, he landed on the ground and took off toward the docks, urging Biggins to keep pace.

They dashed through the paths until they reached the empty dock, once bustling with the day's activity. The hollow echo of their footsteps resonated across the wooden planks, setting Claydon's nerves on edge. Failure was not an option; he had to find them. Disappointment from his brother was the last thing he wanted. "You check that side. I'll take this one," he instructed.

Following orders, Biggins veered away, eyes scanning the crates ahead. Claydon made a beeline for the abandoned factories, ears straining for any clue amidst the dock's eerie silence. Faint cries of a child drifted from one of the buildings. His heart raced as he halted by a weathered red door, listening intently. The sobbing was unmistakable. Taking a deep breath, he nudged the door open, senses alert to the darkness within.

Drawing his revolver, Claydon cautiously navigated the debris-strewn floor. The chorus of infant wails grew louder, propelling him forward. As he approached, he discerned multiple voices mingling in anguish. Adrenaline surged as he pressed on.

Following the sound, he arrived at a padlocked door. It needed to be broken, but gunfire risked revealing his position if Banes and Harvard were nearby. Assessing the door's state, he noted its decrepit condition, juxtaposed with the sturdy lock. Gripping a rusted pole nearby, he wedged it into the lock, applying force to loosen it. With a final thrust, the lock shattered, clattering to the ground.

Without hesitation, he kicked the door open, pistol at the ready. The room greeted him with emptiness, save for the debris littering the floor. The persistent sobbing guided his search, leading him to a hatch concealed beneath an old factory engine.

Wiping his brow, he crouched to move the heavy machinery. His muscles strained against the weight, fuelled by adrenaline as he pushed forward. "Is anyone down there?" he called, muscles burning as he revealed another locked hatch. "Police!" The crying faltered briefly before intensifying. "Please respond!" Claydon gasped for breath.

"Help us!" a child's voice pleaded from below.

Biggins burst into the room, startling Claydon, who reacted instinctively, firing his weapon. Gunpowder filled the air, leaving Claydon disoriented as his ears rang with the aftermath. The children's cries mingled with Biggins's shocked protests.

"Why did you shoot?" Biggins's voice trembled with fear.

Claydon's heart sank as he realised his mistake. "I... I thought I was under attack," he stammered, remorse flooding his veins.

"You'd regret it if you actually shot me," Biggins grumbled, brushing dirt from his knees. His gaze swept the room, searching for the source of the commotion. "What's all that noise?"

Claydon gestured toward the partially hidden hatch. "That's what I'm trying to find out. Can you lend a hand?"

Biggins joined him, both men straining against the weight of the engine. Amidst the children's sobs, their breaths echoed, a symphony of effort and anguish. Biggins couldn't help but chuckle inwardly at the realisation that even his sergeant wasn't immune to physical strain.

"Did you come here because you couldn't locate Banes and Harvard?" Claydon asked.

Biggins nodded, focusing on the task at hand. "Yes, sir. And I heard your call for help, so I hurried over. That's when you took a shot at me."

Claydon's snarl conveyed his disapproval. "That's no laughing matter, Biggins."

Biggins huffed, exerting himself as they pushed the engine aside. "I wasn't joking, sir."

As they caught their breath, Claydon motioned toward the door. "There's an old pipe in the hallway. Fetch it for me, would you?"

Biggins disappeared briefly, returning with the pipe. Instead of handing it over, he gently nudged Claydon aside. "Let me handle this, sir. You need to rest."

Claydon acquiesced, allowing Biggins to wield the pipe against the lock. Each blow vibrated through the floor, sending dust throughout the room. Finally, with a crack, the lock gave way. Biggins swung the hatch open, revealing a group of emaciated children huddled in the cramped space beneath the floorboards. Their eyes pleaded silently, afraid to speak.

Claydon retrieved his police identification from his pocket and displayed it to the frightened children. "You're safe now."

As Biggins reached out to assist them, their expressions shifted from fear to relief. "Let's get you out of there quickly," he assured them.

Claydon surveyed the children's grimy attire, clearly too big for their frail frames, as Biggins carefully lifted them out one by one. "I believe these might be the missing orphans, Biggins. We need to secure this area to gather evidence. Thornton's going down for this!"

A noise from outside interrupted them, halting their movements. They listened intently in the darkness, hearing the faint shuffling of footsteps around the front entrance.

Claydon gestured for silence, motioning the children to stay quiet as he cautiously approached the door to peek outside. Meanwhile, Biggins wiped the dusty window with his sleeve, revealing only darkness beyond.

Suddenly, a bright orange explosion illuminated the entryway, sending shockwaves through the abandoned building. Flames licked up the walls, devouring everything in their path. Biggins's heart raced as he spotted Banes and Harvard fleeing toward a massive cargo ship on the other side of the dock.

"Biggins! Quickly, I need your help!" Claydon's urgent cry echoed from the hallway.

The children huddled together in fear as they whimpered and cried. Biggins struggled to reassure them amidst the chaos.

"Biggins, hurry!" Claydon's voice cracked with desperation.

The scent of oil mingled with burning wood assaulted their senses as the fire spread rapidly, engulfing each level of the building. The night sky blazed with fiery intensity, signalling to the nearby neighbours that the dock was ablaze. Biggins coughed and sputtered, wading through the thick smoke.

Claydon grasped his shoulders, pulling him away from the inferno. "We must extinguish this fire before the entire place goes up in flames!"

Biggins saw the fear reflected in Claydon's eyes and understood that if his sergeant felt afraid, their situation was dire. "But with what, sir? This building is ancient; it'll crumble any minute now. We're trapped."

Claydon's determination remained steadfast. "We can't afford to think like that. We have innocent children in there. We must get them out, no matter the cost. It's our duty."

A section of the ceiling collapsed, narrowly missing Claydon. They both recoiled, fearing they'd be buried alive. Biggins felt panic rising within him. The thought of being trapped beneath rubble was his worst nightmare, now threatening to become reality. Despite his mounting dread, he knew he had to keep a clear head. But the smoke choked him, clouding his thoughts and suffocating him with its acrid odour. It seemed there was no way out.

## CHAPTER FIFTY-EIGHT

# A Horrible Surprise

The house lay shrouded in a sombre darkness, a reflection of the servants' melancholy. With their master recently murdered, they found themselves without employment. Yet, amidst the gloom, a discovery altered their perception of their late mistress. Tucked beneath her bed lay a hidden chest, a trove of Lady Penelope's secrets. Photographs and newspaper clippings chronicled her life, unveiling a side of her unknown to her staff.

In the wake of their master's demise, the servants resolved to organise the household, salvaging items for auction or sale to distant relatives. Shelton's request, made in anticipation of his own death, compelled them to discreetly sift through their belongings. As preparations for his funeral commenced, the servants anticipated a solitary attendance.

Despite the hardship endured by Lady Penelope and Shelton, the photographs revealed a different narrative. Amidst the scattered images, the servants discerned a glimpse of happiness—a testament to the couple's shared joy, captured in moments frozen in time. Though the faces in the photographs remained solemn, the essence of their past happiness lingered, offering a bittersweet revelation to those left behind.

The silence in the room was tangible, disturbed only by the rustling of photographs and the heavy weight of uncertainty pressing down on the servants. Without Jeeves, their stalwart leader, they felt adrift, rudderless in a sea of chaos. Each image laid bare a fragment of their mistress's clandestine life, weaving a tapestry of intrigue and scandal.

As they huddled on the floor amidst the wreckage of their once orderly home, the servants were spellbound by the provocative snapshots before them. Erotic and illicit, the photographs revealed Lady Penelope's clandestine liaisons with a parade of shadowy figures. Though such evidence of her indiscretions was technically illegal, the allure of the black market rendered such concerns moot.

In stunned silence, they pored over every image, each one a damning testament to their mistress's secrets. Signed by their respective suitors, the photographs painted a vivid portrait of a woman entangled in a web of forbidden passion. Among the familiar faces of Thornton and Banes, they discovered a young Lady Penelope, radiant yet vulnerable, cradling a swell of life within her. The revelation left them reeling, confirming whispered rumours of her infidelity.

"So, it's true," Ruth breathed, her voice barely above a whisper as she traced the curve of Lady Penelope's pregnant form. "Evelyn wasn't lying."

Anne, her eyes fixed on Thornton's smouldering gaze, scoffed softly. "You can't trust Evelyn's words, but these pictures speak for themselves. Thornton may be trouble, but there's a certain allure to him in this picture."

"Where do you think the child is now?" Ruth asked, ignoring Anne's comment about Thornton.

She shrugged her shoulders and glanced around at the other servants. "I have no idea. If he was thrown into one of those awful workhouses, he is most likely dead by now. Those places aren't appropriate for a slave, let alone a child."

Another servant girl stepped forward with a fistful of pictures. "There's more. I found these in her drawer over there." She pointed to Lady Penelope's bedside table before dropping them in front of Ruth, covering up the picture of Thornton in the process.

"I believe we should gather these up and deliver them to the police station. This is evidence," Anne said as she began sorting through the new photos.

"I wouldn't rush to that conclusion, Anne. Have a look at this." Ruth displayed a photograph for everyone to see. "Do you recognise him?"

The servants stopped what they were doing and looked at the photo. They stared in shock, wide-eyed and frozen to the spot as Ruth held it up. They knew exactly who it was. It was a photo of Superintendent Landrake sitting on a velvet chair with Lady Penelope wrapped around him, staring straight at the camera with a smirk on his lips. Ruth dropped the picture as if it had caught alight. "I think we should destroy this one."

Amidst the flickering candlelight, tension crackled in the air as Ruth's question hung heavy in the room, cutting through Anne's insistence on preserving evidence. The servants exchanged anxious glances, acutely aware of the precariousness of their situation.

"I don't know, Ruth," Anne admitted, her voice trembling slightly as she clutched the incriminating photograph. "But we can't just destroy it. It's proof of... of something."

Ruth's gaze hardened, her resolve unyielding as she scanned the faces of her fellow servants. "And what good will proof do us if it lands us in even greater danger? If Superintendent Landrake finds out we possess this, we'll be in hot water, mark my words."

A shiver ran down the collective spine of the group as they contemplated the implications of their discovery. The photograph lay on the floor where Anne had dropped it, as dangerous as a ticking time bomb, its presence a silent threat to their security.

"Perhaps Ruth is right," another servant murmured. "We should consider our options carefully."

Anne hesitated, torn between her instinct to uphold justice and the stark reality of their vulnerability. "But... but we can't just ignore it. We have a duty to-"

"Our duty is to protect ourselves first," Ruth interrupted firmly, her eyes full of determination. "We'll dispose of the photograph, and that will be the end of it."

"But it's evidence, Ruth. We can't just give it away. We should take it to Inspector Acker," Anne persisted, picking the photograph up off the floor.

Ruth shook her head, her hands trembling visibly now. "Inspector Acker answers to the superintendent, Anne. If we give him that photo, it'll only end up in the wrong hands. Trust me, we don't want to be on the wrong side of the chief of police."

A murmur of agreement rippled through the group of servants behind Anne. "She's right, Anne. We're just servants. We can't risk our lives over this. It's not worth it."

"But what if he's involved in our mistress's murder? Don't we owe it to her to find out the truth?" Anne pleaded.

Ruth scoffed, her disdain visible. "We don't owe that woman anything. She treated us all like dirt, including you, Anne. Remember that."

Anne's gaze drifted to the faint scars on her wrists, a painful reminder of Lady Penelope's cruelty. "I haven't forgotten."

Ruth seized the photograph from Anne and passed it to another servant, who promptly tossed it into the fireplace. Anne watched in dismay as the evidence of their mistress's secrets turned to ash before her eyes.

Ruth moved to collect the remaining photos. "Let's put these back in the chest. We'll deal with them later, under cover of darkness."

Reluctantly, the other servants followed suit, their actions a blend of obedience and apprehension. Anne joined them, her fingers trembling as she gathered the photographs. But as she reached for another picture, her breath caught in her throat. It was another photo of Lady Penelope and Superintendent Landrake, locked in an intimate embrace. Without hesitation, Anne slipped it into her pocket, her mind racing with the implications of what she had just uncovered.

## CHAPTER FIFTY-NINE

# Trapped

The crackling flames cast dancing shadows across the room, enveloping Mary and Lady Elspeth in a cocoon of warmth as they sat in hushed contemplation. Having returned from the bedroom where Billy still lay, Mary sensed a weighty silence hanging between them, thick with unspoken thoughts and emotions.

The discovery of Billy's birthmark had left a strained tension in the air, and Mary couldn't shake the feeling that Lady Elspeth was grappling with something profound. There was a pallor to her complexion, a weariness in her gaze that spoke volumes. Mary couldn't help but wonder what secrets lay hidden beneath the surface of Lady Elspeth's stoic facade.

Despite her own astonishment at the revelation, Mary couldn't ignore the unsettling atmosphere that had settled over the room. The storm outside raged on unabated, adding an ominous backdrop to their uneasy silence.

"Are you alright, Lady Elspeth?" Mary ventured, her voice hesitant.

Lady Elspeth jumped at the sound of her name, her eyes

flickering with a fleeting expression of surprise before settling back into a mask of composure. "I'm perfectly fine, my dear. Why do you ask?"

Mary hesitated, unsure of how to broach the subject delicately. "You just seem... quiet, now that you know about Billy."

A wistful smile tugged at the corners of Lady Elspeth's lips as she turned her gaze towards the flickering flames. "It's just a shock to me, that's all," she admitted softly, her voice tinged with a hint of sadness. She took a sip of her now-cold tea, the taste unfamiliar and unwelcome on her tongue. She replaced the tea back onto the tray. "But I'm not entirely convinced that Billy is the witch's son. A birthmark, however peculiar, does not make Billy the heir. Many children bear such marks without consequence."

Mary nodded, though her unease lingered like a spectre in the room. There was something more to Lady Elspeth's words, a depth of emotion that Mary couldn't quite fathom. As the storm raged outside, Mary couldn't shake the feeling that they were on the precipice of something far greater than either of them could imagine.

She mirrored Lady Elspeth's action, setting down her untouched tea with a gentle clink against the delicate china. "Lady Elspeth, it's undeniable. Billy fits all the criteria. He's the right age, bears the birthmark, and was left at the same orphanage where Lady Penelope abandoned her child."

Lady Elspeth's demeanour shifted, her eyes betraying a flicker of discomfort. "I'm not convinced of that."

"There's only one way to confirm it—by having someone who's seen the birthmark verify it," Mary persisted.

Lady Elspeth's countenance darkened, her jaw tensing as she fixed a piercing gaze on Mary. "He is not her child!"

Mary recoiled at Lady Elspeth's sudden vehemence, her heart pounding with fear. Though she hesitated, curiosity overpowered her fear. "Why are you so certain Billy isn't Lady Penelope's son?"

"Because I ensured that the baby wouldn't survive. That's why!" Lady Elspeth's voice cracked with fury, drawing the attention of a nearby servant who cautiously entered the room.

"Is everything all right, madam?" the servant inquired, her eyes darting between Lady Elspeth and Mary.

Lady Elspeth's fury intensified as she turned her glare on the servant. "Get out!"

Shocked by her mistress's outburst, the servant hurriedly retreated, leaving the room in an uneasy silence. Mary longed to follow her, to escape the tension that hung heavy in the air, but she remained rooted to her seat, her mind reeling with disbelief.

"Lady Elspeth," Mary began, her voice trembling, "why are you telling me this? I can't imagine someone as kind-hearted as you committing such a terrible act."

"Oh, Mary, there are many things I'm not proud of," Lady Elspeth admitted, her gaze fixed on the tea in front of her. "But when anger consumes me, I say things I shouldn't. I'm sorry you had to hear it. But now you know."

"So, it's true?" Mary's voice wavered as she struggled to comprehend the gravity of Lady Elspeth's confession.

Lady Elspeth nodded, her expression fraught with worry. "It was my butler's doing. Billy cannot be Lady Penelope's son. If he is, my butler has betrayed me and lied." She sighed heavily, visibly distressed by the revelation. "Mary, I'm not a bad person. I couldn't allow Lady Penelope's lineage to continue. She brought nothing but misery to my life, like a dark shadow looming over every moment of happiness I ever had."

Lady Elspeth's struggle with revealing her true nature was evident to Mary, who sensed a deeper turmoil brewing beneath the surface. But Mary's greatest fear wasn't about Lady Elspeth's past—it was about protecting Billy from whatever fate awaited him. "How could you bring harm to an innocent child? It's simply unconscionable."

"Mary, I couldn't bring myself to do it. Though I orchestrated it, it was my butler who carried out the deed. I'm not proud of my actions, but they've transpired, and I cannot change them." Lady Elspeth's gaze turned solemn. "Hence, the child upstairs cannot possibly be Lady Penelope's son."

"But what if he is? What if your servant failed and lied to you?"

"In that case, Mary, I'll have to handle it myself. I refuse to let that wretched woman's lineage persist."

"And what about the orphans you've taken in? What about them? Will you also dispose of them? What will happen when they learn the truth about the kind lady who cares for them?" Mary's voice grew heated as she rose to her feet, leaning over Lady Elspeth's chair with intensity. "I've longed for a child with my husband, but God has blessed me with only one. You're surrounded by innocence and joy, and yet you would strip it away? Lady Elspeth, you don't realise how fortunate you are!"

Lady Elspeth reclined in her chair, her expression serene and contemplative. "Mary, I'm not wicked. If you witnessed Lady Penelope's deeds, you'd understand my actions." She raised her hand, halting Mary's response. "Rest assured, no harm will befall the children. But if the boy upstairs is truly Lady Penelope's son, I'll do what should have been done long ago. Nothing will sway me—not you, nor your husband the detective."

"This is wrong! I won't let you harm him!" Mary's anger surged as she beheld Lady Elspeth's tranquil countenance. This wasn't the woman she knew; this was a twisted version shaped by Lady Penelope's influence. "If you think you can harm my child, you're mistaken. You're worse than Lady Penelope!"

Lady Elspeth's face twisted with rage, her eyes flashing with hostility. Her sudden movement startled Mary, but she held her ground as Lady Elspeth loomed over her. Bitterness dripped from her words like venom. "I am nothing like that witch! I've never stolen someone's husband, or slept with countless men!" Lady Elspeth erupted, nearly knocking Mary off balance. "You have no right to speak to me in such a manner. Besides, the boy isn't even yours. He's not your son."

Her words pierced Mary's heart like shards of glass. She had longed for a son, but after the traumatic birth of her daughter, she couldn't bear another child. Stepping back from the chair, she struggled to compose herself. "He may not share my blood, but he is my son. I've raised him, nurtured him into a fine young man. You acknowledged it yourself!"

Lady Elspeth's indifference stung, but Mary refused to back down. "If that's what you choose to believe, so be it."

The atmosphere in the room grew even heavier, suffocating, and bleak. What had once been a cosy lounge filled with warmth and life now felt like a vacuum, sucking away every glimmer of hope from Mary. It was as though the storm clouds outside had infiltrated the room, staining everything with their fury. Amidst the deafening roar of rain against the windowpanes, Mary's racing heart was the only sound she could hear. She regretted coming here—Lady Elspeth was supposed to offer solace and safety, but instead, Mary felt like she had stepped into another realm. Her mind raced, searching for a way to thwart Lady Elspeth's dreadful intentions as she stared into the woman's grave eyes.

Lady Elspeth cleared her throat, her voice slicing through the tension like a blade. "I believe this conversation has taken an unfortunate turn. Perhaps we should enjoy some more tea and discuss lighter matters for a while." She flashed a smile, her gaze shifting to the servant's bell beside her. "Would you care for some cake as well?"

It was as if a switch had been flipped, and the conflict had never occurred. Lady Elspeth's demeanour softened, and her face regained its warmth, erasing the furrows of concern. Mary was at a loss. Despite being mere feet away, she felt a chilling sense of isolation. Lady Elspeth seemed to possess two distinct personas—the sinister one fading into the background, replaced by her usual cheerful self. Mary couldn't help but wonder who else had witnessed Lady Elspeth's darker side and what other secrets she harboured. Though Lady Elspeth awaited her response, Mary remained silent, fearing to provoke her wrath once more. She could only manage a nod, allowing the servant bell to be rung once more by the woman who claimed to be gentle and caring to all.

This time, a different servant girl appeared, her demeanour bright and cheerful as she carried out her mistress's orders. Oblivious to Mary's distress, she curtsied and left the room.

Mary stole a glance at the tempest outside, longing for escape yet reluctant to abandon the orphans under Lady Elspeth's care.

"Mary, please take a seat. You're cluttering up my lounge," Lady Elspeth remarked casually, drawing Mary's gaze back to her. "Isn't the storm mesmerising? Soon, the wetlands will be flooded. My heart aches for the poor animals without shelter out there."

Mary watched Lady Elspeth closely as she chose a seat far from her. "I must leave soon. My husband will be worried."

"You're not going anywhere, Mary," Lady Elspeth said calmly, her grin widening. She resembled a predator ready to strike. "It's far too dangerous outside."

# CHAPTER SIXTY

## The Photograph

Acker remained immobile in his seat even after Chapman had left to locate Claydon. Bailey's lifeless form slouched in the chair, his once-alert eyes now glazed over, his complexion taking on a waxy pallor with each passing minute. Beyond the confines of the room, the frenetic activity of his officers echoed. Acker's mind buzzed with questions about the unfolding chaos, but his fatigued body refused to cooperate, anchoring him to his seat as he pondered the uncertain future of his career. He couldn't afford for the superintendent to learn about the deaths of the two witnesses from anyone else but him.

Summoning the last reserves of energy, Acker shifted his weary limbs into a more comfortable position before slowly rising to stretch. Joints creaked and protested, a stark reminder of his overdue need for rest. However, the weight of responsibility pressed heavily upon him, urging him to push forward and unravel the intricate web of mysteries shrouding the recent events. While relieved that the case of the missing children had been resolved, Acker couldn't shake the nagging suspicion of its potential connection to Lady Penelope's murder.

Surveying the room, Acker's gaze landed on the communications office through the window of the door, its glass door offering a glimpse of the rarely utilised telegraph within. Now, in this moment of urgency, it became the linchpin of his plan. With a faint glimmer of determination, Acker needed to dispatch a message to the superintendent, summoning him to the station without delay. Hastily draping a nearby woollen blanket over Bailey's body, Acker hoped to conceal the grim sight until he could inform his superior of the horrible developments.

With a silent prayer that his actions would go unnoticed amidst the mayhem of the station, Acker gingerly pushed open the door, wincing at the loud creak of the rusty hinges. Heart pounding in his chest, he darted past his bewildered officers, determined to reach the communications room without attracting undue attention. The thrum of activity masked his hurried footsteps as he slipped into the room, exhaling a sigh of relief as the door slammed shut behind him, muffling the noise from outside.

Time was of the essence as Acker seized the Morse code book from the desk, his fingers trembling. Normally, he would delegate the task of relaying messages, but in the current climate of suspicion and distrust, he dared not entrust this vital task to anyone else. Paranoia gnawed at his mind, casting suspicion on every member of his team, leaving him isolated and alone in his efforts.

As he keyed in the message on the telegraph, a flicker of orange light outside the window momentarily diverted his attention. Intrigued yet pressed for time, Acker quickly refocused on his task, pushing aside the enigmatic glow for later consideration.

The icy touch of the switch sent a shiver down his spine as he tapped out the Morse code, each rhythmic press echoing the urgency of his plea to the superintendent. With each keystroke, Acker could feel the weight of responsibility bearing down upon him, his senses heightened by the adrenaline coursing through his veins.

Finishing the message, Acker stepped back, his chest heaving with exertion, sweat beading on his brow. With a silent prayer, he left the telegraph to work its magic, trusting that his urgent summons would reach the superintendent's ears and prompt a swift response. It was a gamble, but one he had to take in the race against time to unravel the tangled web of mysteries threatening to consume them all.

A sharp knock on the door shattered Acker's train of thought, prompting Symons and Hooper to burst into the room, urgency etched on their faces. "There's a fire at the docks, sir. You must come immediately," Symons announced.

Acker remained rooted to his seat, his brow furrowed in confusion. "What does a fire have to do with us? Can't the Municipal Fire Brigade handle it?" he questioned, his scepticism evident.

Symons tossed Acker his coat, his expression grim. "It's no accident, sir. Chapman is en route, but we need all hands on deck to contain the blaze before it spreads any further. There's not enough of the fire brigade to tackle it."

With a frustrated sigh, Acker begrudgingly rose from his seat. "I'm expecting Superintendent Landrake any minute, and now I'm needed elsewhere," he muttered, retrieving his pipe from his pocket.

Hooper volunteered to stay behind, offering to field any inquiries from Landrake. "What should I tell him if he asks why he's been summoned?" he asked, his tone earnest.

A flicker of a match illuminated the room as Acker lit his pipe, a cloud of smoke filling the air. "Just inform him that I require a private discussion regarding our ongoing case," he instructed, adjusting his jacket before grasping his cane. "Let's not keep the Municipal Fire Brigade waiting."

As they hurried towards the station's exit, a messenger intercepted Acker, delivering an urgent letter addressed to him. "This was just delivered to you."

'Urgent' was scribbled next to his name in small, thin handwriting, and Acker had a feeling it wasn't a letter based on how thick the paper felt inside. "You go ahead; I'll catch up." He gestured to Symons to leave.

"I'll wait in the carriage." Symons announced. He left Acker alone and buttoned up his tunic to go outside, going as slowly as possible, intrigued to see what the envelope held.

Acker ripped open the envelope, pulling out a photograph of Landrake and Lady Penelope together. At first, he stared at it, confused, but when the realisation set in, his face turned pale with shock. Before anyone else could see it, he stuffed the photograph into his pocket, trying to hide the distress from his face. It was already too late. Symons had seen the blood drain from Acker's face and wondered what was in that envelope that scared him so greatly.

"Anything relating to our case?" he asked, curious to see if Acker lied.

Acker looked up, astonished to see that he had been watched. "No. Just some Jack the Ripper nonsense." Before putting on his bowler hat, he patted his pocket, giving Symons a feeble smile. "Let's get out of here."

Symons could tell Acker was lying, attempting to conceal something. It was rare for him to act this way in response to a mysterious letter with no return address, and Symons could see by the way his boss's hands were shaking that whatever it was had unnerved him.

# CHAPTER SIXTY-ONE

## Fire

A swarm of policemen followed Chapman through the tangle of alleyways towards the docks. The smell of smoke was pungent in their nostrils, and the wind from the storm had driven the fire closer to the houses, spreading from rooftop to rooftop. The sky was a dark hue of orange, blending in with the lighting strikes from the dark clouds above. Chapman shivered beneath his coat as he dashed towards the screams, his light steps avoiding every pothole he came across, wary of tripping and falling.

Lives were hanging by a thread, and if Chapman didn't haul his butt there in time, the people of the city would hold the police accountable for the fatalities. That was something he didn't need right now. He clambered over each wall as if the bricks were only a little obstacle in his path, while the other officers trailed after him, their breathing haggard and unfit. He moved like a whippet, using the burning sky as his navigator while the stench of burning wood and rubble lodged in his throat. He grabbed his handkerchief and covered his nose, relying on fast breaths to get through the thickening smoke. He'd always been a fast runner, and now it was his chance to shine and save his people.

"Keep going!" he yelled as he skirted another stack of long-forgotten crates. He hurried into another dark alleyway, shielded by a tiny cluster of abandoned street carts that provided only a narrow crawl space to get through. He didn't care what was on the ground in front of him and got down on his hands and knees, carefully using his hips to nudge the carts aside to create a bigger opening for his officers to pass through.

Another cloud of black smoke stung his eyes, making it impossible for him to see clearly, but the sound of his footfall hitting the wood told him he was now on the docks. Chapman could see black shadows darting back and forth within the smoke, screaming for help, and the heat from the flames lashed at his face as he approached closer. People had already assembled, carrying whatever water they could find to put out the fire. The Municipal Firefighters surrounded the blazing structures, working nonstop to rescue the wounded.

He assembled his officers and sent them in various directions to help put out the fire, fully aware that it was up to him to support the firefighters. He approached a man in a tattered firefighter's outfit. With horror in his eyes, the man turned and stared at Chapman. "The fire is out of control, and there are children trapped inside!"

Chapman's eyes darkened. "Children?"

The fireman grabbed Chapman by the shoulders, perspiration and grime covering his cheeks as he spluttered, "Please help us get them out. We need as many volunteers as possible!"

Chapman removed his jacket and pulled it over his head to protect himself from the flames. "What is the safest way in?"

"Through the rear door. The fire has not yet touched that area. We're doing everything we can to keep it from spreading." He gently nudged Chapman towards the side of the building where the bricks had remained intact. "Take care, sir. Cover your mouth and try to stay as low to the ground as possible. We don't want any more fatalities."

Chapman disappeared into the smoke, keeping his head bowed to the ground. He noticed the dock was starting to become unstable, and the wooden beams had already begun to detach from each other, allowing him to see into the water below. He had mere minutes before the entire structure collapsed beneath him. Chapman would have given up in most circumstances, letting whoever was trapped inside perish in the flames, but these were children. He didn't have any of his own, which fuelled his determination to save the children's lives.

The smoke swirled and twisted around him, engulfing his mind as well as his sight. But the rush of adrenaline pouring through his veins kept his thoughts sharp and alert, allowing him to keep focused on the sounds of crying coming from the front of the building.

A hand stretched out of the haze and grasped Chapman's shoulder, causing him to jump. He recognised the ring on one of the man's fingers and drew him closer. Claydon's eyes rippled with dread and relief as he squinted at Chapman, disbelieving that his friend was even there and that it wasn't simply another hallucination of the fire playing tricks on him.

"Is it really you?" Claydon asked in shock.

Chapman nodded, confused by Claydon's reaction. "Where're the children, Claydon?"

Claydon pointed a trembling finger into the smoke. "Below the stairs," he said before grabbing Chapman's arm and pulling him to the side where Biggins' body lay slumped in the corner. "I think he's dead."

A ticking clock resonated in Chapman's mind, alerting him that their time was running out. He knelt among the wreckage, hoisting Biggins over his shoulder while yelling at Claydon. By the way Claydon was acting, he wasn't sure if he could trust him. The man was in shock, and it was difficult for him to even form a sentence, let alone rescue the children.

The flames were closing in around him, but even with Biggins on his shoulders, he continued to follow Claydon into the smoke to find the children. This was something Acker lacked. It took courage to do what was right instead of fleeing the situation. Chapman could tell that, despite being in shock and unable to walk properly, Claydon pushed into the flames with courage and determination. Chapman admired him for that.

The staircase came into view, and Chapman could just about see the scared little faces of malnourished-looking children cowering as far underneath the stairs as they possibly could.

"Is this all of you?" Chapman asked the oldest child. The boy nodded and allowed Chapman to grab his hand. "I need you all to hold hands and follow me. Under no circumstances should the chain be broken. Keep close to me and bow your head."

They did as they were instructed and formed a line with Claydon at the end, ensuring that no child was left behind. They moved carefully, following Chapman's instructions, and avoiding the debris falling from above. The smoke was thicker than before, and Chapman was having difficulty getting out. Fortunately for him, he had already memorised the twists and turns he had taken on the way in, and it was his sharp memory that would save them from the raging flames.

Biggins' body began to weigh him down, slowing his pace as the door leading inside the building came into view. Relief rushed over him, and he dashed for the door, not realising that the ceiling above him was about to collapse. The chargrilled floorboards, combined with dust and hot iron bricks, began to shake free from the building, tumbling down on top of them and knocking Biggins' body off Chapman's shoulder. As Chapman lost sight of them in the collapsing rubble, the children cried, their tiny pale hands groping through the wreckage for help. Chapman felt disoriented, his mind spinning, and he could feel the warm oozing of blood on his fingertips as he drew his hand away from his head.

"Damn it!" he hissed. He searched for Biggins' body, only to find burning wood and rubble instead.

As the last sections of the ceiling collapsed, the flooring beneath him cracked and gave way, and his life flashed before his eyes. It looked as if someone had pulled the building in from beneath, removing every vestige of what had once been a hardworking factory into rubble. The firefighters couldn't take their eyes off the inferno. Nothing remained, and the docks beneath everyone who had come to assist began to shudder beneath their feet, telling them that they, too, would fall into the waters below if they did not move away quick enough.

Acker emerged through the smoke and ruins, his face filled with thunder. He couldn't help but feel a little guilty for not showing up sooner as he watched in awe at the increasing flames of the fire. As the docks began to collapse beneath them, cracking and splitting from the pressure of their bodies, people surged towards him, their faces filled with horror.

He turned to his officers and barked, "Assist the injured and prevent anyone from returning here. Allow the firefighters to carry out their duties."

The chaos of the inferno consumed the docks, with police officers scrambling to aid the wounded as Acker surveyed the devastation. Across the smouldering wreckage, a cargo ship loomed, its silhouette stark against the backdrop of flames. On its deck, two figures stood, their eyes locked on Acker with an unsettling intensity. Despite the blazing heat from the fire, Acker shuddered as he felt the weight of their gaze, sensing a smirk directed his way.

Suddenly, a silhouette emerged from the smoke, seizing Acker's arm and pulling him towards the heart of the blaze. "Your men are trapped in there, sir!"

As the firefighter guided him towards the collapsing structure, Acker's mind raced. "Who?"

"Chapman and possibly your brother," the firefighter replied, gesturing towards the murky waters below. "The building collapsed with them inside. We've rescued five children, but three men and another child are still missing."

"Children?" Acker's surprise was evident.

"Yes, sir, they were in there," the firefighter confirmed, preparing to enter the water. "I need your best swimmers to assist."

"Symons, gather the others and join us immediately!" Acker's command cut through the mayhem, his urgency clear. Without waiting for a response, he discarded his cane and coat, knowing that time was of the essence. As he lowered himself into the icy depths, the frigid water enveloped him, sending a chill through his bones. The stench of smoke and decay filled his senses, mingling with the dread of what he might find amidst the wreckage.

"We've found another!" a voice echoed above, the tremor

betraying the grim discovery. Amidst the cacophony of screams and weeping, Acker pressed forward, determined to assist in any way he could, even as the flames licked at the crumbling ruins around him.

Something yanked Acker beneath the water's surface, stealing his breath and plunging him into darkness. Panic surged through him as he struggled against the unseen force, his vision blurred and his lungs burning. But then, his fingers closed around a familiar figure, clad in a black coat resembling his brother's. With a desperate heave, Acker hoisted the figure from the water, coughing up the foul liquid that threatened to suffocate him. Symons appeared at his side, aiding in pulling the body from the depths as he shouted orders to the others.

"We have the last one. Keep searching for the child!" Symons's command was a lifeline, freeing Acker from the grim task of retrieval.

"Are they?" he asked desperately as Symons pulled him from the water.

"You should see for yourself, sir. They're over by the alleyway," Symons said, guiding Acker towards the scene with his finger. He delivered a firm strike to Claydon's back, helping him expel the water from his lungs. "There you go. We'll get you dry quickly."

Acker reclaimed his cane and jacket before steadying himself on solid ground. "Who are the children?" he asked.

Claydon drew a laboured breath before responding, his words heavy with exhaustion. "The orphan children who have gone missing, Acker," he explained. Then, his gaze swept the area. "Where are Biggins and Chapman?"

Symons led them in silence to an alleyway where two bodies lay covered by a respectful blanket. Claydon sank to his knees, tears streaming down his face, while his brother stood nearby, his expression stoic. Though grief weighed heavily upon him for his fallen comrades, there were no tears to shed. Hesitantly, he reached out and began to console his brother with a gentle rub on the head, a small flicker of grief betraying the mask of indifference in his eyes.

As they mourned, a voice pierced the desolation of the

burned-down dock. "We've found another! He's still alive!"

They all turned towards the sound of the voice, astonished by the discovery of another body.

"So, who is this?" Claydon inquired. Symons carefully pulled back the blankets, revealing the solemn, drowned faces beneath. One was unmistakably Biggins, his grey face illuminated by the gas lamp above.

"It's Biggins, sir," Symons confirmed, his heart heavy with sorrow for his old friend. He then glanced at the second body, its features obscured by charred flesh. "I can't be certain if this is Chapman. The burns make identification difficult."

"Find out who the other person is, Symons. I need to confirm if it's Chapman." Acker's tone was urgent as he inspected the body's clothing for any identifying marks.

As the firefighters battled the blaze, the collapsing dock served as an unexpected ally, extinguishing most of the flames. With the fire subdued, they had more time to search for survivors. Symons disappeared into the smoke, his senses heightened as he navigated the damaged structure. Following the sound of voices, he carefully made his way across the remnants of the dock, his hands burning from the heat of the charred wood.

Eventually, he reached a firefighter tending to a body. With relief flooding over him, Symons recognised Chapman, though the man appeared worse for wear with half his face disfigured by burns. Nevertheless, he was alive. Symons breathed a sigh of relief, grateful that his colleague had survived the ordeal. But as he glanced back at the second body, his mind raced with questions about its identity.

"We need a medic for him," the firefighter announced, still working to clear water from Chapman's lungs.

"I'll go and inform the inspector," Symons said.

He prepared to stand, but Chapman grabbed his arm and pulled him in before he could move. "Harvard and Banes are aboard the cargo ship. Don't let them escape!" he sputtered, showering Symons with his blood and spit.

Claydon looked on in horror as his brother searched through the body's clothes. "Have some respect!"

"I need to know if it's Chapman!" Acker shouted, his angry stance shocking Claydon.

Acker was stopped in his tracks by a voice from across the water, and he looked over to see where it had come from. "Is that you, Symons?"

They both listened closely, trying to understand what the voice was saying. "Sir, stop that cargo ship! Banes and Harvard are on it!"

It took a few seconds for Acker to grasp what Symons was talking about until he remembered he'd seen two figures staring at him from a ship. He sprang into action, leaving Claydon in charge of the body and headed for the cargo ship. He jumped over the splintered wooden beams like a hyena pursuing its prey. Everything else faded into the background as he concentrated on the leaving cargo vessel. After what Banes and Harvard had done, he couldn't let them go. Not only were they engaged in the case, but Acker's rage spurred his vengeance after they attempted to murder his brother. He wanted them dead, even if it required breaking the law to do so.

His body began to lag, and his legs felt fatigued, causing him to slow down until his body could no longer carry him any further. He'd run out of steam, and as he stood there puffing breathlessly and staring at the two figures snidely waving at him from the cargo ship, he knew it would be the last time he would see them.

## CHAPTER SIXTY-TWO

# Don't Trust Anyone

In the shadows of the cells, the inmates gazed up at the sky, watching as dusk descended like a heavy curtain through the narrow iron-barred window. A scent of burning wood drifted in, mingling with the delicate flakes of ash that danced like miniature snowflakes in the air. What had begun as a mesmerising display of orange hues in the sky now morphed into a sombre, cloudy night, casting a gloomy pall over the jail.

While the others marvelled at the rare sight of colour beyond their drab confines, Thornton remained indifferent. Bent over in agony, his leg throbbed relentlessly, his brow damp with sweat that trickled unnoticed to the filthy ground below. Even Bodmin, typically loquacious since his arrest, failed to spare Thornton a glance. It seemed no one cared about his suffering; not even a cursory check-in from the guards hinted at concern for his well-being.

Each time Thornton lifted his head, the room spun, a nauseating sensation twisting his gut. He had been sick repeatedly, the acrid tang of bile lingering in the stagnant air, but still, no one paid him any mind. The station's doctor, tasked with his care, seemed to have vanished, leaving Thornton to fend for himself in his misery.

Meanwhile, Harvard's daring escape had gone unnoticed by Thornton, who had slept through the commotion. Lacking the means and mobility to replicate Harvard's feat, Thornton knew he was stranded, his injured leg a cruel reminder of his helplessness. As darkness enveloped the jail, Thornton resigned himself to his fate, isolated and forgotten amidst the disorder of the night.

His vision blurred as the hallucinations intensified, his mind teetering on the brink of delirium. Death loomed ominously, a mere breath away, yet Thornton found himself strangely apathetic. All he yearned for in his final moments was a glimpse of his child, a wish he knew would likely go unfulfilled. Memories dissolved into a haze of confusion as the infection ravaged his body, each passing second draining his vitality.

Muffled murmurs from neighbouring cells roused Thornton from his stupor, bringing him back to the bleak reality of his confinement. His gaze darted around, drawn to a mesmerising swirl of crimson silk that danced between the bars, morphing into the ethereal form of Lady Penelope. Disbelieving, Thornton rubbed his eyes, unable to reconcile the apparition before him with reality. Yet, as she materialised before him, no one else seemed to notice her presence.

Though he recognised the illusion, Thornton couldn't resist the allure of the woman who smiled down at him with radiant beauty. Her flawless appearance, untouched by imperfection, captivated him, even as he acknowledged the absurdity of his mind's creation. Her touch was soft and soothing, a balm to his weary soul, as she spoke with a voice that echoed with familiarity.

Struggling to stifle a laugh, Thornton croaked incredulously, his breaths laboured. "Is this the best you could conjure?"

Her eyes sparkled with tenderness as she gazed into his. "This is how you remember me, Thornton."

Shame washed over him as he averted his gaze. "But you were never like this. Cold, distant..."

"No, but you wished it to be so," she interjected gently. "You longed for her love as fervently as you loved her."

Thornton's confusion deepened. "What do you mean?"

A cryptic smile played on her lips as she tapped his hand. "The truth lies within you, waiting to be unearthed."

Exhaustion weighed heavily on Thornton's shoulders as he slumped against the cell bars. "I can't... Everything is too foggy..."

He closed his eyes, allowing the infection to take control of his body. Darkness crept in, causing his body to droop to the side and his head to hit one of the iron bars, attracting the attention of Bodmin from the next cell.

"You don't look too good, Thornton," Bodmin's voice cut through the haze, offering a rare moment of concern.

Thornton's bleary eyes struggled to focus as Superintendent Landrake replaced the ethereal image of Lady Penelope. The stern gaze that met his was far less comforting. "I need to speak with you."

Bodmin's curiosity lingered from his neighbouring cell as Landrake fumbled with the keys, his intentions veiled in secrecy. "Where are you taking him?"

Landrake's retort was sharp, a barb aimed at Bodmin's betrayal. Thornton's muddled mind strained to comprehend the exchange, his body barely responsive as Landrake hauled him from the cell. Weak protests bubbled from Thornton's lips, fuelled by a stubborn flicker of defiance. "I'm not going with you!"

But Landrake's grip was relentless, dragging Thornton towards the stairs with a determination that belied his usual composure. Desperate pleas for assistance fell on deaf ears until the guard, roused from slumber, reluctantly obeyed Landrake's commands.

As they ascended the stairs, Thornton's struggle intensified, prompting Landrake to resort to force. A swift blow silenced Thornton's protests, plunging him into unconsciousness. Landrake's gaze darted nervously, ensuring their clandestine operation remained undetected.

In Acker's deserted office, Landrake's movements were swift and calculated, taking advantage of the station's temporary vacancy. With Thornton's limp form in tow, he navigated the empty corridors, his steps purposeful and determined. Knocking twice to confirm their solitude, Landrake slipped into the office, careful to evade the notice of the lone officer at the front desk.

Alone with his captive, Landrake's expression hardened, his mind racing with the weight of his clandestine agenda. With the station deserted, he had precious time to execute his plan, and he intended to make every moment count.

Landrake had to persuade the young officer Acker had left behind to go and help put out the fire. He didn't go voluntarily, and Landrake knew that if Acker found out he was at the station alone, his stay would be cut short. He still didn't know why Acker had sent him to the station, but the discovery of the two witnesses' bodies led him to believe that it had something to do with why he was there. He had already drugged the last remaining officer at the front desk, hoping that the man would stay asleep while he finished off what he started, and he also had extra for himself after he finished the deed. No one would suspect anything of him if he had also been drugged.

"Sir?" A woman's voice spoke behind him as he shut the door quietly.

He jumped in fright before turning to see Edith and Evelyn sitting in the corner of the office with two empty glasses of whisky on the table beside them.

"Why are you in here?" Landrake demanded, feeling annoyed that his plan had already gone awry. He dropped Thornton's legs and roughly pushed his body against the wall. "You're not supposed to be in here."

Edith, the wise one, sensed something was wrong. She observed the sweat dripping from his brow and the irritation written all over his features. Evelyn cowered behind Edith, her young mind ringing alarm bells, but she couldn't figure out why. She had faith in the police, particularly Landrake. Edith, on the other hand, had suspicions about him.

"Answer me right now!" Landrake yelled, causing them to jump in unison.

Landrake's jaw tightened as he struggled to maintain his composure in front of the unexpected visitors. Edith's piercing gaze bore into him, her intuition sharp as a razor's edge. He cursed inwardly at the disruption to his carefully laid plans, the tension mounting with each passing moment.

With a forceful shove, he pushed Thornton's inert form against the wall again, his irritation palpable. "You're not supposed to be in here," he repeated, his voice strained with frustration.

Edith remained composed, her eyes flickering with suspicion as she assessed Landrake's demeanour. Beside her, Evelyn quivered with uncertainty, her trust in the police waning in the face of uncertainty.

"We were brought here by the inspector," Edith replied evenly, her words measured and deliberate. She sensed the gravity of the situation, her instincts urging caution in the presence of the volatile superintendent. "What are you doing with that man?"

Landrake's gaze darted to Thornton's motionless form, a flicker of uncertainty crossing his features before he regained his composure. "He is an inmate who requires questioning. I need to ascertain how much he knows."

Evelyn's remark cut through the tension like a knife, her youthful candour unsettling in its bluntness. "I don't think he's in any condition to talk. Are you sure he isn't dead? He certainly looks it."

Landrake's facade faltered for a moment, a brief glimpse of uncertainty betraying his usual steely resolve. He clenched his fists, steeling himself against their scrutiny, determined to maintain control over the precarious situation.

His mind raced, concocting a plan to silence Edith and Evelyn without raising suspicion. His grip tightened on Thornton's unconscious form as he eyed the two girls with a mixture of calculation and disdain.

As Edith stared at Thornton's pale, grim face, she couldn't help but feel a little guilty about what she had done. Although he deserved it, she realised that if he died, she'd be classified as a murderer, and that was something that petrified her. "He needs medical attention, sir, or he'll die," she begged, her guilt too much for her to bear.

Ignoring Edith's words, Landrake's gaze darkened, a predatory glint gleaming in his eyes as he addressed the girls with a chilling smirk. "Watch and learn, ladies. You are both in for a treat."

## CHAPTER SIXTY-THREE

# Harvard and Banes

As the vessel glided down the Bristol River, its timbers creaking in protest, Harvard's mind churned with unease. The scent of burning wood hung heavy in the air, a stark reminder of the chaos Banes had wrought back at the docks. Witnessing the old man's callousness had rattled Harvard to his core, casting a shadow of doubt over their partnership.

Banes, seemingly unperturbed by the gravity of his actions, stood stoically by the railing, his grip on his medical bag unwavering. Harvard couldn't shake the feeling of discomfort that settled in his gut whenever he glanced at the man beside him. There was an unsettling aura about Banes, a darkness lurking beneath his benign facade.

Caught in the act of studying his companion, Harvard quickly averted his gaze as Banes shot him a sharp look. The old man's voice cut through the silence, laced with irritation. "What are you looking at, boy?"

Flustered, Harvard stammered out an apology, his cheeks

flushing with embarrassment at being caught scrutinising Banes. "Sorry," he muttered, turning his attention to the rippling waters below.

Banes chuckled, the sound grating on Harvard's nerves. "You should be happy! We're free to do as we please," he remarked, his tone casual despite what he had done. It was a freedom bought with blood, and Harvard couldn't shake the feeling of unease that settled over him like a shroud.

"Where are we heading?" Harvard asked, hoping to get in on Banes's plan.

"I'm returning to London, and you'll be joining me. I have a place there that I occasionally rent out if I'm gone for an extended period. There's a family in it right now, but that shouldn't be an issue. I'll get rid of them," he explained, his face brightening as his plan came together perfectly inside his mind.

Harvard's stomach churned at Banes's causal explanation, the hairs on the back of his neck standing on end. He struggled to maintain his composure, his mind racing with questions and doubts.

"Returning to London?" Harvard echoed, his voice betraying his uncertainty. "And what about the family in your place? How do you plan to handle that?"

Banes's response was unsettlingly nonchalant. "Oh, I'll take care of them," he replied with a dismissive wave of his hand. "Nothing you need to concern yourself with."

Harvard's unease only grew as Banes's words sank in. "What exactly do you mean by 'take care of them'?" he pressed, his tone cautious.

Banes regarded him with amusement, a sardonic smile playing at the corners of his lips. "I simply mean I'll ask them to leave, Harvard," he said, his voice dripping with mock innocence. "No need for alarm."

Harvard couldn't shake the feeling of foreboding that settled over him like a heavy blanket. "With all due respect, sir, your definition of 'taking care' seems rather... vague," he ventured, his gaze fixed on Banes's inscrutable expression.

Banes's chuckle was tinged with something dark and

unsettling. "Ah, you're too tense, Harvard," he remarked, his tone almost jovial. "You'll get used to it. Besides, you're my right-hand man. Nothing to worry about."

Despite Banes's reassurances, Harvard couldn't shake the feeling of dread that gnawed at him from within. As the vessel continued its journey down the river, Harvard couldn't help but wonder what other secrets lurked beneath Banes's enigmatic facade, and what dark paths lay ahead for them both.

Harvard was baffled as to what Banes could possibly be suffering from. He'd seen a lot of unusual things as a mortuary attendant, but nothing prepared him for this. Banes appeared to have two personalities that he struggled to control, resulting in him committing horrible crimes and covering his tracks. The man was very dangerous indeed, and Harvard was beginning to regret his decision to follow him to London. "I don't really know what to say," he finally said.

Banes gave him a sceptical look. "Well, either you come with me, or I have to get rid of you, too. I can't let you go now that you know what my plan is, Harvard. I hope you understand the predicament you've just forced me into." His eyes grew steely as he locked on to Harvard with a harsh, penetrating glare. "Don't make me do something I don't really want to do."

Harvard steadied his breath, trying to remain calm. A cold sweat broke out across his forehead, revealing his fear to Banes. "Uh, well, I promised you that I would look after you. You've been kind to me, doctor. It's now time for me to repay you." He carefully chose his words, trying to keep Banes on his side. He knew he could certainly outsmart the man if necessary, and he was clearly stronger than him, but something inside his gut told him to be cautious. He knew Banes could switch in an instant, but what frightened Harvard the most was not knowing what else Banes was capable of. That terrified him more than anything else. "You can trust me, sir," he finally said, avoiding Banes's leering stare and looking out at the horizon instead.

For a brief while, Banes stayed silent, passively observing Harvard's movements. The man's conscientious look scared Harvard since he couldn't figure out what the man was thinking, but after a few long, agonising minutes, a snarky little smirk appeared on

Banes's lips. "I think we'll get along just fine in London."

## CHAPTER SIXTY-FOUR

# Dinner Laced with White

Mary had been summoned to her chamber to get ready for dinner after her unsettling conversation with Lady Elspeth. Lady Elspeth was determined that the supper would be formal, and that Mary would wear the best dress chosen by one of the servants. She had also witnessed Lizzie being forced to wear a white glittery dress that the eccentric woman had kept in a sealed case for a daughter she had always wished for but unfortunately never got.

The lengthy conversation Lady Elspeth had with herself, compelling everyone to listen as she caressed the fabric of the little dress, made Mary sick to her stomach. She hadn't wanted Lizzie to wear it, but she kept her mouth shut to keep the peace. She didn't want the switch inside Lady Elspeth's mind to flip again, so she trod carefully, looking inconspicuously for an escape route to hopefully come her way.

Now that they were alone, waiting for the clock to strike six for dinner, Mary sat on the edge of the crisply clean bed, watching her daughter twirl in the glittery dress, chatting excitedly about how kind Lady Elspeth was to give her such a beautiful dress.

Mary wanted to scream some sense into her, but she held her tongue. She didn't want Lizzie to know the danger they were in, nor did she want to scare her. She also needed to check on Billy, but Lady Elspeth had appointed a servant to always stand guard outside the door, leaving Mary with little alternative except to sit and wait.

She hoped that by now her husband had noticed her absence and dispatched a search party, but given the police's workload, it seemed impossible that Acker would even return that evening, making the hope inside her diminish little by little as she looked out of the window at the storm and the night sky drawing in.

A knock on the door startled her, and she sprung from the bed to open it. A stodgy little man smiled warmly up at her and said, "Miss, good evening. My name is Bentley, and I've been assigned to escort you to dinner."

His voice was like a singsong, high and trill-like, and despite his efforts to appear taller than he was, he seemed sweet and kind. He kept his back straight and his hands clasped behind his back, taking care not to crease his uniform. She immediately decided she liked this servant and was grateful for his company. The kindness in his eyes as he waited for her response told her he was friendly. They twinkled with mischief, leaving no room for speculation about his personality. He was in his mid-fifties, with receding jet-black hair and bushy brows to match, but when he smiled, he appeared younger, reflecting his mischievous personality. She returned his tentative smile, hoping to win him over. "Thank you, Bentley. You are too kind."

The man bowed and held out his arm, jokingly, for her to take. When she gently lowered his arm, declining his offer, he gave a sheepish grin, as if he thought he had gone too far with his goofiness. Bentley chuckled as Mary pointed to Lizzie, who was staring in admiration at her mother's ladylike manners. "Certainly, madam." He moved quickly towards Lizzie, his hips swaying to an imaginary beat in his head as he took a bow in front of her. She giggled and accepted his extended arm, allowing him to escort her out of the room.

Mary stopped him with her hand and motioned to Lady

Elspeth's room on the other side of the house. "Can you let me check on Billy to make sure that he's okay?"

The air around Bentley instantly turned cold, and she could tell he was nervous as he looked her dead in the eyes and muttered, "I don't think I'm allowed to, miss."

So, it seemed that Lady Elspeth had given her staff strict instructions to prevent her from seeing Billy, which immediately put her senses on guard. "I have to make sure he's alright."

His fingers began to twitch, and his gaze wandered to places other than her. "You'll see him at dinner, miss."

Mary placed a hand on his arm and smiled reassuringly at him, hoping to persuade him to let her see Billy. Her husband had taught her good manipulation skills, which she was now grateful for, even though she thought it was a useless skill to learn at the time. "Please, Bentley. He's still just a boy."

He flinched at her touch. "I'll get into trouble if I allow this."

"I promise I'll be quick." She begged with a slightly aggressive tone in her voice. "She won't find out."

He paused for a few seconds before nodding slowly. "All right, but we need to hurry."

Mary placed a small kiss of appreciation on his cheek, making him blush. "Thank you so much, Bentley."

He pulled her alongside him. "Stay behind me and keep quiet." He then looked at Lizzie. "That includes you, Missy. Consider it a cat-and-mouse game. We must remain hidden from my mistress." He gave her a wink before leading them both to Lady Elspeth's room on the other side of the building. Unbeknownst to Lady Elspeth, he led them through the servant's quarters, allowing them to see the pit they were forced to reside in every night. She couldn't help but feel sorry for the servants as she stared at the simplistic furniture and bare walls. Lizzie was drawn to the half-empty bowls of chunky vegetable broth that sat on the table from earlier. "Why is there still food on the table?"

"Because there's no one to clean up after the servants. They must clean up their own messes," Mary said, casting a sidelong glance at Bentley, hoping she hadn't offended him with her words.

"Can't they employ someone to clean up after them?"

Bentley tried to maintain a straight face. "If we hire someone to clean up after us, we'll be out of work." He took the neglected bowls of congealed food and carried them to a small, shabby kitchen with only a stove and washbasin. "I'll get to it later."

Mary had no idea how fortunate they were until that moment. Her daughter had never experienced hunger or the icy cold touch of her bare feet. Every mess she'd ever made had been cleaned up by a servant, which Mary was grateful for as she gazed at the drabness of the servant's quarters. Bentley moved swiftly on; the swaying of his hips long forgotten as he peered around every corner discreetly to make sure it was safe before entering. The house's creaks and groans matched their footsteps, drowning out the terrible storm outside. Mary became more nervous with each corridor they went down, the interior becoming plusher and posher as they got closer to Lady Elspeth's quarters. The stark contrast between the opulence of Lady Elspeth's chambers and the squalor of the servant's quarters struck Mary with a pang of unease. The gleaming surfaces and absence of dust in Lady Elspeth's domain only served to emphasise the disparity between the lives of the aristocracy and those relegated to servitude.

As Mary traversed the lavish halls, her mind lingered on the grim reality hidden beneath the facade of luxury. She couldn't comprehend why Lady Elspeth would subject her servants to such deplorable conditions, a stark reminder of the cruel injustices that permeated society.

"I know what you're thinking," Bentley finally said after a long moment of only hearing their quick, anxious breaths. "My mistress hasn't always been like this. But over time, as she grew older, she became eccentric and cruel. The servant's rooms have been left in disarray for some time now, and many of us are looking elsewhere for work."

Mary kept her voice low, so Lizzie couldn't overhear. "If you need to get out of here, there's a position at my residence."

Bentley took a moment to reflect on Mary's kindness. "Why would you do something like this for me?" He squinted at her, puzzled as to why she wanted him to work for her. "I don't get it."

Mary's eyes glistened as she fought back tears. "Because I

require your assistance and you need mine. I have to get out of here before your mistress kills us all."

Confusion creased his brows as they drew together. "Why would my mistress attempt to murder you, miss?"

"It's a complicated story. I'll tell you later, but first I need to ensure Billy's safety before putting together a plan." She looked at him through watery eyes, not liking the look of disbelief on his face as his eyes scanned her, wondering if she was telling the truth or not. "Look, Bentley, you've been tasked with following me and making sure I don't leave, correct?"

He nodded slowly, putting the pieces together to make sense in his mind.

"Your mistress is not a pleasant person. You already know this. If you help me and the children escape, I will make sure you have a job after this and better sleeping quarters." Her eyes were pleading and desperate, and she was pinning her hopes on the kind man standing in front of her. "Please, Bentley. My children are in danger."

"Someone is coming, Mummy," Lizzie hissed from the other end of the corridor.

Bentley's jaw tightened as he grabbed both of them and ushered them into an empty room. His skin paled, and Mary could feel his hand shaking with fear beneath his grip on her arm. He pressed his finger to his lips to silence Lizzie, and she stood motionless, scared but intrigued to see if this was a game they were playing. "Is this cat and mouse?" she whispered excitedly.

He pressed his ear against the door, intently listening to the footsteps outside, while Mary covered Lizzie's mouth, preventing her from speaking. Bentley's face lit up with relief. "They've gone." He pressed his face against the door, squeezing his eyes shut, terrified of being caught. "I'm not sure I can do this, miss. I'm not brave enough to do this."

Mary placed a soothing hand on his shoulder and lightly squeezed it. "You are courageous enough. Do you really want to stay in this hell hole for another year?"

He shook his head, knowing Mary was correct. "No, I really don't."

"All right, then, let's proceed." She smiled warmly.

He took a deep breath before opening the door. "Lizzie, keep in mind that the purpose of this game is to be as quiet as possible, okay?" Bentley grumbled as they walked down the corridor.

They arrived at a spiral staircase, and Mary knew they'd reached the mistress's quarters by the way everything was placed neatly. Although the staircase leading to Lady Elspeth's room appeared bleak and plain, someone had gone to great lengths to display a vase of freshly trimmed red roses in the small window above them. Paintings in gold frames were scattered across the walls as they made their way up. The aroma of roses trailed them, reminding Mary of springtime when the flowers were in bloom. It was a nice touch on a rainy day.

A large, bolted wooden door stopped them in their tracks, and Bentley pulled out a slew of iron keys. He knocked before unlocking the door, hoping Lady Elspeth had already started making her way to dinner.

There was no answer.

He pushed open the door to find Billy tied up on the bed, his eyes tightly shut, and his mouth stuffed with a handkerchief. Bentley stared in shock, unable to move from the door. Mary rushed past him to Billy's aid, yanking the handkerchief from his mouth and allowing him to breathe normally. He took a deep breath, and his eyes cracked open a little to see who it was, his face filled with fear.

Mary's attention drifted to a half-empty bottle of peculiar liquid resting on the bedside table, and she reached for it, curiosity piqued.

"It helps her sleep," Bentley explained, ushering Lizzie into the room. His gaze shifted to Billy, a troubled frown creasing his brow. "But it seems she's given some to Billy as well."

Billy's desperate pleas for help echoed in Mary's ears, but his staggering movements betrayed his struggle to stay conscious. With a heavy sigh, Mary returned the bottle to its place. "What do we do now? I can't carry him, and he can barely walk."

"I apologise for not believing you earlier, miss," Bentley confessed, guilt weighing heavily in his voice as he glanced at Billy. "I'll devise a plan. I know this estate like the back of my hand. I can lead you out discreetly, under cover of night. We'll have until morning to make our escape."

Mary glanced out the window at the waterlogged moors, her brow furrowed in concern. "But the moors are flooded. We'll never navigate them by carriage."

"We won't need a carriage, miss," Bentley assured her.

Mary's confusion was evident. "What do you mean?"

"There's a river that flows into the city, about a mile from here. We'll use that route. The groundskeeper has a sizable boat docked behind the estate, big enough for all of us," Bentley explained hurriedly, glancing at the clock with a gasp. "We're running late!"

Panic flickered in Mary's eyes as Bentley dashed towards the door. "But what about Billy?"

"Have no concern for him, miss. I'll handle everything. You and your daughter simply need to attend dinner as usual, or she'll suspect something is amiss." Mary cast one final glance at Billy before Bentley guided them out the door and down the winding staircase. "Return to your chambers after dinner, and I'll fetch you before midnight. No one will be awake by then, allowing us to slip away unnoticed." Leading them through the labyrinth of servant quarters, Bentley ushered them into the foyer through a small entrance. With three purposeful strides, he adjusted his uniform and rapped sharply on the door.

"Come in," Lady Elspeth's commanding voice echoed from the other side.

Bentley swung open the double doors and stepped aside for Mary and Lizzie to enter. Mary's gaze immediately landed on Lady Elspeth, seated at the head of a long table with her arms folded, her expression stern. The table was populated with orphans, each sitting silently with hands folded in their laps, awaiting their meal. Lady Elspeth's lips curved into a smirk as she observed Mary's entrance, Lizzie clinging to her gown with nervous fingers.

"You're tardy," Lady Elspeth's words dripped with disdain. "I expect better from you, Mary."

## CHAPTER SIXTY-FIVE

# Murder At the Station

Acker clambered up the last few steps to the station, with Claydon close behind. His mind weighed heavily from the horrors of the night. Chapman, along with the other surviving children, had been taken to the hospital for examination. Acker had already established that the fire had been started on purpose, and he knew exactly who the perpetrators were. In his eyes, the whole case was a shambles. The more evidence he discovered, the more out of control the case became. People he knew were also involved, leaving him no choice but to arrest them as well.

    He hadn't been home for days, and he was starting to miss his wife and daughter. He hadn't heard from Mary, which was strange, to say the least. She would usually send him a letter or stop by the station if he hadn't returned home for a few days. She'd bring him a homemade meal to make sure he was eating properly. That was one of the qualities he admired in her. Even when she wasn't there, she was always watching out for him. He felt homesick thinking about her, and all he wanted to do was wash the soot off his body and climb into a nice, clean bed with his wife.

As he neared the station, hope swelled within him like a rising tide. Yet, upon arrival, that hope ebbed away like a receding wave. The sight that greeted him shattered any illusions of imminent departure. There lay the superintendent sprawled across the floor, a broken mug by his side. An officer slumbered at the desk, leaving the station vulnerable to intruders who could easily free the prisoners.

Claydon brushed past Acker, reaching Landrake before anyone else. Hope flickered in his eyes as he checked the superintendent's pulse. "He's still breathing."

Mary and Lizzie faded to the recesses of Acker's mind as he navigated through the weary, soot-covered officers toward his office. His heart pounded in his chest, dread mounting with each step. The sight that greeted him was a harbinger of horror. The office door, once securely shut, now stood wide open. With a sinking feeling in his gut, Acker knew what awaited him inside. The scent of death and blood tainted the air, assaulting his senses as he leaned against the door, overcome with weariness.

"What transpired here, sir?" Claydon's voice trembled.

Acker pointed toward the office without meeting Claydon's gaze. "Take a look." His voice remained steady, though turmoil raged within. "We must secure the premises. No one enters, no one exits," he commanded, his determination masking the anguish threatening to consume him.

Claydon's stomach churned at the grisly scene before him. Suppressing a wave of nausea, he steeled himself and began devising a plan. Anger surged within him as he beheld Edith and Evelyn, their forms limp and broken. The room bore witness to unspeakable horrors, crimson staining every surface, and a grotesque message adorning the back wall, covering Acker's certificates of achievements. Claydon fought to contain his revulsion, mindful of the solemn duty that lay ahead. The putrid stench drew the attention of onlookers, who gathered around in shock and horror.

"Should I try to feel for a pulse?" one of the officers behind Claydon questioned him gently.

As he turned to face the officer, Claydon attempted to compose himself, feeling the rage bubbling away from within. "What's the point? Half of their insides have been splattered across the room. No one can survive that." He turned his attention back to the carnage before him and sighed loudly. "Lock this place down. No one can leave. The killer may still be within these walls."

As the officers dispersed, Acker and Claydon remained, grappling with the weight of the situation. With resolve born of necessity, they hoisted the unconscious superintendent and the police officer, ferrying them to a secluded room where they could sleep off the effects of the drug. Claydon sensed an undercurrent of panic and urgency, setting his nerves ablaze with apprehension. Their case was unravelling at an alarming pace, witnesses falling one by one. If this continued, they'd be left with naught but smoke and mirrors, a mere shadow of justice. Claydon's mind raced, grappling with the unsettling realisation that someone within their own ranks was betraying them, sabotaging their efforts from within.

Outside the room, Claydon hesitated, his heart heavy with dread. The air was thick with the pungent scent of death, clinging to his senses like a spectral shroud. The gruesome tableau awaited within, an indelible imprint upon his consciousness. Though no stranger to crime scenes, this macabre display surpassed anything he had encountered before. It spoke of a profound hatred, a visceral loathing that gnawed at his conscience. His thoughts turned to legends of the past, the spectre of Jack the Ripper looming large in his mind. Was this a mere imitation, or the handiwork of a twisted disciple? Unanswered questions swirled like shadows in the depths of his mind, driving him onward.

With Acker incapacitated, the burden of investigation fell squarely upon Claydon's shoulders. Taking a steadying breath, he ventured into the room, his senses assaulted by the nauseating stench of death. Hastily covering his nose and mouth with a handkerchief, he moved to open the windows, inviting the storm's cleansing breath to sweep away the oppressive atmosphere. With the foul odour somewhat abated, he cautiously approached the bodies, gingerly navigating the treacherous terrain of crimson stains that marred the floor. Retrieving his notebook, he set to work documenting the scene with meticulous care, every stroke of his pen a testament to the gravity of the situation.

As his eyes traced the macabre tableau before him, Claydon's gut clenched with unease. The victims' positioning spoke volumes, a grotesque parody of intimacy that sent shivers down his spine. Drawing closer, he noted with a sinking heart the telltale marks adorning their eyelids and throats, grim echoes of the Ripper's handiwork. Dread coiled like a serpent in the pit of his stomach. If this wasn't the Ripper's doing, then it was a chilling imitation, executed with chilling precision by someone well-versed in the horrors of the past.

A sudden rush of warm air at his back brought Claydon sharply back to the present, and he turned to find Acker looming over his shoulder, his gaze fixed on the sketch taking shape before them. Acker's observation drew Claydon's attention to a subtle detail—a faint indent marring the skin of one victim's shoulder. Leaning in for a closer examination, Claydon frowned, his mind racing with possibilities.

"It could be a shoe print... or a ring," Acker mused, his voice tinged with grim uncertainty.

Claydon nodded, his pencil tracing the mysterious mark with furrowed brow. "You think this is the Ripper's handiwork?"

Acker's response was measured, his tone grave. "It bears all the hallmarks... but there's something off about it. This feels calculated, deliberate... as if it's meant to evoke the Ripper's infamy without truly being his work."

Acker's cryptic words sent a chill down Claydon's spine, his mind swirling with a maelstrom of questions. He regarded his brother with a mixture of concern and curiosity. "You speak as though you have a suspect in mind."

Acker's expression remained inscrutable as he turned his gaze towards the makeshift resting place of the superintendent and the officer. "I have my suspicions."

Claydon detected a hint of guardedness in Acker's tone, prompting him to press further. "And what might those suspicions be?"

A flicker of hesitation crossed Acker's features before he

replied, his voice measured. "Observe the nature of the wounds. Unlike the precise incisions characteristic of the Ripper's handiwork, these cuts bear the marks of amateurish violence. They are jagged, haphazard... indicative of uncontrolled rage."

Claydon's brows furrowed in contemplation as he absorbed his brother's analysis. Indeed, upon closer inspection, the distinction was stark. This was no meticulously orchestrated series of murders; it was a frenzied onslaught fuelled by raw emotion.

"But why mimic the Ripper's methods?" Claydon mused aloud, his mind grappling with the implications of Acker's observations.

Acker's gaze hardened with resolve as he met Claydon's eyes. "Whoever perpetrated this act sought notoriety, to cloak their own brutality in the shadow of history's most infamous killer. But make no mistake, Claydon... this individual is no mere imitator. They possess a darkness far more insidious."

Claydon swallowed hard. "Then we must act swiftly to apprehend them before they strike again."

Acker nodded, anger settling over his features. "Agreed. But tread carefully, brother. The mind behind these atrocities is as elusive as it is malevolent. We cannot afford to underestimate them."

"Sir!" Someone shouted from the door. "We've found another body."

When Acker and Claydon turned to see who was speaking, they were met by a tall, gangly boy dressed in an oversized officer's uniform. He was barely a man, his cheeks and forehead covered in acne like a map, but he seemed eager to please, which Acker liked. "Has the body been identified, Chavers?" he asked, sizing up the boy.

The boy shook his head and returned to the doorway, pointing in the direction of the body. "Not yet, sir. When you see the body, you'll understand why."

As if Chavers had punched the air out of Acker's stomach, he was speechless. Claydon jerked his head back, taken aback by Chavers' words. He looked to his brother, hoping that he would lead the way, but Acker appeared despondent and unwilling to even look at the victim.

He took a deep breath and exhaled deeply. "What do you mean?" he asked slowly. His voice trembled, and he couldn't even look Chavers in the eyes.

Despite his youth, Chavers' eyes told a different story. They were filled with remorse and a haunted look, revealing to others the horrors he had already witnessed over the years. "It's best if you look for yourself, sir."

Claydon could only stare in a catatonic stupor, unable to conceal his fear. "Then I suggest that you lead the way."

Acker could only nod in agreement. If the victim resembled the ones they had just witnessed, he would be unable to stomach it. His stomach lurched just thinking about another victim, let alone one that looked like the two butchered women.

Acker found himself trailing behind Claydon and Chavers, their footsteps echoing in the narrow corridor leading to the forgotten file room. Dust particles danced in the dim light, swirling around evidence boxes stacked haphazardly against the walls.

As they entered the musty room, Acker's mind raced with questions. *Why would someone choose this obscure location to conceal a body?* The answer eluded him, shrouded in the mystery of the station's forgotten archives.

"It's as if they wanted to bury the truth along with the evidence," Acker mused aloud, his voice barely above a whisper.

Claydon nodded in agreement, his expression grave. "Perhaps they hoped it would remain hidden forever."

Chavers stepped forward, his voice steady despite the fear he felt. "I stumbled upon the body while searching for old case files. I remembered something about a case that had never been solved a few years ago. I was looking for the files when I almost tripped over his leg. Nobody else is aware of it yet. I assumed you two would want to know first. It was a stroke of luck—or perhaps fate—that led me here."

A flicker of admiration crossed Acker's features as he regarded Chavers. "Well done, Chavers. Your keen eye may have just cracked this case wide open."

Chavers beamed at the praise, his chest swelling with pride. "Thank you, sir. I'll ensure that this discovery remains confidential until further notice."

Acker nodded, his gaze lingering on the young officer with a newfound respect. "Your discretion is commendable, Chavers. We're counting on you to keep this under wraps."

Claydon grabbed Chavers's arm, stopping him from entering the room. "What was the case?"

"There were several similarities between an unsolved case and this one, but I couldn't be certain until I read the file. That's all, sir. I just had a hunch."

"In what case?" Claydon inquired once more, this time with a more assertive tone.

"Remember that servant girl who was murdered in an alleyway about a year ago? It was around the time of the Ripper murders, and Superintendent Landrake imposed a curfew on the city's women to prevent them from going out at night in case it was the Ripper." Claydon nodded and motioned for Chavers to continue. "Well, there are a few similarities between the murders. Despite the fact that the servant girl was not a lady of the night, she was linked to Lady Penelope. She was her servant until she was fired just before she was murdered."

Claydon rolled his eyes, growing irritated by Chavers' lack of information. "I recall the case. What are the similarities, Chavers?"

"Three similarities stood out to me. The first is that the handwriting on the inspector's certificates appears to be nearly identical to the writing on the wall behind the servant girl after she died. It was the same phrase as well. The other two similarities were that all of the victims had the same cut marks on them and that their internal organs were displayed in front of them."

As he took in the information, Acker's eyes glowed with hope. "Chavers, I wish I had more men like you. Excellent work. Locate that case file and place it on my desk. Tell no one what you're up to, but get to work with the case files, and if you come across anything else, then I want you to inform us immediately. I'm assigning you to this case. You seem to have your wits about you, boy."

Chavers' corners of his mouth twitched. "Thank you very much, sir. That means a great deal."

Claydon's suspicion lingered like a shadow, casting doubt on every word that fell from Chavers' lips. As the young officer busied himself with securing the room, Claydon watched him with narrowed eyes, his mind churning with suspicion.

His brother's trust in Chavers was unwavering, but Claydon knew better than to let his guard down. A murderer's cunning could easily disguise itself as intelligence, leading them down false trails and away from the truth. Chavers could be playing them all for fools, using his knowledge to manipulate the investigation and cover his own tracks.

A tug on Claydon's arm brought him back to reality. "Are you coming?" Acker asked, bemused by his brother's suspicious expression. "You looked as if you were a million miles away, brother. Is everything alright?"

Claydon widened his tired eyes, hoping to look normal. "Yes, I'm fine. Let's just get this over and done with, Acker. I think I've seen enough guts for one day, don't you think so?"

Acker pulled his silver cigarette tin from his pocket. "Of course, I understand." He lit a perfectly straight cigarette and puffed away, sending clouds of smoke into the air. "It's our job, Claydon; we have to investigate and close the case, no matter how gruesome it is." He motioned for Chavers to open the door. "Nonetheless, I agree with you. Let us get this done quickly but efficiently."

Chavers exhaled a deep breath and tightly grasped the doorknob, hesitantly opening it. A trace of distress and disgust appeared on his face, but it vanished in an instant, leaving behind a stone-cold expression. To Claydon, it was proof that what the boy had seen had deeply disturbed him, which could only mean that he didn't have the nerve to do something like this. It threw Claydon off guard, casting doubt on his mind. Maybe the boy hadn't done this after all.

Chavers flung open the door, and the smell of blood hit them immediately. Acker noticed Chavers' knees trembling as he approached the body slowly. He felt sorry for the kid and put a reassuring hand on his thin shoulder. "We can make our own way. Just find the file and leave. You've seen enough for the day."

Claydon's mind was quickly overcome with jealousy. He

pouted at his brother, irritated by his remark. "Can I leave too? I think I've seen enough guts to open up a butcher shop."

Acker laughed. "Sorry, Claydon, but I require your vision. You have better eyesight than I do."

As Chavers sifted through the musty files, a sense of unease settled over him like a shroud. The weight of the task ahead pressed down on his shoulders, the stakes higher than ever before. He couldn't afford to let his nerves get the best of him, not when this was his shot at proving himself to the inspector.

With determined focus, he pushed aside his doubts and zeroed in on the task at hand. Each file he touched felt like a delicate relic, threatening to crumble at the slightest touch. He handled them with care, his fingers tracing over faded labels and smudged ink as he searched for the elusive document.

Despite the overwhelming odour of death that hung in the air, Chavers forced himself to stay focused, his mind racing as he counted the seconds ticking by. He knew that every second counted, every file scrutinised bringing him one step closer to his goal.

As he scanned the titles, a flicker of hope ignited within him. This could be his chance to shine, to prove that he was capable of more than anyone had ever imagined. With renewed determination, he pressed on, driven by the desire to make his mother proud and to carve out his own place in the world.

Chavers's keen eyes spotted a loose piece of paper wedged between two folders. Carefully, he extracted it, causing two other files to tumble to the ground in a disorganised heap. "Sorry," he muttered, swiftly gathering up the fallen documents and returning them to their place.

Skimming through the initial pages, Chavers felt a surge of excitement as a couple of old photograph negatives slipped out. Holding them up to the light, he realised they were crucial pieces of evidence. With a satisfied smile, he tucked the files securely under his arm.

Turning to Acker, who remained engrossed in studying a bloodstained footprint, Chavers announced, "I found them, sir."

Acker's response was distracted, his attention still fixated on the floor. "Make sure no one sees you, Chavers," he instructed. "I'm sure Claydon will let you use his office, but take the back staircase." A brief pause, then Acker glanced at Chavers's shoes. "What size shoe are you?"

Chavers's cheeks flush. "Size eight, sir, but I'm still growing."

Acker raised his brow at him, amused. "I'm sure that you are." He returned his attention to Claydon after concluding his conversation with Chavers. "Take out your notebook and begin sketching."

It was Chavers' cue to leave, and he quietly slipped out unnoticed by the other two as they both stared at the floor, engrossed with the footprint.

Acker watched his brother sketch, commenting on the likeness and making sure that everything was correct. He wanted no mistakes. "What do you reckon, size tens?"

Claydon shook his head. "No, they're bigger than that. Possibly a size eleven or twelve, an average-sized foot. Most men are that size around here, Acker. It doesn't mean anything."

Acker knelt to Claydon's level, his eyes scanning the print for detail. When he noticed an oddity on the side of the print, his lips twitched into a smirk. "Look over here, Claydon. A scuff mark indicates that the perpetrator walks with a slight limp."

"He could have been attempting to avoid the blood. What leads you to believe it's a limp?"

"If he was avoiding the blood, he would have seen the footprint and destroyed the evidence."

"I guess you're right." He got up and flipped his book shut. "I've finished. Let's carry on."

Acker's and Claydon's footsteps were hesitant on the stone-cobbled floor, like a clock ticking slowly. As they approached another narrow bookcase full of rotting folders, they exchanged a sidelong glance. The smell became more malodorous as they got closer to the body. Acker caught a glimpse of a foot through the crack of the casefile box shelves. He recognised the shoe but couldn't quite place who it belonged to. He didn't realise it was Thornton's body until he noticed the gammy leg lying motionless on the hard stone floor, nestled in between two large boxes of files.

He was the first to round the corner and face the horror scene. Thornton would have been unrecognisable if it hadn't been for the infected leg. There was nothing left of him to suggest he was Thornton at all. It was even worse than the previous crime scene. Whoever was responsible had a murderous streak in them. This individual was lethal and malicious in ways that could only be described as pure evil. Even Acker was having difficulty inspecting the crime scene as it looked so unrealistic. He couldn't accept that someone in his force was perfectly fine with such aberrant behaviour. No one was safe, not even him.

Claydon made a retching sound and dashed away, his hand covering his mouth. *He was always the weakest link*, Acker reflected as he returned his gaze to Thornton's lifeless, mangled body.

"Sir, the superintendent is starting to stir." From behind Acker, an officer called out from the doorway.

"Don't come in here. I want this room locked." Acker demanded as he retreated hastily away from the crime scene.

The officer's nose twitched. "What's that smell?"

"Nothing to be concerned about." Before the officer could look in, he slammed the door behind him. "Please direct me to the superintendent."

The officer motioned for Acker to follow him with a nod. Along the way, they came across a green-skinned Claydon, and Acker yanked on his arm as they passed him, "He's waking up."

Claydon groaned but followed Acker. "Fine," he murmured.

The station appeared to be chaotic. The officers whirled back and forth everywhere Acker looked, their faces permanently etched with fear. Screams and yelling could be heard just outside the station's doors. The mob of city dwellers was getting out of hand, and Acker could sense the tension in the air. It was strained and stiff, like an elastic band that had been stretched too far before snapping. He didn't like where this was going, and he needed to act quickly before things got out of hand. If the people of the city found out that not only had there been five murders at the station, but the culprit was also a part of his team, then there wasn't going to be a police station left by the time they'd finished with it. Acker felt adamant that the superintendent was the murderer; he just had to prove it, and that's what he was about to do, but he needed the officers on his side.

The officer pointed to a closed door near the front desk. "In there, sir."

Acker turned to his brother. "Round everyone up, Claydon. I need every able-bodied officer here. Also, make sure that door is locked tight." He pointed to the front door being rocked back and forth by the mob outside. "Get the barracks up. It looks like we're going to be in for a rough night."

"Should I send a telegram to the chief?" Claydon asked nervously.

Acker slowly nodded, petrified of what their chief was going to think. "Yes, but don't tell him about the murders."

Acker adjusted his jacket before entering the room, where the superintendent was sprawled on a small sofa in the corner. The other officer had been placed on the floor, covered by a blanket, with a glass of water sitting beside his head.

Landrake groaned, clutching his head in pain. "What happened?"

Acker glared at him, not bothering to participate in the man's games. "I think you know, sir."

He bolted upright in his chair and looked at Acker innocently. "Come again?"

The officers behind Acker stared at him in confusion, wondering what their inspector could possibly mean.

"Can I see your left foot?" Acker asked.

The superintendent tilted his head quizzically at Acker. "My foot? Why?"

Acker rolled his eyes, already tired of the front Landrake was putting on. He marched up to him and removed his shoe in one swift motion. "All I need is your shoe, sir."

Landrake began blinking rapidly, sweat forming on his brow as he attempted to reclaim his shoe. When Acker noticed the blood encrusted on the bottom of the shoe, his chest tightened. He pointed to it, indicating to Landrake that the game was over. "Could you please explain this to me?"

The blood drained from the superintendent's face in an

instant, and he slumped back into his chair, speechless.

The officers were puzzled and shaken as the room became deathly quiet. They had no idea what was going on but judging by the look on their superintendent's face and Acker's aggression, something bad was about to happen. The atmosphere surrounding them was the epitome of bewilderment. No one said anything, not even Acker, who was still holding the evidence in the air for all to see.

Claydon appeared and stopped beside Acker. "Is it the same print?"

Landrake stared bug-eyed at Claydon, chewing over his words as Acker gave Claydon the shoe. "It's the same shoe. It even still has Thornton's blood on it."

Landrake's eyes darkened. "He's been found?"

"Didn't you think no one would find him so you could dispose of him later?" Acker asked, his voice tinged with sarcasm.

"I have no idea what you're talking about, and if you continue to speak to me in that manner, I will have you removed from this case and arrested," Landrake threatened, his eyes leering and condescending. "Now, give me back my shoe."

Claydon clutched it tightly. "No, sir; I'm afraid not. This is sufficient evidence to place you at the scene of a crime that you have just committed."

"What in the name of God are you talking about, sergeant?" He glared at Claydon sternly, trying to get to his soft side. "The only thing I remember doing is making myself some tea, and then I woke up on this couch."

Landrake only needed a glimmer of doubt to sway Claydon's opinion. Acker would be more difficult to persuade, but his brother was weaker and easier to control. "Claydon, your brother is trying to put thoughts into your head yet again. I have nothing to do with whatever it is you're both up to."

There it was—a glimmer of doubt in the man's eyes as he looked back and forth between Landrake and Acker, trying to figure out who was right.

Acker stared at him, stunned. "Are you really going to trust this man over me, Claydon?"

Claydon shuffled his feet, trying to avoid his brother's gaze. "Well, um..." he stammered.

"Claydon, are you serious? Mother was right. You're extremely easy to persuade." Acker then remembered something crucial that would put an end to this ridiculous facade. He pulled the photograph from his pocket and handed it to Claydon. "This should make up your mind."

When Claydon saw Lady Penelope and Superintendent Landrake grinning in the photo, his face fell. His hand began to tremble as he held up the photograph for the superintendent to see. Landrake felt his fear ripping the air from his lungs like an avalanche, suffocating him.

"Where did you get that?" he asked slowly, unable to believe that they were holding the only piece of evidence that could tie him to Lady Penelope's murder. It wasn't until now that he realised Lady Penelope might have kept one back when he thought he had burned them all.

The image of them both in an erotic position was permanently etched in his mind, and he could see his life disintegrating before his very eyes. He still had vivid memories of that day, complete with the invigorating scent of bluebells and the crisp, clean sheets that had been freshly made for Penelope's bed that morning. He had never felt happier than he did on that day. Penelope revealed to him a side of himself that even he was unaware of. Penelope knew every detail of his life, which he only shared with her, in a way that his wife could never have achieved with him.

His body grew icily cold with remorse and horror as the memory of Penelope's blood on his hands popped into his head. He wondered whether Acker and Claydon could sense his feelings of regret and what they would do if they learned what he had done. The inspector was simply too good and had found practically every piece of evidence that could put him on the receiving end of a noose, despite his best efforts to slow the case down. His hands were stained with so much innocent blood that even he had lost count of how many lives he had taken to cover up his past.

He began to tremble and squirm in his chair as paranoia crept up on him. His eyes darted erratically between Claydon and Acker and even briefly glanced back at the other officers who were standing behind them. He had wronged them all. A harried look matched his pale complexion as he started to stutter, "It's not what it looks like, I promise," while holding his hands up in defence. He purposefully balled his fists to give the impression that he was unafraid of his colleagues in an effort to calm his trembling palms. Under his hostile expression, he was petrified. For the first time in his life, he felt inferior to Acker.

"Then what is it meant to look like, sir?" Acker spat, glaring at the superintendent.

Landrake's tone altered, becoming overly combative and stressed: "Look, there was not, nor has there ever been, anything going on between me and the victim. This is a fake, cruel joke to deter you from the truth and help you find the real killer. I am the superintendent. Why would I murder someone?"

A smirk formed on Acker's lips. "I didn't say you murdered her, sir, but you've just confirmed my suspicion."

With their shoulders drooping in disgust, the officers behind Acker nodded in agreement. They all looked chapfallen, their eyes telling Landrake that he had just lost their trust. An air of disconcertment surrounded them, making Landrake feel even more on edge than he already was. He could tell by the way Acker was licking his lips in satisfaction that it wouldn't be long before the man found every piece of evidence that would implicate him as Lady Penelope's murderer.

Although he had intentionally hurt her the night she died, he was sure that he had left her alive. She was going to tell his wife about them, and he couldn't have that, so he gave her a little warning that if she opened her mouth about their affair, he would hurt her a lot worse than he already had. He was only supposed to scare her. From what he saw in the case files, her throat had been slit, which he definitely didn't do.

But he wasn't innocent either. He had taken at least five lives to stop the case from being solved, and now, as he sat in the chair, wishing that the floor would open up and swallow him, he knew that his time as the superintendent was up. Even if he claimed innocence, no one would believe him. He had left behind vital evidence near one of his victims, and now Claydon was holding it in his hand, ready to file it away and use it against him when the time was right.

Claydon pulled out his cuffs. "I'm sorry, sir, but we are going to have to arrest you."

The glint coming off the cuffs sent a violent shiver through Landrake, and he suddenly stood up, not knowing what he was doing, and headed straight for the door. His mind still felt hazy from drugging himself earlier, impairing his ability to think straight. The air surrounding him began to suffocate him, making him choke and splutter. Claydon came towards him, cornering him like an animal. The other officers rushed towards him in an attempt to wrestle the superintendent to the ground. They couldn't keep him down due to his irascible demeanour, and he shoved them aside as easily as blowing a feather away. He then sprinted for the window, slamming his body through the panes of glass, and plunging into the swell of people below.

Acker's heart raced as he approached the window, steeling himself for the sight that awaited him outside. The cacophony of screams and cries reached a crescendo, echoing through the room and sending shivers down his spine. Peering out, he grimaced at the scene unfolding below.

There, sprawled on the cobbled street, lay Landrake's slumped body, his form entangled with another man. A pool of dark crimson stained the ground, mingling with the cobblestones in a gruesome tableau. Acker's gut churned with unease as he struggled to discern whose blood it was, unable to distinguish between the superintendent and the other man in the chaos.

"I want every able-bodied officer outside right now! We are going to have a riot on our hands if they realise who it is!" Acker hissed, his veins protruding from his head and neck in anger.

The officers vanished in a flurry, snatching their batons as they dashed out of the station, poised to confront the surging crowd. Acker felt the onset of a stressful headache, each throb in his temples mirroring the rhythmic pounding of fists against homemade signs. His mind churned with turbulent thoughts, a tempest of unrest and violence swirling within him.

In the flickering glow of a nearby gas lamp, Acker advanced towards the seething crowd. The city's inhabitants had erupted into chaos, pillaging shops and shattering windows in a frenzy of protest against the authorities. Though Acker recognised the opportunism behind the looting, he also empathised with the undercurrent of rage and anxiety pulsing through the mob. It hung thick in the air, a palpable taste of fear lingering on his tongue as he surveyed the swelling throng from the elevated steps. Claydon stood steadfast beside him, nostrils flaring at the tang of sweat and stale beer. If the police didn't tread carefully, the city might soon be consumed by flames, ignited by the public's desperate search for a phantom culprit while the true perpetrator lay prone at their feet, possibly lifeless.

Amidst a scuffle in the heart of the crowd, Acker intervened, raising his hands for silence before addressing them. "Citizens of our city, I require your full attention before I can provide an update on the case." The sound of Landrake's groan halted his speech momentarily. Without looking, he turned to Claydon, murmuring, "Get Landrake and the other injured man out of here. Take them to the hospital, but ensure Landrake's face remains unseen. I want the superintendent under round-the-clock guard, understood?"

Claydon nodded, signalling nearby officers to assist him with a click of his fingers.

Taking a deep breath, Acker refocused on the crowd. "My fellow citizens, the perpetrator responsible for Lady Penelope's murder has been apprehended and is now in custody. You may rest assured this evening."

"Who is it?" someone shouted.

"It could be any one of us!" came another voice amid the clamour.

A shiver ran through Acker beneath his jacket as a creeping anxiety enveloped him. To calm his nerves, he swiftly retrieved his cigarette tin and lit one. "I implore everyone to remain calm," he urged. "For now, know that the culprit has been caught."

A man swaggered forward, his demeanour oozing with confidence amidst the crowd's tension. With a pencil tucked behind his ear and a faint scent of whisky wafting around him, he bore the unmistakable aura of a reporter. As he drew closer to Acker, his stylish waistcoat adorned with multiple pencils and a glinting silver pocket watch caught the light. Before he even uttered a word, Acker could sense trouble.

"What about the additional homicides and the station escapees, Inspector?" the man inquired, his voice smooth and probing.

Acker suppressed a sigh, his patience wearing thin. "Back off, vulture. This isn't your place."

Raising a perfectly arched eyebrow, the man persisted, "But aren't you obligated to address the public, Inspector?"

Before Acker could respond, a woman chimed in, her curiosity piqued. "What other murders? How many more are there?"

With a sly grin, the man nodded, relishing the attention. "Oh, at least five that I know of, but who knows? There could be even more." He emphasised the word "even," savouring its impact. "And let's not forget the mysterious man who fell from the supposedly safest spot in the city. Quite a story, wouldn't you say?" His sarcasm dripped like honey, enticing the crowd's intrigue.

Acker clenched his fists, struggling to contain his anger. Instead, he focused on maintaining composure. "Further details will be disclosed in due time. For now, I urge everyone to disperse. There's nothing more to see here."

The man gave Acker a mocking glance before focusing only on the woman. "You see, they don't want us to know the truth. They're hiding something." As he carried on talking, interest grew in the others surrounding him, wanting to know more. "We're being lied to! Don't you want to know what's happening in our city? Don't we deserve to hear the truth?"

Acker realised right then that he wasn't going to be able to silence the gathering. They were beyond saving from the reporter's rowdy words. As everyone started clamouring for more information, fear and horror filled the air, spreading beyond the people and onto the officers. The throng of people grew increasingly hostile as they slowly approached the officers while they paused with their batons, ready to attack if necessary.

Acker was beyond worried and unsure of what to do. The superintendent typically handled situations like this, but now it was left up to him to sort them out. Everything was falling apart, and this was all down to Landrake being behind every murder that took place in connection with the Penelope case. Acker wasn't sure if Landrake was indeed involved in Lady Penelope's murder, but he was sure as hell going find out. He just needed to get rid of this mob before they destroyed the station and every piece of evidence in the case that went with it.

## CHAPTER SIXTY-SIX

# Keep Awake

The elegant clink of silverware on fine china reverberated through the room, accompanied by a soft murmur of conversation as the children eagerly savoured each bite of their meal. Around the table, plates and bowls brimmed with steaming delicacies, meticulously arranged to entice the eye and the palate alike. Every conceivable side dish adorned the table, garnished with edible petals that added a touch of sophistication to the feast.

Servants moved gracefully, presenting each bottle of red wine with practised poise, their impeccable service a testament to the grandeur of the occasion. To the surprise of some, even the children partook in the wine, their youthful enthusiasm matching their elders' as they drank with abandon.

Lady Elspeth's eyes gleamed with anticipation as a servant poured a glass of wine for Mary, a subtle smirk playing on her lips. Yet Mary, sensing a subtle undercurrent of treachery, declined the offer, her suspicions casting a shadow over the lavish affair. Aware of the dangers lurking beneath the veneer of opulence, she remained vigilant, refusing to succumb to Lady Elspeth's cunning schemes.

Mary sensed the weight of Lady Elspeth's gaze bearing down on her, like a relentless heat that seemed to seep beneath her skin and settle in her bones. It was as if every glance from the woman was a sharp blade, slicing through the layers of her composure with precision. She dared not meet Lady Elspeth's eyes directly, fearing the intensity of the scrutiny, yet couldn't resist stealing fleeting glances to gauge the woman's interest.

Throughout the evening, Lady Elspeth's unwavering attention remained fixed on Mary, an unspoken tension hanging heavy in the air between them. With each passing moment, Mary's unease deepened, her nerves fraying under the relentless scrutiny. It was as if she could feel the weight of Lady Elspeth's expectations pressing down on her, suffocating her beneath their oppressiveness.

Large, handcrafted paintings of Lady Elspeth and her ancestors lined the walls of the exquisitely furnished hall. The paintings were wrapped in gold and depicted them peering down on them with beady eyes. A tinge of jealousy persisted in Mary as she imagined magnificent balls being displayed within the hall. She felt awed by the expensive vases and decor in every corner of the gigantic room.

A large, centrally placed marble hearth sat high and mighty, blowing out wave after wave of heat to warm the room. Even the stained-glass windows that were embellished with gold radiated importance in the hall's audacious declaration of wealth and power. Who would believe Mary's dramatic account of being imprisoned inside Lady Elspeth's home given that the woman had everything—wealth, influence, and grace?

"I hope that you've settled in well." The sound of Lady Elspeth's voice filled the quiet hall.

"Thank you, madam, I have," Mary muttered, fiddling with the food on her plate with her fork in an attempt to divert her attention away from Lady Elspeth's leering gaze. She glanced discreetly at the clock, wondering where Bentley was and hoping that he was setting things into place for their escape.

She peeked around the table, noticing that the orphans were eating with their forks rather than their hands. Lady Elspeth had taught them well, and she admired her for that. She was paving the way for a bright future for them, beginning with how to eat sensibly instead of like barbarians.

As Mary plucked up the courage to ask Lady Elspeth a question, her heart fluttered wildly in her chest. "Will Billy spend the night in your room?"

Lady Elspeth paused in the middle of cutting her chicken and raised her brow at Mary. "What a ridiculous question, Mary. No, of course not. He's been relocated to the opposite room from mine. He'll stay there for a day or two until I figure out a humane way for him to disappear."

Mary tried to hide the ghastly feeling she was feeling inside. She remained quiet, wishing that she could just disappear into a painting on the wall.

Lady Elspeth cleared her throat and raised her wine glass to the ceiling, "To cutting off Lady Penelope's family line," She began with a smirk. The orphans looked at her with confusion. "If there's one thing I can teach you, children, it's that you have to take action if you want something done." She looked around the table, grinning from ear to ear at each and every one of them, stopping at Mary. "To my future victory."

Mary's heart leaped into her throat at the words. "To your future victory, Lady Elspeth," she said with a forced grin while fighting the mounting panic. She firmly grasped her knife and fork while oblivious to the faint crying coming from Lizzie. "I'm glad you're going to be at peace soon, " she finished with another raise of her wine glass before setting it back down again, still untouched by her lips.

Lady Elspeth sent her a doubtful glance from her seat across the table. "Mary, you won't drink to my triumph?"

Mary hesitated. She gave the glass a long, suspicious look before picking it up very slowly. Her hand felt cold and clammy against the crystal glass as she took the smallest sip that she could muster in order to please Lady Elspeth. Without Lady Elspeth noticing, she dabbed at her lips and spat the wine back onto the serviette. The taste was sweet, yet tangy, which Mary didn't particularly like.

She wasn't sure if it was all in her head, but after being closely watched while she drank some of the wine, everyone had calmed down and stopped paying attention to her, including Lady Elspeth, who was now chatting with the young child next to her.

With a subtle gesture, Mary set down her knife and fork, a silent cue to the staff that she had finished her meal and was ready to leave. Beside her, Lizzie followed suit, albeit less discreetly, allowing the utensils to clatter against the dish with an intentional noise. It was a calculated move to draw attention to their readiness to leave, a small act of defiance amidst the stifling atmosphere of the dinner table.

"And where might you two be going?" Lady Elspeth's high-pitched voice trilled.

Mary feigned a yawn. "I'm all of a sudden feeling very sleepy, so I think me, and my daughter, should turn in for the evening. I'll see you in the morning." Before Lady Elspeth could react, she loudly scraped her chair back and stood up. The woman gestured for one of her servants to follow them with a nod, something Mary fully anticipated happening. For Billy's sake, she had to maintain her normal behaviour; otherwise, she would ruin the entire plan, and Billy would perish at the hands of the wicked old hag.

False-faced and leeringly staring at Mary, she nodded and snootily chuckled, "Well, I hope to see you bright and early tomorrow morning. We'll go horseback riding if the weather is nice!"

Mary's lips twisted into a rictus. "Of course, madam. As you wish."

Mary wasn't sure how long she could maintain her phoney persona. Lizzie's cheeks ached from all the fake smiling, and she looked as perturbed as ever. She was like a leech sucking blood from her mother, clinging to her arm as if her life depended on it. Mary could feel her little girl trembling beneath her grip, which made her feel guilty about the whole ordeal. When the doors to the great hall closed, she knelt at Lizzie's level and said, "I know you're frightened, but you have to put on a brave face for Billy. I promise we'll leave as soon as it is safe."

"Alright, I can do that." The little girl nodded, her eyes subdued and tearful.

Mary ruffled her curly hair as the doors reopened, revealing the servant to whom Lady Elspeth had earlier nodded. He looked down at Mary, surprised that they were both so close to the door. He cleared his throat, embarrassed that he was discovered. "Please excuse me, madam." He quickly exited through a side door into the servant's quarters.

"He's on his way to our room. Let's move quickly." Mary hissed, dragging Lizzie along with her.

They hurried up the shiny, marble steps, pausing just outside the room where Billy had been placed. Mary shook the door to see if it was locked. Her last ray of hope faded as the door remained firmly shut. "We'll come and get you soon, I promise," she whispered loudly, placing her hand against the hardwood. She moved on, quickly pulling Lizzie up the hallway and towards the opposite side of the mansion to their room. Mary could feel the servant's eyes on them as they rounded the corner, peering through whatever orifice he had found to hide. She clutched Lizzie's shoulders and guided her in the right direction, keeping her close by her side.

Mary had always found the velvety colours of the walls to be exquisite and breathtaking, but as she passed by the immaculate wallpaper, which proudly held up beautiful paintings that must have taken hours to paint, they now seemed dull and foreboding. The blood-red wallpaper appeared to be dripping from the walls, submerging them as they walked by. Mary knew it was all in her head, but she couldn't help but shiver as she let her imagination run wild, transforming everything she saw into Lady Elspeth's evil presence. She couldn't quite tell if she was losing her mind or not, and the thought of her mind playing tricks on her frightened her. She needed to keep her mind sharp and alert.

The beady eyes of the paintings' figurines followed them from above. The gleaming white ceiling paint with intricately hand-carved patterns had turned bleak, like a barren wasteland. Normally, Mary could see beauty in everything. She was usually very optimistic, but not this time. Lady Elspeth had melted and moulded everything she touched into something heinous and dark, even if it still looked the same as before. The glimmer and glitz were gone, Lady Elspeth reminding Mary of a black widow, and they were heading straight into the centre of her spiderweb.

A glimpse of the servant's mop of dark hair caught her attention from up the hallway, and she looked down at the soft, plush carpet, hoping that he hadn't noticed her staring. They arrived outside their door, but something made Mary stop. Faint footsteps could be heard from behind the door, putting Mary's senses on high alert. She gripped the door handle and slowly opened the door, fully expecting to see someone snooping around.

Except for two squeaky-clean glasses of warm milk neatly placed on each of the bedside tables, the room was as it had been before. The beds had been redone, with plump-looking pillows atop boutique-embroidered covers. A see-through crystal vase filled with fresh lilacs released a faint but sweet floral scent into the room. A newly varnished bookcase with classics mixed in with freshly dusted China ornaments appeared to have been moved recently. The footsteps had vanished, but a faint odour of sweat lingered in the air, giving Mary the impression that someone had been in there recently.

"Wait here," Mary whispered, gently nudging Lizzie back into the hallway. She turned on her heel and headed straight towards the bookcase. Everything appeared to be in its proper place at first glance, but as Mary knelt, she noticed two indents where the case used to sit. She carefully pushed the bookcase away from the wall, which felt surprisingly easy to her. Someone had purposefully attached small wheels to the bottom of the case, allowing it to glide effortlessly across the wooden floorboards.

She peeked behind the case, allowing her eyes to adjust to the darkness, before noticing a small wooden door that was completely concealed by a purple velvet curtain that slid along a pole above the door.

"I knew it." She scornfully muttered, disappointed with her lack of awareness. She yanked the curtain away and entered slowly through the strange, enthralling door. She recognised her surroundings immediately. Bentley had taken them through these passages earlier. "You can come in now, Lizzie." She hissed as she shut the secret door.

Lizzie appeared next to her, sulking with her head hung low. She pursed her bottom lip and crossed her arms tightly to express her annoyance at being left outside. Mary rolled her eyes and wrapped her arm around her daughter's shoulders before lightly squeezing them. "Lizzie, don't be like that. I just wanted to make sure it was okay for you to come in."

Lizzie huffed, silently resenting her mother's prudence. She'd been mollycoddled her entire life, never allowed to act like a normal child, and only allowed to play when she was in her mother's line of sight. Although Mary believed she was acting in Lizzie's best interests, Lizzie had other ideas. This was yet another example of her mother's lack of faith in her.

Mary glanced above Lizzie's head at the clock above the fireplace, "We should start packing right away. We have to pretend we're sleeping in our beds to avoid suspicion if anyone looks in." She caught sight of the decorative pillows on top of the bed and pointed them out to Lizzie. "These can be used to form a body shape in the bed. Help me with them."

Lizzie began to pull the pillows off the bed in a destructive manner, following her mother's guidance. Mary scowled at her before stuffing the pillows beneath the quilt and moulding them carefully into a body shape. She moved swiftly and elegantly around each bed, plumping and pulling each pillow until she was satisfied with the way they looked.

Lizzie picked up the glass of milk on the bedside table, licking her lips at the sight of the creamy texture.

"Don't!" Mary snapped, slapping the entire glass to the floor, causing it to shatter into tiny fragments. Lizzie looked at her with wide eyes, bewildered by her actions. "Look, Lizzie, they were placed there for a reason. They might be tainted with something. I forbid you to drink it."

Although her mother was likely right, the other glass of milk looked so appealing that she had to clasp her hands behind her back to keep from reaching for it. Lizzie smacked her lips together as perspiration slithered down the glass, forming a small pool on the wood, and wondered if it would be ladylike to lick the water from the table. She knew her mother would give her one of her famous disapproving looks, so she bit her tongue and walked away from the temptation before she got into trouble again.

Her mouth felt as dry as the Sahara Desert or the sandy places she'd read about in books. She desperately needed to wet her lips and quench her thirst, but all she had was a glass of milk that was quite possibly laced with a sleeping drug, which was becoming more appealing to her as time passed. Even the bowl of water for washing their hands had vanished. Lizzie began to suspect that Lady Elspeth had hidden something in her food to make her thirsty. She cast a discreet sidelong glance at her mother to see if she would notice her licking the perspiration from the glass in a desperate attempt to get some sort of liquid into her, but instead saw her panting like a dog in heat as if she was also as thirsty as her.

"Are you thirsty too?" she anxiously asked, hoping her eyes were deceiving her.

"How did you know?" Mary asked, pausing to see what she was doing.

"Because I'm thirsty as well," she puffed, resisting the urge to drink the milk. Her throat was dry and sore, and each lungful of air felt like she was swallowing knives.

"This must be another of her ruses," Mary grumbled, irritated that she hadn't paid enough attention to their food. She sagged into a chair next to the window, allowing her body to sink into the silky, smooth fabric, and closed her eyes. "We'll rest until Bentley returns." She murmured to Lizzie. Before Lizzie could reply, she was already drifting off into a deep sleep.

Wrapped snugly in the blanket, Mary drifted into sleep with a contented smile, her soft snores filling the room. Lizzie, however, found herself unable to shake off the feeling of unease creeping over her. She eyed the glass of milk on the nightstand, its creamy allure taunting her parched throat. Each glance intensified her thirst, making her mouth feel like it was filled with sand. Something felt off about her mother's sudden slumber. Back home, Mary's restless pacing would echo through the house, a familiar soundtrack to Lizzie's own struggles with sleep. But here, in this unfamiliar place, her mother had succumbed to sleep with unsettling ease, leaving Lizzie to wonder what secrets lay behind her serene facade.

She nervously twiddled her fingers as she paced up and down the room, looking for any kind of distraction to keep herself from drinking the glass of milk. She took a book from the bookcase and sat beside her snoring mother. She opened it to the first page and began to read quietly to herself. She couldn't focus on the words. Her gaze kept being drawn away from the pages and towards the bedside table displaying the glass as if it were a crown full of jewels.

Her vision began to blur, and she realised she was fighting a losing battle. She couldn't take it any longer and stood up, tossing the book on the floor which narrowly missed her tiny feet. She was aware that her mother would be disappointed, but she couldn't care less as she held the glass up to inspect its contents. She wondered if she would be able to taste anything different if there was something mixed in with the milk. The thirst from whatever Lady Elspeth had put in her food to get her to drink the milk was now overbearing, causing her to become apathetic towards what her mother would do if she found out, which Lizzie knew she would.

She detached herself from the instinctive thoughts in her mind and raised the glass to her mouth. As soon as she felt the moisture on her lips, she began gulping the milk down as if she couldn't get enough of it. The sheer luxury of feeling the liquid slide down her parched throat was intoxicating. She closed her eyes and let the milk pour into her mouth and dribble down her chin.

A black shadow behind her caught her off guard, and she didn't have time to react before a gloved hand swooped out and smacked the glass from her mouth in frustration. "You stupid girl, don't drink that!" A man's voice rang out. Lizzie opened her eyes fully to see Bentley standing in front of her, tapping his foot, and glaring at her with disapproval. "Lizzie, you should not have drunk that. It's laced with a sleeping pill."

"I'm sorry, but I was ever so thirsty," she sulked, turning away from his cold, sharp eyes and looking guiltily at the ceiling. "I needed something to drink." She then lowered her gaze to his hand holding a silver tray. There were two glasses of water on the tray. "Oh."

"I brought these because I suspected her plan, Lizzie. You should have listened to your mother and waited." He then cast a glance over her shoulder at Mary slouching in her chair. "It appears your mother had some as well. Is that correct?"

Lizzie grabbed the two glasses from the tray and, without thinking, gulped them down one after the other. She finished with a lick of her lips and shook her head. "No, sir, she did not, but I believe Lady Elspeth may have also laced the food as well."

He raised a brow at her unladylike manners and set the tray down on the table. "Why would you think that? I've only ever seen her lace the drinks."

"Because my mother suffers from insomnia. She's always antsy before bedtime, but as you can see, she's snoring soundly."

"Okay, this may be a problem, but I believe I have a solution. Stay put and try to stay awake. I'll get back to you as soon as possible. Everything is ready for our journey."

Lizzie watched him walk towards the bookcase that had been pushed to the side to reveal the secret door. "Is that how you entered?"

"Yes. Everyone is turning in for the night, and I can only sneak around for so long without being seen." He began sliding the bookcase back into place before giving Lizzie a mischievous grin. "Be good and stay awake."

Lizzie heard the door close with a creak, leaving her alone again. Without Bentley keeping her mind occupied, it began to shut down. The drug began to take control, pulsing through her veins and making her feel odd on the inside. She staggered over to her mother and began tugging her arm in an attempt to get her attention. Mary sighed and turned away from Lizzie, still fast asleep. Her little legs gave way beneath her, and she collapsed beside her mother's chair, trying to keep her eyes as wide as they could be as she struggled to keep awake.

Lizzie's consciousness began to fade slowly, like a boat drifting calmly over the waves of the sea. Her thoughts, which had been clear and concise just moments before, had become jumbled as she struggled against the drug's effects. She couldn't fight it any longer and decided instead to just give in and allow her body to succumb to the exhaustion. Her head drooped to one side, nestled deep into her mother's puffy evening gown, and as she drifted off, darkness engulfed her mind, leaving a calm, serene dream in its place.

"Lizzie!" Bentley and Billy emerged from the shadows of the bookcase, immediately noticing them both sleeping. Mary jumped, startled awake by Bentley's booming voice, and leaped from her chair in terror. Without her mother's leg to lean on, Lizzie flopped to the floor, oblivious to her surroundings. Bentley raced over and shook Lizzie's shoulders to wake her. "Come on, Lizzie. I told you to keep awake!"

Mary rushed to her daughter's aid, half asleep and bewildered: "Lizzie! Oh, my goodness, what's happened?" She then noticed Billy, "Billy! Thank goodness you're safe!" She threw her arms around him and squeezed his body against hers while repeatedly thanking Bentley.

"Getting Billy isn't the hardest part, madam. What comes next in my plan is going to be the hardest part." He warned her, giving her a look of caution. "Lady Elspeth has laced both of your drinks and food, and it looks as if it's taking more of an effect on Lizzie than on you, but I'm sure that's because she has double the dose inside her."

Mary felt a pang of guilt. She brushed off his remark, trying not to let it bother her. "Based on your words, I'm assuming she drank the milk I specifically requested for her not to drink." She emphasised the word 'specifically,' letting it roll off the tip of her tongue slowly.

"I see that I've upset you. Forgive me, madam." He edged closer to Lizzie's slumped body and picked her up, throwing her over his shoulder in a quick, swift motion as if she were as light as a feather. He turned to Mary and directed her hand to grasp Billy's arm. "I'll need you to try to stay awake. Make use of Billy to keep yourself going. We must get moving. Everyone is now in bed."

Mary felt nauseous as the ground beneath her spun. Her head beat like a drum—loud and constant. Billy held her up, cushioning her with his arm to stop her from collapsing. She was grateful for his presence, but she felt a twinge of guilt for him having to witness her frail and feeble side. She could tell that he was still in pain from the burn but failing miserably in trying to hide it behind a fake smile.

"Let's get started. I want to put as much distance as possible between us and this place." Bentley's expression said it all; his words were matched by the disgusted look on his face as he took one last look around the room before ushering Billy and Mary through the secret door.

Every groan and creak from the floorboards reverberated through the still, silent air. In the dim light, the servant's quarters appeared even worse than before. To Mary, the walls seemed to be closing in on them, edging closer and closer as they muddled their way through the narrow maze of corridors.

Bentley halted abruptly in his tracks, almost colliding with Billy. He muted everyone with a wave of his hand and listened intently to a muffled sound coming from behind them. It sounded like the ruffling of a nightgown rubbing against skin as someone approached them through the darkness.

Bentley hissed, "Someone is awake." In a panic, he turned his head every which way, looking for a hiding place. "We must act quickly!" He shoved Billy with Mary attached into a nearby room and quietly shut the door behind him.

In the fading light, you couldn't see anything except the shadows cast by the furniture lining the walls. Bentley took a step into the moonlight streaming through the window and pressed his fingers to his lips to keep them quiet. He then pointed to the bed, and Mary could see a bulge in the blankets through her sleepy eyes, understanding what Bentley was trying to say. The hushed sound of bare feet scurried past with an amber glow from a night lamp illuminating the crack beneath the door. Bentley's heart returned to normal as the light faded back into the darkness. He couldn't tell who that was, but he knew they shouldn't have been out at that time of night. He began to shake as a sense of dread overcame him.

Lizzie, despite her small stature and light weight, was

beginning to irritate his shoulder. He gently tossed her over to his other shoulder before glancing at the nearby clock on the mantelpiece, illuminated by the silvery moonlight. "We must move," he said in a low voice, hoping not to wake up whoever was in the bed next to them.

"Who was that?" Billy whispered, his voice cracking slightly from fear.

"I'm not sure, Billy. I suggest we move quickly but keep as quiet as possible. This is our only chance to escape." The iciness of the doorknob sent a shiver down Bentley's spine as he grasped it tightly. He held his breath, half expecting someone on the other side of the door, and slowly opened it, hoping it wouldn't creak. He peered out slowly, "All clear."

They trailed after Bentley, Mary's head swimming with dizziness from the spiral staircase's ascent. Billy clung to her, offering support as she struggled to maintain her balance. The twisting stairs only added to her disorientation, leaving her feeling as though she were caught in a whirlwind. Lady Elspeth's treatment had left her feeling weak and vulnerable, a sensation she detested yet found herself unable to shake. Despite her pride, Mary was grateful for Bentley's assistance. His kindness had been a lifeline in this bewildering ordeal, guiding them through the labyrinthine corridors of the estate.

Bentley's patience wore thin as Mary lagged behind, her steps faltering with exhaustion. He muttered under his breath, his frustration evident as he juggled Lizzie's limp form while urging Mary forward. Finally, they emerged into yet another narrow corridor, Bentley leading the way with purposeful strides. With a sense of urgency, he navigated through the maze of passages until they reached the servant's kitchen. Relief washed over Mary as they entered, grateful for a moment's respite from the chaos that surrounded them.

"What're you doing, Bentley?" Someone with a thick Northern accent hissed from beside the stove.

Bentley's heart leapt into his throat, and he froze, panic-stricken. His face became ashen as he turned slowly towards the voice. His breathing accelerated in time with the beat of his heart. Wide-eyed and terrified, he spoke with a tremble, "Please don't tell our mistress that you've seen us, James."

The man stepped out of the shadows into the light, a smirk on his lips. "Should I or should I not?"

Mary recognised him right away. He was the servant Lady Elspeth had requested to follow her and Lizzie back to their room earlier. With a contemptuous look, he smiled at Mary. "Lovely to see you again, madam." His words wreaked of sarcasm, and Mary wanted to slap the snide look from his face.

The man's icy blue eyes looked as if they could pierce through flesh. He was fresh and rosy-cheeked, with damp hair dripping onto his nightgown. A pan of hot water began to boil over, diverting James's attention away from them. He moved quickly, removing the pan from the heat. "Well, I'm sure you can imagine what would happen if our mistress discovered you were escaping with her guests." He turned away from them to clean up the spill on the stove. "What's in it for me if I keep quiet for you, Bentley?"

Bentley's shoulders sagged in defeat, knowing exactly what James was after. He sighed loudly and thought for a moment before responding, "I'll give you our grandfather's watch." He juggled Lizzie's body while reaching into his pocket for a silver-chained pocket watch.

"Our?" Billy asks, bemused. "He's your brother?"

Bentley nodded, ashamed. "Yes, he's the eldest."

James grinned with satisfaction as he snatched the watch from Bentley's grasp. "At last! Finally in the hands of its rightful owner."

"Now will you let us leave?" Bentley asked bluntly.

James held the watch up to the light, beaming with delight. "Well, you can't go without taking something to keep you warm out there." He said, carefully inspecting the chain. "I'll make you a beverage; you can take it with you."

Before Bentley could object, James busied himself preparing hot tea, enough for all of them. Mary watched with growing unease as he added a sprinkle of suspicious-looking white powder from a dusty tin, his movements furtive as if trying to conceal his actions. Quickly stirring the tea, he poured it into a flask and sealed it tightly. Ignoring Bentley's presence, James handed the flask directly to Billy. "Here you go, son. Now be on your way," he said briskly, urging them to leave. Mary's heart pounded with apprehension, her instincts warning her that something was amiss.

His brother's discourteous attitude put him on edge. His eyes were dead, void of any emotion as he glanced towards Bentley. But once his eyes were on Mary, they filled with lust, lingering on her bosom just long enough for her to notice. In embarrassment, she turned away from his lewd stare. James' grin didn't reach his eyes, giving him a psychotic appearance that Bentley found disturbing.

His brother hadn't always been so cruel, but since being in Lady Elspeth's presence, she had warped him into one of her many slaves, willing to do anything she asked. James was her most loyal servant, and Bentley wanted to kick himself for getting caught by him. He couldn't trust his brother, nor did he want to. James' snarky attitude influenced most people, allowing him to force his way into their minds with his persuasive attitude and crumble their walls to allow himself in. He posed a threat. A leech that needed to be squashed. His mind was as sharp and cunning as a fox, and Bentley knew that if his brother used his mind against them, they would have no chance of survival, let alone escaping Lady Elspeth's clutches.

Before returning to the stove to clean up, James winked at Billy. He stood tall and confident in front of the shabby kitchen sink, his shoulders broad and threatening. Unlike his brother, who stood stiffly with his back permanently curved, revealing to all that life had dealt him many blows, James had an arrogant attitude about him. He was someone not to be messed with.

"What would happen if you were caught?" James asked, his face mockingly innocent.

Bentley's eyes narrowed with a sullen look on his face. His heart sank, knowing all too well where this discussion was heading. James had always enjoyed playing the cat-and-mouse game. "You know what would happen if we were caught."

James cast another snide glance at his brother. "I know. I just wanted to make sure you were aware as well."

"Didn't you just say you wouldn't?"

"I told you I wouldn't," James repeated, exaggerating the last word to muse himself.

Bentley was as white as freshly ironed linen. His face was stricken with fear, and he appeared to be fighting back tears. "If you still have any emotion inside that rotting flesh that houses your evil soul, you will let us go peacefully," he spat.

James' face lit up with surprise as he heard his brother's words. His face then twisted into a mocking frown. "Oh, my dear brother, such harsh words come from your mouth. I'm hurt in many ways." He turned away from them and pretended to cry.

"Drop this silly facade, James," Mary said confidently, having grown tired of his ridiculous performance.

James turned to face Mary, his eyes sneering and condescending. "Keep your mouth shut, madam. You're a woman. You have no right to address me in that way!"

Before anyone could react, Billy dropped Mary and strode the two paces over to James. He grabbed the large cast-iron kettle from the stove and hurled it at James' head.

There was no time for James to react or duck. The kettle's handle caught him on the side of his head, splattering scalding water everywhere. As a trickle of blood appeared, dribbling slowly down his forehead, he stared at the boy in shock. His legs crumpled beneath him, and he fell to his knees. "Why?" He uttered before passing out.

Billy's expression was unlike anything Mary had ever seen in a boy. As he stared down at James's slumped body, it was pure hatred, spiteful, and cruel. Nobody said anything. Nobody moved. The air around them was heavy and still. Like long, bony fingers caressing your leg, it felt unsettling.

Mary was wide awake now, suffocated by the bleak, gloomy environment. What she saw in Billy for those few seconds stayed with her like a blemish that would not go away no matter how hard you scrubbed at it.

Lizzie's soft groan brought them all back into the room. "Is he still alive?" Mary trembled, her voice high and squeaky.

Billy shrugged as if nothing mattered. He took a step back, staring blasély at the kitchen wall, showing no remorse for what he had just done. She brushed past him and knelt beside James to check the pulse on the side of his neck. She blew out a huge sigh of relief. "He's still alive."

"We have to hide him," Bentley finally muttered, "It'll give us more time to escape." He lowered Lizzie gently to the ground before yanking his brother's limp body across the cold, stone floor as if he were just a doll, indifferent to the fact that he was dragging his brother. He opened the door to a walk-in cupboard in the far-left corner of the kitchen. It was packed to the brim with food, with barely enough room for someone to walk in. Bentley hurled his brother in with an uncaring expression on his face. "All right, let's go," he mumbled as he picked Lizzie up off the floor.

Mary, stunned and disturbed by what had just occurred, quietly followed Bentley, declining Billy's offer of assistance. For a split second, a look of sadness appeared on Billy's face, quickly replaced with another shrug of his shoulders and a brisk walk past Mary to catch up with Bentley.

Mary trailed behind, unwilling to be near Billy. She was wary of him; a slight trepidation hung over her like a dark cloud. She couldn't shake this perturbed feeling, but she was also curious about what else Billy was willing to conceal from her. The flask in Billy's hand reminded her that her mouth was beginning to feel like sandpaper. She desperately needed a drink but didn't want to waste any more time by stopping, and in the case, it was laced with drugs. Bentley scurried through the maze of corridors like a hungry rat. He treaded carefully, avoiding every creak in the floorboards, as he had done a hundred times before. To Mary, every corridor and every door appeared to be the same. Bentley's sense of direction impressed her, and as they hurried down the last flight of stairs leading out to the back of the house, a wave of relief washed over her.

The storm had long since passed, leaving a trail of destruction in its wake. Despite the fact that it was still quite windy, Mary appreciated the feeling of clean, fresh air on her face. She took a deep breath, allowing her eyes to adjust to the darkness.

"There isn't time to relax. We must put as much distance as possible between ourselves and this place," Bentley called out above the wind.

The darkness was like a veil around them. Everything looked as if it were covered in soot, with only strange-looking mounds and shapes visible instead of the landscape. The atmosphere was tenebrific and obfuscating, circulating and blanketing everything. Mary could hear the whistling through the trees, the swish and sway of the leaves, and bits of rubble being blown about in the wind. Her senses were still hazy from the sleeping pill, but as she concentrated harder, the smog began to lift from her mind. Bentley walked on, wasting no time. He dodged and darted through the obstacle course of abandoned carriages, heading straight for a back gate. The storm had ripped the latch off the gate, allowing it to smash against the fence like a drum beating in time with the wind.

Bentley's eyes widened in fear as he looked back over his shoulder at the mansion. Mary turned to see what he was looking at and noticed a glow of orange moving soundlessly past each window on the top floor, where Lady Elspeth resided.

CHAPTER SIXTY-SEVEN

# Superintendent Landrake

The soft toss and throw of the stretcher being carried up the hospital steps nearly put Landrake to sleep. He could already smell the faint chemical odour wafting out through the hospital's double doors, and it sickened him to think that he was going to be among death and disease. Instead of focusing on the pain pounding from the side of his head, he fought the oncoming waves of exhaustion, desperate to stay focused on his new plan of escape.

None, not even those closest to him, including his colleagues and wife, were privy to his true capabilities. Time was ticking before the media twisted his story, tarnishing his image beyond repair, despite his conviction that he wasn't inherently evil. Acknowledging a dark streak within, he believed it could be controlled. In his mind, the killings were justified, a pact with the voice in his head to eliminate threats to his safety. Responsibility eluded him, even for his failing marriage. He saw himself as flawless, willing to do whatever necessary to maintain that facade. To him, the murders were merciful, safeguarding his reputation. No one would dare challenge him in court; he had too much to lose.

"I'm leaving him in your care. I'm going back to the station to help the detective. Make sure nothing happens here." Landrake recognised Claydon's voice right away as he listened to a set of footsteps hurrying away. There was a sigh of exasperation and then silence for a while until another set of footsteps stopped a metre from the stretcher he was lying on.

"He needs to be watched. He cannot be let out of sight," A low male voice spoke above his head, like dead leaves rustling in the breeze.

His stomach churned as two pairs of rough hands seized him, hoisting him into the air. Though he longed to protest their rough handling, caution prevailed, and he feigned unconsciousness. With a jolt, he hit a frigid, unyielding surface, unmistakably a gurney. The icy metal seeped through his clothing, chilling him to the bone.

"Does he pose a threat?" another voice asked, timid and nervous.

"Don't ask questions, madam. Just do as I say. There will be an officer outside his door at all times, but I ask that the hospital staff also remain vigilant and keep very wary of this man."

All eyes fixated on Landrake, curiosity tinged with suspicion as to why he was the centre of attention. A frigid hand gripped his face, prompting his eyelids to flutter open as it pried them apart for inspection. Maintaining composure, he allowed the scrutiny. A murmured exchange between someone and the officer preceded a forceful tug of his head, directing attention to his wound for further examination.

"Take him to room 104," another voice spoke, stern and proper, and Landrake knew immediately that it was the doctor. He could feel the man's stringent presence next to him—powerful and calm, with a hint of arrogance. Landrake liked this man already. He knew that he could get him on his side if he had the chance.

The gurney's wheels squealed against the hospital's smooth, shiny floor, alerting Landrake to the fact that they were on the move to his new home. "I demand to know if this man will be a danger to my staff. I have the duty to protect them, officer," The stern voice spoke up again, this time more forcefully.

"I've been instructed not to say anything, doctor. You'll just have to sit tight for the moment until I know what's going on."

The gurney abruptly came to a stop, causing Landrake's body to slide downward towards the edge. "I'm not stupid, and neither is anyone else here. He will be recognised as the superintendent. The word will get out, and before we know it, the hospital will be surrounded by reporters."

"Doctor, take your hand off me!" The officer barked. "As I previously stated, Inspector Acker has instructed me not to say anything until he says so."

"Then, I suggest you find out quickly before this place is overrun by the papers. If word gets out, I'm sure your inspector will be furious." As they wheeled the gurney through the corridors, Landrake noticed a slight snide tone in the doctor's voice. "I don't want my nurses bombarded by reporters!"

"They won't if your staff keeps their mouths shut!" The officer bellowed, his voice attracting the attention of nurses and patients. Eyes darted back and forth, trying to remain unnoticed while being curious about what all the fuss was about.

Landrake could feel the officer's angry grip on the gurney beneath him. Even though he kept his eyes closed, pretending to be unconscious, he could feel the tension between the doctor and the officer rising. He would have told them off by now if he wasn't on house arrest, abusing his title as superintendent and treating them like they were beneath him. To him, everyone was below him, apart from a few close colleagues of his, whom he treated with the utmost respect.

He needed them now more than ever to get him out of this mess he was buried in. They controlled everything in the city, from every city dweller to the judge. They were the tax collectors, the idle, merry men you see sitting behind large, lavish desks in the finest silk suits. They were egotistical, and they knew every secret hidden within the city, which they used to their advantage.

He wished he could be like them. To sit behind a freshly varnished desk with maids attending to his every need was a dream come true for many men, let alone him. He was well aware that he was merely a pawn in their game of controlling the police force. There would be chaos if the people of the city knew what was really going on and who was running it.

Landrake could feel himself drifting off into his mind, away from the heated argument above his head. His thoughts returned to Acker and how his life was hanging by a thread as a result of him. Acker was the only person who could bring him down and ruin his life. He couldn't have that, and he couldn't have his reputation tarnished among his peers. If he was to survive this ordeal, then Acker would need to be dealt with quickly.

His foot slammed into the side of the door, yanking him from his daydream of strangling Acker. The officer pushed the gurney into room 104, unconcerned about whether Landrake was okay or not. Anger welled up within him as pain seared up his leg. His leg throbbed, and he struggled to keep his eyes closed. The argument faded away up the corridor, leaving him alone for the first time. He squinted, checking to see if the room was empty, before fully opening his eyes and rubbing his now sore leg.

The corridor was bustling with activity, but in his room, there was a serene atmosphere. He relaxed his muscles one by one until he was completely immersed in the silence. For the first time in a long time, his mind was silent, and he began to drift off to sleep. The low hum of people's conversations rocked and comforted him like a lullaby, and as he began to coast into the darkness of his mind, he sensed another presence watching him from within the room.

## CHAPTER SIXTY-EIGHT

# The Wrong Shoe

Since Landrake had been whisked away to the hospital, the crowd outside the station had begun to get increasingly volatile. Agitation mounted among the crowd, manifesting in the shattering of two windows. Officers stationed inside guarded the breaches, meting out swift retribution to any attempting to breach further. Meanwhile, Acker retreated to his office, locking himself in, his pacing punctuated by disgusted glances at the bloodstained floor. Anticipation gripped him as he awaited a breakthrough from Chavers, desperate for any lead in the case files. Yet, amidst his restless movements, the boy remained absorbed in his reading, indifferent to Acker's frantic pacing.

The mortuary had received the bodies, yet the lingering scent of death hung heavy in the air, casting a pall over their surroundings. A sense of hopelessness pervaded, offering no respite from their grim reality. Acker couldn't help but rue his decision to take on the case; its difficulty surpassed any he'd faced before. Despite the apprehension of the murderer, a gnawing uncertainty clawed at him. Trust was a scarce commodity; with one colleague hospitalised and another guarding the superintendent, only a handful remained dependable—a fledgling boy just beginning to show signs of maturity, and Symons.

His mind drifted to his wife, Mary, a pang of concern gripping him. Her prolonged silence troubled him deeply, as did the absence of Billy, who failed to report to the station for two consecutive days.

As Claydon's head peeked into the room, Acker greeted him with a quizzical expression. "How did you manage to return? The area's crawling with troublemakers."

Claydon's smirk hinted at his resourcefulness. "Went around the back, sir."

Acker's brow furrowed. "You took that risk? The place is practically besieged."

Undeterred, Claydon continued, "Three officers are safeguarding the superintendent, so I figured I'd be of better use here. Any more news on the found torso in the morgue?"

Acker sighed, shaking his head. "Let's focus on one thing at a time. We're stretched thin as it is." Then he turned to Chavers, his tone serious. "No, we haven't found any evidence related to another torso. Our priority remains on this case."

Chavers looked up from his reading, confusion evident. "What torso?"

Acker's frown deepened. "There have been previous discoveries. One was found on the docks months ago."

Claydon's disappointment was palpable. "Why wasn't I informed?"

Acker's response was firm. "I need everyone's focus on our current investigation. We'll address it in due course. Right now, let's concentrate on gathering evidence against the superintendent."

Claydon's shoulders slumped, his frustration evident as he sank into a chair, flipping through case files with a mixture of dejection and annoyance. The room fell into a heavy silence once more, broken only by Acker's restless pacing.

The room had fallen into a heavy silence once more, broken only by the rustle of papers until Claydon's discovery prompted a flurry of activity. A sense of anticipation hung thick in the air as he presented the photograph of the bloodied footprint, questioning the whereabouts of the superintendent's shoe.

Without hesitation, Chavers retrieved the shoe and tossed it to Claydon, who wasted no time scrutinising its sole. A spark of hope ignited in Acker's eyes as he awaited Claydon's revelation.

After moments of intense examination, Claydon's puzzled expression spoke volumes. "The prints don't match. It's not the same shoe."

Acker seized the shoe and photograph, studying them intently. "But how is that possible?"

Claydon interjected, his tone thoughtful. "If you look closely at the bloodied print, there's a distinct feature—a hole in the shoe. Whoever killed Lady Penelope was wearing footwear with a hole."

Chavers jumped up in excitement. "Which could mean that whoever the culprit is has no means of money."

Open-mouthed and staring blankly at the certificates on the wall, Acker could only stutter, "It's not the superintendent."

## CHAPTER SIXTY-NINE

# London

As they neared London, Banes couldn't ignore the distinct scent that greeted them, a pungent embrace from the city. The acrid odour had assailed them the moment they disembarked, with Harvard quickly spotting the countless chimneys billowing black smoke into the sky. Open sewers snaked through streets, mingling with the putrid rivers and thick smog that enveloped the city. Channels carried away a grim concoction of waste—human, animal, and refuse from butchers—intermixing to form a noxious brew. Both men instinctively covered their noses with handkerchiefs to ward off nausea.

Despite the olfactory assault, Harvard found himself taken aback by the vibrant hues and opulent surroundings of London's streets. Meanwhile, Banes navigated through the throng with practised ease, avoiding direct paths in favour of shadowy alleys and narrow passages teeming with the destitute. Their attire drew curious glances, but Banes remained unfazed, preferring to remain concealed within the city's depths.

The streets of London reverberated with the clamour of horse-drawn traffic clattering over cobblestones, intermingled with the ceaseless activity of its inhabitants. A constant stream of carts laden with goods traversed the thoroughfares, infusing the air with the rich aroma of freshly baked pastries. Amidst the cart traffic, hackney coaches darted back and forth, ferrying passengers along the narrow pathways to various destinations. Sedan chairs glided through the streets, transporting affluent individuals to their places of business, while throngs of pedestrians jostled past, eager to seize the day's best bargains.

Though reminiscent of Bristol in its bustling energy, London bore a bleaker countenance, its skyline dominated by towering factories and its streets populated by downtrodden figures coming and going. Children, their faces drawn with hardship, sought alms from passersby, and Harvard observed with dismay as one youngster deftly pilfered a gentleman's purse without detection.

Banes smirked and tapped his pocket, "Keep your possessions close to you."

After witnessing that interaction, they both avoided the slums and blended in well in the wealthier part of the city. Men tipped their hats to Banes after spotting his medical bag clutched to his side. Harvard felt a twinge of jealousy as he looked down at his meek attire, wishing to be just as respected as Banes, but no one batted an eye at him.

The rush of city traffic accelerated Banes as they hastened towards his long-forgotten home. He stared with admiration at the ladies dressed handsomely in their finest silk dresses, attempting to impress their suitors. Banes had forgotten it was matching season, but as his fingers twitched in desire to touch their snowy-white skin, he couldn't help but feel a little depressed that he was too old to find himself another woman.

Banes' residence was much like Harvard's old room, situated above a shop. The place looked bleak and rundown, which was the opposite of what Harvard was expecting. He was expecting something a lot cleaner and fresher than what lay before them. The doctor was wealthy enough to afford better accommodation than the one Harvard was witnessing before him.

"I own both the shop and the apartment upstairs, but I rarely rent out the shop." Banes had said as they walked in through the back door. "This was a family-owned business that I abandoned many years ago to pursue a career in medicine."

Harvard could only nod as he scanned the haggard, old shop, full of thick layers of dust and walls covered from top to bottom with cobwebs. His nose began to twitch as a result of it all.

"It could use a good cleaning." Banes chuckled as he noticed Harvard's surprised expression. He climbed the creaky wooden steps to the apartment above and waltzed in without knocking. But much to Banes' surprise, his tenants had already left some time before, leaving the place in shambles. As he looked around at what was left of his home, a snarl crept from his mouth. "I don't understand how they could have done this to me."

Harvard felt a little sorry for the old man, yet there was a hint of ignorance about him that he couldn't ignore. It gave him pleasure to know that Banes had been wrongly done over, and he struggled to keep his smirk hidden as he looked at the old man's features. "What should we do now?" he asked, fully expecting to be shouted at, but instead, Banes turned away from him and inspected the damage.

The furniture had been beaten to a pulp and was no longer repairable. The flowery wallpaper was ripped in places as if clawed by a wild animal. The fireplace was covered in charred newspaper and soot, and the air still smelled faintly of pipe smoke. Harvard followed Banes into the bedroom and stood there, watching him pat out the lumps in the mattress on the bed. "This is mine," he said, then pointed to the ground. "You can sleep on the floor for now until we find you another bed."

Harvard expected nothing less from his new master. He nodded and tossed the few belongings he had on him to the floor.

The bedroom had remained untouched, and it exuded a delicate, feminine presence. Vases of dead flowers had been scattered around the room as if someone were attempting to brighten the atmosphere. The bed had already been stripped, exposing the stains underneath. The wallpaper was the same, but there were no rips or marks this time. A stained chamber pot protruded from beneath the bed, and a bowl still full of stagnant water sat on a table alongside an abandoned hairbrush devoid of bristles.

"Welcome home," Banes muttered mockingly.

He stood up and walked out before Harvard could respond. His footsteps echoed through the floorboards until they came to a halt, and a screeching sound from an unoiled door sounded out, which piqued Harvard's curiosity. He followed the sound downstairs and into the old shop, where a hatch had been opened. As Harvard made his way down the stone steps into the basement, an old, rusty lock and chain swung from the latch, captivating his interest even more. He wondered why Banes felt the need to lock the basement hatch for his tenants and what he had down there that he didn't want anyone else to see.

Stepping into the dimly lit basement, Harvard's heart hammered against his ribs, the sound reverberating in his ears. Banes stood at the centre, a disturbing tableau unfolding before him—walls adorned with a collage of newspaper clippings, his hands clasped behind his back as he swayed with palpable excitement. A cluttered desk, strewn with papers and jars concealing ghastly contents, occupied the space below the macabre display. Photographs of mutilated torsos, meticulously arranged alongside the news articles, lent an eerie semblance of order to the scene, as if they were morbid works of art.

The sight chilled Harvard to his core; he had always sensed a sinister undercurrent in Banes, but witnessing his malevolence laid bare on the wall before him sent shivers down his spine. The revelation that the doctor was the notorious torso killer struck him with a profound sense of dread, shattering any illusions he had harboured about his colleague's true nature.

"You shouldn't be in here, Harvard," Banes said without turning around. His tone was snide and contemptuous, as if he were reprimanding a schoolboy.

"What is all this?" Harvard questioned.

Banes chuckled. "It's my treasure trove. I collect trophies from a hobby of mine." He knelt before the desk as if it were an altar. "I really missed this, Harvard. It's like a thirst that must be quenched." He then sneered as he looked back at Harvard's disturbed expression. "Don't be concerned about yourself. My desire is only for women—well, good-looking women, to be precise. I'm not particularly interested in your torso."

Harvard was relieved, but he couldn't believe the situation he had found himself in. He thought he had odd hobbies, but the doctor's hobbies were truly insane. He had nowhere else to turn, and no one would accept him into their home. He was in a strange city, and the only person he knew was a raving lunatic with a murderous skill against all women.

## CHAPTER SEVENTY

# Escape

The woodland in front of them was rich in plushness and opulence. As they passed through the gate, black shadows hung in the groves, making Mary nervous. The hairs on the back of her neck stood stiffly on end, indicating that someone was nearby, probably watching their every move. The shaggy heads of the oak trees were encircled by coils of ephemeral mist. They writhed around them, tantalising and dubious, like a hot beverage sitting on the table, ready to be consumed. The mist caressed the lichen-encrusted bark, dipping and diving into every crack and nook. It glided with a mysterious intent, adding its astral vapour to the damp breath of the countryside. It muffled sounds, haunted the dunes, and touched every surface with its wispy breath. It was what Mary called 'morning mist', beautiful yet icy to the touch.

The tree's woody incense was the result of years of snapping branches crashing to the woodland floor and decomposing. Like a miasma, the composting, organic odour rose in waves, wafting up their noses. Every verdant tree they passed under looked as if its branches were reaching out to snag at their clothes. Bentley decided to go deeper into the dense heart of the woods, following the winding path as if he had taken it many times before.

The early morning peace was soul-soothing, infiltrating Mary's muscles and relaxing them one by one until she felt completely calm. The feeling that someone was watching them had faded, and she began to enjoy their walk to the river that led back into the city.

Every now and again, she cast a glance at Billy, searching for the aggression she had witnessed only moments before. She'd never seen that in him before, and she began to wonder if she knew him completely or not at all. But he was only a child. A young man in need of her support. She couldn't deny him a place in her heart simply because he was prone to rage. After all, he was only trying to keep her safe.

The wind howled through the trees, swishing and swaying back and forth until a blizzard of leaves fell to the floor in front of them. The silvery hue of the moon peered through the clouds, providing them with some light as they hurried through the woods.

Little Lizzie groaned slightly in her sleep as her head bounced around on Bentley's shoulder. Mary was washed over with guilt. She had not been there for her daughter when she needed her the most. She was lucky Bentley had a good heart; otherwise, she had no idea where they'd end up.

"Just a little bit farther," Bentley yelled above the wind.

After a few more minutes of trudging through the undergrowth, the woodland cleared, revealing boggy marshes and rotting vegetation. Bentley had to slow down and tread more carefully than usual as the low, curling mist slithered its tentacles through every wet, dewy weed and entangled vine. Mary could feel the moist air on her skin, and with each step, she had to avoid the sound of slurping mud and burps of trapped air from beneath the surface.

The marshland was a dangerous place to be, full of death traps and poor animal skeletons protruding from the wasteland as if to warn travellers of what lay ahead if they ventured any further. Before them, soggy yellow iris and branched burdock appeared.

The deeper they went, the more of that they saw. Blackened pools bubbled and squeaked among the low-lying shrubs, emitting a moss-like stench into the air. Mary shivered from the sound of animal cries nearby. Her feet were getting soaked, and she was shivering from the cold. This was her first experience in such a dire situation, and she didn't like it one bit. Nor did she like her clothes getting ruined and her hair becoming an entangled mess. She felt less lady-like.

When she caught sight of the drink Bentley's brother had given them, her mouth began to water. She desired it so badly that it was all she could think about.

A gunshot rang out behind them, causing the ground beneath them to shake. Bentley had already thrown Mary into the long, overgrown weeds before she could even turn around.

"Keep down!" He hissed as he pulled Billy down with him. "They've found us."

"What do we do now?" Billy asked nervously.

"Keep heading west. The boat is just over these weeds. Stay down and keep Lizzie's head afloat."

Mary looked at him, confused. "Wait, what about you? Aren't you coming with us?"

"I'm going to have to try to keep them away from you, or you won't make it." He put a comforting hand on Mary's shoulder. "Don't worry, the river will flow directly into the city. It will not take long." He cast a glance behind him before gently nudging Mary deeper into the weeds. "Bring your husband to Lady Elspeth's house and explain what has happened. Now, Mary, go."

With a fake smile on his face, he waded through the water away from them and headed toward Lady Elspeth's men. Billy snatched Mary's arm and pulled her forward. "You heard him. Let's go."

They moved quickly west toward the small dock that held the boat, pushing their way through the tangle of weeds with their bodies half-covered in Marsh water. Billy kept Lizzie close to him, carrying her over the bogs to keep her dry. Every time a gunshot rang out, they flinched in unison, watching the sky turn bright orange. Lady Elspeth's sniffer dogs were tracking them down like foxes. Mary had just then realised why Bentley had pushed them both into the mucky water: to confuse their scent and allow the dogs to follow him instead.

A wave of guilt and appreciation washed over her, and she stopped, looking back to see if Bentley was still alive. Across the horizon, she could just make out a dark figure ducking into the woods away from Elspeth's men, and another round of shots rang out, lighting up the sky once more and revealing Bentley's face just before he vanished behind a tree.

"Come on, or we'll get caught!" Billy shouted, pulling at her arm again to get her to move.

She yanked her arm back. "I need a drink, Billy."

He sighed and tossed the flask at her before moving on without her. She savoured the hot, sweet taste of the tea, forgetting that James had poured powder into it. She licked her lips, before catching up with Billy and handing it back to him. "Have some as well. You need the energy."

He nodded and drank the rest of the tea before tossing the flask into the weeds. "We don't need that any longer."

She wrinkled her nose in disgust. "You shouldn't litter."

"Sorry," he muttered, unfazed.

They continued through the undergrowth, taking care to avoid the sinking bogs and rotting vegetation. The water had reached their hips and was getting deeper as they went. The smell made Mary's eyes water, but that wasn't the issue. She wasn't sure if it was the stench of the marshes or fear, but something was making her feel very dizzy. She collided with Billy, knocking him off balance and pushing him deeper into the vegetation. "I apologise," she stammered, clearly struggling to keep her cool.

A giggle came from Billy, surprising Mary, as she expected him to be angry. She pulled him out of the tangled vines while he stumbled into her, letting go of Lizzie and allowing her to sink beneath the murky water. He laughed even louder as he watched Lizzie's head vanish, alerting Lady Elspeth's men from a distance. Mary quickly caught Lizzie before she disappeared completely and pulled her back up, angry at herself for not protecting her daughter.

"What the hell is wrong with you, Billy?" Mary hissed,

attempting to silence him. "Be quiet!"

As if he were drunk, Billy's eyes rolled to the back of his head. "Please accept my apologies, your Majesty," he chortled.

Another wave of dizziness knocked Mary off her feet, and she collapsed into the water, still clutching Lizzie. Billy laughed again, much louder this time.

"Seek them out!" A distant voice called out.

Fear seized Mary as she watched the towering weeds before them being mercilessly hacked down. An ominous sense of foreboding gripped her; she couldn't shake the feeling that something was amiss. Bentley's brother's peculiar tea suddenly seemed suspicious. Determined to stay alert, she fought against the drowsiness threatening to overtake her. Billy, incapacitated by whatever was in the tea, was beyond assistance, leaving Mary with no option but to take charge. With determination, she hoisted Billy upright, all the while ensuring that Lizzie remained safe in her care.

"Billy, I need you to pay close attention to me," she slurred. "I'll hold Lizzie's legs while you hold her arms. We must continue, or we'll get caught."

Billy nodded slowly, as if unsure of what Mary was trying to say. They stumbled on, both holding each other up through the murky water, still trying to save Lizzie from drowning. Lady Elspeth's men were closing in on them, chopping down everything in their path.

They eventually arrived at a small clearing with a dock large enough to hold one boat. Bentley was right. The river's current was strong, and Mary realised right away that they were going to win.

"Get in," Mary commanded, her mind reeling with unease. Billy stumbled into the boat, his balance precarious, threatening to overturn it. "Watch it!" Mary snapped, frustration tinged with impatience as she steadied the boat. With delicate care, she lowered Lizzie into the boat, swiftly untying it from the post. Barely managing to board herself without tumbling into the river, Mary felt her pulse quicken, the world around her blurring into a dizzying swirl of colours.

Straining her eyes, Mary could just discern the heads of Lady

Elspeth's men amidst the tall grass, their presence fleeting as they drifted downstream. A pang of guilt tugged at her heart for Bentley, hoping fervently for his safety. Despite the looming threat of capture, Mary harboured a glimmer of assurance that Lady Elspeth wouldn't bring harm to him.

As they sat in the boat, exhaustion weighing heavy upon them, Mary leaned heavily against Billy's trembling form. His muttered words were a jumble, incomprehensible to Mary's ears, while Lizzie slumbered softly in her lap, oblivious to their peril. Feeling Billy shiver beneath her arm, Mary drew him closer, shielding him from the biting wind as she watched the scenery slip by.

The boat swayed gently with the current's embrace, navigating the water's surface with ease. Mary's own fatigue began to overwhelm her, her thoughts slipping into a haze of weariness. Just as she felt herself succumbing to the darkness, Billy's sudden burst of tears jolted her awake. His anguished sobs wracked his frame as he clung to Mary, his confession shattering the silence. "I killed my mother."

Mary's blood ran cold, the weight of Billy's confession sinking in amidst the fog of her mind. "But you never knew your mother?" she queried, incredulous at the revelation that he had committed matricide. Billy's sobs intensified, his words muddled and unintelligible amidst his anguish. With a gentle touch, Mary rubbed his shoulder, a soothing gesture born of maternal instinct. "Billy, take a deep breath. Try to calm down and tell me slowly."

Meeting her gaze with tear-streaked eyes, Billy hiccupped between sobs, his vulnerability stirring a newfound tenderness within Mary's heart. For the first time since Billy had entered her life, she felt a surge of warmth and affection towards him, akin to the love she would feel for her own son.

"Lady Penelope is dead because of me," Billy confessed, his voice barely above a whisper. Mary's affection for him dissolved in an instant, replaced by a chilling cocktail of shock and dread. Vivid images of the crime scene flooded her mind, each more gruesome than the last, painting a vivid picture of the heinous act that had claimed Lady Penelope's life. It was no accident; someone consumed by psychosis and rage had mercilessly ended her existence.

"What do you mean, Billy?" Mary stammered, unable to meet his gaze, her mind reeling with the implications of his admission.

Closing his eyes, Billy's voice trembled as he muttered, "It was me. She rejected me as her son, and I... I lost control. I didn't mean to, but I killed her."

As the drug in the tea took hold, enveloping them in a haze of disorientation, reality warped into a nightmarish dreamscape. Billy's confession echoed in Mary's mind as she slumped against him, both succumbing to the sinister grasp of the drug.

# CHAPTER SEVENTY-ONE

## The Breakthrough

After what felt like an eternity, Acker resumed pacing his office, his agitation mounting with each passing moment. "I can't believe this. We're right back to where we started."

Claydon raised a calming hand to halt the detective's pacing. "It's not all bad, sir. The superintendent is still accountable for the other murders. We just need to retrace our steps and ensure we haven't overlooked anything."

Acker's curiosity piqued. "Are you suggesting we revisit the alleyway?"

Claydon nodded, gathering his belongings. "Exactly. Let's tie up loose ends and close this case."

With resolve, he opened the office door. "Let's finish this."

Acker grabbed his coat, turning to Chavers. "Bring the files. They might come in handy."

Chavers sprang into action, gathering the files into a stack.

"Yes, sir."

"I need to check on Mary before we head back to the crime scene," Acker stated, sliding into his coat. "I haven't heard from her in a while, and I'm starting to worry."

"You haven't mentioned this before, sir," Chavers began. "We all just assumed you were stressed about the case. Should you be worried? What's happened?"

Acker gave him a deadened look before putting his hat on. "I rarely bring my home life into my place of work unless I have the need to worry, and yes, Chavers, I have the right to worry. Something is wrong. I can feel it."

"Has she ever done something like this before?" Claydon asked as he followed him out of the office.

Acker exuded fear. "Barely a day goes by without hearing from her, Claydon. Billy hasn't shown up to the station either, which is also out of the ordinary."

"I noticed that as well, but I assumed you didn't need him and told him to stay at home," Claydon admitted, feeling stupid for not thinking clearly.

As they navigated through the corridors toward the station's rear exit, curious officers glanced their way, wondering about their urgent departure.

Acker's fear for his family swelled rapidly within him. He berated himself for entrusting Mary and Lizzie to Billy, a near stranger with an unknown past. His decision to extend sympathy to the boy and offer him sanctuary under witness protection now seemed naive and reckless. A sense of foreboding gnawed at his gut, compelling him to hasten to his home with an urgency born of instinct, driven by the need to uncover what could be amiss.

"How much can we trust young Billy?" He asked abruptly, piquing Chavers' interest from behind Claydon.

He looked at him, puzzled. "Acker, he's just a kid. What exactly do you mean by that?"

"Claydon, just answer my question. How much do you trust the boy?" Acker asked once more, this time more sternly.

Claydon sighed. "I wouldn't put my life in his hands, if that's what you mean. What are you trying to say, Inspector?"

Acker stared intently at his brother. "We don't know anything about the boy. What if he's wronged my wife and daughter?"

"You're not thinking clearly, sir. Your wife and child are probably fine. We'll double-check on our way to the crime scene to give you peace of mind." Chavers rested his hand on the detective's shoulder. "Try not to let your mind spiral out of control, sir. We need your mind to be sharp before checking the crime scene again."

Acker hated to admit it, but Chavers was right. They all needed to step into that alleyway with a fresh mindset. There must be something there that the murderer accidentally left behind. It was a slim chance, but a chance, nonetheless.

Their jobs dangled by a slender thread, the absence of the superintendent leaving Acker solely responsible for presenting evidence to the judge. A single misstep could spell their swift dismissal. A heavy sigh escaped Acker as he requested the door keys, burdened by the weight of his colleagues' expectations. Claydon swiftly acquiesced, eager to flee the station's oppressive ambiance and the lingering scent of death.

A gust of wind assaulted their faces as Acker swung open the back door. Claydon shivered, the chill penetrating his jacket. "Do you think the torso will become our next case?" he inquired, his mind drifting to the grisly photograph of the dismembered body.

To Claydon, the image had resembled a slab of meat, awaiting the knife of a butcher. Were it not for the tiny heart tattoo adorning the shoulder and the discoloured, sagging breasts, he might have mistaken it for animal flesh.

Acker didn't even bother to look Claydon in the eyes before responding. "All in good time, sergeant." He took a step into the alleyway and waited for the other two to follow. "Keep your head down and try to blend in," he warned before yanking the door shut and locking it. "We only have one chance at this."

Chavers clung to the files as if his very existence depended on them. He had a hunch that they would soon be crucial, and as he trailed behind the detective and sergeant through the maze of alleyways in search of a cab, he couldn't help but wonder if they regarded him in the same light as they did Billy. Despite still being labelled as a "boy" within the police force, Chavers had consistently outshone every officer, establishing himself as the group's intellectual powerhouse. Through sheer determination and effort, he had earned Acker's recognition as a "smart" individual. Now, he was determined to demonstrate to Acker that he was more than capable of cracking this case.

Just beyond the alleyway, the cacophony of the mob's cries for justice reverberated through the air, assaulting the men's ears. As they approached the throng, their hearts pounded erratically in their chests, akin to a fluttering swarm of butterflies. Nerves gnawed at them, leaving them on edge by the time they reached the alley's end, where the crowd's fury seemed palpable.

Acker understood the importance of maintaining composure, knowing he would be the most recognisable to the city dwellers. Yet, despite his efforts to remain composed, fear caused him to tremble uncontrollably beneath his jacket. Even amidst the chaos, his attire stood out, exuding a sleekness that contrasted sharply with the rabble surrounding them.

"Chavers, you sneak out first and call a cab. We'll wait here." Acker ordered, his gaze shifting from the mob to the empty carriages waiting for passengers up the street.

Chavers stepped back nervously. "Why should I, sir? I'm the one dressed in the uniform. I'm going to stick out like a sore thumb!"

Acker looked Chavers up and down before yanking his brother's jacket off and handing it to him, much to Claydon's disagreement. "Here, take this and cover yourself up. Try and keep to the shadows."

Chavers shrugged his jacket on, avoiding Claydon's angry stare, before covering up the pile of files in his hands. Acker then gently nudged him in the direction of the carriages, smiling encouragingly. The boy looked as if he was about to cry as he took a hesitant step towards the mob. Once he realised the angry protesters were taking no notice of him, he began to walk normally around the crowd, weaving in and out to get to the cabs. No one paid him any attention. They were too focused on the police station, shouting and brandishing the officers as incompetent.

Acker and Claydon watched Chavers like a hawk as he snuck through the crowd. They both let out a huge sigh of relief in unison once Chavers reached one of the carriages safely and put a thumbs up to them.

"So far, so good," Acker muttered more to himself than to Claydon as he followed in Chavers' footsteps to meet the cab halfway.

The carriage slowly made its way through the back of the crowd, the coachman keeping a large enough gap away from the people to avoid scaring the horses. As he listened to the hesitant hooves on the cobbled walkway, Claydon could sense the horses' fear. Even the coachman regarded the mob with caution, his brows drawn together and a bite of his lip showing the worry on his face.

A sense of relief washed over Acker and Claydon as they settled into the safety of the carriage, believing themselves to have evaded the watchful eyes of the mob. However, their respite was short-lived. Suddenly, a familiar voice pierced the air, the loud-mouth reporter from before singling them out with a boisterous shout. Panic surged within Acker as he watched the enraged faces of the mob converging upon them.

In the back of the crowd, the reporter stood with arms crossed, a malevolent grin etched upon his face. His eyes glinted with mischief as he made a menacing gesture, sending a chill down Acker's spine. As the mob closed in, the reporter's colleague captured the chaotic scene with a camera, immortalising what would become a notorious photograph of the century. Acker winced, realising the devastating blow the journalist had dealt to their already fragile careers. The man revelled in their downfall, eagerly scribbling notes for his article, undoubtedly embellishing the events to sow further chaos.

Amidst the turmoil, Acker's thoughts raced back to his wife and child, the reason for their hasty departure from the station. As the chaos intensified, a loud screech echoed through the air, followed by the sound of hooves thrashing wildly. A horse, overcome by panic, lashed out, sending the coachman tumbling from his seat and striking a member of the mob with its powerful hooves, splattering blood in its wake.

As the reporter continued to scribble down notes, his face lit up with excitement, his hands moving quickly across the notepad.

Acker was well aware that they were doomed. He could already see the dreadful headlines on tomorrow's front page: 'Man Injured in Mob Caused by Police'.

"Let's get out of here!" Claydon yelled, slamming Acker's wolf's head cane into the carriage's roof.

The horses, overcome with terror from the mob's onslaught, emitted another piercing squeal, causing the carriage to lurch violently. Ignoring the coachman's plight as he dangled precariously from the carriage, ensnared in the reins, the panicked horses bolted down the street, leaving the furious protesters in their wake. The coachman's cries for assistance were drowned out by the chaos, his desperate attempts to avoid being dragged along the ground falling on deaf ears.

"Get those horses under control before we have a disaster!" Acker barked, his concern solely focused on the safety of their precarious situation.

With determination, Chavers swiftly deposited the files onto the seat before clambering out of the window to take charge. Acker and Claydon watched in astonishment as the young man sprang into action, seizing the coachman and hauling him back onto the seat, freeing him from the entanglement of reins.

The mob had long since vanished, but the shock of what had just occurred lingered. After taking command of the horses and slowing them down to a trot, the coachman pulled over and pulled a flask of whisky from his pocket. He handed it to Chavers after swigging just enough to regain his composure and stop shaking. Chavers turned it down and passed it on to Acker, who eagerly accepted it and gulped it down before handing it to his brother, leaving only a drop behind. Claydon gave him a stern look before handing it back to the coachman. "Thank you very much, brother," he spat, growing annoyed with Acker's ignorance.

"Where to, gentlemen?" the coachman asked in a gruff tone, still feeling shaken from his near-death experience.

"44, Royal York Crescent," Acker replied, closing his eyes and settling back into the cushioned seat.

With a soothing click of the coachman's tongue, the horses resumed their journey, their pace considerably calmer this time.

The remainder of the trip passed without incident, with Chavers keeping the coachman company, engaging in conversation that swiftly diverted their attention from the recent chaos. Meanwhile, Claydon stewed in silence, his thoughts consumed by concern for the injured member of the mob.

As Acker's townhouse loomed into view overlooking the city, his heart quickened its rhythm, pounding loudly in his chest. Beads of sweat formed on his brow, his features contorted with tension. His breaths came in rapid succession, his body already in motion as he leapt from the carriage and dashed up the steps to his front door, leaving the coachman to bring the vehicle to a halt.

Claydon rolled his eyes, unfazed by his brother's erratic behaviour, and jumped down from the carriage, slowly making his way up the steps. Chavers paid the coachman with one silver coin. "Wait here," he said before joining Claydon and Acker. The coachman tipped his hat to Chavers before turning his attention back to the horses.

The house was deafeningly quiet, and a chill lingered in the air. There were no lamps lit, nor were there any servants present. But it was the cold stove that struck Acker the most. It looked as if it hadn't been used in days. Fresh kindling had been piled inside the oven, yet there was no one around to light it. Everything had been cleaned and neatened, yet there were no servants around. There wasn't even a letter to say where they had gone.

"There's something wrong," Acker muttered as he rummaged through the house. "This house hasn't been occupied in days."

Claydon's ears perked up, eager to hear what his brother had to say. "I see what you mean. What do you think happened to them?"

Acker ignored his brother's question and turned his attention to Chavers. "You have a keen eye, Chavers. Search this house and see if you can find any evidence to suggest where my family is."

Chavers nodded and set the files down on the table before proceeding upstairs. "I'll start in your room and work my way around," he called out from the stairwell.

"This is very unlike Mary to do something like this," Acker said, his voice quiet and hoarse.

Claydon stepped back from Acker and moved toward the kitchen door. "I'll look through the kitchen for a letter. She must have left you some sort of note."

As they meticulously searched every corner of the house, scouring for any clues that might shed light on Acker's family's disappearance, their efforts led them to Billy's room, a task Acker delegated to Chavers. Acker, meanwhile, gazed out of the lounge window, straining his eyes for any sign of their return, but the street remained empty. Battling to suppress his emotions, he turned away, unwilling to let his men witness his struggle. Retreating to the kitchen, he sank into a chair at the table, his back turned to them, hiding the telltale signs of his reddened eyes.

His foot grazed against something beneath the table, prompting him to bend down and retrieve it. As he beheld his wife's handwriting on the paper, a surge of relief washed over him. "I've found a letter!" he exclaimed with a mixture of joy and relief as he began to read its contents. The letter provided a detailed account of their temporary absence, explaining that they had ventured to Lady Elspeth's residence for a brief sojourn, during which the servants were granted leave. With this revelation, everything suddenly clicked into place for Acker.

"Well, sir, that's a relief," Claydon remarked, peering over Acker's shoulder as he read the letter. However, his relief was short-lived as he noticed the date at the top of the letter, prompting a furrowed brow. "They should have returned by now," he observed, gesturing to the date. "We ought to organise a search party."

Acker's gaze hardened as he locked eyes with Claydon. "And who would we send, Claydon? We don't have many men left!"

Before Claydon could respond to his brother's pointed question, Chavers burst into the room, clutching a shoe in his hand. "Sir, you need to see this," he urged, thrusting the shoe sole in Acker's direction. He pointed out a distinctive hole in the sole. "This matches the shoe print from the crime scene." Chavers then directed Acker's attention to a dark splatter of blood on the shoe's side. "And this appears to be blood."

Acker yanked the shoe from Chavers and inspected it closely. "Who does this shoe belong to?"

"I found it in Billy's room. They look like his workhouse shoes before you took him in," Chavers responded.

Acker's gaze bore into Chavers, his brow arched in scepticism. "And what, pray tell, are you insinuating, Chavers? That this boy is Lady Penelope's killer?"

Chavers nodded eagerly, thrusting a photograph of the crime scene under Acker's nose. "Yes, sir," he affirmed. "Take a closer look. The shoe print and the hole match perfectly. He's our prime suspect."

Acker felt the air grow thin, his hands trembling as if grappling with an invisible force. The kitchen seemed to shrink around him, its walls closing in, suffused with an ominous darkness. His lungs constricted, each breath a struggle against the weight of the revelation. The stress pulsed through his veins, throbbing in his temples. How could it be that the culprit they sought had been hiding in plain sight all along? "Suspect? He's just a boy, Chavers, like you, just a boy," Acker muttered, his voice laced with disbelief.

Claydon watched his brother's reaction closely, pondering if the strain of their work had finally taken its toll. "What's your take? Are they a match?"

Acker's gaze shifted from the photograph to the shoe, scrutinising every detail before nodding to his brother. "They're identical," he confirmed, sinking into a chair with a bewildered expression. "I can't fathom it. I've been harbouring a fugitive."

Chavers offered a reassuring smile. "You couldn't have known, sir," he interjected softly.

Acker rubbed his eyes wearily, the weight of the situation bearing down on him. "Thanks for the sentiment, Chavers, but I doubt the newspapers will be as forgiving."

Claydon paced the room, his mind racing with possibilities. "Let's not rush to judgement. Being at the scene doesn't prove guilt," he mused aloud.

"You may be onto something, but why keep silent about it?" Acker's voice was muffled as he buried his face in his hands, grappling with the weight of their discovery.

Chavers made a rustling noise, causing Acker to sit up and

observe. Papers flew everywhere as Chavers quickly scanned each document until he found what he needed. He set it on the table for them to read. "According to Bodmin, Lady Penelope had a son with a very distinctive birthmark whom she gave away at birth. Sir, I bet you he's Lady Penelope's long-lost son. I can just feel it."

"And what if he is?"

"Then that's obviously his motive. Rejected by his mother and thrown into an orphan house to work till death would make anyone resent their parent, don't you think?"

Acker's lips formed a grin as he realised Chavers was onto something. "If he is the murderer, we need to find him and question him."

Claydon paused his pacing and looked into Acker's tired eyes. "You have a much bigger issue than that, Acker."

"What's that?"

"Your wife and child are with the murderer, and they could be anywhere by now," Claydon warned.

As Claydon's words sank in, Acker's smile faded as quick as it had come. He jumped from his chair and dashed out the door to the carriage.

The coachman tipped his hat to him and took the reins. "Where to, sir?"

Claydon and Chavers rushed into the carriage, bewildered by Acker's sudden burst of energy but also unsurprised. They would have acted in the same way if their family were in the company of a murderer unbeknownst to them.

"21, Moorland Lane," Acker called to the coachman. He then turned to Claydon and Chavers. His expressionless, hard face looked cold. His only emotion was a stern, condescending, and angry look in his eyes. Claydon had only seen this expression once before, and the events that followed nearly cost them both their jobs. Claydon didn't want that to happen again, but from the way his brother gripped the velvety seat's edge, digging his nails deeply into the cushion, told him that whatever was about to happen wasn't going to be pretty. "We're going to pay Lady Elspeth a little visit to find out where my wife and daughter are."

## CHAPTER SEVENTY-TWO

# Landrake's Plan

As the early evening breeze drifted through the hospital window, it stirred Landrake from his deep slumber, dragging him reluctantly back to consciousness. He cursed his lapse into sleep, berating himself for losing precious time. But now fully alert, he began to devise a plan. The hospital buzzed with activity just beyond his room, urging him to find an alternative escape route if he wished to evade capture successfully.

Across the corridor, he could glimpse into the neighbouring room. Chapman lay motionless in his hospital bed, cocooned in pristine white sheets. The gentle rhythm of his snores harmonised with the faint whistle of the breeze, lulling Landrake into a false sense of security. Then, with a pained groan, Chapman shifted, his face contorting in agony. He turned towards Landrake's room, revealing the grotesque visage of his badly bandaged, burned features. Landrake's breath caught in his throat. He had been unaware of Chapman's severe injuries from the fire. Guilt washed over him like a tidal wave. He held a genuine fondness for Chapman, admiring his intelligence and education. But now, his once-familiar face was marred beyond recognition, a twisted mask of charred flesh beyond any hope of restoration by even the most skilled surgeon.

Landrake averted his gaze, unable to bear the sight any longer. The weight of guilt pressed heavily upon him, urging him to turn away from the charred remains of Chapman's once-human face. With a heavy sigh, he shifted his attention to the officer slumped in the corner, apparently oblivious to the world as he slept. It was the perfect opportunity to slip away unnoticed.

The hospital bustled with frenetic activity, a whirlwind of nurses and doctors navigating the chaos with urgent determination. Clipboards clutched tightly, they darted back and forth, their movements a frantic dance in response to the influx of fire victims from the docks.

The cacophony of squeaking wheels and agonised cries grated on Landrake's nerves, fuelling his disdain for hospitals. The stench of blood mingled with stale hospital food turned his stomach, prompting an involuntary bout of nausea. He hunched over the edge of his bed, retching quietly, hoping to avoid drawing attention from the passing medical staff who seemed oblivious to his distress.

Rules and regulations plastered the walls like authoritarian graffiti, imbuing the sterile environment with an air of institutionalised oppression. Landrake felt suffocated by the hospital's stifling atmosphere, the infantilising decor amplifying his growing sense of frustration. Every fibre of his being screamed for escape, the familiar corridors and monotonous rows of identical doors only intensifying his desire to flee this dreary prison.

Hospitals, in Landrake's eyes, were like barren landscapes in a forgotten painting, devoid of colour or life. The labyrinthine corridors stretched endlessly, punctuated by clusters of antiquated hospital beds that cluttered the floor like discarded relics of a forgotten era, obstacles for the hurried medical personnel navigating the maze.

Landrake remained still on his bed, a silent observer amidst the chaos unfolding before him. Victims of the dock fire were being ferried into the hospital through the double doors, each one a grim reminder of the tragedy that had unfolded. With a surge of anticipation, he leapt from his bed, peering out in search of familiar faces among the injured, hoping to catch sight of Acker's men among them.

The hospital, a cesspool of disease and suffering, felt suffocating to Landrake, its walls closing in around him like the bars of a cage. He longed to break free, to escape the confines of this wretched place and breathe in the fresh air of freedom once more.

Returning to his room, his eyes were drawn to the open window beckoning him from behind. It was his only chance. Rushing to the window, he surveyed the bustling street below, alive with the energy of a new day. Stallholders haggled over their wares, while shoppers prowled the streets in search of bargains, their eyes glinting with the thrill of the hunt.

The stench of sickness threatened to overwhelm him, causing him to recoil from the window in disgust. Abandoning his escape plan, he backed away, narrowly avoiding a puddle of vomit on the floor, and nearly stumbling over the slumbering officer in the chair. With a muttered curse, he stepped back, eyeing the officer's peaceful expression with a mixture of revulsion and opportunity.

A sinister idea began to take shape in Landrake's mind, a plan both horrifying and desperate. With a ruthless resolve, he seized a pillow from the bed and pressed it firmly against the officer's face, his heart pounding with adrenaline. As the struggle ensued, Landrake watched with grim determination, waiting for the final breath to leave the officer's body.

Finally, the officer fell limp, his life extinguished. With trembling hands, Landrake stripped the uniform from the corpse, donning it in place of his own clothes. Carefully arranging the body in the bed to resemble his own unconscious form, he took a moment to survey his handiwork, his mind racing with the implications of his actions.

Excitement surged through Landrake as he donned the officer's uniform, feeling a rush of adrenaline at the prospect of his daring plan succeeding. Hastily grabbing the police hat from the floor, he pulled it low over his face, concealing his identity as best he could without drawing suspicion.

With a final glance around the room, Landrake darted into the corridor, seamlessly blending into the bustling throng of nurses and doctors. Like a shadow, he slipped between them, his movements swift and calculated, evading notice as he made his way through the hospital corridors.

Approaching the staircase leading to the upper levels, Landrake hesitated, his hand hovering over the doorknob. Unsure of the best course of action, he weighed his options, knowing that time was of the essence. Without hesitation, he pushed through the door, narrowly avoiding a collision with a nurse ascending the stairs.

The nurse stumbled backward, dropping her medical files in surprise. Ignoring her protests, Landrake scooped up the scattered papers, his eyes scanning the contents for any valuable information. Chapman's name leaped out at him from one of the files, seizing his attention.

Forgetting the nurse at his feet, Landrake delved into the file, his focus consumed by the revelations within. Startled by his disregard for her, the nurse regained her composure, demanding an apology for his brusque behaviour.

Landrake's lip curled in disdain as he met her gaze, his tone dripping with contempt. "You collided with me, madam. The fault lies with you, not me."

Disgusted, she snatched the file from Landrake's grasp, her voice laced with disdain. "You're a law enforcement officer, sir. Act like one." Wiping her brow, she gathered the remaining files, her movements tense with apprehension. Mid-action, her gaze flickered down to Landrake's shoes, where she noticed dried blood, her confusion evident as she looked up at his face.

Before she could react, Landrake produced the officer's pistol from his pocket, his voice a low hiss as he silenced her protests. "Don't even think about screaming," he warned, keeping his tone subdued to avoid drawing attention from the passing medical staff.

Despite the fear etched on the nurse's face, the bustling hospital corridor remained oblivious to their exchange. Landrake's grip tightened on her arm as he instructed her to rise slowly and follow him, the threat of the gun hanging between them. "I won't hesitate to shoot if you resist," he warned, his tone leaving no room for argument.

The nurse, a petite woman with a cherubic face, cast desperate glances at the passing doctors and nurses, silently pleading for help. Sensing her reluctance, Landrake tightened his hold, positioning himself behind her with the gun pressed against her back. "Move," he commanded, his voice firm as he propelled her forward.

Her legs wobbled like a marionette whose strings had been cut as she clutched the bannister, her grip desperate as she quietly prayed under her breath. With a sharp tug, Landrake yanked her arm and pushed her forward, causing her to stumble but catching her before she hit the ground. "I said walk, damn it," he growled.

As they descended the stairs, the nurse's cheeks flushed brighter with each step, leaving sweat stains from her hands on the bannister in her wake. Her breaths came in shallow gasps, and she fought to maintain her composure, her fear palpable.

A concerned doctor blocked their path, his hand reaching out to touch the nurse's brow. "Are you alright, matron? You seem overheated."

Feeling the gun's pressure against her back, the nurse flinched but managed to keep her voice steady. "I'm fine, just a bit warm," she replied, forcing a weak smile.

The doctor's gaze shifted to Landrake, suspicion flickering in his eyes. "And who might you be?"

"Law enforcement," Landrake bit out, his irritation evident.

The doctor's scrutiny lingered for a moment longer before he nodded, his attention returning to the nurse. "If you need to rest, take a break. I'll cover for you."

With a nod of gratitude, the nurse didn't reply, her heart pounding in her chest as she feared the consequences of speaking out. Landrake maintained his calm facade, his words masking the threat beneath. "I'm taking the matron outside for some fresh air. She needs it."

The doctor took a deep breath before stepping to the side to allow them to pass. "Thank you for accompanying her." He lowered his tensed shoulders and gave them one last look before carrying on up the stairs. "See you in an hour!" he shouted down to them as he rounded the corner out of sight.

The matron let out a small whimper as Landrake pushed her forward. "Where are you taking me?" she demanded, her voice rising in desperation, hoping for a rescue.

He jabbed the gun into her back with more force. "Keep quiet, woman. Your tricks won't work on me. I am the chief of police."

She halted, eyeing him with defiance. "I know exactly who you are."

"Then you know not to provoke me," he snapped, shoving her again. "Move!"

Outside, Landrake flagged down a passing cab. "Get in," he ordered.

"I won't tell anyone, I swear. Just let me go," she pleaded, scanning the street for help.

He sneered, brandishing the gun. "Get in."

With one last glance at the hospital, the matron's hope dwindled. She spotted the doctor who had intervened earlier, but before she could shout for help, Landrake shoved her into the carriage and urged the coachman to leave. As they sped away, the matron cowered in the corner, trembling with fear, while Landrake muttered to himself, plotting his next move.

"Where to, sir?" The coachman called down to Landrake.

Landrake shot a glare at the sobbing matron. "Silence, you old crow. I'm thinking."

She fell quiet, avoiding his gaze as he tapped his foot impatiently. "Would you release me if I helped you escape the city?" she ventured, her voice trembling.

His lips curled into a sinister grin as he assessed her. "Attempting to bargain, are we?"

"Where shall I take you, sir?" the coachman asked again, growing impatient.

Landrake's frustration flared. He seized the matron's head,

forcing her to look at him. "Get me out of here, and I might consider it."

She nodded eagerly and signalled the driver. "To the docks, sir, as swiftly as possible."

"The docks?" Landrake mused, intrigued.

"My brother has a boat there," she explained softly. "You can flee the city via the river."

He leaned back, contemplating her proposal. The river—a clever escape route he hadn't considered. He decided to keep her close; her resourcefulness might prove useful again. As for letting her go, well, that was out of the question. He couldn't risk her leading Acker to him.

The journey to the docks passed without incident, the matron counting each bump in fearful anticipation. Her eyes remained fixed on the gun, fearing its sudden use. Tears streaked her cheeks as she imagined her family's anguish if she didn't return home. She wished desperately to be among the onlookers outside, rather than trapped in the carriage with a madman beside her.

The carriage careened to a stop at the docks, narrowly avoiding the charred remnants of the fire.

Landrake surveyed the desolate scene, the once bustling dock now reduced to a haunting graveyard of burnt wood and broken dreams. The matron's eyes widened in horror as she took in the devastation. "So much death," she murmured, her fingers tracing the scorched remains as if searching for signs of life.

Impatiently, Landrake yanked her away, dismissing her sentimentality. "Show me the boat."

With a resigned sigh, she pointed to a cluster of vessels tethered to decrepit posts. "The blue one."

He tightened his grip on her wrist, a silent reminder of his control. "I'm not done with you yet."

Her heart sank, tears threatening to spill as she felt the weight of his dominance. "But you promised..."

"Not until I'm safely away," he snapped, pulling her closer with a cruel grip. "Who will row if you're not with me?"

Reluctantly, she complied, each step feeling like a march towards her own demise. With every tug and shove, she prayed for rescue, despising the man who held her fate in his hands. She couldn't shake the feeling that she was merely a pawn in his twisted game, destined for a fate worse than death.

As they reached the boat, she braced herself for what lay ahead, the chilling realisation sinking in that she may never escape the clutches of the man she now knew to be a monster in disguise.

She couldn't shake the curiosity gnawing at her. *What had he done to warrant such vigilant guarding, even as he commandeered a boat they'd provided?* It wasn't until they were adrift on the river's gentle currents that she summoned the courage to inquire. The smirk on his lips sent a shiver down her spine, his eyes alight with a disturbing glee as he relished her fear.

"I've done a bit of harm here and there, and the detective took offence," he quipped, his tone dripping with sarcasm.

The mere mention of the detective sent a chill through her, his sinister aura lending credence to his words. She watched his hands grip the oars with a vice-like hold, as though they were instruments of death stained with blood. A whimper escaped her lips as he loomed closer, revelling in her terror.

"Easy there, Matron. I've no intention of causing you harm," he assured, though his unsettling gaze belied his words.

Her hope dwindled as his reassurances fell flat, his eyes dancing with malicious intent. Shaking violently, she clung to the soaked fabric of her uniform, each droplet of sweat a testament to her escalating panic.

Throughout the journey, she sat in stunned silence, a silent witness to the bustling activity on land, a stark contrast to her perilous situation. Landrake's frustrated curses at the ageing engine went unnoticed, her focus consumed by the grim reality of her predicament. Her brother's neglected boat struggled against the tide, its sluggish pace a grim reminder of her vulnerability.

Landrake's gaze bore into her, a silent interrogation as he sought to decipher her thoughts. But she remained inscrutable, her expression a mask of resignation as she braced herself for whatever lay ahead.

As the river narrowed, overgrown weeds and grass snagged at the boat, impeding its progress. The matron silently prayed for some intervention to halt Landrake's course. Once-rural landscapes had transformed into soggy marshlands, with dilapidated buildings peeking out from the encroaching foliage.

The distant cries of wild animals echoed through the trees, a haunting serenade amidst the encroaching vines. Despite Landrake's menacing presence, the rhythmic sounds of water against the boat offered a fleeting sense of solace to the matron, a brief respite from her mounting fear.

Landrake's attention suddenly shifted to a lone boat drifting downstream. With a swift manoeuvre, he brought their boat alongside it, his expression morphing into one of recognition. Mary, Lizzie, and Billy lay asleep in the boat, their serene faces belying the danger they were in.

"Are they..." Landrake's voice trailed off, his eyes narrowing as he observed them.

The matron, sensing his intentions, silently boarded the other boat to check on them. She touched Billy's cold skin lightly, relief flooding her when she felt a faint pulse. Landrake's orders to bring them aboard his boat sparked a debate about their urgent need for medical attention.

But Landrake had other plans. His cold gaze fixed on Mary, his intentions clear. "They're coming with us. She'll be my leverage," he stated, his tone brooking no argument.

There was that look on his face again as he stared down at Mary's defenceless body. The matron quickly huddled over her, shielding her from Landrake's piercing gaze. He chuckled and sat back down, amused by the matron's sudden burst of bravery. "Get the girl."

She kept a close eye on him as she gently picked up Lizzie and placed her next to Mary. The boat rocked back and forth as she made her way onto the other boat for the final time to get Billy. Landrake suddenly grabbed her and dragged her back into his boat. "Leave the boy. He is of no use to me."

"He might perish out here!" She cussed, disgusted by his lack of concern for the poor boy.

Ignoring her protests, he powered up the boat's engine, his grip on her tightening. "It's not our concern," he dismissed, his tone chilling.

The matron watched Billy's boat drift away, a sense of guilt weighing heavily on her. She turned to Landrake, her gaze demanding answers. "Who are they?" she pressed.

With a smirk, Landrake revealed his sinister plans. "My escape plan. They're the detective's family. And you," he declared, his eyes gleaming with madness, "are coming with me."

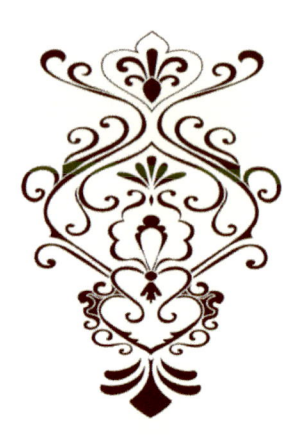

# CHAPTER SEVENTY-THREE

## Schizophrenia

The day had evolved into a tumultuous journey for Acker, his emotions riding the peaks and valleys like a roller coaster. Anxiety gripped him tightly, manifesting in the trembling of his leg as they sat in the carriage, swaying with each turn guided by the coachman. The path ahead twisted and turned, the coachman skilfully steering the horses to avoid obstacles strewn by the recent storm.

The once lush greenery that enveloped the marshland now lay battered and broken, the remnants of trees and shrubbery scattered by the tempest. The horses, sensing the lingering tension in the air, grew increasingly restless, their unease mirrored in Acker's furrowed brow as he impatiently twiddled his thumbs, yearning to move forward without delay.

Acker's stomach churned with a sense of impending doom, his

thoughts consumed by the fate of his wife, Mary. There was an unsettling sensation lingering just beyond his grasp, intensifying the weight of guilt and anxiety pressing down on him. Chapman's condition, his body swathed in bandages, served as a constant reminder of Acker's own narrow escape from the flames. The thought gnawed at him, fuelling his impatience to reach Lady Elspeth's estate before his emotions erupted like a volcano.

His patience, already stretched thin, frayed further with each passing moment. Images of his loved ones in peril danced through his mind, stoking the flames of his fury. Acker, a man not known for his patience, felt the tension coil tighter within him, a ticking time bomb ready to detonate. Even Claydon, his own brother, could sense the volatile atmosphere hanging heavy in the carriage.

"Is there no end to this journey?" Acker's voice sliced through the air, thick with frustration and cold resolve.

Claydon, caught off guard by his brother's outburst, could only offer a helpless shrug in response, hoping it would suffice.

A surge of rage coursed through Acker's veins, his fist colliding with the carriage's wooden frame in a thunderous blow. "Damn it, Claydon! We've been confined to this infernal box for hours! All I see is endless fields of misery and dampness!"

His brother's retort cut through the air like a blade, laced with bitterness and regret. "And whose fault is that, brother? If you weren't so consumed with chasing down every criminal in the city, perhaps you would have noticed sooner that your wife and daughter were missing!"

The words hung heavy in the air, a painful reminder of Acker's failures, etched onto his face like scars.

Chavers winced, feeling the sting of Claydon's cutting words like a physical blow. He clutched the files tightly to his chest, seeking solace in their weight, before turning his gaze to the window. Outside, the landscape stretched endlessly, a vast expanse of fields and trees that seemed to mock his desire for escape.

As the heated exchange between the two brothers escalated, Chavers retreated inward, seeking refuge in the recesses of his mind. It was a coping mechanism he had learned from his mother, a way to shield himself from the cacophony of noise and conflict.

His fingers twitched involuntarily, a familiar urge to cover his ears and block out the world rising within him.

From a young age, Chavers had known he was different. His peculiar habits and sensitivities had drawn ridicule from others, making him retreat further into himself. But he had persevered, channelling his unique qualities into academic success and a promising career in law enforcement. Still, the scars of childhood taunts lingered, shaping him into the reserved and solitary figure he was today.

His family's wealth had afforded him some measure of comfort, allowing him to indulge in the finer things in life and accommodate his eccentricities. Yet, despite his mother's hopes for grandchildren and societal expectations of companionship, Chavers remained content in his solitude. Relationships held little appeal for him, preferring the sanctuary of his own company to the complexities of human connection.

But now, as the clamour of the argument reached a fever pitch, Chavers abandoned all pretence of normalcy. Dropping the files to the floor, he pressed his hands firmly over his ears, rocking back and forth as a low, mournful sound escaped his lips. In that moment, he allowed himself to embrace his true self, however unconventional it may be.

Acker halted mid-sentence, his gaze fixed on Chavers, who was exhibiting peculiar behaviour. Claydon furrowed his brow, perplexed, as Chavers rocked back and forth, eyes squeezed shut and sweat glistening on his forehead. Acker leaned forward, his voice edged with concern. "Chavers, what's going on?"

Chavers seemed oblivious to their presence, lost in his own world of distress. He continued to sway, his movements growing more frantic by the second. Acker's patience wore thin, and he resorted to a stern slap to jolt Chavers back to reality.

"What the devil are you doing?" Acker demanded, his tone sharp.

Startled, Chavers blinked rapidly, trying to regain his composure. "I-I'm sorry, sir. Loud noises... they unsettle me."

Claydon interjected, his tone incredulous. "But the rocking? That's a bit extreme, isn't it?"

Acker's eyes widened as realisation dawned. "You're one of them, aren't you?"

"One of who?" Claydon interjected, confused by the cryptic exchange.

"Are you saying you're... one of those eccentric types?" Acker asked cautiously, unsure of how to broach the subject.

Chavers nodded sheepishly, his gaze fixed on the floor. "Yes, sir. I've always been a bit... different."

Claydon leaned back in his seat, processing the revelation. "Well, I'll be damned. And here I thought you were just a green recruit."

Acker rubbed his temples, feeling a headache coming on. "So, what exactly triggers these... episodes?"

Chavers shifted uncomfortably in his seat, reluctant to divulge too much. "Loud noises, mainly. They overwhelm me, and I lose control."

A moment of silence hung in the air as the brothers absorbed this newfound information. Acker's mind raced with possibilities, wondering how best to accommodate Chavers's needs while also fulfilling their mission.

Acker let out a deep, disappointed sigh. "It would be a shame to lose a good officer because of his eccentricities." He paused for a moment to consider the best solution. He then rubbed his palms together and looked at Chavers sternly. "You must maintain control of that and not allow anyone to see that side of you. You're smart and loyal. That's what I need on the force. Keep yourself together, Chavers; I mean it."

"Why aren't you institutionalised?" Claydon asked, disturbed.

Chavers sighed, his cheeks growing redder by the second. "Because I'm good at hiding it."

Claydon broke the silence with a sigh. "Well, we can't have you falling apart on us every time there's a commotion. We'll need to come up with a plan."

Acker nodded in agreement, his mind already formulating strategies to support Chavers while maintaining operational efficiency. "Indeed. We'll have to make some adjustments, but we can't afford any distractions, especially now." Acker finished their conversation by turning to look out the window, not wanting to hear any more. His face brightened when he noticed Lady Elspeth's manor house in the distance. "We're here." After a pause, he added, "Right; I want this place searched from top to bottom and the servants questioned," Acker said, his gaze fixed on the impending manor house. "I'd like to know where my family is."

The manor house loomed against a sombre sky, its facade casting a foreboding shadow over the grounds. The carriage trudged along the rugged path, its wheels grinding against the rocky terrain with a cacophony of noise that mirrored the tension within. As they approached, the butler emerged from the doorway, his expression as sour as the gloomy weather.

Acker leaned in, his voice a low growl of command. "Check every inch, from the highest tower to the lowest cellar," he instructed the men.

With a determined stride, Acker led the way, the other two trailing close behind as they entered the imposing manor. The butler attempted to intercede, but Acker brushed past him with a forceful shove, his eyes ablaze with determination.

Inside, Lady Elspeth sat unperturbed before the crackling fire, her demeanour serene despite the intrusion. Acker's approach was like a tempest, his demand for answers reverberating through the room as he confronted her with a steely gaze. "Where are my wife and child?"

She raised her finger to silence him. "There's no need for that aggressive tone, sir." She closed her book and set it down beside her. "They left yesterday morning to go home."

With an air of ennui, she finally turned her gaze towards them, her eyes scanning each of them in turn. Clad in a midnight-blue gown that seemed more suited to a grand ball, she wore a thick layer of powder on her face, adding years to her visage. Leaning back in her chair, she casually revealed a cane hidden behind it, her fingers tracing the smooth leather strap as she locked eyes with Acker.

Acker regarded her warily as she delicately lifted her teacup, taking a refined sip. "Lady Elspeth, do not test my patience."

Her eyes narrowed, and she set the cup back onto its saucer

with precision. "Sir, I find your tone rather offensive. Miss Acker and Lizzie sought refuge in my home due to the storm. I extended them hospitality, for which you should express gratitude, not disrespect."

Acker's frustration boiled over, his hand slamming onto the table with force, causing the tea set to tremble. "I grow weary of this! Madam, where are my wife and daughter?"

The butler burst into the room, brandishing a shotgun and rushing to Lady Elspeth's defence. "Sir, I must ask you to step back from Lady Elspeth," he commanded, his eyes blazing with defiance as he aimed the weapon at Acker's forehead.

Lady Elspeth raised a hand to halt her butler's advance. "The firearm is unnecessary," she declared before returning her attention to Acker. "You cannot simply barge into my home uninvited, Detective. It is highly impolite."

"I demand to know my wife's whereabouts!" Acker's voice rose with frustration, his patience wearing thin with Lady Elspeth's haughty demeanour.

She tsked disapprovingly. "As I've already stated, your wife departed yesterday morning after the storm had subsided. Where they are now, I cannot say."

"Then, what of Billy?" Claydon interjected from behind Acker.

Lady Elspeth's eyes darkened at the mention of the boy's name. "He left with the inspector's wife and daughter."

Acker loomed over Lady Elspeth, his hands gripping the armchairs as he leaned in close, casting a shadow over her. "You're concealing something, madam," he growled, his voice a low rumble.

Her lips curled into a sneer as she met his gaze defiantly. "I have no reason to deceive you."

"Then, you won't mind if we conduct a search of your premises?" he pressed, his tone edged with a veiled threat.

Lady Elspeth's facade faltered for a moment, a flicker of fear crossing her features before she composed herself with characteristic haughtiness. "Do as you please, Detective."

It was a small crack in her composed demeanour, but it was enough to confirm Acker's suspicions. Stepping away from her, he exchanged a knowing smirk with Claydon. "Chavers, check upstairs. Claydon, search downstairs. I'll take the servant quarters."

As the servant's quarters were mentioned, a hint of apprehension flashed across the butler's face, his hand inching toward the shotgun. But before he could act, Chavers and Claydon intervened, blocking his path. Acker seized the shotgun, fixing the butler with a steely gaze. "Move aside, or I'll have you charged with obstruction."

With a resigned sigh, Lady Elspeth motioned for the butler to step aside, returning her attention to her book. "You'll find nothing, but if it amuses you, feel free to search."

Acker shot her a defiant look before leading the men away, leaving her to her reading. "Get Bentley out of here and stash him in the stables," she instructed her butler swiftly once they were out of earshot.

Acker pressed his ear against the door, listening intently as Lady Elspeth spoke. He had baited her into revealing something, and now he waited in the shadows, poised to uncover the truth.

Claydon glanced at his brother, perplexed. "What's the plan, sir?"

Acker pushed them towards a cupboard beneath the marble staircase. "Just follow my lead," he whispered, closing the door quietly, leaving it slightly ajar for observation.

As expected, Lady Elspeth's butler emerged and made his way towards the servant quarters. Acker motioned for Claydon and Chavers to follow, keeping a discreet distance behind the butler. As they watched him disappear through the servant quarters' door, realisation dawned on Claydon and Chavers. Impressed by Acker's cunning, Claydon couldn't help but feel a pang of jealousy, overshadowing his admiration.

Once again, Acker had outsmarted them all with his meticulous planning and sharp intellect, a feat Claydon could only envy. They lingered in the shadows, blending into the dim, dreary atmosphere of the servant quarters. The meagre daylight struggled to penetrate the grime-coated windows, casting everything in a dull hue. Chavers found himself yearning for the comfort of his modest cottage on Chamberlain Street. Passing by the worn furniture and peeling wallpaper, he entertained the thought of adding a splash of colour with a can of paint.

"Chavers, stay focused," Acker hissed, breaking Chavers from his reverie.

With determination driving him forward after his earlier misstep in the carriage, he hastened to follow the detective closely, ensuring he didn't lag behind again. As they pursued the butler through the labyrinthine corridors, the gloomy, cramped passageways grew wearisome, their walls blending into an indistinguishable mass of grey. Each numbered door and attached name tag seemed like a copy of the last, adding to the monotony of their surroundings.

A sudden halt from Acker brought them to a standstill, his raised arm signalling the others to pause. "Where did he disappear to?"

The corridor lay deserted, save for a faint trace of the butler's scent lingering in the air. Acker, adopting the focus of a bloodhound, sniffed delicately, tracking the scent to a door labelled "Bentley." With a satisfied grin, he motioned to the others. "The pieces are starting to come together."

Pressing his ear against the door, he strained to catch any sound. A scuffle from within jolted him, prompting a quick retreat, pulling the others along. "Someone's approaching."

As the door swung open, the butler emerged, dragging a struggling figure behind him—presumably Bentley. "Stay put," the butler growled, producing a rope from his pocket. Bentley fought against the bindings, his face etched with desperation as he resisted. An impatient swipe from the butler silenced his struggles momentarily.

Stepping into the light, Acker revealed himself, his smirk evident. The butler's surprise was palpable as he released Bentley, his hands still clutching the rope.

"Busted," Acker declared, relishing the moment.

Claydon seized the butler's wrists, securing them with the rope. "Don't even think about escaping. You're under arrest."

Bentley, now by Acker's side, appeared both surprised and relieved, extending his hand in gratitude. "You arrived just in time. I appreciate it. How are Mary and the children? Are they safe?"

Acker's gaze sharpened. "They're not here?"

Bentley's handshake faltered. "Didn't Mary send you?"

A shake of Acker's head followed. "We're searching for her. Who are you?"

Ignoring Acker's query, Bentley turned to the butler. "Where are they?"

The butler shrugged indifferently, unperturbed by his arrest. "I don't know."

A surge of impatience gripped Acker, his hand tightening around the butler's throat, demanding answers. "Where have my wife and daughter gone?"

The butler clawed at Acker's arm, his eyes almost popping out of their sockets. "I... don't...know." He croaked.

Bentley touched Acker's arm gently. "I don't think he does know, sir."

"He's right," Claydon said from behind Bentley. "If you kill him, then we won't know the truth."

Bentley guided Acker's hands away from the butler's neck and down to his side as the detective stood motionless, staring into the distance. "So, where have they gone? What happened to my family?" His eyes were sad as he took a step back from the butler to calm down. "All I want to know is where they are."

"They must have escaped on the boat. They're almost certainly on their way back to Bristol." Bentley said, his gaze fixed on Acker. "Lady Elspeth had kept them here against their will, and I assisted them in escaping, but I was apprehended before I could join them."

"Why would she want to keep them here?" Chavers asked, his brow furrowed while looking directly at the butler for an answer.

The butler looked away in embarrassment. "Gentlemen, my mistress suffers from schizophrenia. She occasionally sees things that aren't real." He stared at the floor, scuffing his shoe on the worn carpet. He could feel their eyes on him, making him feel uneasy. "The whole thing has gotten out of control."

"Then why did you go along with it?" Acker demanded.

"I was just following orders."

Acker turned to Chavers and Claydon. "Search this place. If

they're here, we'll find them." He then returned his attention to the butler. "You, sir, are coming with me." He took ahold of the man's shoulders and marched him back the way they came. "I need you as a witness, Bentley," he called over his shoulder.

Bentley nodded and rushed after Acker, who by now was trying to shove the butler into the foyer with as much force as he could without breaking his bones.

Lady Elspeth's smile dropped when she noticed her butler being forced into the lounge by Acker. "What is the meaning of this?" she growled, scowling at them.

If looks could kill, Lady Elspeth's dagger glare would have killed them all. She wasn't the frail, kind woman she used to be. It was as if her personality was changing her features. Her face was etched with lines as if her skin were a map. Her eyes had darkened significantly since Acker first saw her, turning a deep obsidian colour that matched her scowl. Her skin had also paled, presenting her as an old hag and making her appear older than her years. No longer did she appear friendly and welcoming. Her face screwed so tightly in rage that even Bentley could no longer recognise her as his mistress.

It was as if something had snapped in her, and her usual chirpy self had vanished, replaced by a bitter old woman, ready to pounce. The atmosphere in the room was so thick and heavy that even Acker was struggling to keep his cool.

"What the hell have we gotten ourselves into?" he murmured in Bentley's ear.

The man looked up at Acker, his eyes full of fear. "I've never seen her like this before." He peered over at the butler, and he, too, had the same expression plastered on his face. They were filled with fear and panic as he stared at his mistress, who sat stiffly in her chair, her face twisted in anger.

Acker swallowed hard and cleared his throat. "We know you're lying, madam. Everything has been revealed to us by your butler." He lied, hoping to provoke a reaction from her. He wanted her to be so angry that she would reveal where she was keeping his family. Where else could they be if they weren't here?

Lady Elspeth slowly turned towards her butler. He gulped loudly, as if a ball had become lodged in his throat. Her eyes narrowed into slits, and she pursed her lips like a sulking schoolgirl. "Well, is this true?"

The butler nodded, avoiding her gaze. "I'm afraid it is, madam."

"Very well then," she said, reaching behind her back for something. She pulled out a pistol and pointed it directly at the butler's heart before firing, filling the room with smoke and bursts of gunpowder essence. "I don't like being betrayed."

Acker screamed in shock, clutching the butler as he collapsed to the floor. He pressed on the man's wound, watching as the blood drained from his shocked face and his white shirt turning dark red. Bentley rushed over to his mistress and yanked the pistol from her grip while she sat amusedly staring at her butler's corpse on the floor.

"I don't like being betrayed," she repeated, turning her head sideways so she could get a closer look at the hole in his heart.

Claydon and Chavers moved in, guns drawn and ready to fire. "What in God's name is-"

"Arrest her right now!" Acker screamed, pointing to Lady Elspeth, who was smirking calmly in her chair, her book resting open on her lap.

They leapt on her, pushing Bentley to the side. She didn't fight back. Instead, she stood up and turned around, pulling her wrists together behind her back, allowing them to cuff her. "Lady Elspeth, I'm arresting you for murder," Claydon stated, tightening the cuffs until she winced in pain. Only then did he stop.

Chavers attended to Acker and pulled him away from the butler. "He's gone, sir. There's nothing we can do for him now." He led the detective to a chair and forced him to sit down before pouring him a glass of brandy from the drink cabinet. "Your wife and child are nowhere to be found. They must still be somewhere in the marshes," he said, while handing over a half-full glass of golden liquid.

Acker downed it all at once. "Then we'll have to search the marshes," he spluttered.

"More men will be required," Claydon said as he pushed Lady Elspeth in the direction of Acker. "I'll go back and book this witch in, and you can continue your search for your family. I'll only be gone for a day, and I'll come back with more men."

"That's the best idea you've had all week, Claydon." Acker managed to smile while pouring himself another glass of brandy. "Take the carriage. We'll make a start on foot," he said before turning to Bentley. "You'll help us search, won't you?"

Bentley bowed. "It'll be my honour, sir. We'll check the lake first. That's where they were heading before I lost them. We can take the mistress's horses."

"When was the last time you saw them?" Chavers inquired.

"Early in the morning. I was supposed to join them on a boat returning to Bristol, but I was apprehended before I could reach them."

Chavers paused for a moment. He paced up and down, mentally calculating something, before turning to Acker. "If my calculations are correct, your wife and daughter should arrive at the Bristol docks within a few hours."

Claydon nodded towards the door, indicating that he was leaving. "Then we must return to Bristol."

Acker placed the crystal glass neatly on the table before heading into the foyer. "Then, what are we waiting for? Let's go!"

## CHAPTER SEVENTY-FOUR

# Fate

Superintendent Landrake had orchestrated a daring escape for Acker's family and the matron, navigating the treacherous streets of London with precision honed by years in law enforcement. His reputation opened doors, but it was his determination that saw them through. With bribes and false promises, he secured their passage, knowing the payoff would be worth it.

As the boat Landrake managed to secure after train rides, and carriage journeys drifted into London, its passengers still unconscious from whatever concoction he made the matron give them, Landrake surveyed the cityscape. Smoke billowed from factory chimneys, blending with the grey clouds above. The streets teemed with people, a chaotic dance of fashion and anonymity.

Under cover of darkness, Landrake ushered Mary and Lizzie to a seedy hotel, where discretion came at a price. Mary's composure impressed him, a stark contrast to Lizzie's tearful outbursts. Frustration boiled within him, leading him to threaten the girl with a pistol, only to be swayed by Mary's plea for mercy.

Watching Mary tend to her daughter stirred a mix of emotions in Landrake. Her strength and compassion evoked envy for the affection he had never known. Loneliness gnawed at him, memories of neglect echoing through the halls of his childhood home. In that moment, a solitary tear betrayed the hardened facade he had crafted.

He wiped the tear from his cheek quickly, replacing it with a stone-faced expression. "I'll shoot her if she cries again."

"Why are you doing this?" Mary sobbed, unable to hold back her own tears.

Confused, Landrake looked at her. "You have no idea?"

She shook her head, still tucking Lizzie into her side and shielding her with her body. "You're the superintendent. Instead of committing crime, you should be fighting it."

"That is correct, and I would have gotten away with it if your husband hadn't interfered in my life." He glanced out the smudged window at a passing woman dressed in rags. "Don't worry, I've got a plan that will get me out of this mess, and it involves all of you," he said, grinning from ear to ear.

The matron's eyes widened in disbelief. "You said you'd let me go."

Landrake scowled. "You're so naive."

He stood by the window, the gun in his hand a symbol of his power and control. With a twisted grin, he mimicked the act of violence, a chilling display of his disregard for life.

"Do not shed innocent blood," Mary said through clenched teeth.

He looked over his shoulder at her to see her cuddling Lizzie on the bed. "And why not? It won't make much of a difference to my record."

"They've done nothing to you. Allow them to live. Besides, doing so will reveal your location," the matron reasoned with him, and she knew she was deterring him from his morbid plan by the way his brows raised up in surprise.

Mary's words cut through the air like a knife, a reminder of morality in the midst of his dark intentions. The matron's plea echoed her sentiment, appealing to his sense of reason. Surprise flickered across his face, a moment of clarity breaking through his clouded mind. Their words struck a chord, stirring a conflict within him.

"You're completely right, matron." He resumed his gaze out the window. "I'd better not give myself away too soon. This will be your temporary residence." He motioned with his hand around the shabby-looking room, which was in desperate need of a fresh coat of paint. "So, I suggest you start getting comfortable."

His eyes bulged at the sight of something outside, and he stared intently out the window, leaning as far out as he could at two men walking up the street. His eyes widened in surprise.

"Banes," he muttered in shock. As he watched them walk up the road, his smile widened into a grin. "This is getting a lot more interesting."

As he spotted the familiar figures outside, excitement coursed through him, electrifying the air. With a newfound sense of anticipation, he addressed the women.

"It seems our plans have changed," he announced, a glint of mischief in his eyes. "There's something far more intriguing awaiting us."

## CHAPTER SEVENTY-FIVE
# The Time Is Up

The scene at the muddy dock was a grim tableau, illuminated by the flickering light of torches held by officers. Billy lay motionless in the boat, unaware of the storm brewing around him, a storm of accusations and revelations.

For Billy, the murder he had committed weighed heavily on his soul, a burden he had carried in silence for far too long. His secret, gnawing away at him, had driven him to the brink of despair. Even the fleeting relief of confiding in Mary had been overshadowed by the overwhelming guilt and remorse that consumed him.

His mother's rejection had been the catalyst for his descent into darkness, a moment etched into his memory with chilling clarity. The rush of violence, the sickening satisfaction that followed—moments that had shattered his fragile facade of normalcy.

As the blood seeped into the cobblestones beneath her, reality crashed down upon him like a tidal wave, drowning him in dread and fear. The spectre of punishment loomed large, a constant reminder of his heinous act.

Yet, amidst the turmoil, Billy had found a precarious sanctuary in his position at the station. It was both a stroke of luck and a calculated move, allowing him to manipulate the investigation and cover his tracks.

But fate had a cruel twist in store for him. As Detective Acker's imposing figure loomed over him, Billy's facade crumbled, the weight of his deeds crashing down upon him once more. In that moment, he knew that his carefully constructed world was unravelling, and there was nowhere left to hide.

"You're under arrest, boy," Acker growled as he lowered a pair of handcuffs to his face. He motioned for the officers to grab Billy, then grasped his shoulders and pulled him up onto the dock. "How could you, Billy?" he yelled at him.

"I'm assuming Mary told you?" Billy asked, keeping his face expressionless.

Acker looked taken aback by the boy's lack of remorse as he cuffed him. "No, she didn't. Where are my wife and daughter, Billy? What have you done with them?"

It was Billy's turn to look confused. "She isn't with you?" He then peered over the dock at the empty boat below. "They were both in the boat with me before I passed out, I swear!"

"Well, they're not there now, so where are they?" Acker screamed directly in the boy's face.

The tension crackled in the air as officers surrounded Acker, their eyes trained on him to ensure he didn't lose control of his fury towards Billy. Acker's anger was palpable, evident in the bulging veins on his forehead, a sign of his struggle to contain the rage threatening to consume him.

Claydon's timely arrival provided a moment of respite. He stepped in, a pillar of calm amidst the chaos, and forcefully separated Billy from Acker. "Easy, brother. Let's not escalate this any further," he urged, his voice a soothing counterpoint to Acker's seething anger.

Acker's gaze bore into Claydon's, the intensity of his frustration evident. "How can I stay calm when my family is missing?"

he demanded, his voice tinged with desperation.

"We will find them, but we must handle this situation with care," Claydon reasoned, his tone measured. He gestured for the officers to take Billy into custody, ensuring he would be closely monitored. "Lock him up and keep a close eye on him, 24/7."

Turning to Heath, Claydon emphasised the importance of managing the situation delicately. "This will attract attention from the press. Acker won't be giving any statements for now," he instructed, his voice firm yet composed. "Make it clear that we have apprehended Lady Penelope's murderer."

Heath nodded, ready to carry out his orders. "Understood, sir. What should I tell them?"

Claydon paused for a moment, considering his words carefully. "Inform them that the suspect is in custody, and further details will be provided in due course," he replied, his tone authoritative. "We need to handle this with caution."

"Don't give anything away. We just need them to back off for a little while until we can figure this out. Don't mention Billy's name. In fact, cover Billy's head with a sack so no one can identify him. If this gets out that the murderer was under our noses the entire time, we'll be a laughingstock of the city." Claydon glanced over Heath's shoulder at Acker being restrained by the others as he tried lunging for Billy. "I'll be giving you orders from now on. My brother is unfit to handle this case, and I don't want any of this to make the news. I'll look after my brother while you hold down the fort at the station. Understand?"

"Yes, sir, I understand." He grabbed Billy's arm and led him over to the carriage to be taken away.

Acker's desperation reached a crescendo as he watched Billy being escorted away, his voice cracking with emotion as he pleaded for answers. "Where have my wife and daughter gone? What did you do to them, murderer?" His words were a mixture of anguish and accusation, fuelled by the torment of uncertainty.

Claydon held onto his brother, offering what little comfort he could. Tears mingled with sweat on Acker's cheeks as he fought against the restraint, his heartache pouring out in waves. "You're going to the noose! I'll make sure of that!" Acker's voice trembled with raw emotion as the carriage pulled away, carrying Billy and a whirlwind of unanswered questions.

"All I want to know is where they are," Acker repeated, his voice muffled against Claydon's shoulder, his despair echoing through the empty dock.

Claydon's touch was gentle as he stroked Acker's head, his own heart heavy with the weight of their situation. "We'll find them, Acker. I promise," he vowed, his words a beacon of hope amidst the darkness that threatened to engulf them.

But their moment of solace was shattered by the urgent cries of an approaching officer. Acker's eyes snapped open, his attention instantly drawn to the new threat. "What is it?" he demanded.

"The superintendent has gotten away!" The officer's words sent a jolt of adrenaline coursing through Acker's veins. "Landrake has escaped!" The gravity of the situation hit Acker like a physical blow, his mind racing to comprehend the implications.

"Say that again?"

"Landrake has escaped from the hospital, accompanied by one of the nurses. He was last seen on this dock, heading in that direction." He indicated the direction of London. "And get this: another witness has stated that not only was he with the nurse, but there was also another woman and child with him too."

"Where was this?" Acker demanded, grabbing the officer's arm and pulling himself away from Claydon's shoulder.

"The witness saw them heading towards London, sir."

"And what about Chapman? Is he safe?" Claydon asked.

"Yes, sir," he said, "but there has been no improvement in his health."

"London," Acker muttered, a plan already forming in his mind. "He has my wife and child and is heading to London." His gaze hardened with determination as he turned to Claydon. "We need to go after them. Pack your things; we leave for London immediately."

Claydon nodded, his expression mirroring Acker's resolve. "I'll gather what we need. We won't let them slip through our fingers." With a shared understanding, they set their sights on London, their determination unshakeable in the face of adversity.

THE END

Book Two Coming Soon

ABOUT THE AUTHOR

Willow Hewett is the author of the 'Past My Time' series, as well as 'The Taranock' (Horror), 'Chamberlain Street' (Historical Crime), 'The Wishy-Washy Curly-Wurly Dragon' series (Children's Picture Book), 'The Leviathan' (Thriller).
She writes in her spare time and has won multiple awards for her Young Adult series, and her Television scripts.

www.willowhewettauthor.co.uk

www.facebook.com/storiesthatspook

Thank you to –

<a href="https://www.vecteezy.com/free-photos/hand">Hand Stock photos by Vecteezy</a>

<a href="https://www.vecteezy.com/free-photos/jack-the-ripper">Jack The Ripper Stock photos by Vecteezy</a>

<a href="https://www.vecteezy.com/free-photos/screaming-woman">Screaming Woman Stock photos by Vecteezy</a>

<a href="https://www.vecteezy.com/free-photos/scary-background">Scary Background Stock photos by Vecteezy</a>

<a href="https://www.vecteezy.com/free-photos/sensuality">Sensuality Stock photos by Vecteezy</a>

<a href="https://www.vecteezy.com/free-vector/18th-century">18th Century Vectors by Vecteezy</a>

## MORE BOOKS BY WILLOW HEWETT

Find them on Amazon, Waterstones, Barnes & Noble, and many others.

*The old house at the end of the street has a dark history. For centuries, locals have talked of strange events and disappearances within its walls. Wild tales have been woven into folklore, told at night to scare children.*

*For Arthur and Amelia, the house was a bargain, in need of some repair but big enough for their growing family.*

*They hadn't heard the rumours. They didn't know about the people vanishing. They had no idea that moving to this quaint little English town might not be the fresh start they were hoping for.*

*Something has been disturbed. Something waits, trapped in the shadows, craving the souls of the unwary.*

*Tick tock. Tick tock. Beware the thirteen on the clock.*

*www.willowhewettauthor.co.uk*

*Find it on Amazon, Waterstones, Abe Books, Barnes & Noble, and many others.*

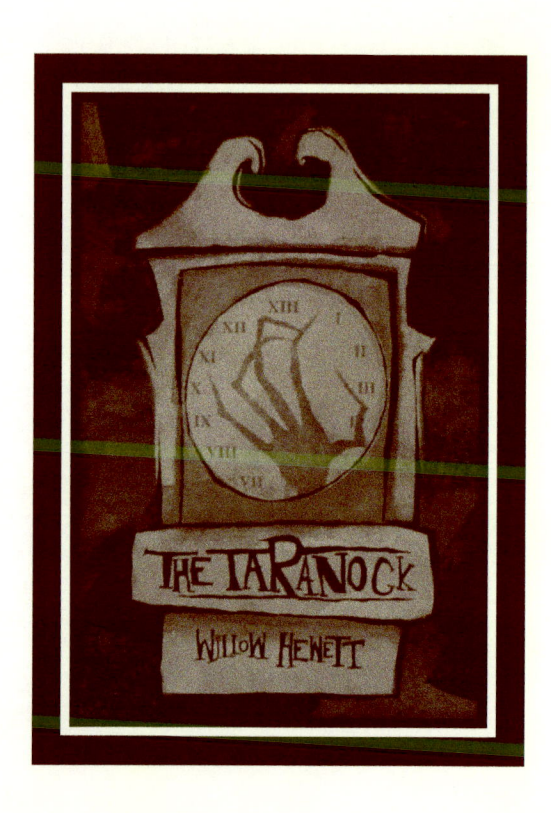